CECIL CAMERON grew up in the S... and read history at London Uni... Children. She began her work... during the Vietnam war. She continued to be involv... charity for many years and was awarded an OBE in 2002. Cecil has always loved writing – entertaining her five brothers and sisters, then her own children. She started to write professionally when she retired, drawing on her own family history in Sicily. Cecil is married to a highland clan chief and spends her time between the beautiful west coast of Scotland and London. She has four children and is currently working on her second novel.

An
Italian
Scandal

CECIL CAMERON

Harper
North

HarperNorth
Windmill Green,
Mount Street,
Manchester, M2 3NX

A division of
HarperCollins*Publishers*
1 London Bridge Street
London SE1 9GF

www.harpercollins.co.uk

HarperCollins*Publishers*
1st Floor, Watermarque Building, Ringsend Road
Dublin 4, Ireland

First published by HarperNorth in 2021
This paperback edition first published in 2022

1 3 5 7 9 10 8 6 4 2

A catalogue record for this book
is available from the British Library

ISBN: 978-0-00-849402-5

Printed and bound in the UK using 100%
renewable electricity at CPI Group (UK) Ltd

MIX
Paper from
responsible sources
FSC™ C007454

This book is produced from independently certified FSC™ paper
to ensure responsible forest management.

For more information visit: www.harpercollins.co.uk/green

GARIBALDI'S HYMN

Come join them. Come follow, o youth of our land!
Come fling out our banner, and marshal our band!
Come with cold steel, come with hot fire,
Come with the flame of Italia's desire
Begone from Italia, begone from us now!
Stranger begone, for this is our hour!

HISTORICAL NOTE

Before 1860, the Italian Peninsula was made up of separate states. Apart from the liberal kingdom of Piedmont, the Austrians occupied the north and the Spanish Bourbon king, Francis, ruled the kingdom of Naples and the Two Sicilies in the south. A campaign to liberate and unify Italy had been underway for decades, including the ill-fated revolution in Sicily of 1848. In May 1860, the scene was set for General Garibaldi, with his famous Redshirts, to sail from Genoa to Sicily and join the Sicilian patriots in a final attempt to free the nation from foreign occupation and oppression.

In Britain, Queen Victoria and her German consort, Prince Albert, reigned over a prosperous nation. The Industrial Revolution was at its height, creating wealth for a few and mass migration to the cities for many others. Society was divided between the very poor, the aristocracy and a new middle class who followed a strict code of etiquette and propriety.

PROLOGUE

'Sirocco! The sirocco is coming!'

The words spread through the streets and everywhere there was activity. Men scurried to and fro, clearing pavements and packing up goods on the open stalls. Boats in the harbour were secured and the great doors of the cathedral shut and bolted. By the time the sun reached its peak, the busy squares and boulevards of Palermo were deserted and the ancient capital still as a doomed city awaiting its fate.

The Devil's Wind, they called it, and it brought with it madness and despair. Moaning and whistling against shuttered windows, the sirocco rampaged in fury. Tiles were torn off roofs and rubbish tossed in the air. Barrels and crates were sent crashing against walls or spinning into the sea. Children cried while the old took to their beds and waited for the *tempesta* to pass.

Late in the afternoon, the sound of hooves on the cobbles brought a woman to her window. She made the sign against evil as a lone horseman passed below. Only the Devil would be abroad at such a time and the rider looked like Satan himself going at such a pace. He was bent over the saddle, hat pulled down low, as he galloped down the narrow streets. On he went, past the naked statues of the Fountain of Shame until he reached the old quarter of the city where the alleys were narrow and steep. Flecks of lather flew from his horse's neck but he spurred it on until he came to a palace high above the city.

The horseman pulled up beside a barred gate. He dismounted and threw his hat and cloak across the saddle. Then he put his foot on the bar and hauled himself up. There was a gap at the top and he squeezed through, dropping down on the other side. For a moment he stood, his gaze scanning the front of the house. Then he began to walk. Every few paces he glanced up to the balustrade running along the floor above until he found what he was looking for. A window, left unlocked by a careless servant, had blown open, its lace curtain billowing in the wind. The interloper climbed branches of a wisteria, vaulted over the balustrade and slipped into the house.

Taking the scarf from his neck, he wiped the dust from his mouth. Hazy light caught his reflection in an old glass, revealing a face that was lean and hard. There was a deadly purpose in the blue eyes that looked back at him. He waited, listening intently. The only sound was the banging and rattling of shutters, and rugs on the floor muffled his footsteps as he walked to the door.

Prince Riccardo Scalia was dozing on his bed. He sensed, rather than heard, the turning of the door handle. Instinct, born of years of conspiracy, jolted him awake. Before the door was open, he was on his feet with a dagger in his hand. Seeing the tall man silhouetted in the entrance, his eyes narrowed. The raw look of vengeance was written on the intruder's face. How long could he hold him at bay? How long before someone heard them and sent for the guards?

'Ben Mavrone! My doormen have instructions not to allow revolutionaries into the house.'

'Your servants are asleep and I didn't wake them. We shall be left undisturbed.'

'May I enquire as to the nature of your visit?'

'You know why I'm here.'

'I know you were involved in the revolution. There remains a warrant for your arrest. However, I recall you ran off to Ireland or some such place to escape.'

'Yet you tried to capture me. You tried everything from spies to hired assassins. When you failed, you took my brother instead. You didn't care that he was innocent. You used him as bait to get me back to Sicily.'

As he spoke, Mavrone's hand moved to the hilt of his knife. He held it against the light, running his finger along the blade. Every move was calculated in the war of nerves between the two men. Prince Scalia placed his feet squarely apart. Mavrone was younger, but he was the one with the cooler head. He only had to reach his loaded pistol in the drawer.

'Come now! Your brother was tried and found guilty of treason. He would have been shot if King Ferdinand, in his mercy, hadn't spared his life. His death in prison was an accident. Although, had you returned earlier, I dare say it might have been prevented.'

Scalia accurately anticipated his opponent's reaction. As Mavrone sprang forward, he stepped aside so the strike glanced off his shoulder. Both knives were up. Scalia had the advantage with the light behind him. With one arm bent to shield his face, he began to edge sideways. Mavrone followed, step by step, as they circled the floor. As they neared the corner of the room, Scalia began to gain confidence. The drawer was half open – no more than an arm's length away. Then Mavrone made his move.

He was playing with him like a cat with a mouse and black fury rose in Prince Scalia. He hurled himself at Mavrone with his blade aimed for the heart. He expected the knife to penetrate flesh, but the weapon was sent spinning out of his hand. Mavrone hit him, whipping the side of his knife against his head and Scalia's knees gave way. He staggered and fell against a heavy screen, knocking it over and taking both men to the ground. Mavrone's weight came down on him, straddling his chest with his knife pressed hard under Scalia's chin.

'My God! What are you doing?' A woman's cry rang out.

Bianca! Prince Scalia had thought his wife was sleeping in her own rooms. She must have been woken by the noise. He prayed she was an angel signalling his reprieve, but Mavrone did not move.

'Leave us, Bianca,' he said, tersely.

'For mercy's sake, have you lost your senses?' Bianca was tugging at Mavrone's shoulder.

'Leave us, unless you want to see your husband killed before your eyes.'

'Why, in the name of heaven? What has he done?'

'Alex is dead. He was murdered in prison.'

Prince Scalia winced as the blade broke the surface of his skin. Blood trickled from his chin and he looked at Bianca. Why hadn't she the sense to call the guards? Why didn't she scream instead of standing there as if turned to stone? The stupid bitch! Couldn't she see there was no mercy in Ben Mavrone?

'I don't believe you! Riccardo told me his sentence had been reduced.'

'I assure you there is no mistake. I saw his body for myself. He was killed the day I returned to Sicily.'

'Dear God have mercy …'

Prince Scalia's gaze fixed on his wife's face and her voice was a whisper. 'Is it true?'

He gritted his teeth as Mavrone grabbed his hair and forced his head back.

'Tell her the truth,' Mavrone said.

'It's true.' A dry croak came from his lips. 'He was executed … on my orders.'

Bianca fell to her knees and caught hold of Mavrone's arm. For the first time he turned to look at her.

'Spare him, Benito. They will only kill you as well.'

'They've never succeeded before.'

'But this would be murder! Without a trial, it's a crime as evil as his. Don't you see?' Her fingers clutched frantically at his sleeve. 'Is this what Alex died for? Don't condemn your soul to eternal damnation. I beg you, if you still have any love for me.'

She was weeping and Scalia held his breath. Mavrone would never commit murder in front of Bianca! He thought he was saved until he saw Mavrone push her aside. In that instant, Riccardo Scalia knew the terror of death.

Mavrone hesitated no longer. He lifted his knife and cut the prince down one cheek and then the other. Blood spurted out, streaming down his neck and staining his shirt scarlet. Scalia screamed, clutching his face. His cries echoed around the room, diminishing along with his strength, until finally there was silence. Mavrone bent down and picked up a piece of torn tapestry. He cleaned the blood off his knife and dropped the fragment beside Scalia's unconscious body. Bianca buried her face in her hands as he touched her hair.

'I spared him for your sake, Bianca. I'll take this as a memento of your devotion.'

For a moment, he held her hair like a lover. Then he sliced off a curl and crushed it in the palm of his hand. When Bianca raised her head, Ben Mavrone was walking away. He did not look back. The door closed behind him and the wailing wind deadened his footsteps as he left the apartments of Prince Scalia as stealthily as he had come in.

CHAPTER ONE

LONDON, DECEMBER 1859

It was different now. Different from how it had been this morning when Oliver Temple's note arrived on her breakfast tray. The stiff white envelope was propped against the teapot with her name, Miss Carina Temple, scrawled in her uncle's hand. Carina waited until she was up and dressed before she opened the letter. There was no 'be so kind' or 'at your convenience', only a single line summoning her to attend upon him at three o'clock of the afternoon.

All the way there, Carina promised herself she would be civil. Her uncle, Oliver, was also her guardian with total control over her finances. Their dislike for each other was mutual, but on no account must she lose her temper. Oliver's brusque note had nothing to do with the other matter, she was sure.

The carriage turned the corner of Hyde Park and a recent conversation flooded her mind.

'What possible harm is there? Lord Danby's lonely with his wife tied up at Court,' Carina had argued with her aunt, Alice. 'We keep each other company, that's all. There's no impropriety in our friendship.'

'It is nothing to the purpose. Lord Danby is a married man.'

'He has always behaved impeccably.'

'That's not the point! My brother, Oliver, will come to hear of it and I will be held responsible. If you refuse to consider your own reputation, please have some consideration for mine!'

Alice had ended the conversation by getting up and going over to the piano. She was upset and played too fast, Carina recalled with a pang of guilt. She was happier when Aunt Alice was content, but she had continued to meet with Danby. Why shouldn't she? Her long period of mourning was finally at an end and she was starved of life. It was unnatural to be shut up, entombed in black crêpe and seeing no one. The gloomy ritual imposed by society couldn't bring back her father and, when it was over, Robert Danby had been the first person to take an interest in her. He was self-assured and worldly and she enjoyed his company – at least, that was so, until last week.

The weather had turned cold and Lord Danby escorted her to the picture gallery at Stafford House. He was knowledgeable, pointing out the best paintings and greeting various acquaintances with a nod of the head, not stopping to speak to them. Then, as they walked out of the front door, he slipped his arm around her waist and pulled her to him. Right there in the middle of St James's Street! Carina freed herself and glared at him.

'I'm only helping you down the steps, Miss Temple. We don't want you to slip and twist your pretty ankle, now do we?'

How easily he laughed it off, but Carina was appalled. Just imagine if anyone had seen them! It only took one person and rumour would spread like wildfire. They would be talked about in every salon and ballroom of London. Robert Danby had overstepped the mark, but he wouldn't be blamed. Oh no, the man was never guilty. His misdemeanour would be shrugged off and her character vilified.

She mustn't fear the worst, Carina decided as they arrived at the mansion in Belgrave Square. A footman ushered her into her uncle's study and Oliver Temple did not stand up. He sat behind his desk, indicating the chair opposite with a wave of his hand. Before Carina had time to arrange her skirts, he began.

'You know why I've sent for you?'

'I expect you wish to talk about my overdraft.'

'No, Carina, not this time. You're here to explain your conduct over these last weeks.'

Carina looked her uncle straight in the face. Oliver was a stocky man and had put on weight since she last saw him. Ginger side-whiskers could not hide the folds of his chin and his cheeks were as red as the claret he had consumed over lunch.

'I refer to your acquaintance with Lord Danby. What do you have to say for yourself?'

'Nothing. It is entirely my own affair.'

'There, you're mistaken.' Oliver leant forward and placed his hands on the desk. 'I had words with Lord Danby in White's club last night.'

He was bluffing, Carina thought. He must be! Robert Danby despised her uncle. He would go out of his way to avoid him. Her heart beat faster and Oliver continued.

'Rumour has it that you are intent on breaking up his marriage.'

'I'm surprised you take notice of such gossip.' Carina made an attempt to sound indifferent. 'Lord Danby is merely an acquaintance.'

'Merely an acquaintance? His wife is lady-in-waiting to Her Majesty, does that mean nothing to you?'

'As I've not been presented to the queen, I've not the slightest interest in either her or her courtiers.'

She had struck home, Carina saw by the way Oliver's mouth thinned and he shifted uncomfortably in his chair. Her uncle had no intention of arranging her presentation at Court. He was determined to keep that privilege for his own children.

Oliver picked a letter from his tray and read it through before he placed it face down on the blotter.

'Has Lord Danby been invited to your home?'

'No, he has not.'

'But you accompanied him to Lord Stafford's house last week, contrary to my sister Alice's prohibition?'

'Alice did not prohibit me. She knew nothing of it—'

'So you deceived your aunt in order to have an assignation with a married man?'

He gave her a hard stare, but Carina had herself in hand. She sat straight, a sea of blue velvet skirts around her, and kept her face blank. So they *had* been seen! And whoever recognised them, had gone straight to Oliver. *But why*, Carina wondered? She had no enemies as far as she knew. Who could have informed on her? Certainly not Alice or her friend, Harry Carstairs. They were the two people she trusted most in the world. It was possible Oliver might have had her followed. She wouldn't put anything past him and now he was speaking again.

'You're a great disappointment to me, Carina. Since your father's demise I've done everything in my power to take care of you. How do you repay me? By dragging the family's name through the mud!'

Carina's expression did not change, but her lips went white. She couldn't bear Oliver talking about her father. You pompous little man, she thought. Papa was worth a hundred of you. You're only my guardian because he died unexpectedly – not because he respected you. Hot words bubbled up and she forced them down for Alice's sake. Putting her hands on the arms of her chair, she made as if to rise.

'I will not remain here and be insulted, sir! Please would you order my carriage?'

'You will stay until I've finished and pay attention to what I have to say! News of your liaison with Danby is bandied about by every gossipmonger in London. So much so, I felt obliged to ask His Lordship if there was any truth in the allegations.'

He was trying to catch her out, Carina thought. She didn't believe him but a knot tightened in her stomach.

'Lord Danby claims you threw yourself at him and have pursued him relentlessly. He went so far as to describe you as an unscrupulous hussy. What he meant by *that*, I dread to imagine.'

Oliver was poisonous as a snake and hot colour washed Carina's cheeks. It was a preposterous allegation. How dare Danby say such a thing when she had ignored his overtures in the beginning and only accepted an invitation for luncheon when his wife was present? Admittedly, it had gone on from there but they both knew the rules. She had broken with Lord Danby immediately after the incident at Stafford House. Since then, his letters had been returned and his calling cards ignored. But none of this was Oliver's business. Let him think what he liked. She was under no obligation to justify herself.

'Well, do you deny it?'

Carina fixed her gaze at a point over Oliver's shoulder, looking at a landscape of cows in a field on the wall behind him.

'For shame, Carina! You're a disrespectful young woman!'

Oliver pushed back his chair and stood up. Walking over to the window, he opened the latch and let a stream of cold air into the room. Carina infuriated him and he blamed his brother for her unruly nature. Why John had married a foreigner in the first place, he didn't know. When Sonia died in childbirth, he had failed to find himself a suitable second English wife to discipline his only child. John may have taught Carina to ride and shoot as well as a man, but she had her way for the asking. As a consequence, she was as wild and wilful as the wind.

This was the age of the self-made man and Oliver Temple was not about to give way to a girl of eighteen. Unlike his older brother, he was the one who had worked, overseeing the cotton mills that provided prosperity for the Temple family. Apart from Melton, the family home, everything he owned had been gained by his own endeavour. Last year he had received a knighthood from the queen and was proud of his success. If Carina thought she could jeopardise all he had achieved on a whim, she was mistaken.

Oliver closed the window and gave himself a moment to study his niece. Carina was striking with her sloping eyes, so like her father's and sea green as a Russian cat. Her mouth was delicately curved and her copper hair pinned high above her collar to show off her slender neck. She was slim like her Sicilian mother, a small waist accentuated by the tight-fitting jacket. He could understand why a man like Danby might be attracted to her. On the surface, Carina appeared delicate as a spring flower, but he had seen the fire in her eyes moments before. Tempestuous blood ran in her veins and this time she had gone too far.

Carina wondered what Oliver was thinking. The muscles of her face were stiff from keeping still and she lowered her eyes as he returned to his chair.

'I've decided you're to go to Sicily until this unfortunate business has blown over.'

Carina's head came up, her chin lifting. For a brief moment the only sound in the room was the ticking of a clock. Then, hardly trusting herself to speak, she asked him to repeat what he had said.

'I dispatched a letter to your grandmother this morning, informing her you will arrive in Palermo early in the New Year.' Oliver paused, his voice dropping reverentially. 'Her Majesty is most concerned for Lady Danby's welfare and I'm charged with resolving the matter. A sojourn in Sicily is the obvious solution.'

'Damn the bloody queen and damn you, Oliver Temple! You've no right to order my life!'

As the words came out of her mouth, Carina leapt to her feet. In response, Oliver slammed his fist down on the desk.

'You'll not speak of our beloved sovereign with such disrespect! You're a spoiled and ungrateful child. I can think of nowhere to suit you better than a barbaric island like Sicily!'

'I'm not going to be sent away!'

'Then I shall cut your allowance with immediate effect.' Oliver collected himself swiftly. 'Not only will you be penniless but homeless as well.'

As if he expected her to jump across the desk and attack him, Oliver reached for the hand bell and rang it loudly. The door opened and the footman marched in carrying her cloak. Her uncle had manipulated the interview from the beginning, Carina thought, and the man had probably been standing by the door throughout.

'Your Aunt Alice will travel out with you as your chaperone.' Oliver stood up. 'Your passage is booked for the first week of January. That's all I have to say to you.'

Carina snatched her cloak from the footman and slung it over her arm. Without another word, she marched out of the room, her footsteps clattering on the marble stairway as she went down. She heard the footman hurrying after her, but did not stop. The front door was open and she ran through the hall and down the steps to where the brougham was waiting.

The lamplighters were already at work and, once inside, Carina took off her bonnet and threw it on to the seat. She wrapped her cloak tightly about her. Her heart was beating so hard in her chest it hurt. Oliver was a liar. Care for her indeed! When her father died, he couldn't wait to get his hands on Melton, the home where she had lived all her life. The house in Mount Street had been acquired with undue haste and she and Alice packed off to London within a month of her father's accident. For that alone she would never forgive him.

Tears pricked the back of her eyes and Carina squeezed them shut. She hadn't cried since leaving Melton and she would not now. Anger drove out pain and she flexed her fingers until the joints cracked. The conversation with Oliver had been a charade! He knew the dalliance with Danby wasn't serious – only a diversion to pass the time, easily begun and as easily ended. Her uncle had been looking for an excuse to send her away and Lord Danby had handed him one on a plate.

Carina was seized suddenly by panic. What was she going to say to Alice? It was all a pack of lies, but her aunt would be mortified. Fresh anger struck her. Robert Danby had behaved despicably and Oliver was ruthless – but they wouldn't get away with this! 'I won't let them bully me,' she swore under her breath. 'I'll think of a way to stop them before I talk to Alice.'

CHAPTER TWO

Carina entered the house quietly and crept past the drawing room where Alice was playing the piano. Her maid, Rose, was waiting in the bedroom and she undressed and climbed into the bathtub. She lay soaking in the warm water and by the time she returned to the bedroom it was six o'clock. Without much interest, she picked out a gown of blue crêpe and stood while Rose fixed the lacing on her corset. Then she went to sit at the dressing table.

Rose brushed her hair with long, smooth strokes as thoughts went tearing round her head. Oliver had said Alice was to travel with her as chaperone and Carina was swept by resentment on her aunt's behalf. Why should poor Alice have to journey half-way across the continent at his behest? What did Oliver think would happen to her if the house were closed?

'Your aunt's given up so much to care for you. She's still a young woman. I hope she finds happiness for herself one day.'

Carina recalled the words of her friend, Harry Carstairs. For sure he was referring to Sir Anthony Farne, a widower from Northumberland. He had become a frequent visitor to Mount

Street and, for the first time in her life, Alice was in love. Harry's understanding of human nature was uncluttered by experience, but, for once, Carina agreed with him. If their courtship foundered, then she would be to blame.

How had it all gone so wrong? She should have listened to Alice, but it was too late now. She had to think herself out of this mess and an idea took shape in her mind. She would ask Harry to speak to Robert Danby. They belonged to the same club and he might be able to extract an apology. Oliver wouldn't be able to send her away then. What was it Danby had called her? An unscrupulous hussy? Carina shook her head hopelessly. Lord Danby's priority was to save his own skin and he would never back down.

Two oval miniatures stood on the table and Carina picked up the one of her father and held it to her lips. It brought back to her the grief she suffered when he died. She had wanted to run with the pain and coped in the only way she knew how. She was young, her spirit of survival strong, and she had pursued everything and anything that filled the void inside. Living on the bright edge of life, nothing mattered so much that it could hurt her again – and this was the result.

Carina put the miniature down and studied the portrait of her mother. Sonia Temple had the expression of a woman who knew her own mind. How would she advise her daughter, she wondered? Would her mother tell her to submit to Oliver?

You will go to Sicily. The knowledge came to Carina with an absolute certainty she had experienced before. For as long as she could remember, she had been susceptible to a sixth sense – a voice in her head telling her what would happen. Her premonitions were rarely wrong and she drew a surprised breath.

'Are you feeling unwell, ma'am?'

'I'm fine, thank you.' Carina saw Rose's worried face in the glass and forced a smile. 'I will write my journal and ring when I'm ready.'

Rose left the room and Carina pressed her hands to her cheeks. It was so unfair, but life was unfair and self-pity never helped anyone. Alice had been both sister and mother to her. She was the most important person in her life and, if the outcome of this afternoon couldn't be undone, then she must come first.

So, why not go to Sicily? Her grandmother – the Contessa Denuzio – was eighty and a visit long overdue. Once Carina was safely in Palermo, Alice could return to England while she stayed on under the contessa's protection. There was one condition. She would let it be known this was her decision and had nothing to do with Lord Danby or Oliver Temple. A winter in the Mediterranean was hardly a life sentence, after all. Hadn't Byron and Shelley taken refuge in warmer, friendlier climes when society turned against them?

Lord knew, she was weary of London. Hot houses smelled sweet, but they suffocated you if you stayed in them too long. Alice was her closest companion and Carina had few girlfriends. Young women of her age were mostly concerned with the pursuit of a wealthy husband while her ambition was to be a poet. She read every piece of verse she could lay her hands on and knew most of the Romantics by heart. Carina wasn't sure that she was any good, but Alice had always encouraged her.

There was time before dinner and she went over to the bureau and took a small bound volume from the drawer. She held it under her nose, smelling the soft leather, before she began to turn the pages. Along with a first edition of Byron's *Childe Harold*, her journal was her most treasured possession. Quotations were interspersed with scatterings of verse and she skipped to the first blank page. Picking up a pen, she stroked the feathered end against her cheek. Then she dipped the nib in the inkwell and began to write.

If I am to trace the footsteps of my hero on his Pilgrimage—

Here, she broke off and neatly scored through the line. She thought for a moment and then wrote beneath:

Remember thee, remember thee!
When exiled far in Sicily,
O false uncle, doubt thee not
A fiend like thee is best forgot!

Her mood brightened for the first time that day. Writing stilled the clamour in her head and she felt calmer. She blew on the ink and closed the journal, returning it to the drawer before she rang the bell for Rose. It was time to finish dressing and go down for dinner.

CHAPTER THREE

She was going to be late, Carina thought as she hurried downstairs the next morning. Harry Carstairs had sent a note saying he would call at noon and she dozed off after breakfast so they had to rush. Rose was flustered and kept dropping hairpins. Then Carina couldn't decide what to wear. She dithered, picking one outfit after another and finally settled on a tarlatan promenade dress. Its hem was high enough to show off her new Moroccan boots and the crinoline so wide her skirts brushed both sides of the staircase as she went down.

The tall-case clock in the hall was chiming twelve as she walked into the morning room and went to stand by the fire. She loved this room with its red wallpaper and brocade curtains. She would miss it while she was away, she thought. She would miss Alice and Harry too and she wondered how she could have been so confident the night before.

Sir Anthony Farne was just leaving when she went down and, once he had gone, she told Alice about the meeting with Oliver.

'Oh dear, oh dear!' Her aunt's hands fluttered like two white birds in her lap. 'I'll call on him first thing tomorrow and persuade him to change his mind.'

'It won't do any good. You know Oliver! He would hang rather than incur Her Majesty's displeasure.'

'I can but try—'

'Please don't! I've quite made up my mind to go.'

Sitting across the hearth, Carina was sharper than she intended. Alice was twelve years older than her and as refined as her brother was coarse. She looked pretty in a plush velvet dress with a wide collar that complemented her china-blue eyes. Her auburn hair was pinned under a trimmed tulle cap and, for all her concern, there was colour in her cheeks. Carina felt comforted in her presence. She hadn't meant to snap at her.

'I'm sorry you're obliged to travel with me. I promise to make sure you return to England just as soon as I'm settled.'

'Hush now, dearest. I'm delighted to accompany you. I was very fond of your mother. It will be good to see something of her home.' Alice smiled and smoothed the scalloped trim of her cuffs. 'By chance, Anthony and I were talking about Sicily earlier. He reminded me that Miss Parsons is cousin to the British Consul in Palermo and intends to visit him in January. Do you think we might travel out with her?'

Recalling the small, energetic spinster who was Alice's friend, Carina's heart sank. There was nothing to dislike about Miss Parsons except that she talked a good deal and mostly about politics. Last month she persuaded them to spend a whole morning in a draughty hall in Kensington, tasked with sorting clothes for veterans of the Crimea. Carina had longed to be out riding in Rotten Row. The smell of camphor clung to her for days afterwards and when Harry suggested she continue the good work, she told him smartly he could go in her place.

There was a knock at the door and Thomas, the footman, showed Harry into the room. Carina held her hands out to the blond young man who came towards her.

'Harry, what a pleasure.'

Carina led Harry to the sofa and patted the seat next to her. She studied him as he sat down, noting the smart cut of his coat and buff trousers. Every detail of his dress, from his embroidered waistcoat to the ruby solitaire nestling in the folds of his cravat, was up to the mark. Harry had become quite the man about town and was good-looking with his thick moustache and hazel eyes. Although he denied it, she knew of several young ladies in London who were in love with him.

'As well as can be expected under the circumstances.' Harry rubbed his hands on his knees. 'It's all over London this morning, you know.'

'What's all over London, the Great Stink of last summer?'

'Don't be frivolous, Carrie. It ain't one of your railway novels. This is real life, where actions have consequences.'

Real life? Oh yes, she knew what that meant for women – staying at home with a brood of children while your husband was free as air. Well, it wasn't the life she wanted. She had tried to explain this to Harry so often. Why couldn't he understand? He was forever pulling her up and Carina hoped he hadn't come to give her a lecture for she wasn't sure she had the patience to endure it.

'How many times did I tell you Lord Danby was untrustworthy?' Harry asked.

'So many that I don't recall a time when we spoke of anything else. You said I would lose my reputation and now I have. Are you satisfied?'

'Of course I'm not satisfied! I bumped into Sir Oliver in White's last night and he told me he'd spoken to you. Is it true that you're banished to Sicily?'

Carina stood up and walked to the centre of the room. Picking up a newspaper, she opened it to hide her face. The idea of Harry talking to Oliver behind her back made her furious. He professed himself her champion but, when it came to it, members of the gentlemen's clubs of St James's stuck together like clams. And to think she had almost asked him to appeal to Robert Danby!

A stinging retort was on her lips, but Carina caught herself. There had been too many arguments lately and, afraid of saying something she might regret, she skimmed through the paper instead. A leading article caught her eye. She glanced over it and then read aloud: 'Our correspondent writes from Sicily that revolution is in the air and Palermo is a hotbed of intrigue and conspiracy.'

Carina lowered the broadsheet and looked across the room at Harry. 'Do you hear that? Palermo sounds almost as bad as London.'

Before she had finished, Harry rose to his feet and walked over to the hearth. His brow was furrowed and his shoulders hunched. There was a bruised look in his eyes and Carina's irritation left her.

'I'm only teasing, Harry! I don't mean it.'

'Don't you? Difficult to know what you mean these days. You're like a stranger most of the time.'

'I should have taken your advice and I'm sorry I did not. Now, please will you stop being cross?'

Carina went to stand beside Harry as he flicked through the invitation cards stacked on the mantelpiece. She had said she was sorry. What more did he want? Harry was still frowning and when he took the fob watch from his waistcoat and snapped it open, she laid a hand on his arm.

'I've finished with Robert Danby. It's over and done with.'

'But the scandal's not over. It's the talk of the town.'

'Next week someone else will behave outrageously. Then you'll talk about them instead.'

Harry covered her hand with his. He was beginning to weaken, Carina thought, but his grip tightened.

'It's no good, Carrie. Can you imagine, my father's forbidden me to call on you? I shouldn't be here now, in truth.'

The Carstairs had been her family's closest neighbours in Yorkshire and Carina was shocked. Mr Carstairs had been her father's best man. How could he take Robert Danby's side against her? The betrayal cut deep and she withdrew her hand as Harry ploughed on.

'Too many people heard Danby talking to your uncle. You can't imagine some of the things he said. They were beyond the pale—'

'Are you here to tell me you're no longer my friend?' Carina cut in.

'Of course I'm your friend.'

'Then you should trust me! I never encouraged Lord Danby. He lied to my uncle—'

'So why are you being sent away?'

Oliver had been at work and the damage was done. What a time they must have had of it, Carina thought – all those so-called gentlemen listening to the salacious gossip! She waited until coolness came back and then lifted her shoulders in a dismissive shrug.

'You can tell your friends that the trip to Palermo is entirely my own idea. I've always wanted to visit my mother's family.'

'But you don't know your maternal relations!' Harry stated as if it was good reason never to do so. 'Sicily's a wild and uncivilised place. I don't like the sound of it. Don't like it at all.'

'My grandmother's lived in Palermo all her life. It's not the least uncivilised …' Carina trailed off, uncertain of what Harry was thinking. He ran his hand through his hair and there was a taut look on his face.

'Listen to me, Carrie. It's crucial that you regain your good name. You must promise me your conduct will be irreproachable while you're away!'

'I thought you said my reputation was damaged beyond repair—'

'People will forget once you've gone. If you behave impeccably, Sir Oliver will relent. Then I'll be damned if I don't come to Sicily and fetch you home myself!'

Harry's tone was vibrant, his expression so full of hope that goose bumps pricked the back of Carina's neck. She enjoyed other men's admiration, but Harry was her oldest friend. He had switched from disapproval to passionate intensity so fast and she didn't know how to answer. If it had been anyone else, she might almost have mistaken the pleading look in his eyes for something quite different. The world had turned topsy-turvy in the last twenty-four hours and she was desperate to return to normality.

'That is most gallant of you, sir. Pray tell me, what would your father say *then*?'

Carina spoke lightly but Harry's head went down. He slipped the fob back into his waistcoat as the door opened and Alice walked in. 'I'm sorry. I didn't know you were visiting, Mr Carstairs. What a pity, for I am just on my way out.'

Carina did not hear Harry's reply. She was wondering why Alice was dressed in funeral clothes. How she hated those scratchy dresses and heavy veils! Her weeds had been burnt months ago and she thought Alice had done the same.

'I'm due at a service of remembrance at one o'clock.' Alice answered her unspoken question. 'I would offer you a ride, Mr

Carstairs, but I'm already late. No doubt you'll be glad of a breath of fresh air.'

'Indeed, Miss Alice. I am going to White's. The walk will do me good.'

'And what do you have planned for this afternoon, dearest?' Alice turned to Carina.

'I'll finish my shopping and then write to my grandmother. I know she will take my word for the truth – unlike some other people I know.'

When Alice left the room and Harry followed without saying goodbye, Carina could have bitten off her tongue. Harry brings out the worst in me, she thought. What does he mean I'm like a stranger? He's the one who has changed, not me. One minute he's scolding me and the next … And the next … he's looking at me like a lovesick schoolboy.

The workings of a man's mind were an enigma to Carina. Too often they said one thing when they meant another. How could anyone know what they were really thinking? She had spent so much of her childhood alone, there were times she felt ill equipped in her dealings with people and her confidence wavered. Could she have everything the wrong way around? Was it possible she had unwittingly given Robert Danby a false impression? No, it wasn't so! Danby had made all the running. She had never led him on – not to the slightest degree!

Carina dismissed the idea and went over to the window, looking down to the street as Harry helped Alice into the brougham. She tapped on the glass pane, but Harry strode off without a backward glance. His cane made a spotted pattern in the snow on the pavement and she watched until he disappeared round the corner.

As she turned back into the room, a chill touched her. Harry and Alice were the bedrock of her life. She would never intentionally hurt either of them. The strain of yesterday was playing on her mind and she had read too much into Harry's words. He was only trying to cheer her up and she must write at once and apologise for her asperity. Thomas could take her letter this afternoon so he had it when he came home and by tomorrow they would be friends again. There was no need to be afraid.

CHAPTER FOUR

The Burlington Arcade was filled with Christmas shoppers and the crush of people made it difficult to move. Despite Alice's instruction to take Rose with her, Carina was alone. Footmen, their arms stacked high with parcels, followed customers to their carriages, while her purchases would be delivered to the house the next day. The arcade was sparkling with Christmas decorations and she was content to make her way slowly towards Piccadilly where a queue of people were waiting for Hackney cabs.

The thin gauze veil of her bonnet fluttered against her cheek as she searched for one that was free. It might be quicker to walk, but she was without a chaperone and the pavements were wet with snow. It would be a shame to ruin her new boots. As she deliberated, a familiar voice spoke from behind her.

'Miss Temple! This is a fortunate coincidence.'

A hand dropped on her shoulder and she was spun round to find herself facing Robert Danby. Carina saw at once he looked dreadful. He was unshaven and leaning heavily on his cane.

'I've been trying to call all week.'

'I have been greatly occupied.'

'Too occupied to read my letters? They've all been returned, don't you know.'

'I cannot delay, sir. My aunt is waiting for me—'

'How very strange.' Danby's expression darkened. 'My cousin, Mrs Vere, told me she was accompanying your aunt to a remembrance service this afternoon. I believe she invited her for tea afterwards.'

'You may believe whatever you like! I don't want to talk to you or to stand here all afternoon.'

'Dear girl, I've no intention of keeping you here. My carriage is at the north entrance and I will drive you home.'

'I told you my aunt is expecting me—'

'And you, Miss Temple, are a very poor liar.'

Robert Danby released her shoulder and tucked her hand under his arm. Carina was obliged to walk with him back up the arcade. He elbowed his way through the crowd and she noticed people turning their heads and whispering behind their hands. She could imagine what they were saying and kept her head low until they came to the north entrance. The landau, drawn by the famous Danby matching greys, stood waiting and group of young men in greatcoats were admiring the equipage.

Their encounter was no accident, Carina thought with a twist of alarm. Robert Danby had followed her to the arcade and had been waiting to catch her on the way out. His subterfuge infuriated her. She wanted to shout at him and throw off his arm, but didn't dare risk a scene. If she wasn't careful, news of this latest debacle would wing its way across London and Alice would come to hear of it.

The monkey boy unfolded the steps and she had no choice but to let Robert Danby escort her to the carriage. He gave instructions to the coachman and Carina lifted the side of her cloak to cover her face as she climbed in. The distance to Mount Street was no more than ten minutes' drive and she could handle Lord Danby. She would tell him exactly what she thought of him and that would be the end of it.

When he joined her, Danby sat down clumsily, ignoring the fact he was crushing her skirts. He knocked on the roof with his cane and then slumped back and stretched out his legs. He was staring into the middle distance and Carina stole a glance in his direction.

Grey light from the window fell on his face and the dark stubble on his chin. He had taken off his gloves and her gaze was drawn to the thick hairs on the back of his wrists. Robert Danby was a big man and everything about him displayed the arrogance of inherited wealth. He wore the best clothes, owned the best horses and gambled his money away. Looking at him now with his florid complexion and full red lips, Carina couldn't think how she ever thought him attractive. Then Danby turned his head. His gaze swept boldly over her as it had the first time they met. Recalling that occasion and her own unaccountable reaction, her heart missed a beat.

'I believe you owe me an explanation, ma'am.'

'And you, sir, owe me an apology.'

'Do I now? And why is that?'

'Because you are no gentleman! You lied to my uncle and defamed my name! Is it true you told him that I pursued you shamelessly?'

'I don't deny it. And I'll lay a hundred to one it was that upstart uncle of yours who stopped you seeing me.'

'Your behaviour is contemptible, sir. You have caused myself and my family the greatest distress.'

'Well, there's a thing! You never cared tuppence for your

family before.' Robert Danby's mouth twisted in a smile that did not reach his eyes. 'What's your game, Miss Temple? Do you have ambitions to become the second Countess Danby? Are you playing fast and loose in order to ensnare me?'

Carina was struck dumb by the question. She could smell brandy on his breath. Danby was drunk and she stiffened as he shifted closer.

'I hoped our relationship might be different. But one way or another, I will have you.'

There was a gale blowing through her head and Carina struggled to keep calm. Robert Danby had discarded his air of sophistication and she sensed violence beneath the surface. Any provocation might be dangerous. She was terrified she might laugh – the shocked, hysterical laughter that comes with panic. Her pulse raced so fast it was difficult to breathe and she pressed her hand to her heart to slow its frantic pace.

'It was never my intention to mislead or encourage you, sir.' Her voice was husky with nerves. 'If I have led you to believe otherwise, then I apologise most sincerely.'

She hoped to pacify him, but Danby did not answer. He was looking out of the window and, following the direction of his gaze, Carina saw they were in Berkeley Square. Thank heavens, she was almost home. Then, just as she expected the landau to swing left into Mount Street, it swerved in the opposite direction. She was thrown back against the cushions and, by the time she leant forward, exclaiming that the coachman had missed the turn, they were increasing speed.

'I'm not taking you home yet.' Robert Danby leant across her and pulled down the blind. 'You and I shall enjoy ourselves first.'

'Turn around at once, do you hear! You—'

She was silenced as Robert Danby's hand went for the ribbons of her bonnet. He undid them roughly and tossed it to the floor. One arm went around her shoulders and she let out a cry as his hand grasped her chin. His fingers squeezed her jaw and his mouth smothered her lips. As Carina clawed wildly at his face, she felt herself being bent over backwards. Her cloak was caught beneath her and Danby's weight bent the hoops of her crinoline until they snapped.

'I know this is what you want …'

Danby began combing his fingers through her hair, mumbling wild, incoherent sentences until he bent his head again. This time his kiss was indescribably worse. His wet mouth traced a path across her cheek and his tongue pressed her lips apart. He had broken the frogging of her jacket and reached inside for her bodice. Carina grabbed a handful of his hair and pulled, hard. Danby groaned, but did not lift his head. She pummelled at his shoulders and arms. She would kill him rather than let him do this! She would kick and bite until he was forced to let her go, but Danby was too strong and she could not get free.

Her arm thrashed outwards. If she could reach the strap, she might pull herself up and get to the door. Her hand touched the cane lying on the floor. She tried to get hold of it, but Danby caught her arm and trapped it by her side. He attempted to kiss her again and Carina sank her teeth into the side of his cheek. As his neck jerked backwards, she flung out her hand. Fumbling along the floor, her fingers closed around the cane. She raised it above his head and, using all her strength, brought it down across the back of his skull.

Carina hit him so hard that the cane cracked in two. A look of astonishment crossed Danby's face, but, for a moment, the blow seemed to have no effect. Then the pupils of his eyes rolled upward and he slumped forward. His body was a dead weight on top of her and Carina struggled to get from underneath him. She pushed with her hands and knees until a final shove sent him to the floor.

Lord Danby lay so still she thought he was dead. Violence had answered violence and she had killed him! Carina was close to hysteria, half laughing and half crying until she saw the fingers of one hand twitch. Not only was he alive, Danby was already regaining consciousness! There was no time to lose and she scrambled over his legs and banged on the front partition with her fists. They were travelling at such a speed no one could hear, so she picked up the broken cane and hammered on the roof. At last, there came a shout from above and the landau began to slow down.

Carina found the catch and swung the door open. Hanging onto the straps, she glanced back. Robert Danby lay sprawled on the carriage floor but his eyes were open, the glassy look in them changing from bewilderment to rage as his gaze came into focus. He moved his hand in a feeble attempt to grab her skirts and, before the carriage came to a halt, Carina jumped.

She landed awkwardly, falling onto her knees in the snow. The monkey boy leapt down and tried to help her up, but she shouted at him and pushed him away. Seconds later, she was on her feet and sprinting down the street. She had no idea where she was going, no thought but to get away. Her hair fell across her eyes, half blinding her, and when her petticoats caught between her legs, Carina hitched her skirts above her knees and ran on.

Danby would come after her and she could hear a carriage travelling fast behind. Carina pressed back against a wall, terror squeezing her heart until the vehicle went past. It was only a Clarence cab, but she had to dig her fingers into the palms of her hands to control her panic. For a long time she stood motionless. Then she plucked up her courage and looked back.

Dense fog thickened the night and there was no sight or sound of the Danby landau. Gas lamps spread soft pools of light onto the pavement and at the far end of the street she made out the skeleton of trees. Was it her imagination or were they the trees of Berkeley Square? By some miracle, had her flight led her in the right direction?

Coming closer, Carina recognised the houses that led into Mount Street. She was safe, but the cramp in her side made her bend double. As fear and revulsion gave way to shock, she began to shake so violently she had to cling to the iron railings for support. She kept her neck bent until the nausea and faintness passed. Then she straightened up. Her jacket was torn and there was no sign of her bonnet. She must have left it in the carriage or dropped it along the way. With trembling hands she looped her hair into a knot at the back of her head before she turned her attention to her dress. There was nothing to be done about the broken frogging of her jacket. The snapped bones of her crinoline stuck through her skirts like knitting needles – but now her only thought was of Alice.

Her aunt must never discover what had happened! Carina had lost all track of time. Alice might not yet be home. If she was lucky, she might get upstairs before her aunt returned. She would enter by the basement door and swear Thomas and Rose to secrecy. She would say she had been attacked by pickpockets and Carina didn't care that she lied. She would do anything to prevent Alice finding out what a narrow escape it had been.

You damned fool, she swore under her breath. You stupid, stupid fool! Why, for once, couldn't you do as Alice asked? It was madness not to take Rose with you this afternoon. Flirtation is not a game and you brought this on yourself! Incensed by her own folly, blood coursed through her veins and strength returned. She could see the house and light from downstairs rooms shining onto the street. There would be time for self-re-crimination later. The only thing that mattered was to reach her bedroom without meeting Alice. Cold flakes touched her cheeks and Carina realised it was snowing. Pulling her hood over her head, she picked up her skirts and broke into a run.

CHAPTER FIVE

SICILY, JANUARY 1860

Carina stood on deck as the steamer that brought them from London approached Palermo harbour. The city nestled beneath a crown of gold-topped mountains and she could see palm trees and rose-coloured domes. As they came into the shelter of the bay, the light was so dazzling she tipped the rim of her bonnet down to shade her eyes.

There was time before disembarkation and her mind went back to that fateful afternoon. Whenever she thought of Danby's assault, Carina felt sick to the pit of her stomach. There was no one she could tell and she dared not report him to the police – for who would take her word against a peer of the realm? Alice was still out when she had reached home and Rose the only person who witnessed the state that she was in. Rose had come from Yorkshire with her and Carina trusted her completely.

'If you want my opinion, miss,' she had remarked as she inspected the jacket. 'Good thing I be coming with thee to Sicily. Folk in those parts wouldn't put up with this kind of thing.'

There had been no further letters or calling cards from Lord Danby and a week later Carina read in the Court Circular he had been received by the queen at Buckingham Palace. No matter how badly he had behaved, Danby was welcome back in the fold. The hypocrisy of the court disgusted her and, from that day on, she couldn't wait to get away.

It had been raining on the day of their departure and Harry Carstairs drove with them to the docks. She had looked back from the ship to his tall figure standing under an umbrella and thought: Harry is a good man and I will always disappoint him.

'Born with a devil in your heart.' The words of Paddy O'Brien, the head groom at Melton, came into her head. 'Let's hope your guardian angel catches him quick. Then you'll be a saint!'

It was strange to think of Paddy after so many years – but she would never be a saint. Carina understood herself too well for that. She was aware of her faults – her quick temper and impulsive nature that led her into trouble. She had wasted four years in mourning and then made a fool of herself. How could she have been so naive? Don't look back, she told herself. There's no room for bitterness or regret. You're eighteen years old with your whole life in front of you. You made a mistake and have learned your lesson. Now you've been given a second chance. Think only of the future.

Ahead lay an exotic city that filled Carina with hope. After two weeks cooped up on board, how she longed to be ashore! The passage through the Bay of Biscay had been rough. Alice, and Jane Parsons, suffered from seasickness and stayed in their cabins until past the Straits of Gibraltar while Carina walked on deck every day. She had never left England before and loved the adventure of a sea voyage, the spray in her face and taste of salt on her tongue. When the weather improved, she found a sheltered spot close to the bridge. There, Jane Parsons discovered her one morning reading *Childe Harold*.

'Could any man have written with such feeling without experiencing *life*?' Jane's tone was passionate. She was dressed in the same corduroy jacket and skirt she wore every day with her hair scraped back beneath a poke bonnet. She might have been considered drab were it not for her bright brown eyes and eager expression.

> *What is there wanting to set thee free,*
> *To show thy beauty in its fullest light?*
> *Make the Alps impassable; and we,*
> *Your sons, for Italy – Unite!*

'Lord Byron believed Italy must become one nation. He was a prophet as well as a poet. On the Continent he is admired above all others!'

Of all people in the world, Carina would never have guessed Jane Parsons shared her love of Byron. Her opinion of her changed in that instant. Jane wasn't the dull woman she had thought in London and they would surely be friends! Carina wanted to learn about Sicily and the closer they came to their destination, the more animated Jane became. Walking on deck or taking supper in their cabin, she spoke of the island's troubled past.

'The revolution in Sicily of '48 was suppressed with dreadful brutality. Hundreds of people were executed or imprisoned and many more forced into exile. You cannot imagine the suffering the patriots have endured. Mind you, my cousin, the consul, says it's only a matter of time before the Sicilian people rise up and cast off the Bourbon yoke!'

Carina thought of the newspaper article she had read to Harry in London. The idea of revolution had seemed far away then, but Jane's words last night had sent a shiver down her spine.

'You promise to call on me at the consulate as soon as you are settled?' Jane's voice beside her now made Carina start. She had come up on deck with Alice and was leaning over the rail, pointing to the beach. 'Our baggage will be taken to the Passport Office. Make your way there and wait for whoever the contessa has sent to meet you.'

They left the steamer in groups, clambering down steep steps to the long boats that were to row them ashore. Alice hung on to Carina's arm and sat close to her on the narrow bench with Rose hemming her in on the other side. They were packed so tightly together her new turquoise dress would be ruined. She should have worn a travelling habit like Alice, Carina thought, but she wanted to make a good first impression on her mother's family and she was too excited to care.

Arriving on the beach, the women were surrounded by men eager to offer them assistance. Carina had learned Italian, but they spoke in a dialect she couldn't understand. Somehow they had become separated from Jane, and Alice was pale with anxiety. Carina stood on her tiptoes, searching over the heads of the crowd for the Passport Office but the beach was so crowded it was impossible to see beyond the shoreline. She was wondering what to do when someone called her name and she turned so quickly she almost knocked into the young man who had come up behind them.

'Carina, it is you! I knew the minute I saw your dress. What a sensational colour! I'm your cousin, Paulo Denuzio.'

He bent over her hand, brushing it with a kiss and as he looked up Carina's gaze met a pair of laughing brown eyes.

Paulo was about her age with dark curling hair. There was a becoming droopiness to the corners of his eyes and his smile was that of a mischievous boy.

'Well, are you going to present me to your aunt?' he asked.

'I'm very pleased to make your acquaintance. How very kind of you to come.'

Alice's response was heartfelt and Carina was delighted to meet her cousin. She was aware her mother's brother was married with children, but believed they lived in Naples.

'Gabriella is with me. She's waiting in the carriage.' Taking for granted they knew who he meant, Paulo offered both Carina and Alice an arm. 'Gino will take your maid to identify your luggage and drive her home. Please be so kind as to come with me.'

A coachman in livery stepped forward and Carina was relieved to let Paulo guide them through the melee. The energy in the air was exhilarating and she did not mind the chaos and noise. The sun was warm and the sky bluer than any sky she had ever seen before. It was a world away from dismal, grey London. I'm going to be happy here, she thought with a thrill of pleasure. I'm not going to miss England one little bit.

They came to the road where a landau stood open in the mild air and a girl of about sixteen was peering over the side. Gabriella was pretty with large dark eyes. Her hair was coiled in thick plaits around her head and she wore a plain linen smock. Carina hoped her turquoise dress, with its low décolletage and petticoats peeping beneath the skirts, wasn't too risqué. At least a fur-trimmed mantle covered her arms and no one could disapprove of her bonnet. With its cream silk lining and wide ribbon tied under her chin, it was modest enough. She smiled at Gabriella and her cousin's cheeks dimpled shyly.

'Behind us is Mount Pellegrino, and there's the marina.'

Paulo pointed out the sights as they set off and came to a street lined with elegant houses. 'This is the Toledo. When the nobility lived here it was considered the finest boulevard in Sicily. Now the houses are all religious establishments and it's gone to the dogs—'

'Paulo, don't you talk so!' Gabriella spoke for first time.

'It's perfectly true. They were built for pleasure – and what have they become? Convents for celibates!'

Paulo went on to tell them about his family. He was a student of Law at the University of Perugia while Gabriella was being educated at a convent in Naples. They were in Palermo on vacation and their parents due to arrive the following week.

'My sister's going to be a nun,' he explained. 'Unless, that is, she's rescued from the religious life by one of my bachelor friends.'

At that moment, as if on cue, a young man on horseback rode up beside the carriage. He removed his hat and made a sweeping bow as Paulo introduced him.

'May I present Enrico Fola? Enrico belongs to one of the noblest families in Sicily, yet, for all that, he's a rogue! Do you know our friend is in danger of becoming a Liberal?'

The words had an edge to them that made Carina look at Enrico Fola more closely. Apart from his wide-brimmed hat and long hair, he didn't appear very different from Paulo. With his pale face and deep-set eyes, he was handsome in a romantic way and she noticed how Gabriella blushed when he spoke to her.

'And that,' Paulo declared after Enrico Fola took his leave, 'is the reason my little sister will not become a nun. She's been in love with Enrico all her life.'

Gabriella shot him a look that would have silenced most people, but Paulo was irrepressible. 'There's no use denying it, Ella. The whole world knows it's true.'

'Be sure we won't take notice of him,' Alice intervened mildly. 'Brothers always love to tease.'

Her aunt was more relaxed already and Carina was impressed by Palermo with its fine churches and statues in pretty squares. The citizens were smartly dressed, their carriages drawn by horses in harnesses adorned with plumed feathers. Painted donkey carts drove alongside stylish phaetons and on every corner were flower stalls and women selling fruit. At Paulo's insistence they stopped for iced sherbet brought to them in the carriage before setting off again.

The open boulevards were left behind and the streets became narrow and dark. Lines of washing were strung from one side to the other, blocking out the sun. Instead of the scent of flowers, the air was close and fetid and Carina sensed hostility in the silent stares of the women and children who crowded in doorways. Barefoot urchins ran after the carriage calling out for money and when an old man spat under the wheels, the coachman cracked his whip. No one spoke until the slums were left behind and they came out above the city and trotted across a piazza with a church. As they rumbled through a barrel-vaulted entrance, she glimpsed the Denuzio coat of arms and Carina knew they had arrived.

Her first impression of the palazzo was of a large honey-coloured house with shuttered windows. They alighted in the inner courtyard and Paulo and Gabriella escorted them up a flight of steps to enter on the first floor.

'This is the *piano nobile*,' Paulo explained. 'It's where we meet, eat and entertain. The bedrooms are above, rather less *nobile* but a good deal more comfortable.'

Carina glimpsed a series of rooms, leading from one to another, before they ascended a second staircase. Alice was shown into her suite and then Gabriella led Carina down the passage. She beckoned her into a bedroom with a balcony over-looking the city, where Rose was already surrounded by boxes and giving orders in uncompromising English to the young girl helping her to unpack.

A note awaited her from her grandmother saying she was looking forward to welcoming her once she was settled. An hour later, Carina set out to find her. Her hand gripped the banister rail as she went down. What would they make of each other, she wondered? If only she knew what Oliver had said in his letter! He was bound to have written a damning indictment. How would she answer if her grandmother asked about Robert Danby? She must tell her the truth, she decided as she reached the gallery.

A footman was waiting and there was no chance to think further. Carina followed him downstairs, through an arched doorway and along a dark corridor with shadowy portraits gazing down from the walls. Presently, they arrived at her grandmother's apartments and Contessa Denuzio rose stiffly from her chair and held out her arms.

'My beloved child, welcome home.'

Carina had a miniature of her grandmother as a young woman and took in every detail of her appearance. She was small and, apart from a lace cap, dressed entirely in black. Nonna was thin as a sparrow – Carina felt her shoulder bones as she embraced her – but her grasp was strong as she led her over to sit by the window. Her skin was like parchment and Carina had a strange urge to run her hands over her face. This was the closest she had ever come to her mother and all she could think was: Sonia was hardly older than me when she left Sicily. I should have come before. Why did I leave it so long? Tears filled her eyes and her grandmother held onto her hand so she couldn't reach her handkerchief. Too overcome to speak, the two women sat in silence until there was a tap at the door and a maid entered with a tray of refreshments.

Carina sipped her lemonade and then, prompted by her grandmother, began to talk about her childhood. She was hesitant at first, gradually becoming more confident. She told her of Melton and the Yorkshire dales, how she loved horses and her passion for reading and poetry. As she was speaking, she had the sensation she was describing someone she hardly recognised or remembered. There was a vital, undiscovered part of her in this room and she longed to ask about her mother. Do I remind you of her? What was she like? Would she have approved of me?

Her grandmother's sharp old eyes never left her face. It would be too painful for her to speak of Sonia now, she thought, and her questions must wait. She was trying to think of something else to say when Nonna asked about her life in London.

Carina took a quick breath before she answered. 'I believe my uncle wrote to you regarding the circumstances of my visit.'

'Oliver Temple's correspondence was private.' Nonna put up her hand, waving the question away. 'I'm grateful he decided to make an old woman happy, but your mother didn't care for him. I weighed his words accordingly.'

So that was it. She had read Oliver's version of events and had no wish to talk about it. The topic Carina dreaded the most was dismissed and Nonna continued briskly, 'I'm delighted your Aunt Alice is to stay with us for a few weeks. Sonia wrote of her with great affection and I look forward to meeting her. Now, let me tell you what I have planned for you …'

She went on, speaking of picnics in the gardens of La Favorita and visits to the Teatro Santa Cecilia. The Princess del Monti had invited them to her box at the opera the following week, thus ensuring her entrée into Palermo society, and Paulo promised to escort them around.

'We're not as sophisticated as you are in London, but Sicily is never dull. I'm sure you'll be happy here, my dear.'

Carina felt a glow of warmth radiate through her. How could one not respond to such a welcome? She already felt more at home than she ever had in London. There was an immediate understanding with her Sicilian relations. The sense of kinship buoyed her up, and when she came downstairs later she was pleased to find Paulo waiting in the salon.

He poured out two glasses of chilled wine, handing one to her, and raised a toast. 'To my beautiful cousin, who has come to set Sicily alight! The whole of Palermo is asking about you. "Will Miss Temple be allowed out of the house?" "When may we be presented?" I've never been so popular in my life.'

'Why so, I cannot imagine.' Carina looked at him questioningly.

'Don't say you thought to arrive in Palermo and not find your reputation gone before you?'

There was mischief in his eyes and Carina dropped her gaze. She shouldn't mind, but her grandmother had made her feel all the unpleasantness was left behind. She hadn't expected this of Paulo and answered coolly. 'Does our grandmother listen to the same gossip as you?'

'Nonna would never hear a word against you.'

'So what's your opinion of my reputation?'

'Should I denounce a scandal if you don't yourself?'

Carina did not answer and Paulo went over to the side table to refill his glass. He continued without looking round. 'It's really of no significance. Papa thought it advisable to apprise us of certain rumours, that's all.'

To be sure, he was an impudent young man! What did he expect her to say? Did Paulo think she'd admit or deny anything to him? If so, he was a fool as well as a prattler. She had liked him so much that morning and was now disappointed. When he came and sat down beside her, she turned her back and picked up a small enamel box from the table.

'Are you annoyed with me?'

'Not in the slightest,' she said shortly.

'Yes you are. Of course indiscretions are only acceptable as long as they remain discreet.'

Carina imagined Paulo smiling at his own wit and turned the box over in her hand. A hint of vulnerability usually did the trick and she sighed.

'I'm sorry you choose to think badly of me. I hoped we might be friends.'

'Of course we're friends. Why ever not? And I don't think badly of you. I'm full of admiration!'

Before she could think of a suitable retort, he slipped off the sofa and knelt on the floor with his arms across his chest. 'I didn't mean to offend you. Please will you forgive me?'

He was being ridiculous and Carina refused to answer.

'Tell me what I can do to appease you? I'll challenge anyone who casts doubt on your honour. Pistols at dawn – whatever you demand! I will risk life and limb to prove my allegiance.'

It was all an act, but Paulo was hard to resist. His antics made her want to laugh and Carina struggled to keep a straight face.

'How you behave is up to you. Now, will you please get up?'

If her attempt at coolness worried him, Paulo did not show it. He was back on his feet, a smile lifting the corners of his mouth even as he tried to prevent it.

'You'll never refer to my life in London again. Is that understood?

'Upon my honour, I swear to be your most loyal champion. However ...'

Just then a footman entered carrying a tray of olives, which he placed on the table. The setting sun threw beams of light across the room, turning the walls from gold to pink and through the open door came a murmur of voices. Alice and Gabriella were talking as they approached, their silk skirts rustling on the marble floor as they came down the gallery.

'Silence is my bond, dear cousin.' Paulo placed his hand over his heart. 'But know this: in Sicily a scandal attached to one's name is a greater asset than a fortune. If it turns out that you have neither, you'll be considered a nonentity!'

CHAPTER SIX

In the days that followed, Paulo was good as his word. When they were not admiring sights in the city, they drove into the countryside and Alice painted watercolours while they explored local villages and markets. Carina admired the jewellery and fine silks from Catania and bought a quantity of both, watching intrigued as Paulo haggled with the merchants. Nothing seemed too much trouble for him, even when she ordered a case of coral to be sent on approval and he had to arrange a substantial deposit. He obliged her every whim and Carina was as captivated by her cousin as she was by her mother's childhood home.

Apart from the universal ringing of church bells, there were as many different aspects to Palermo as mosaics in the cathedral. It was a city of light and shade where delicate arabesque arches stood beside baroque churches and solid Norman buildings. There were twisted trees and donkeys in straw hats. Grand palaces were hidden behind doors in filthy streets and puppet shows performed next to the outright macabre. Despite Paulo telling her it wasn't to his taste, Carina insisted they visit the famous Cadaveri. Alice declined to join them and Carina was appalled when she saw the mummified bodies dressed in clothes and hung up in alcoves. In Sicily, it seemed, people were in love with death as much as with life and Palermo was mysterious, shabby and magnificent.

They had arranged to call on Jane Parsons and Carina was in the best of spirits as they set out. The sun was shining and her new bonnet with its long ribbons was a sensation. She couldn't help noticing how many young men turned their heads to look as they drove by.

'Do you like my flirtation ribbons?' she asked Paulo.

Paulo smiled, but gave no reply. He had business in town and would drop them off on the way. He had been quiet all morning and Carina was content to absorb the atmosphere. It was a festival day and broughams and phaetons jostled for space with speedy *caleffini* to the sound of pipes and drums. Families were gathered on balconies, the men smoking cigars on the first floor while women stood above, waving to their friends, and children pressed forward to get a better view.

'There was a great rumpus at the opera last night,' Paulo announced as they turned into the Toledo, pausing until Carina and Alice gave him their full attention before he continued. 'A demonstration broke out during the overture. The police dragged out the culprits, but the entire performance was cancelled. The teatro is closed until further notice.'

'But we're invited for tomorrow night! Who was responsible?' Carina and Alice spoke simultaneously.

'The usual troublemakers – so-called patriots and rebels.'

'Why at the opera, of all places?' Alice enquired.

'The composer of *La Traviata* is a supporter of Italian Unity. His name's their slogan. V.E.R.D.I. for Victor Emmanuel Re D'Italia.'

'But I don't understand. You already have a king in Naples.'

'Oh, they want rid of *him*. Their ambition is to create a united Italy with the king of Piedmont as figurehead.'

'I see ...' Alice began, and then trailed off.

'What will happen now?' Carina asked, a small frown creasing between her eyebrows.

'The police are taking no chances. The theatre will remain closed until all those responsible are behind bars. I'm afraid your entrée into Palermo society must be postponed.'

Carina remembered Jane Parsons telling them about the chief of police. Jane said Count Maniscalco ran a system of spies, using torture to extract false confessions and that he was the most hated man in all of Sicily.

'What a pity. We were so looking forward to the evening,' Alice remarked. '*La Traviata* caused a furore when it opened in London, albeit for different reasons.'

Alice did not elaborate as they swung through the gates of the British Consulate and the carriage pulled up in front of a white stucco house. A Union Jack hung above the portico and they were greeted by an official who took them up a wide flight of stairs. Sheffield sconces adorned the walls and Carina noticed all the furniture was English. When they reached the drawing room, a large portrait of Queen Victoria met her eyes. It was so vast it dominated the room and she thought: how ridiculous when everyone knew the queen was tiny.

Beneath the painting stood Jane Parsons, who hurried forward to greet them. The consul was instantly recognisable in white tie and morning coat with his wife beside him. She had a hesitant way of moving, peering short-sightedly in front of her as she approached. There was another gentleman with them. He had intelligent eyes and a distinguished air, Carina thought, as Jane presented Baron Riso.

'It is a great pleasure to meet you, Miss Temple.' The baron spoke English in an attractively stilted fashion. 'Miss Parsons tells me you're the daughter of Sonia Denuzio. I'm glad you have returned to her homeland.'

'Did you know my mother?' Carina asked in Italian.

'I met her on several occasions. She was a beautiful and clever woman.'

The baron's words made Carina's heart swell. Her father had been too heartbroken to ever speak of her mother and Alice was the only person who had told her about her. There's so much I don't know, she thought. Until now, I've been afraid of letting myself think too much about her. Why do I feel such a sense of loss for someone I never met?

They went outside to sit on the terrace and Baron Riso was placed between Alice and Carina. The baron paid her great attention, asking her opinion on a number of things and listening attentively to her answers. Carina found him charming and was sorry when Alice announced it was time to leave. Paulo was collecting them on his way home, she explained. On the way down, Baron Riso offered her his arm and complimented her on her bonnet.

'I'm pleased you approve.' Carina bestowed on him a dazzling smile. 'My family consider it a little *de trop*.'

'Nothing is ever too much in Sicily. We are a nation in love with excess.'

They walked through the front door into the sunlight and Carina caught sight of Paulo standing beside the carriage.

'Please come here, Paulo!' she called to him. 'I would like to present you to our friends.'

Paulo walked over slowly, even reluctantly, it seemed to Carina, and when he shook Baron Riso's hand did not look him in the eye.

'My wife and I are hosting a ball at our home next week. It would give us great pleasure to extend an invitation to you. We would be honoured by your attendance.'

'Most civil of you, sir, but I'm afraid we can't accept,' Paulo interjected.

'We'd be delighted to receive your invitation.' Aggrieved by Paulo's interference, Carina immediately contradicted him. 'Would you be kind enough to write to my grandmother?'

'I will send a card to the Contessa Denuzio today.' Baron Riso smiled and bowed. 'It's been a pleasure to make your acquaintance, Miss Temple. Good day to you all.'

The baron strode off and they took their leave. They were barely out of the gates before Paulo rounded on her.

'Do you always accept invitations from *anyone* who asks you anywhere?'

'The British Consul and Baron Riso aren't just *anyone*! What's wrong with you today? I've never been so mortified in my life. Don't you agree, Alice?'

Alice would not be drawn in and the two cousins glared at each other in silence, neither of them prepared to give way until Paulo said in a superior tone of voice. 'The demonstration at the opera wasn't a random event. It was planned by certain rebels, including your new friend, Baron Riso.'

'I don't believe you! If so, then why hasn't he been arrested?'

'Because the police don't have enough evidence against him—'

'I'm sure because there is none!'

'Saints have mercy, do you have to be so stubborn?' Paulo leant forward, lowering his voice. 'Baron Riso has powerful friends and the authorities don't dare touch him. However, I'm convinced this soirée is cover for a secret meeting. He's done it before, you know, using the rank of society to camouflage a conspiracy.'

'Really, that's too much!' Alice responded so sharply that Carina stared at her. 'Respectable people such as the British Consul would never—'

'Respectable?' Paulo did not let her finish. 'That's *not* how Mr Goodwin is perceived in Palermo. His sympathies are well known. General opinion is that the British should keep their nose out of what doesn't concern them.'

In the split second that followed, Carina thought Alice might lose her temper. Two bright spots of colour appeared on her cheeks, but she remained silent.

'Unlike my parents, I've no affection for our current leaders.' Paulo continued undaunted. 'But these people are fanatics. Given half a chance, they would stir up another revolution.'

'Is your friend, Enrico Fola, one of them?'

'Enrico's a dreamer. He may support their ideals, but he would never act against the king.'

'So why is he permitted to call on your sister?'

'My parents are old friends of his family. I've known Enrico all my life – but sometimes despair of Gabriella's crush on him. If he's not careful, she'll be left with a broken heart.'

Most likely, Paulo suspected Enrico's involvement in last night's events, Carina thought. Why, only yesterday Gabriella let slip that Enrico declared the inspection of private houses for weapons unlawful! Her cousin believed everything Enrico said and had made Carina promise not to tell for fear of getting him into trouble.

They travelled on and, as they entered the old quarter, the landau was brought to a halt. There was a commotion in the street ahead and, leaning out, Carina saw a phaeton tipped on its side blocking the way. The horses were uncoupled and men were pushing from behind while others hauled with ropes from the front. A crowd had gathered and everyone was shouting different instructions.

Then an old woman, eyes bright with malaria fever, stepped forward. Her bony hands clutched the carriage door. '*Poveretta – more di fame! Fata la carita. O boni servi di Dio, facite la carita!*'

Paulo had instructed them never to carry money and neither Alice nor Carina had a purse. Alice sat with her hands clasped, her spine not touching the back of the seat and Paulo took out his watch and started fiddling with the mechanism. Carina glanced to the other side of the street and her gaze locked with that of a young woman standing in a doorway. She had the hollow-cheeked look of starvation and held a small, motionless bundle to her breast. Looking straight at Carina, she began to unwrap the blanket. A tiny, dark head emerged, but the baby lay so still there was no way of telling whether it was dead or alive.

Seconds passed. Carina was terrified the girl meant to give her the baby. Then a man's voice barked from within and she pulled the blanket back over the child. Not taking her eyes off Carina, she drew one finger across her throat before she turned and went inside.

There was no mistaking the gesture and Carina blushed scarlet. She wanted to snatch off her new bonnet and throw it after her. It would sell for good money – but the girl was too proud – and most likely it would end up on the fire. The only other thing she had was a new coral brooch and she twisted her neck to look past Alice. The old woman was still hanging onto the door and while Paulo talked to the coachman, Carina grappled with the pin on her corsage. With a wrench she had it off and passed it to Alice, indicating to the woman with her eyes. As soon as the brooch was handed over, she was gone. At the same time there was a loud cheer and the phaeton was pulled free.

They were on their way and Carina's head was spinning. How could such misery exist in the heart of the city? And why had Paulo instructed them never to give alms? There was great poverty in London too, but they didn't have to drive through slums every time they went out. Their carriage and fine clothes felt like an insult in the face of such misery. Whether Paulo approved or not, she would take her purse with her in future. Anything would be better than what had just happened!

Her enjoyment of the visit to the consulate evaporated and Carina felt depressed. She didn't like to see Paulo in a bad mood. It wouldn't do to end the morning on a sour note, so she smiled at him.

'We don't wish to compromise you, Paulo. Alice and I are happy to go Baron Riso's ball on our own.'

'That would be extremely unwise.'

'I've brought my best ball gowns from London and not had a single occasion to wear them,' Carina paused. Paulo would probably think she was being reckless, but she was tired of constraint and added, 'I'm sure it will be a splendid adventure.'

'The kind that ends up in the Vacaria prison?'

'One can't be arrested for dancing a waltz.'

'Carina's right,' Alice put in graciously 'You've been very kind to us. The last thing we want is to place you in a difficult situation.'

Paulo did not answer immediately. He leant back with his arms behind his head and then, when they were crossing the piazza, remarked as if the thought had only just occurred to him,

'I expect you'll sweet-talk Nonna into giving you permission, Carina. For my part, I'll wait until my parents arrive tomorrow and let them decide. No doubt, I'll be obliged to escort you just to keep you out of trouble.'

Paulo wasn't as reluctant as he made out, Carina thought. His tone was too languid and artificial and he was dying to go. Suddenly she longed to dance and for the music and gaiety of a party. Which dress should she wear? There were a dozen to choose from, but the white organza was her favourite. Her gloom was forgotten and she was excited, looking forward to the evening already. If Baron Riso were a man of his word, which she was sure he was, the invitation should arrive this afternoon and she would speak to her grandmother just as soon as she was home.

CHAPTER SEVEN

If sweetly you love me and deeply you care
When Autumn is falling and Winter is bare;
If you are constant in Spring's rushing tide
When Summer is calling, you stay by my side,
In all seasons true, our life will we share;
For sweetly I love you and deeply I care.

She had thought of the first line on the day she left England and the poem found its voice today. Carina had spent all afternoon finishing the draft. A handful of women were celebrated poets in England. Would anyone consider her verse worthy of circulation, she wondered? It wasn't enough to rhyme and scan. Poetry should express true emotion. What was it like to experience true passion? I don't want to die a spinster, she thought. One day I will fall in love – and then poetry will flow from my pen like water.

Stiff from sitting so long, Carina stretched her arms above her head. Dogs were barking and she could hear a flurry of activity downstairs. Her uncle and aunt must have arrived from

Naples. She would go down with Alice later, she decided. It would be easier to meet them when everyone was gathered together before dinner.

The door to the grand salon stood open and Gabriella was playing the piano as Carina and Alice walked down the gallery. She stopped as they entered and put away her music. Before Carina could speak to her, the door at the far end opened and her uncle and aunt entered, followed by Paulo.

Her mother's brother, Carlo Denuzio was of medium height with dark hair thinning on the crown. His expression was difficult to read behind thick-rimmed spectacles, while his wife Anna Maria was friendly and vivacious. She had a pretty, round face and bombarded Carina with questions about the latest fashion news from Paris.

During dinner, talk was livelier at her aunt's end of the table but Carina did her best to pay attention to her uncle. Surreptitiously observing her cousins as he droned on at her, she was glad to see Paulo had recovered his spirits. Gabriella, on the other hand, was subdued. She barely touched her food and, when they withdrew to the salon, went to sit by herself in a corner, taking no part in the conversation.

As soon as the others retired and the three of them were alone, Paulo was on to her.

'What's the matter, Ella? The cat got your tongue this evening?'

'Don't pretend you don't know.' Gabriella looked at him, her black eyes glistening. 'You were there and you heard Papa. He has no right to speak so, denouncing all patriots as criminals and traitors to the king.'

'Papa's entitled to his opinions – as we are to ours. How else would Enrico Fola be allowed in this house?'

Carina watched as Gabriella stood up and walked over to

her brother. She was tiny beside him, the top of her head barely reaching his shoulder, and there was a quiver in her voice.

'Don't you dare bring Enrico into this! At least he has principles – which is more than anyone can say about you.'

'Well, I'm glad he wasn't caught up in last night's shenanigans.' Paulo put a hand across his mouth to stifle a yawn. 'All words and no deeds with Enrico. Let's hope it stays that way.'

'Are you blind as well as partisan? Do cruelty and injustice mean nothing to you?'

'Dear Ella, I may be blind but I'm certainly *not* partisan. We're to entertain Prince Scalia for lunch on Friday and I'm dragooned into attending. To top that off, I must then escort Carina to a ball at the Palazzo Riso next week. There are no greater political extremes in the kingdom. I don't know which I dread most. On balance, I dare say Prince Scalia's probably the worse of two evils.'

Carina ignored the slight on Baron Riso for she was interested in the lunch party. Paulo had spoken to her of Riccardo Scalia, Duke of Pallestro. The prince was a friend of his parents and a powerful member of the Bourbon court. He was also in charge of law and order in Sicily and Paulo did not like him.

'Is Prince Scalia really the monster that you say he is?'

'Scalia's an agent of the Devil,' Gabriella exclaimed.

'I wouldn't trust him as far as I can spit,' Paulo grimaced, wrinkling his nose. 'I hope you're not squeamish, for Mama's bound to place you next to him. His face is scarred as a butcher's block.'

'Why? What happened to him?'

Paulo looked mysterious and made no answer. He would string her along for his own amusement, Carina thought. She would ask Gabriella later. As she returned to her chair, Paulo announced he was going out. Without giving them a chance to ask where he was going, the door closed behind him.

'Paulo's studying Law – but he doesn't understand the meaning of justice,' Gabriella stated flatly.

'I'm sure he cares more than he admits.'

'I'm afraid he does *not*! Many of his friends are liberals but he refuses to get involved. Enrico's given him evidence of illegal executions and he takes no notice ...'

Gabriella dropped her crochet needle on the floor and knelt down to search for it. When she had it, she stood up, her face flushed as her sentences tumbled over each other. 'Papa's even worse! He has the ear of the king and yet denies the atrocities committed in his name. He knows Scalia and Maniscalco are acting outside the law, but he's too weak to denounce them! I'm ashamed to be a member of this family and that's the truth!'

Gabriella was so upset Carina was afraid she might burst into tears. Her cousin was blinded by her love for Enrico, she thought, while Paulo was a cynic and she didn't know which one of them to believe.

'Sicily's a rich island, but the people aren't permitted to grow enough food to feed themselves.' Gabriella went on, anger running in her voice.' The government hope to break our spirit, but they'll never succeed!'

The girl and baby came into Carina's mind and she said nothing. Gabriella possessed a quality she admired. Her cousin would always do what she believed to be right. And then there was Jane Parsons. Why should a sensible woman like Jane make similar allegations if they were untrue?

'I'm sure Paulo's going to the ball on the orders of Prince Scalia!' Gabriella announced suddenly.

'Why on earth? He detests the man ...'

'Promise me you won't let him out of your sight. He will try to gather evidence against Baron Riso and you must stop him.'

Carina was too tired to argue. As they made their way upstairs, she took her cousin's hand.

'The idea of Prince Scalia makes me quite nervous. You will stay by my side at this lunch on Friday, won't you?'

'I've volunteered to keep Nonna company. She doesn't care for the prince either, although she speaks well of his wife. She says it's a shame Bianca married him. Something happened a long time ago but Nonna's never really explained. I'm sure you could find out. You're good at winkling things out of people.'

On the morning of the lunch party Carina woke up early. Through the open window came the cries of street vendors and she could hear footsteps on the stairs. The household was up and yet she was no wiser about Princess Scalia. When she questioned her grandmother, her only comment was that Isabella del Angelo had been a friend and she knew her daughter, Bianca, as a child.

Anna Maria was in charge of preparations and the palazzo had been turned upside down. Rugs were hung out of windows to be beaten, the best table linen pressed and the courtyard scrubbed until the cobbles shone like marble. They were to eat in the blue salon and footmen had been hurrying up and down all of yesterday, bringing the best wine and gold plate from the cellars. Extra staff had been drafted in to help and blocks of ice and flowers had been arriving since dawn.

Carina had wanted to show off her latest creation from Mr Worth, the finest dress designer in London, but Alice insisted she wore a less flamboyant outfit and suggested the green bombazine. It was too bad, Carina thought as she studied her reflection in the Venetian glass. Her hair was parted down the middle in a severe style and the dress buttoned to the chin with a starched white collar that scratched her neck. It made her look positively dowdy. Why not the turquoise silk with its pretty neckline and scalloped hem? Alice wouldn't even be there – she was confined to bed with a chest infection. Carina was tempted – but she had promised to obey Alice in future and couldn't go back on her word so soon.

To make matters worse, when she went downstairs, Carina found everyone else decked out in their finery. Anna Maria's friend Donna Marcella was encased in gold satin with rows of pearls draped over her bosom and her aunt bright as a peacock in blue crêpe. Even the bishop was arrayed in a riot of episcopal purple. She wanted to run upstairs to and change, but there was no time for the guests of honour had arrived.

As she curtsied to the princess, Carina took in her fair hair and soft blue eyes. Bianca Scalia was dressed to the height of fashion. Her silk skirts seemed to float in the air, her mantle trimmed with agate, and on her head sat the prettiest veil pinned over a comb in the Spanish style. Never again, even if Alice were on her deathbed, would she heed her fashion advice, Carina vowed; and then, before she was quite ready, she was being presented to the prince.

'*Molto piacere,*' Prince Scalia murmured as he lifted her hand to his lips.

The prince was of a slight build with a narrow face and hooded eyes. He was impeccably dressed in a cutaway coat and crossover cravat. His scars were partially concealed by a trimmed beard, but they were impossible to ignore. From beneath each earlobe, a ridge ran down his cheek to the corner of his mouth so that when he smiled his upper lip lifted in a sneer. The prince held her hand longer than was necessary and

Carina pretended not to notice. Determined not to stare, she kept her eyes down until Anna Maria fetched her over to talk to the princess by the window.

With her high cheekbones and flawless complexion, Bianca Scalia was undeniably beautiful. Was this her first visit to Sicily, she asked Carina? And how long did she plan to stay? Carina answered vaguely, distracted by the constant movement of the princess's hands. She fiddled with everything she touched, her fingers plucking the lace of her cuffs or straying to the heart-shaped locket that she wore around her neck. She would hold it for a moment and then let it drop, clasping her hands on her lap. A few moments later she would start again. It was a disconcerting habit in a woman so outwardly sophisticated and a relief when the party moved through for lunch.

The blue salon had been transformed. Winter light filtered through the windows so the stamped wallpaper shimmered like seawater and the table was weighed down with gold plate and glass. A liveried footman was posted behind each chair and Carina was placed next to Prince Scalia. They stood with heads bowed as the bishop said Grace and, when they sat down, the prince turned to her first.

His manners were as polished as his conversation, but Carina didn't remember afterwards what they talked about. His unblinking gaze stayed on her face and she was increasingly aware of his dark eyes lingering on her lips. Prince Scalia was old – at least forty – and she was the only single woman present. His unabashed flirting embarrassed her. When she dropped her napkin, the prince waved the footman away and picked it up himself. His hand brushed against her arm and Carina withdrew it hastily.

'I hope you'll come to visit us at the Villa Pallestro.' The prince was undeterred by her awkwardness. 'It will be a pleasure to show you our country estate. Rarely are Sicily's shores graced with such grace and beauty as your own.'

It was a flowery speech with a nuance that Carina recognised. It made her think of Robert Danby. Despite Scalia's exquisite manners, she sensed a predatory, ruthless personality and gave him a cold look before she turned to talk to Paulo. She had already noticed how often her cousin beckoned the footman to refill his glass. Carina saw the devil-may-care look in his eyes and prayed he would behave himself. Surely Paulo wouldn't dare stir up trouble in such elevated company? Then, as Anna Maria was about to rise from the table, he made a remark that was like a small explosion. 'I'm told Captain Mavrone has been seen in Palermo.'

The statement was directed at no one in particular, but Paulo might have danced a jig on the table for the effect it had. There was an audible intake of breath followed by a tense silence and, for no reason at all, Carina looked at Bianca Scalia. She was staring at her husband, her features frozen in shock before she had time to compose herself. What had Paulo said to provoke such a response? Carina dared not enquire. Time seemed to stand still until Prince Scalia spoke from beside her.

'Paulo is obviously au fait with all the gossip in Palermo. Where does he pick up such tittle-tattle, I wonder?' The prince's tone was quietly malevolent. 'I hope he doesn't frequent the establishments of ill-repute where conspiracy and treason are rife in our city. I advise you to keep a closer eye on your son's proclivities in future, Carlo.'

The prince looked around the table, his gaze resting briefly on each of them before it settled on her uncle. Carina saw Carlo Denuzio's cheek twitch and a film of sweat break out on his forehead. He lifted his napkin, dabbing his lips, and Anna Maria signalled to the butler. Chairs were pulled back, scraping the parquet floor as the ladies rose and withdrew to the gallery. Her aunt was visibly flustered, using her fan with vigour, and Donna Marcella began talking about a sculpture exhibition in Naples. Bianca Scalia pretended to show an interest, occasionally inclining her head, but conversation was stilted, and, when the men joined them, Paulo was not with them.

It was not until later that Carina saw him again. She had been with her grandmother and was taking a stroll in the garden. Following a path between hedges of myrtle to the fountain with a satyr dribbling green water from its mouth, she came across Paulo and Enrico Fola.

'By the saints, the roasting I've just had! Their Excellences were hardly out of the house before my father let fly!' Paulo rolled his eyes dramatically. 'If Enrico hadn't arrived, it would have been the rack and thumbscrews.'

'I gather Paulo's been shooting off his mouth again.' Enrico fell into step beside Carina. 'He can't resist taunting Prince Scalia, but should have more sense than to do so in his own home.'

'He certainly set the cat among the pigeons! And I was the only one there with no idea what it was about.' Carina directed her tone of accusation at Paulo. 'Who is this Captain Mavrone, anyway?'

'Enrico can tell you. The captain is one of his comrades.' Paulo kicked a pebble off the path. His tone was sulky, bringing a swift retort from his friend.

'Mavrone and I may share the same views on the future of our country, but we have little else in common.'

'Don't be a humbug!' Paulo laughed in his friend's face. 'What you mean is the man isn't the same rank as yourself.'

'Who is he?' Carina persisted. When Enrico didn't answer, she turned to Paulo and repeated the question. He was silent and she stood in front of him until he gave a hitch of his shoulders.

'Ben Mavrone is Riccardo Scalia's arch-enemy. There's been a deadly vendetta between them for years.' Paulo's eyes lit up at Carina's astonished expression. 'After the '48 revolution, Scalia put a price on his head. Mavrone escaped from Sicily so the prince incarcerated his brother, using him as bait to make Mavrone return.'

Carina gazed at him. Was he making it up? One never knew with Paulo, but he was getting into his stride and she was too curious to stop him.

'The brother met with an accident and died in prison. Scalia then disappeared from Palermo, supposedly on a political mission to France. When he returned, the surgery had been performed on his face. You're free to draw your own conclusions.'

'Do you mean they fought a duel?'

'I doubt it was so honourable. The odd thing is why, when Mavrone had him at his mercy, didn't he finish him off? A life for a life and all that?'

'Because there's no greater humiliation for a man like Prince Scalia than to owe his life to his enemy,' Enrico offered.

'Maybe, but there's another theory.' Paulo dug his hands into his pockets and strolled onward. 'It's rumoured Captain Mavrone was, and possibly still is, Bianca Scalia's lover.'

'Really, that's outrageous!' Enrico Fola interjected forcibly. 'There's no foundation—'

'And no smoke without fire. You have to admit, my friend, being a rebel has a dangerous attraction for the ladies.'

Carina saw Enrico scowl and Paulo changed the subject. The story of murder and revenge was the stuff of Gothic novels, she thought; yet Prince Scalia exercised a sinister power that was hard to throw off. They had all heard the menace in his voice and Paulo had better watch himself. He shared her own impulsive nature and the prince would make a dangerous enemy.

Carina walked on, lifting her skirts high and unconsciously showing off her ankles as she climbed the stairs to the veranda. She thought Paulo and Enrico were behind her, but when she looked back there was no sign of them. Paulo must have taken his friend off to apologise – and so he should! She didn't believe half of what he said. The idea of the nervous creature at lunch having a liaison with an outlaw was beyond credibility.

'A rebel has a dangerous attraction for the ladies.' The sentence echoed in her mind. It was a mild evening, but a shadowy feeling touched Carina. Something strange had happened at lunch, something she didn't understand. She was accustomed to premonitions, but this was different. Until just now she had no idea about the vendetta. So what was it that impelled her to search out the princess when Paulo mentioned Captain Mavrone? And why, in that briefest of moments, had she been convinced the look she saw on Bianca Scalia's face was one of unguarded terror?

CHAPTER EIGHT

It was past seven o'clock when their carriage drew up outside the Palazzo Riso. Lights blazed from the upper windows and they could hear music as they waited in line in the street. The courtyard was packed with vehicles dropping off their guests and by the time Alice, with Carina and Paulo, reached the reception, the party was in full swing.

Liveried footmen met them at the door and ushered them upstairs. Carina was both excited and apprehensive. Paulo had said news of the scandal in London had reached Palermo. If so, would she be lionised or cut dead? She was longing to dance, but she wouldn't tolerate being snubbed. If that seemed likely, she would plead a headache and ask Paulo to take her home. At any rate, no one could criticise her appearance. Her hair was pinned up in a chignon, threaded with ribbons, and her dress cut wide across the shoulders with a daringly low neckline. Her arms were bare and her waist tiny above skirts that billowed out in a cascade of flounces.

They waited in line behind a group of chattering girls and Carina fidgeted with her fan. Through the doorway was a room full of people and the hum of conversation. At last her name was announced. As she stepped over the threshold, there was a sudden hush. Carina was aware everyone was looking at her and gripped her fan hard between her fingers. Then, with a lift of her chin, she extended her hand first to his wife and then to Baron Riso.

Baroness Riso was a handsome woman with a warm smile and grey hair. Carina would have liked to talk to her, but others followed behind. Paulo had disappeared and she stood with Alice by the door until the baron offered them both an arm. As he led them to the centre of the room, the hubbub of voices started up again. Within moments, they were surrounded by young men pressing for introductions. Baron Riso returned to his post by the door and Carina was pestered by suitors until every polka, mazurka and waltz was taken and her dance card was full.

'I reserved the first dance for you. And the supper dance.' Carina waved her programme at Paulo as he made his way through the crowd to her side.

'I thought it was polite for a lady to wait until she was asked?'

'You'd have been too late so I filled them in myself.' Carina turned to Alice. 'Why did you refuse every dance? We're at a ball, don't you know?'

'I've been waiting for you.' Jane Parsons came over before Alice could answer. 'We've secured a table over there. Do please join our party.'

Jane indicated to where Mr and Mrs Goodwin were sitting with another couple. Alice nodded and smiled at Carina and Paulo. 'You two go off and dance. I'm more than happy in the company of my friends. We shall meet for supper.'

'Come on, Paulo. It's time to do your duty!'

With Alice settled, Carina hurried Paulo towards the dance floor. Chairs and sofas were arranged for sitting out and in one corner men were playing rouge et noir with ivory chips. Paulo suggested they might join them, but she dragged him on, too eager to admire the pictures and fine Florentine tapestries until they came to the ballroom. Beneath the candle-lit chandeliers, couples swept by in a fast, spinning waltz. Paulo led her onto the floor and bowed as she dropped a curtsy. Her cousin was an accomplished dancer and after him came a stream of others until Carina was breathless and begged to sit down.

Her latest partner, a young man with soft brown eyes, went in search of refreshments and Carina looked around. The ballroom was gold and white with a carved ceiling and mirrors reflecting the swing of the men's swallow-tailed coats and the girls' dresses as they danced by. Heavy chignons were balanced on the girls' shoulders and fans tied to velvet ribbons dangled from their wrists. The men were elegant although there was hardly a uniform to be seen – no epaulettes, sashes and shining boots. Carina missed the bright colours of the military – but she was at a ball, the first she had been to for months. Her heart thrilled to the sound of music, her foot tapping in time as Enrico Fola appeared beside her.

'Your curiosity about Captain Mavrone is about to be satisfied. He's over there. A warrant for his arrest and he shows himself openly in public. I believe he does it deliberately to provoke the authorities. Word will be all over Palermo by tomorrow.'

The music stopped and Carina looked in the direction Enrico indicated. A group of men stood talking at the far side of the room and her attention was drawn to a tall man with his back to her. Dark hair curled over the top of his collar, and, unlike other guests in tailcoats, he wore a jacket and breeches. As he turned to greet a fellow guest, his eyes caught her inquisitive gaze. They were a startling blue against his tanned skin and his regard was bold. The captain was clean-shaven, the lines of his mouth finely shaped and there was cool recklessness in his handsome face. He was the kind of man who would break a woman's heart and walk away unscathed, Carina thought as her dancing partner returned.

She presented him to Enrico, and, when she looked again, Mavrone was still watching her. Carina opened her fan, peeping over the top, and saw him turn to one of his companions. Then he looked back and smiled, the invitation in his eyes as clear as if he had spoken the words out loud.

He was flirting with her, but not in the way practised in London. She was familiar with the tricks for attracting a man – the sideways glance and fluttering eyelashes – but she sensed Captain Mavrone had no time for frivolity. He appeared relaxed, but there was a tension in his pose that reminded her of a soldier away from his regiment in time of war.

Warning bells rang in her head. Look away now. Don't encourage him! Oh, but he was so good-looking … His gaze was magnetic and Carina couldn't help herself. She lowered her fan and their eyes locked again. Mavrone bowed his head and raised his glass. Was he toasting her health or admitting defeat? There was no way of knowing, for a naval officer stood in front of her to claim the next dance. By the time it was over, both Baron Riso and Captain Mavrone had left the ballroom.

'Enrico tells me you spotted the infamous captain,' Paulo commented as he led her in to supper. 'Were you bowled over like every other woman in Palermo?'

'In my opinion he's a rogue with too high an opinion of himself.'

At the far end were tables laden with dishes of meats and salads and her cousin declared he was famished. He filled their plates before they went to find Alice with Jane and the

Goodwins. They sat down at their table and conversation picked up from where it had left off. When she had finished, Carina emptied her glass of wine and smiled at Paulo.

'So, are you enjoying yourself? I hope you've dispensed with your reservations?'

'It's a grand affair, but there's more to it than meets the eye. Don't you find it odd Captain Mavrone attends a ball where he's in danger of arrest for the sake of a few waltzes?'

'Enrico says he does it to taunt Maniscalco and Prince Scalia.'

'Enrico's my oldest friend, but he's not always right. And I've seen other disreputable characters who don't normally attend occasions like this.'

'Why shouldn't they be here if they're friends of our host?'

'Then tell me where they've all gone! Before the last dance I walked through the reception rooms and didn't see any of them. Baron Riso doesn't appear to be mingling with his guests.'

That much was true. Every table was occupied and Baroness Riso sat close by, surrounded by a large party. But her husband was not with her and Captain Mavrone nowhere in sight.

'So where do you think they are? Making bombs in the basement or hatching a plot upstairs?' Carina was glib.

'I wouldn't be surprised if they were doing both.'

Paulo placed his hands on the arms of his chair and Carina gave him a suspicious look. 'I hope you're not planning a reconnaissance?'

'The idea never entered my head, sweet cousin.' Paulo smiled disingenuously. 'It's warm in here and I need some fresh air.'

Paulo stood up, excusing himself to Alice, and Carina watched as he made his way through the oncoming tide of guests. Waiters brought puddings to their table and Jane announced that the small pink mounds were shaped like breasts in honour of the martyrdom of St Agatha.

'How utterly awful!' Alice declared, and put down her spoon.

'They're made by the nuns in the Convent of Santa Maria and are quite delicious. Do please try some.'

Carina did not hear her aunt's response. She was wondering where Paulo had gone. Gabriella said he was capable of espionage and perhaps he was, after all. She imagined him creeping around, taking notes on his host's activities to report back to his father. Coffee was served and he should be back by now. It was exactly as Gabriella had feared. Paulo was searching the house and she must find him before it was too late! Looking down at her programme, Carina said the first thing that came into her head.

'Forgive me, but I'm engaged for the next mazurka. When Paulo returns, please tell him I'm on the dance floor?'

As she left the table, Carina realised the mazurka was over. The orchestra was playing a polonaise and she hoped Alice and Jane were too occupied by the pudding to notice. The dance was underway and it was easy to slip unnoticed into the next room. The sound of laughter came from an alcove where a couple was sitting but most of the guests were at supper and when she reached the landing the hall was deserted. Where was Paulo? It was far too chilly for him to have stayed outside all this time. Had he gone to search the upper floors or was he down in the cellars?

Carina peered cautiously over the bannister. The hall below was empty and she made up her mind and started up the stairs. She prayed she wouldn't run into Baron Riso or anyone else. What possible reason could she give for coming up here? She was doing nothing wrong, she told herself. If she were caught, she would think of some excuse. The wine she had drunk with supper gave her courage and when she reached the upper floor she stopped and listened.

She could hear the orchestra playing far off, but all around her was quiet. A passage leading off the stairwell disappeared into a void of blackness and the stillness made her apprehensive. Perhaps she should return to the anteroom and wait for Paulo there? But before she did, she must make certain he wasn't up here. She would take a quick look along the passage and then go back downstairs.

Running her hand along the panelled wall, Carina walked down the corridor. There were no illuminations and every few paces she peered over her shoulder to the stairwell. On one side, the windows were draped with heavy curtains and there were doors on the other. The bedrooms must be on this floor, she thought, and all their occupants downstairs. Soon maids and valets would come to tend the fires. She was about to retreat when she glimpsed a crack of light beneath a doorway ahead.

Carina crept forward, her shoulder pressed against the wall. She heard voices and held her breath as she tried to make out what they were saying. The name 'Denuzio' was enunciated in a slow, distinctive drawl and anxiety flashed through her. Had Paulo been caught? Was he inside the room being interrogated?

As she concentrated, trying to distinguish her cousin's voice from the others, she began to catch the drift of the discussion. Count Maniscalco's name came up and then another she recognised, Francesco Crispi. Where had she heard that name before? Jane had spoken of him, she remembered. Francesco Crispi was a Sicilian exile in London and an outspoken advocate of revolution! Carina felt the hairs stand up on the back of her neck.

'Why wait?' someone asked.

'Because we're not ready.' Baron Riso's voice was unmistakable. 'We need Francesco Crispi to rally the support of our countrymen. Without him the revolution will fail.'

There was no doubt that he was in charge and Carina clasped her hand over her mouth. She had done exactly what she suspected of Paulo and spied on Baron Riso! She couldn't bear to hear another word and, flattening the sides of her skirts with her hands, sped back along the passage. She was in sight of the landing when she heard the click of a door and the soft tread of footsteps. Someone had left the meeting early. Whoever it was, they would see her the moment she came into the light of the stairwell! She must find somewhere to hide, and, as her arm brushed against fabric, Carina remembered the concealed windows.

She slipped behind a heavy curtain, heart skittering as the footsteps came nearer. Please don't let them stop! Don't stop! As she willed the footsteps to go on past, she noticed the hem of her skirt was caught beneath the curtain fringe. She bent down to pull it back out of sight, then let out a yelp of fright as a hand grasped her wrist and the curtains parted to reveal the unsmiling face of Ben Mavrone.

'So what have we here? A mouse skulking in a corner or a new recruit for Count Maniscalco?'

His eyes went over her and Carina's mouth turned dry.

'Has complicity deprived you of the power of speech, Miss Temple?'

'I lost my way. I'm looking for my cousin. He's … he's unwell …' she stammered. 'I believe he came up here to lie down in the library.'

'And you expected to find the library up here? Surely you passed through it downstairs?' Mavrone's grasp tightened.

'I meant Baron Riso's private library.'

She was improvising wildly and Mavrone took a step forward. The curtains closed behind him and Carina was acutely aware of the proximity of his body in the cramped space. Her chest rose and fell in rapid breaths but, apart from the way he held her, Mavrone seemed relaxed.

'Did you come up here to spy on Baron Riso or to meet a lover for a secret tryst?' he asked, studying her with faint curiosity.

'I told you I was looking for my cousin.'

'I don't believe you, ma'am. Please will you try again?'

'I heard nothing, I tell you!'

He hoped to force an admission from her and Carina responded in a fierce whisper, 'I've told you the truth. Now let go of me!'

'You don't really expect me to do that, do you? Perhaps you'd rather tell Baron Riso why you were eavesdropping on his private party?'

'Take me to the baron if you wish. I know he will believe me. I *know* him to be a gentleman and not an ill-mannered bully!'

When Mavrone released her, Carina experienced a moment of triumph. She had made him back down. If she were prepared to explain herself to Baron Riso, then he could detain her no longer. She would tell the baron just what she told him. Unless they had found Paulo, she was in the clear. So why didn't he move out of her way?

'Are you in such a hurry to leave?'

The question was an enticement, echoing the silent exchange of earlier and Carina could barely breathe. There was danger here, a dark enchantment to which she was susceptible and she swallowed hard.

'Will you please let me pass?'

Mavrone nodded, but did not move. Only the bulk of her petticoats kept the lower half of her body from touching his as Carina began to edge past him. Later, when she dissected the manoeuvre in detail, she couldn't think why, when she had to move sideways, she did not turn her back. It was awkward in any case and made more difficult by the width of her skirts. One of his buttons snagged the ribbon of her corsage. Carina felt his hand brush against her breast as he broke the thread to release it.

Captain Mavrone was testing her to the limit and waited until the last moment. As Carina's hand reached for the curtain, his arm went round her waist. He pulled her back and Carina did not resist or cry out. Moonlight turned the colour of his eyes metallic and she gazed at him, spellbound. He ran his fingers lightly down the side of her cheek and then his mouth came down on her lips.

The memory of Robert Danby ripped across her mind and vanished. Mavrone's kiss induced a different sensation altogether. She could feel the warmth of his body beneath his jacket as he kissed her deeply and passionately. Her eyes closed and her head fell back against his arm. Mavrone's hand tangled in her hair, the other caressing her neck and Carina melted into his embrace. Wrapped in the dark night, she was aware only of the exquisite feel of his lips and the touch of his fingers. When he stood back, she swayed unsteadily against him. He placed his hands on her shoulders to look down into her face.

'By God, ma'am, you're certainly worthy of your reputation.'

As his words penetrated her trance-like state, rage and humiliation flowed through Carina and she drew back her hand and slapped him hard across the cheek. She would have hit him again but Mavrone caught hold of her wrists. Maddened by the way he held her, she shouted at him.

'Damn you to hell! Damn you, let me go!'

'I believe you came up here looking for me and I'm flattered.' In contrast to her own, Mavrone's voice was level. 'It's been a pleasure to make your acquaintance. When you're ready, I shall escort you back downstairs.'

Carina's hands shook as she straightened the line of her bertha. Unable to think of an insult crushing enough, she pushed past him and stepped into the passage. The hem of her skirt caught and she jerked the fabric so hard a panel of organza split from hem to waist. She couldn't go back to the party looking like this! She must tidy her hair and find someone with a needle and thread to repair her dress. There would be a retiring room, most likely on the ground floor, and she walked swiftly to the landing.

Gathering up her skirts, she heard Mavrone's footsteps behind her as she ran down the stairs, fury bursting within her, until she was halted by the sight of Paulo in the hall. Her cousin was staring at her as if she had fallen out of the sky; he appeared so surprised that at first he didn't notice who followed.

'Angels defend us, where have you been?'

'The young lady was looking for you upstairs,' Mavrone answered before Carina could utter a word. 'Miss Temple was concerned for your welfare. So much so, in fact, she was oblivious to the compromising situation in which she placed herself. She was searching the bedrooms. You can imagine my surprise when she entered mine.'

Paulo's mouth dropped open and Carina's gaze swung from him to Mavrone. What the devil was he talking about? Was the captain afraid she might tell Paulo of the conversation she had overheard? Mavrone wanted to ensure her silence and didn't care if he traduced her – but what could she say in defence? To admit she'd been upstairs was bad enough, but the sight of her hair and torn dress was explicit condemnation. If she gave the conspirators away, he would surely let it be known she had been in his bedroom. Gossip was the meat on which the appetites of

Palermo fed and the look in his eyes implied the story would be embellished in the telling.

Left speechless by his audacity, Carina turned her back on the men. She heard Paulo answer, his voice tight with the effort of controlling himself. 'My cousin's not feeling herself tonight. I'll find her aunt and take her home immediately. We would be grateful if you'd keep this unfortunate incident to yourself, sir.'

'That would certainly be best for all concerned.' Mavrone's easy tone was deceptive. 'However, my discretion comes at a price. I will only remain silent if the bargain is kept by all three of us.'

'You have my word upon it.'

'And that of Miss Temple?'

'Miss Temple will gladly forget she ever made your acquaintance,' Paulo answered firmly. 'As far we're concerned, we didn't see you here this evening, Captain Mavrone.'

Without giving her a chance to gainsay him, Paulo took Carina by the arm, his fingers pinching above the elbow as he marched her across the hall to the front door and called for a man to bring their cloaks.

'Stay here and don't speak to him again, do you understand!' he hissed in her ear. 'I will go and fetch Miss Alice.'

When a footman brought her cloak and placed it over her shoulders, Carina did not take the trouble to thank him. Seething with rage, she waited in the cold draught for Paulo to return with Alice. Their carriage was summoned and, once hidden in the dark interior, she looked in the direction of the hall and saw Mavrone had gone.

Oblivious to the frost between the cousins, Alice chatted happily on the way home while Carina huddled in a corner. She wondered how an evening that began with such high hopes could end so badly. If Paulo hadn't gone wandering off, the encounter with Mavrone would have been avoided. And what was he doing in the hall when she came down? He should never have given in to the captain's blackmail! If he believed in her virtue, then he should have followed her example and kept quiet. She would talk to him in the morning, she decided, but, when they arrived back and Alice went upstairs, Paulo caught her before she could escape. 'What, in the name of heaven, do you think you were up to?'

'I was looking for you. I bumped into Captain Mavrone. He accused me of trespassing and we had a brush.'

'A brush! A brush?' Paulo looked at her as if she had lost her wits. 'Is that what you call it – when you turn up looking for all the world as if you've been rolling in the hay with a farm boy?'

'It wasn't my fault! You were away so long I was worried about you.'

'Enrico and I played a few hands of piquet. When I came back, I was told you were on the dance floor.'

Paulo would never admit he was guilty and maybe he wasn't – but he had an alibi, which was more than she could say for herself. If she alienated him further, he might go to his father and that would be a catastrophe. She would be locked in a nunnery or worse. An apology was in order.

'I'm truly sorry, Paulo. I beg you not to say a word, please! There was no harm done. I swear I'll die if you betray me.'

'I'm beginning to understand why you were banished from London.' Paulo searched her face to assess how much sincerity was in her words. 'We've standards in Sicily, too, you know. It's a grave mistake to ignore them.'

'Oh, Paulo, you told me all those things and they went to my head. If it were the other way round, I would never give you away. I would stand by you, even on pain of death.'

Carina hung her head as she stood in front of Paulo, trying

to look ashamed, and finally he touched the back of his hand to her cheek. She kissed him goodnight and, halfway up the stairs, stopped to look down. There was a gleam of amusement in Paulo's eyes. He had a fair idea of what had happened, she thought, but her cousin wouldn't betray her. They were two of a kind and she could trust him.

Rose was waiting in the bedroom to help her out of her dress and untwine the ribbons from her hair. The delicate watch-spring steel of her new crinoline had survived and when Rose left, her arms full of organza and stiff petticoats, Carina went to sit by the hearth.

She closed her eyes and felt again the pressure of Mavrone's arms around her and the taste of his lips. The memory of his kiss sent tremours down her nerves. She would like to think he had taken advantage of her, but she couldn't deceive herself. The moment their eyes met, a charge of electricity had leapt between them. For the first time in her life, she had experienced a physical response that was beyond her power to control. Yet equal to the fire she had felt, was the heat of her indignation. Mavrone was a hardened soldier – but to throw her reputation in her face was contemptible. How could she have let him kiss her?

She needed fresh air and Carina slung her shawl about her shoulders. Opening the shutters, she stepped out on to the balcony. Palermo was spread out below, its slender spires silhou-etted against an indigo sky and lights bobbing in the harbour as fishing boats set out for the early catch. Down there, men like Ben Mavrone and Baron Riso were plotting revolution. She had learnt their secret. Did that make her an accomplice to the crime? There was no real evidence. She had only overheard a few words. Besides, if Gabriella was right, then Baron Riso was on the side of the angels. And for all she knew, she was too ...

It was time for bed and Carina turned back towards her bedroom. Her thoughts returned to Ben Mavrone and it struck her then that the whole of the conversation upstairs had been in English. Mavrone was Sicilian, but when they were alone he had spoken in her native tongue and she hadn't noticed until now because his accent was perfect, his use of the language as fluent and natural as her own.

CHAPTER NINE

PALERMO, FEBRUARY 1860

The noise of rain, coming in a sudden downpour, made Carina look up from the letter she was writing. She went over to the window and stood with her fingers absently tracing the pattern of raindrops on the glass. It was on days such as this that she missed Alice most. The morning her aunt left for England, she hadn't gone to see her off. Alice said it would be too upsetting, so Anna Maria went in her place. When they had said goodbye at the house they had both wept. Then, yesterday, a letter arrived from Alice announcing her engagement to Sir Anthony Farne.

Alice wrote that a small wedding was planned in March and there was no need for her to come home.

'The timing is most propitious now that you're settled, dearest. We are to live in Northumberland, but Anthony appreciates the close bond between us. When you return I will travel south to be with you in London. The house in Mount Street will remain open and everything just as it was before ...'

No, it would not! How could it be? Last night Carina had hardly slept. She paced her bedroom until dawn. Alice hadn't abandoned her, she told herself over and over again. It was only because she was lonely that she was upset. She loved Alice and this was what she wanted for her.

> *'I am delighted to receive your wonderful news.'* She began her reply. *'I know that you and Anthony will find true happiness together. My only sadness is that I will miss your wedding … I'm not sure when Oliver expects my sojourn in Sicily to come to an end – but my grandmother has asked me to stay for as long as I want. I have no desire to return to London, at present, and expect to remain in Palermo until after the summer.'*

How she wished Paulo and Gabriella were still here. They had returned to their studies a week after Baron Riso's ball. Paulo did not mention the evening again, but he hadn't forgotten, Carina was sure. She tried not to think about him, but Ben Mavrone was constantly on her mind. Where had he gone? Which part of Sicily was his home? How could she find out more about him? He had become an obsession and she couldn't get him out of her head.

She was too much alone, Carina decided, and sent a card to Jane Parsons. A note came back informing her Miss Parsons was in Rome. Palermo was deserted and her only consolation was the time she spent with her grandmother. They talked about her mother and Nonna gave her Sonia's letters to read. Her mother wrote with verve. She was outspoken and confident, in love with her husband and looking forward to the birth of her first child. That part brought tears to Carina's eyes and Nonna patted her hand.

'Sonia would be very proud of you, Carina. You're like her in so many ways. Once she decided on a course of action, she never wavered from it.'

One evening, to give her granddaughter some younger company, the contessa invited a group of Paulo's friends, including Enrico Fola, to dinner. Carina bit her tongue through the social niceties until she could venture the one question she wanted to ask: if there was news of Captain Mavrone.

'He's not in Palermo. No one knows if he's even in Sicily.'

It was obvious Enrico didn't want to talk about Mavrone and Carina wondered if Paulo had said anything. She would kill him if he had, but she was not to be put off. She could have no peace until she tracked him down and placed her hopes in her budding friendship with Bianca Scalia. The princess had come for tea and invited her to stay at their country villa. She had also spoken of her mother.

'When I was growing up, Sonia was the person I admired most in the world. She was both beautiful and kind. It was so romantic when a dashing naval officer swept her off to England! All of us girls swooned with envy.'

The sound of a dog barking broke into her thoughts and Carina went back to the bureau. She had wasted half the morning dreaming and would finish her letter to Alice this afternoon. There was just time before lunch to dash a line off to Harry. She had told him of the vendetta between Prince Scalia and Captain Mavrone, mentioning in passing she had met them both.

Harry's response was typical.

'Do take care, Carrie. Remember your promise and leave this matter well alone.'

Carina reached for a fresh piece of paper. Harry was right not to trust her, she thought as she wrote in a fast, sloping hand.

*I have been invited to stay at the Villa Pallestro by Bianca Scalia.
The visit is a timely diversion, although I doubt I will discover the
truth. Have no fear, dear Harry. I shall act decorously and with the
utmost discretion.*

'There is the Villa Pallestro!'

Bianca Scalia leant forward, pointing out of the carriage
window. They were bowling along the coast road towards the
village of Bagara and Carina saw a large house standing on a
hill. The ride from Palermo had taken less than two hours and
as Carina straightened her gloves, smoothing the soft leather
between her fingers she realised Bianca had asked her a
question.

'I'm sorry. My mind was far away.'

'I was wondering if you miss your family and friends in
England?'

'I miss my aunt, but Palermo is more agreeable than London
at this time of year. The *carnivale* was a delight and I enjoyed
the ball given by Baron and Baroness Riso.'

'May I ask you a favour, Miss Temple?' Bianca hesitated. Then
looked at her squarely. 'Please would you refrain from mentioning that evening to my husband? He is no friend of Baron Riso.'

It was the opening Carina needed, but there was no chance
to take the conversation further. The carriage rattled through
iron gates and up a cypress-lined avenue, coming to a halt in
front of a large villa with a columned facade. Two lines of servants bowed and curtsied as they entered and Bianca led the way
through salons scented with flowering lilies to the drawing
room.

Wherever her eye alighted, Carina saw the Scalia emblem of
a dragon entwined in the Bourbon fleur-de-lys. It was carved
into marble, engraved on brass and every inch of plaster on the

walls was painted with frescoes. There were animals and birds, gods and goddesses reclining on celestial clouds, and a ceiling painted blue with a scattering of gold stars. The villa was far grander than she had expected, and when the butler took Bianca aside, Carina wandered over to the window to look out.

The garden was laid out in the classical style, with topiary and statues. Beyond it, the road to Palermo stretched like a ribbon through green fields.

'I'm afraid there's been a delay,' Bianca said, coming up behind her. 'Your maid and luggage have only just arrived. They left Palermo before us and I don't understand.'

'I am more than happy to wait—'

'Riccardo never said anything! I'm so sorry.'

'Please don't worry on my account. I will refresh myself later.'

'Are you sure?'

Bianca's restless gaze scanned the road to Palermo and Carina had no idea why she was so concerned. After a light lunch, she was shown to her room and lay down on a chaise longue, listening to Rose's mutterings as she hung up her dresses.

'I've never known such a palaver! You'd have thought Old Nick was under the seat the way the soldiers carried on. Gino told them we were on our way to the Villa Pallestro, but they took not a blind bit of notice!'

'What do you suppose they were looking for?'

'Revolutionaries and such like.' Rose held up a skirt, assessing it for creases, her tone as matter of fact as if she were discussing the traffic in Piccadilly. 'Gino says the authorities discovered a hornets' nest in Palermo. The military are rounding suspects up from here to Messina, but they're wasting their time. The rebels are far too slippery to be caught by a bunch of idiots! He told me so – right in front of the soldiers.'

And that, no doubt, was why the Denuzio carriage had been held at the side of the road for most of the morning, Carina concluded. A nervous frisson ran through her. Was it also the reason Bianca was so agitated? Thoughts and questions darted through her mind; she had to speak to Bianca before Prince Scalia arrived.

With this in mind, Carina changed for dinner early, but when she arrived downstairs it was Prince Scalia and not his wife who awaited her in the drawing room. A footman served champagne on a silver salver and the prince took a flute and handed it to her. The bubbles tickled her nose and she made an attempt to be gracious.

'You're most indulgent, Your Excellency. Champagne is quite my favourite of all the French wines.'

'I'm delighted to hear it. We don't stand on formality at the villa. I hope you will consider yourself on intimate terms with us.' Prince Scalia twisted the stem of his glass between his thumb and fingers. 'I've arranged to take you riding in the morning. It will be a pleasure to show you our estate. Bianca is happy to provide you with the suitable attire and will lend you her mare.'

Carina might have prevaricated, but just then the door opened and Bianca came in, accompanied by a black-frocked priest. Father Domenico had soft, plump hands and she caught a whiff of rosewater as he was introduced. He embarked on a long story about her uncle and Carina saw the prince greet Bianca with a kiss on the cheek before he gave her his arm and led them into the dining room.

Dinner was a sumptuous meal of pasta followed by fish and then meat. The moment Carina finished one course, her plate was whisked away to be replaced by another and she lost count of how many times her glass was refilled. She felt light-headed as she listened to Prince Scalia and Father Domenico discussing local matters. There was no mention of roadblocks and when the footmen withdrew, she remarked casually, 'My maid tells me they were held up on the road due to trouble in Palermo.'

Carina folded her hands together as Prince Scalia took a cigar from the box and held it under his nose. She was surprised he didn't wait for the ladies to withdraw, but customs were different in Sicily. He struck a match and inhaled until the end glowed.

'I apologise for any inconvenience, but we're obliged to enforce extra measures of security.'

'Not more arrests, Your Excellency?' Father Domenico asked.

'The action we take is not of our choosing, Padre. If the rebels continue their subversion, then we use all our powers to destroy them.'

'What extra measures, precisely?' Bianca's hand reached for the heart-shaped locket. Her fingers clasped it briefly.

'Every man of working age will be questioned and anyone who can't provide evidence of employment or lodging taken to Palermo for investigation. Not a single traitor will slip through our net this time.'

For a time no one spoke. The atmosphere in the room seemed to close in and Carina glanced at Bianca. She was completely still, not even her hands moved, and her eyes were veiled by lowered eyelashes.

'It's been a successful exercise,' the prince continued. 'Once we get the prisoners to Palermo, we have the means to make them confess. I'm confident we will extract all the evidence necessary to condemn them.'

In the first instance, Carina was not sure she had heard him right. For Prince Scalia to confirm the allegations made against him so complacently outraged her. She couldn't let him get away with it! She meant to speak calmly but anger sharpened her voice.

'Surely you don't have authority to arrest innocent men when no crime has been committed?'

'If the security of the State is threatened, all men are guilty until proved innocent. Those who speak against the king must answer for their opinions – even if they expound only hot air.'

Prince Scalia dropped a column of ash into a dish and inclined his head towards her.

'The more prominent the rebels are, the greater danger they present. Liberals like Baron Riso believe they live a charmed existence, but they're not beyond our reach. Take your friend, Enrico Fola. His family enjoy the trust of our beloved monarch and yet he belongs to a secret society bent on treachery.'

'I've never heard Enrico Fola speak against the king!'

'We've placed Baron Riso and Enrico Fola under close surveillance.' Scalia ignored her intervention. 'It's only a question of time before they become careless and then we'll have them.'

So the prince had been informed of her visit to the Palazzo Riso. Was he also aware Ben Mavrone had been there that evening? Carina could feel Bianca's gaze across the table, willing her to stay silent, but caution was swallowed by indignation.

'My grandmother gave me permission to attend the reception. Am I to infer you've also placed her under surveillance?'

'I believe the Contessa Denuzio was misled as to the nature of Baron Riso's invitation. I shall write and advise her to put an end to your association with such people – and the sooner the better.'

'I'm not given to jumping at shadows, Your Excellency. There were no traitors in Baron Riso's home—'

'My husband isn't implying you did anything wrong, Carina. He's only concerned for your safety.'

'Well said, Bianca.' The prince looked approvingly at his wife. 'Miss Temple doesn't appreciate having her friends chosen for her. Indeed, we're privileged that she honours us with her presence.'

'We live in difficult times, Miss Temple. It's hard to know who one can trust.' Father Domenico sounded flustered.

'Thank you, Padre, but I'm quite capable of looking out for myself.'

'Of course, you're a woman of the world and should be respected as such.'

The bite of malice in Scalia's words was not lost on Carina. The wine had made her rash, but as they went through to the salon, she saw his expression change. No longer supercilious, the prince's regard was hard and intense and it seemed he was attracted by her defiance. He said goodnight at the bottom of the stairs and she followed Bianca down the corridor to her bedroom.

Rose helped her undress and Carina sat down to brush her hair. Prince Scalia is a calculating, clever man. I must keep him at arm's length, she thought. I will be aloof but not unfriendly. I will simply ask him why Paulo dislikes Captain Mavrone. That should be enough to provoke a reaction. It won't get Paulo into trouble – and by this time tomorrow, I will have learnt something.

CHAPTER TEN

Rose drew back the curtains and, as she had every morning that Carina could remember, gave a succinct account of the weather.

'It will be fine today, ma'am, but sharp, mind you.'

It couldn't be seven o'clock already! Carina had drunk too much wine and her head ached, but it was too late to change her mind. She downed two cups of strong coffee before Rose helped her into Bianca's riding habit.

The jacket was on the small side and she held onto the bedpost as Rose tugged the lacing of her corset until it was tight enough to fasten. The skirt was a little short, but the hat was pretty, with a veil and streamers, and the boots a perfect fit. Carina's footsteps resounded on the marble as she went down to the hall where Prince Scalia was waiting.

His gaze travelled from her neck down to the tip of her black boots and then returned to her face.

'My wife's habit fits you like a glove, my dear. The outfit is most becoming.'

What he meant was that it was rather too tight, Carina thought irritably. Her mood improved when the horses were led up to the front door. Bianca's mare, Pabla, was pure Arab and pranced delightfully. It took two grooms to hold her head as Carina mounted. She arranged her skirt over the saddle horn and Prince Scalia offered her a riding crop, with a vicious-thong attached to the end.

'I don't need a whip. The mare is raring to go.'

'Take it, all the same.'

Prince Scalia thrust the crop into her hand and they set off, trotting down the drive and out through the gates. Pabla's narrow neck arched as she danced sideways and when they had turned off the road, Scalia called to her,

'Give her head! I'll catch you up …'

She loosened the reins and the mare leapt forward, flattening her neck to reach full stride. Carina experienced a thrill of exhilaration. This was what she had missed, the wind in her face and the fluid movement of a horse beneath her. The Arab's speed was breath-taking and she did not slow down until Pabla began to blow. They drew up near a ravine, where wild flowers peeped between rocks. Prince Scalia was a long way behind, keeping the bay at a steady canter. She might have lost him altogether, Carina thought, but the gallop had dispelled the stagnation of drawing rooms and her mind was clear.

She was aware her cheeks were flushed as Prince Scalia drew level. 'Did Pabla bolt with you?'

'I wanted to try her paces and she responded magnificently.'

'And you were in control all the time? I'm impressed by your horsemanship.' The prince nudged his horse closer and leant over to brush a straggling hair off her face. 'You're an unconventional young woman, Miss Temple. Do you approach everything in life with such abandon?'

'It depends on what I want to achieve.'

'Were you trying to get away from me?'

'No, of course I wasn't … I knew you would catch up. Your horse has more staying power.'

'A quality I greatly admire.'

His knuckle was hard beneath his glove and there was hot, keen look in his eyes. This was her chance. The question was on the tip of her tongue, pressing against her lips, when a burst of gunfire exploded above their heads. Pabla shied so violently Carina was almost thrown off and Prince Scalia dug his spurs into the bay's flanks.

'Some fool's shooting rabbits! Follow me!'

Carina followed close behind as they climbed a steep bank. The ground was littered with stones so the horses stumbled and slipped until they came out of the gully on to a high plateau. Thorns stuck out their spiky heads between scattered boulders and she saw a circle of army tents positioned on a slope to the left. The sun was in her eyes and when she looked more closely, Carina realised what she had taken for rocks were prisoners in chains. There were hundreds of them, sprawled over the wasteland like an army in disarray. A chill ran through her but she was determined not to show Scalia that she was shocked.

'Quite a catch, don't you think?' The prince touched his thumb to his nose.

'I offer you my commiserations. There can't be many loyal Sicilians left at liberty.'

'Come now, Miss Temple.' Scalia gave her a stern look. 'This is not the time nor place to propagate your liberal opinions.'

'You misjudge me, Your Excellency. I'm merely commenting on statistics. How can you suspect so many men are a threat to the state?'

'Because every Sicilian peasant is born with treachery in his soul. Discipline is the only way they learn it's not worth their lives to support the rebels.'

Scalia meant to reprimand her, and Carina did not answer. Her gaze passed over those prisoners close to the roadside. They were a pitiful lot, with manacles on their wrists and ankles, and she felt sorry for them. Watching her face, Scalia's mouth twisted in a distorted smile.

'I must speak to the commandant. If our methods of law enforcement offend your sensibilities, you had better wait here.'

The words were thrown over his shoulder as he touched his whip to the bay's neck and Carina watched him go with simmering resentment. There was a guard post along the road and a soldier stepped forward to challenge him. Prince Scalia leant down. She hoped he was giving instructions for her safety, but the soldier returned to his companions without so much as a glance in her direction.

The guards were a damned sight too complacent, Carina thought. She could easily ride away, but Scalia would take any form of retreat as weakness. So she stayed where she was, speaking softly to the mare to calm her. Wild fowl hooted in the distance and she could hear a low murmur of voices behind her. The prisoners seemed to be closer than before and sensing the stealthy approach to her rear, Pabla struck the ground with her front hooves. Now, Carina clearly made out the clanking of leg-irons and shuffling footsteps on the track. Her hand tightened around the riding crop and when a stone was kicked carelessly, rolling along the ground under the horse's hooves, she could bear the suspense no longer.

'If you come any closer, I'll set the guards on you!'

'We only want to pay our respects, lady.'

The answer came in a guttural voice, and was followed at once by another. 'So *you're* Scalia's new favourite – and not ashamed to be seen out riding with him.'

Carina wouldn't be intimidated. If she ignored them, they

would tire of their jibes and leave her alone. Then, from the corner of her eye, she saw one of the prisoners step forward. She had the impression he was taller than the others and, despite his chains, moved with agility.

'Why don't you get off your horse, Miss Temple?'

She heard the words before she saw him, but Carina would have recognised the voice anywhere. It was the same drawl that had mocked her before and her breath caught in her throat as Ben Mavrone moved to Pabla's head. With a quick movement he took hold of the bridle.

'We have met, or don't you remember?'

A thick layer of dust covered his face and there was blood on his wrists. Mavrone was as filthy as his companions, his appearance so far removed from the picture in her mind, Carina wouldn't have known him apart from his voice and the colour of his eyes. His regard passed over her as if he could see through her riding habit and her heart jerked unsteadily.

'Yes, I remember,' she said, finally finding her voice. 'I don't know why you're here – but I'd be grateful if you would let go of my horse.'

'I'm sure you understand the circumstances under which I'm detained.' Mavrone did not release Pabla's bridle. His hand slid along the rein close to her own. 'It's a pity I wasn't aware you were an intimate of Prince Scalia when we last met.'

'I'm not ...'

Carina faltered. Mavrone's eyes were like the sea on a bright day, only colder, and the contempt in them undisguised. He thought she had betrayed their conspiracy and seeing her with Scalia confirmed his suspicions. He would never accept she was innocent and a combination of shock and nerves kept her silent.

'You find us in desperate circumstances. I hoped you might offer us some assistance.'

Refusing to answer, Carina fixed her gaze on a point between Pabla's ears.

'What's the delay, Capitano?'

One of the men came to stand beside Mavrone and Carina remembered the others. Three of them had formed a semicircle in front of Pabla. She saw the way they watched Mavrone, waiting for his command. The captain had instigated the manoeuvre. Did he plan to steal the horse and make his escape? Surely, he couldn't ride in shackles? No one could – yet he would manage somehow, she thought. He would haul himself over the mare's back and gallop off, leaving her to the mercy of his companions.

Carina let her gaze roam over the men. They were close enough for her to smell the stench of stale sweat and she wrinkled her nose.

'Miss Temple doesn't like the scent of patriots, Ruffo.'

'Get your men out of my way or I'll use the whip on you,' she commanded in a low voice.

'Will you indeed? Has Prince Scalia initiated you already?'

Carina ignored the question. With a flick of her wrist, she uncoiled the leather thong to its full length. Her heart was tight in her chest as she waited for Mavrone to step out of the way, but he did not move.

'I order you to release my horse!'

'I don't take orders from Prince Scalia's—'

What happened next was like a nightmare. As she lifted the leather thong above her head, Mavrone forced Pabla's head round towards him. He grabbed the heel of her boot and wrenched her foot out of the stirrup. In a panic of terror, Carina lashed out. The whip caught Mavrone across the face. She saw blood on his forehead, but still he hung on. Then someone yanked the whip from her hand in a grasp that almost broke her

wrist and Mavrone's arm went around her waist. He was dragging her from the saddle and, knowing she was about to fall,
Carina screamed.

Terrified by the commotion, Pabla reared up on her hind
legs. Then her hooves touched the earth and she jumped
forward, whinnying with fright as she bolted. The reins
snapped, flapping uselessly, and Carina clung on to the mane
as they careered along the track. There was a crack of rifle fire
and she bent down, her arms around the horse's neck. Bullets
whistled overhead and the saddle horn pressed painfully into
her stomach but she hung on until Pabla lost her footing. The
horse's head went down and Carina was thrown from the
saddle.

She landed so hard the air was knocked out of her body.
Carina lay still, gasping for air until the feeling of suffocation
lessened, then checked the movement of her arms and legs.
Nothing was broken and she opened her eyes to find Pabla
standing over her. They had reached the army encampment
and she staggered to her feet. She leant against the horse as a
soldier marched towards her. He demanded identification.
Carina shook her head and he turned on his heel and began
shouting orders. Suddenly there were soldiers running in all
directions. The flap of the nearest tent lifted and Prince Scalia
emerged. He stood for a moment, and then strode to her side.

'Did the mare run away with you? Are you hurt?'

'You're guilty of gross negligence, sir!'

'But the guards?'

'Your guards are blind and incompetent! They were shooting
at me, for heaven's sake!'

'My dear girl, you're concussed. Come and lie down until
you are recovered.'

'Don't be a fool! I've fallen off a horse before,' she replied in a harsh whisper. 'What was your purpose, sir? Did you mean to punish me for my political views?'

Prince Scalia's face went taut until every feature was rigid and Carina turned her back on him.

'Miss Temple believes her accident was due to the actions of your guards, Falcone.' He spoke loudly so that she would hear. 'If she can identify the culprits, you will ensure they're severely punished.'

The broken rein lay across her palm and Carina turned round slowly.

'I wish to return to the villa at once. I take it those responsible will be reprimanded?'

'Certainly, ma'am. My officers are down there already.'

'There's only one way to deal with them, Falcone. Single out the ruffians and send them ahead to Palermo. Count Maniscalco will deal with them personally. You know the procedure.'

Was he talking about the prisoners or guards? Carina did not know. The prince's face was hard and his tone chilling. 'And get me a fresh mount. Miss Temple will ride my horse. I'll send a groom to collect the mare this afternoon.'

Prince Scalia took hold of her arm as if he expected her to resist, but Carina was too shaken to respond. She waited while the side saddle was put on the bay and the prince gave her a leg up. As they left the camp she was beyond feeling anything except fiery hatred for both men. Scalia was a sadistic monster and Ben Mavrone a rough and abusive criminal. The image that possessed her had been an illusion and she should have known better. The cold wind went through her and Carina shivered. She hadn't given them away, but the guards would blame the prisoners and it wouldn't take them long to identify Mavrone. Once Scalia discovered he was among the captives, his fate would be sealed. She would never see him again.

CHAPTER ELEVEN

Carina leant back against the cushions as the Scalia carriage sped along the road back to Palermo. She had managed to escape a day early and the rest of the visit had been torture. By this morning she had reached breaking point.

She made sure she was never alone with Prince Scalia, but felt his eyes on her wherever she went. Her remarks to him were caustic and ill-tempered; yet the more she repudiated his advances, the more cloying he became. The prince made no attempt to conceal his interest and Bianca spent most of the time in her private apartments. On the few occasions she joined the party, she was nervous and distracted. Carina had hoped they might be friends, but understood her no better the day she left than when she arrived.

Was Bianca slightly unbalanced, Carina wondered? She was beginning to think she was losing her mind herself. A string of sleepless nights had left her nerves shattered. Now anger had faded, she was tormented by guilt. Every time she thought of the encounter with Ben Mavrone she felt ashamed. She had beaten a man in chains. How could she have acted with such violence? She wasn't a bad person, Carina told herself. She was proud of her courage and Mavrone had frightened her – but she should never have breathed a word to Scalia. If she only she'd said Pabla bolted and she fell off, he might have escaped.

A tear slipped from her lashes and slid down her cheek. She wished she had never gone to the villa. And never set eyes on Captain Mavrone. Prince Scalia had received an urgent summons and departed for Palermo last night. Carina was terrified of what it might mean. She must warn Enrico and Baron Riso! Whatever she felt for Mavrone, she hated Prince Scalia more. If she could save her patriot friends, then at least one good thing would come out of the visit.

Worn out by the conflict of her emotions, she fell asleep, not waking until they reached the outskirts of Palermo. The storm that had threatened all day broke over the city and a battery of rain hammered on the roof. Torrents of water gushed down the streets so it took forever to reach her grandmother's house. When they drove into the courtyard, Carina didn't wait for the coachman to bring an umbrella. She was out the minute the steps were down, running to the porch with her face turned up so rain fell on her cheeks.

She could see Pietro, her grandmother's footman, reading a newspaper as she tugged the bell rope. He swung the door open and Carina dumped her bonnet and cape on a chair and set off down the passage. The curtains were drawn in the sitting room and Nonna was installed by the fire with game of patience laid out on a table in front of her. She looked up in surprise.

'My dear! I wasn't expecting you until tomorrow. Why, you're wet through!'

'It's only a drop of rain. I thought you'd be pleased to have me home.'

'I'm delighted to see you.' The contessa paused, studying Carina's face, as she rang the bell. 'First, you must have something to eat. Then you can tell me everything.'

Pietro was dispatched to the kitchen and Carina stood warming her hands in front of the fire. Nonna picked up the cards, shuffling the pack, and then set it down with a slap.

'Scalia has the habits of a tomcat. I hope he didn't misbehave in any way?'

Pietro came in with a tray, which he placed on the table, and Nonna waited until he had gone before she continued, 'I expected him to act properly with his wife in residence but one should never underestimate Riccardo Scalia. He's a strange, unpredictable man. Carlo says it's because his parents showed him no affection and he was bullied at school. In my opinion, he was born devious and your uncle is a little afraid of him.'

'It wasn't because of *the prince* I left early. There was an odd atmosphere about the place, Nonna. I couldn't make head or tail of Bianca. She was like a different person there …'

Her grandmother began to lay her cards down on the table, turning them over slowly. The fire crackled in the grate and Carina took a glass of wine from the tray and drank it. The wine warmed her and she crossed her ankles, looking at the toes of her boots glowing in the firelight.

'They're an ill-matched couple. I can't understand why Bianca married him. She must have had a hundred suitors.'

'It wasn't a love match, if that's what you mean. Isabella del Angelo was a good woman, but not wise. She regarded the proposal as a golden opportunity for her daughter. On the surface, Prince Scalia offered everything – wealth and a high position in society – everything except happiness. The child was only seventeen, how could she know better?' The question was rhetorical. 'Bianca was also very susceptible at the time. She was recovering from a broken heart.'

'So she married Prince Scalia after her engagement to Captain Mavrone was broken off?'

'What makes you think that?'

'Paulo told me. Well, he didn't say they were engaged exactly. He implied they were …'

Carina couldn't get the word out and Nonna answered without looking up. 'I'm sure Paulo puffed a lot of nonsense! Bianca was never *engaged* to Mavrone. It was a childhood attachment and brought to an end the moment her mother found out. The Mavrone boys were sent abroad and within months she was married to the snake.'

'And Mavrone never forgave Prince Scalia. Was that the beginning of the vendetta?'

'No one knows. Mavrone was a wild young man, but he respected Donna Isabella. He and his brother were orphans and she brought them up out of the kindness of her heart. Her only mistake was to allow Bianca to spend her holidays with them. Can you imagine, the daughter of Count del Angelo falling for the son of a peasant?'

At once everything became clear – Bianca's strange behaviour and her relationship with her husband. Theirs was an arranged marriage embittered by the memory of her first love. And Bianca must have known Ben Mavrone was near the Villa Pallestro! That was why she had been distressed about the roadblocks. It was the only possible explanation. Mavrone had come to meet with her and been captured, quite by accident, along with the others.

A quiver of jealousy darted through Carina. Ben Mavrone was Bianca's responsibility – so let her save him! Bianca wouldn't have the nerve, she thought. Then a new idea occurred to her.

Bianca might appear fragile, but there was resilience beneath her fragility. There must be, and cunning, too, to carry on with her lover under her husband's nose.

Suddenly Carina was furious. Furious with herself and furious with all of them. Her infatuation had been madness, a stupid girlish fantasy, and thank God it was over! She didn't care what happened to Mavrone. She wanted nothing more to do with the whole wretched business. And yet, she must speak to Enrico and warn him. She would ask Nonna to send a card, requesting he call upon her at his earliest convenience.

Refreshed by a good night's sleep, Carina felt better as she waited for Enrico in the garden. The storm had passed and the sun was out, warming her as she sat on the stone bench. She wanted to speak to Enrico outside so they wouldn't be overheard. Should she say she had seen Ben Mavrone? Only if absolutely necessary, Carina decided. She didn't want to think about him and Enrico was in enough trouble already.

A bird was nesting in the viburnum bush close by, darting in and out and Carina looked up to see Enrico walking down the path. How attractive he was with his pale face and limpid eyes, she thought. No wonder Gabriella was in love with him. Enrico was far nobler than the man who branded him a traitor.

'What's so urgent that I'm summoned here post-haste?' Enrico sat down beside her.

'A matter of the greatest importance. It concerns Prince Scalia. He claims you're a member of a secret society and a traitor to the king!'

'Does he really?'

The look in Enrico's eyes was guarded and his stiffness made Carina feel awkward. Did he think this meeting was a contrivance on her part to entrap him? Why, the very idea was absurd! She caught her lower lip between her teeth and waited a minute before she spoke.

'The authorities discovered a plot involving Baron Riso. You're suspected of treason and are under surveillance. You could be arrested at any time!'

A smudge of yellow pollen fell on Enrico's sleeve and he blew it off, his tone indifferent. 'I'm sure Scalia was keen to impress you, but they have no evidence.'

'They don't need evidence, you know that! Please listen to me, Enrico! You must consider your safety and that of your family. Think of Gabriella.'

'Gabriella would want me to stay.'

Lord, he was being difficult! If she'd known he'd be so stubborn she might not have bothered. Carina twisted her hands to contain her frustration.

'How does it serve your cause if you are imprisoned?'

'It testifies to the world there are men in Sicily prepared to sacrifice themselves for their country. It gives the people hope.'

'Fiddlesticks! The people don't want martyrs – they want food! The revolution failed last time. How can you prevail against the might of the Bourbon army?'

'In '48 we were alone. If we demonstrate the courage to rise up ourselves in the name of unity and freedom, Garibaldi will come ...'

As if he had said too much, Enrico gazed up to the palm fronds swaying in the breeze. Carina had read about Garibaldi in the newspapers. He was a charismatic leader whose aim was to unite Italy. Enrico's no dreamy idealist, she thought suddenly. He's in far deeper than any of us ever imagined. Heaven protect him, does he have any idea of the risk he is taking?

'Not even Garibaldi can perform miracles. Whatever it is

you're planning, you must postpone until circumstances are more fortuitous. It would be folly to act now.'

'If we delay, every free-thinking man in Sicily will be silenced.'

'And if the revolution fails, you'll achieve the opposite of what you hope. The injustice and suffering will only be worse—'

'Forgive my impertinence, but you've only been in Sicily a month.' Enrico lowered his head to look her in the face. 'What do you know of injustice and suffering?'

'I know you cannot fight suffering and injustice with the sword. They are only be defeated by endurance, using pain as your weapon and courage your strength.'

Enrico looked at her curiously, but said nothing. He was impatient to be gone, Carina could tell. She had failed to convince him and must play her last card.

'Captain Mavrone has been arrested,' she said in a low voice. 'I saw him with other prisoners on the Scalia estate. He's on his way to be interrogated in Palermo.'

There was a moment of silence and then Enrico swung round. 'Are you sure it was him?'

'I'm absolutely sure. And if they have Mavrone, they'll soon arrest you. You must leave Palermo before it's too late!'

He stood up and Carina followed suit, disconcerted by the shift in his reaction.

'Please forgive my lack of civility earlier.' Enrico extended his hand. 'We dare trust nobody – not even our own families. You're a true friend and I thank you.'

'Will you warn Baron Riso?'

'I'll warn Francesco, but we cannot run away. It's our patriotic duty to win Sicily her freedom.'

For all his fine words, Carina would have done anything to stop him. Tears welled up in her eyes and Enrico dipped his head beneath her bonnet and kissed her cheek. Then he stood back.

'Don't lose faith in us, Carina. And stay away from Prince Scalia. That man would move heaven and earth to have you in his power.'

Enrico's resolve was unbreakable. Did Paulo have any idea of his friend's commitment, Carina wondered? More importantly, was Gabriella aware of the danger he was in? Her cousin would be proud of him, she thought. And what of herself? Enrico's passion stirred her heart. The patriots had right on their side, but revolution was a bloody business and the odds stacked against them. They must be certain, she thought as she watched his slim figure disappear towards the house. They must be sure that their sacrifice is not in vain.

CHAPTER TWELVE

Dearest Alice
Palermo is a different city without you and my cousins. I miss you
and am less confident now than when we first arrived. Sicily has a
cruel and savage side that is hard to understand. I would like to
speak to Jane, but she is in Rome and I dare not visit the consulate
on my own. I wonder if I truly belong here? Please write soon. My
grandmother is in good health and sends you her blessing on your
marriage.

A little over a fortnight later, Carina received an answer.

Our separation is a bitter pang, dearest. I understand you are
lonely without the company of Paulo and Gabriella – but please
don't be too downhearted or discouraged. These weeks of winter
will pass and when your cousins return for Easter, your spirits will
revive. I have never seen you so happy as in the company of your
mother's family. Sicily is in your blood and will never leave you …

Alice understood her better than anyone and Carina was reassured. Still, Enrico's remark about Scalia troubled her. Was he referring to her in particular, or anyone acquainted with Baron Riso? She was safe under her uncle's protection and it was Enrico who was in danger. Where was he now?

A wall of silence surrounded the palazzo and she was desperate for news. Anna Maria had returned to Palermo and called twice at the Palazzo Scalia already. She must have learned something, but Carina could not question her in front of her grandmother. It was impossible to discover anything until, out of the blue, Anna Maria suggested she accompany her on a pilgrimage to the monastery of Santa Fiore in the mountains.

When Nonna expressed reservations, her aunt brushed them aside. Prince Scalia had assured her that the roads were safe, she declared; and even been so kind as to offer a mounted escort.

'It's only for our peace of mind. Count Maniscalco's been busy all winter. The brigands who caused us so much trouble are all under lock and key.'

So it was settled. Nonna gave way and Carina rose early on the morning of the excursion. Anna Maria had stipulated nothing too ostentatious, so she chose a dress of dove-grey crêpe without a crinoline. Despite Rose's admonitions, she refused to wear a corset. Tightly laced stays were unnecessary on a pilgrimage, she argued. Besides, it would be cold in the mountains and flannel pantalets were warmer than petticoats.

Carina's arrival in the courtyard preceded that of her aunt by a few seconds. Anna Maria was rigged out like a ship in full sail, with a gold crucifix pinned to her chest and clasping a jewel-encrusted prayer book. Observing her difficulty in negotiating the narrow doorway into the carriage, Carina wondered if they would both fit inside. Once she was in, Anna Maria gathered as many folds of her skirt about her as she could and Carina squeezed in opposite her. A sea of black taffeta filled the space between so she could hardly breathe, but when they reached the city gates the horses were whipped up and a breeze came in through the window bringing relief.

Scalia's two outriders, with their distinctive cockaded hats, were with them and Anna Maria announced she was going to say her prayers. Her lips moved silently as the beads passed through her fingers and the smell of wild herbs by the roadside made Carina think of Melton. Alice had told her how Sonia instructed the gardeners to pick sweetly perfumed leaves, laying them out in trays to dry before they were brought into the house. The custom had carried on after her death but it only occurred to her now that it came from Sicily.

'What are you dreaming about? Some young man perhaps?' Anna Maria put away her beads as the landau jolted over a bad patch of road.

'I was thinking about the brigands who've been arrested. What will happen to them?'

'If they're found guilty, they'll be sentenced accordingly. Now let me see, where are we?'

'Will any of them be executed?'

Anna Maria was gazing out of the window and turned her head, her face crumpled with disapproval.

'You forget we're on a pilgrimage, Carina! Such morbid fascination does not become you. You make me feel faint with such talk. Now, where are my smelling salts?'

Anna Maria searched in her pouch for a bottle and waved it under her nose. Then she leant back and shut her eyes. She didn't look faint, but it was an effective way to put an end to questions. She must wait for the return journey, Carina decided. Then she would pester and cajole Anna Maria until she extracted every morsel of information she had to offer.

They had come to the foothills and were lumbering up a narrow road between rocky escarpments. Judging from the position of the sun, it must be almost midday. If her calculations were correct, they would arrive at the convent of Santa Fiore within the hour. The thought of shady cloisters and the fresh mountain air made Carina drowsy. She was half asleep when a loud noise jolted her awake. For a confused moment she thought she was dreaming. Then she heard shouts and a rattle of gunfire. The horses plunged forward and the landau lurched, tilting precariously. As it came to a shuddering halt, both women were thrown to the floor.

The carriage was tipped on its side, making it difficult to move, but Carina managed to heave herself up on to the seat. As she leant down to help Anna Maria, a high-pitched keening came from outside. It was a spine-chilling sound and silenced by a gunshot. One of the horses must have broken a leg! They had shot one of the horses! As Carina tried to get to the door, Anna Maria clutched her skirts. 'We've been attacked! *Madre de Dio*, we've been ambushed!'

'We've had an accident. I expect a wheel's broken off. I'm going to open the door. You stay here.'

Anna Maria began to intone a prayer and Carina grasped the door handle. Where was Gino, the coachman? He should be here by now. The door was jammed fast and after a couple of attempts she gave up. Reaching for the blind, she undid the catch. Then she hauled herself up, resting her elbows on the rim as she looked out.

They had crashed at a point where the road was only wide enough for a single vehicle to pass. Just as she had thought, one of the wheels had sheared off. Carina could see the coachmen gathered in a group ahead. One of them – she thought it was Gino – was giving orders and waving his arms. Squinting her eyes, she counted the men. There were too many figures! Then, with a lurch of her stomach, she looked up and saw others standing at the top of the bank.

Anna Maria was right – they had been ambushed. Carina stared in horror at the bandits. Cartridge belts were slung over their jerkins and they carried knives with wide blades that caught the sun as they scrambled down the escarpment. The man she had mistaken for Gino was herding the coachmen to the side of the road. He prodded them onto their knees with the butt of his gun as they were tied up and made to lie face down on the ground.

Where was Scalia's escort, for God's sake? Carina twisted her neck and searched back along the road. Two bodies were sprawled on the ground and one lay close to the carriage. He had been trampled under its wheels and his hat, bearing Prince Scalia's cockade, was soaked in blood by his head. Nausea rose in her throat and Carina let go of the window ledge and sank back onto the seat.

'Holy Mary protect us!' Anna Maria raised her head. 'Santa Rosalia, come to our aid. Jesus save us—'

Carina was brought to her senses by her aunt's wailing. 'We must give them money if they come for us. How much do you have?'

'I don't know. It's in my purse …'

Anna Maria fumbled in her skirts and Carina saw the purse first. It had fallen out and was lying on the floor. She picked it up and spilled the contents on to her lap. Among the bottles and handkerchiefs were a few coins and a roll of banknotes tied to a large white piece of parchment.

'What's this?'

'A letter from Prince Scalia—'

'Well, we won't have need of that.'

Carina detached the notes and stuffed the letter into her pocket. She squeezed the banknotes in her palm as footsteps approached. The handle of the door was shaken and then the whole panel wrenched off its hinges. The gaping hole was filled by the shadow of a man who caught her by the shoulders and dragged her out.

She landed on her feet, a knife held beneath her chin so her head was forced back. The brigand's arm was tight beneath her ribs and a strangled sound came from her throat. The pressure eased and Carina breathed in air as the bandits crowded around her.

'What brings you to Santa Fiore with a mounted bodyguard?'

'We're on our way to the monastery. We'll give you money.'

'Sure you will – but maybe we want a bit more.' One of the men made an obscene gesture with his hips. 'Shall we have us some sport, my friends?'

'You forget our purpose, Paco. Where's the money, lady?'

Carina's arms were pinioned to her sides and the one called Paco took her hand and opened her fist. With a yell of triumph, he waved the bankroll in the air before digging into the pockets of her skirt.

'What's this?' He held up the letter from Prince Scalia.

'Tell us what it says!' one of them shouted.

Paco dropped the paper to the ground and the bandits laughed.

'Didn't you go to school, Paco? Can't you read?'

They had discarded the document and Carina saw greedy delight on their faces as the money was distributed. The knife beneath her chin was removed as the man who held her took his share. She momentarily forgot about Anna Maria until, like a signal from hell, Carina heard a scream as two bandits lifted her aunt out of the landau. The crucifix had been torn from her dress and tears streamed down her face. She tripped over her long skirts and a rough hand sent her to the ground.

'Time to say your prayers, you old cow!'

'Let's hear you beg for your life—'

'Leave her alone! Stop it! Stop it at once!'

Carina shouted at them, but she was forced to listen as the bandits goaded Anna Maria. Her aunt was on all fours, her vast crinoline billowing behind her. She was weeping and pleading until suddenly her sobbing ceased. She had seen Prince Scalia's letter and Carina's blood slowed in her veins. No, she wouldn't be so stupid! Even Anna Maria couldn't be such a fool! As she willed her to ignore it, Carina saw her fingers stretch out for the roll of parchment.

'Come on! Kiss my boots and I might let you live.'

'Never!' Anna Maria waved the letter in the air. 'We're under Prince Scalia's protection. This is—'

She was silenced as Paco hit her across the face. Blood dripped from her mouth and when his arm went up to strike her again, Anna Maria fainted at his feet. Paco reached down and snatched the letter from her limp fingers.

'Do you know who they are? They're Scalia's friends. It was in her possession, Ruffo! She knows what it says. Make her read it!'

He strode over and thrust the document in front of her face. Carina was turned about so she was staring at her captor. Above the thunder in her ears, she heard him say her name. 'Miss Temple, if I am not mistaken?'

Shifting his gaze from her, he looked over her head to the others. 'Leave the woman to me. Keep the letter, Paco. I know someone who'll have use of it. Search the carriage and search well. Make sure no more of Prince Scalia's spies are hiding inside.'

The orders were given and darkness swirled in Carina's brain. The brigand who held her was the same man she had seen with Mavrone near the Villa Pallestro. Anna Maria had placed them in mortal danger and such terror seized her. Carina cried out as Ruffo pushed her back against the broken wheel. Her aunt lying unconscious on the ground; her neck was bent sideways and her eyes closed. A lizard scuttled by, its tail touching her hand and her fingers twitched. Thank God she was alive – but what had they done with Gino and the others?

Scalia's men lay dead on the road but Carina couldn't see Gino. Where was he – and how could she save any of them? She must try to bargain with the bandits. Apart from Ruffo, they were swarming over the landau, ripping up seats and tearing off brass fittings and she twisted round to look at him.

'We're on a pilgrimage. It would be sacrilege to do us injury.'

'Sacrilege, do you say? Isn't whipping innocent men sacrilege?'

What was he talking about? Carina stared at him blankly. The rim of the wheel bruised her spine and she winced as Paco emerged from the carriage, grinning toothlessly.

'Is she too much for you, Ruffo?'

'Get the weapons on the horses and hurry up! You can keep the money – but the woman is mine.'

'What do you want to take her for? Get on with it here. Save yourself the trouble.'

They spoke in dialect, but Carina understood enough. The bandits were desperate and there was no hope of bargaining with them. She must escape and ride for help. With a suddenness that caught Ruffo off guard, she threw her body sideways and ducked under his arm. Her long legs streaked out as she sprinted towards the uncoupled horses. When she reached the first, she grabbed hold of its mane and had one leg over the withers before Ruffo caught her and threw her to the ground. Paco held her down as a foul-smelling wedge of material was stuffed in her mouth and her wrists bound with rope.

Ruffo slung her over the horse so her head hung below its flanks. When he mounted, he pulled her up to ride astride in front of him and Carina looked around in panic. Anna Maria was on her knees, clinging to the broken axle and Ruffo shouted over to her.

'Tell Prince Scalia we have his whore! If he wants her back he'll have to pay! Otherwise, she's dead!'

Her skirts were hitched up and Carina kicked her heels at the horse's shoulders. Her boot caught in the reins and she yanked the bit, trying to bring the animal over backwards. The next instant a hard object slammed into the side of her head. There was a blinding flash before everything went black and the last thing she heard was Anna Maria's voice, fading, calling out her name.

CHAPTER THIRTEEN

The horse stumbled and Carina groaned as consciousness forced itself upon her. Her head ached and she was astride a horse, slumped against a man's chest. Her hands were tied but the gag had been removed and the air she breathed was cool. It was almost dark, but she made out a column of riders ahead and the serrated edge of a mountaintop. How long had she been unconscious? Too weary to search for answers, her eyelids dropped and closed.

Occasionally in the hours that followed, she heard Ruffo talking and, when they stopped, the sound of running water. A stream gushed down the hillside and the bandits dismounted and waded in alongside their horses, scooping water into their mouths. Ruffo remained in the saddle while one of the men filled a skin and handed it up to him. He took long gulps and finished with a grunt. Then Carina's head was pulled back and he prised her mouth open, pouring water down her throat.

Paco's hand slid up her leg, pinching her calf through the thin material of her pantalets.

'Keep your filthy hands off her. She's mine,' Ruffo growled.

He pulled up the horse's head and took the lead, following a path no wider than a sheep track. Carina felt lather from the horse's flanks, hot and sticky on the inside of her legs. Her head throbbed as she forced herself to think. They had been on the move for half a day and were far away from Santa Fiore. The bandits intended to use her as a hostage and would do her no harm, she told herself. She tried to be brave, but her teeth chattered. Where were they taking her?

Ruffo guided the horse carefully and when they reached a small clearing he reined in and dismounted. Reaching up, he grasped Carina around the waist and lifted her down. Her legs were cramped and he gripped her arm, steadying her.

'Stay close to me – if you try to run, I'll let Paco have you,' he muttered.

She hated this man with his thick body and bull-like strength, but she feared Paco more. As she followed Ruffo, loose shale made her stumble and he squatted down beside her. Not knowing what he meant to do, Carina drew her legs up away from him.

'No need for fancy shoes where you're going.'

Her boots were pulled off and Ruffo helped her to her feet. With his hand heavy on her shoulder, they passed through a thicket of thorns. When they came out the other side, she glimpsed the outline of tumbledown shacks. A fire had been lit and Ruffo cupped his hands to his mouth and gave a long, warbling whistle. There was no responding signal and he swore.

'*Merda!* He's a suspicious devil. Stay here.'

'I'll take care of her.' Paco's arm encircled her waist and Carina fixed her gaze on Ruffo. She saw a man standing by the fire and Ruffo raise his arms as he came into the light. Then he turned to point in their direction.

'So, lady-whore, it's time to get you ready.' Paco's fingers pulled her hair loose and moved to her collar.

'Behave yourself, Paco! You heard what he said,' one of the others whispered.

'Ruffo's a fool if he thinks he can keep her for himself.'

She would scream if he touched her again, but Paco let her go for Ruffo was coming back. With his fist in the small of her back, he pushed Carina ahead of him and when they reached the campfire, took her by the shoulders and turned her round.

'Here she is, my friend. A worthy prize, eh?'

Ice fingers of shock reached down inside her as Carina stared at Ben Mavrone. She must be delirious, she thought. He was being interrogated in Palermo. How could he be here? Then hope leapt in her heart. Mavrone was a friend of Baron Riso. He wasn't a murderer and would come to her rescue! There was a distant look in his eyes as they went to her face. Didn't he recognise her? How different she must look in dirty, torn clothes with her hair hanging loose – but surely he would save her? Then Carina thought of their last encounter and all certainty vanished.

'I told you how we captured the horses. She was in the carriage,' Ruffo said. 'She's the one we saw with Scalia! He'll pay good money for her!'

Mavrone turned to Ruffo without speaking to her and Carina watched as the other men come forward. They shook his hand, greeting him in turn, and she sensed his authority. He only had to tell them to free her and they would do so. What was he waiting for? A bottle was passed from one to the other but her attention was only on Mavrone as she strained to hear what he was saying.

'You've money and horses enough. Tomorrow, when you're rested, you'll make your way to Marsala.'

'What about the woman?' The question came from Paco.

'She's the property of myself and my friend,' Ruffo answered. 'That's right, isn't it, Capitano? It was on Miss Temple's orders you and I were picked out for punishment.'

That's *not true!* Carina shouted inside her head. This couldn't be happening. She felt her grip on reality slipping and at any moment might become hysterical.

'Read this, Capitano! Tell us if she's a Bourbon spy.'

Paco stepped forward with Scalia's letter and gave it to Mavrone. He looked at it, frowning as he scanned the page, then held it up and read aloud.

I, Prince Riccardo Scalia, Duke of Pallestro, authorise Contessa Denuzio and Miss Carina Temple to travel to the Convent of Santa Fiore. If anyone impedes their progress or causes them unnecessary delay, they will be reported to the Office of Justice and prosecuted accordingly.

'There you are! The whore was doing penance for her sins.'

'She's a spy!'

'What ransom will Scalia pay for her?'

A cacophony of voices rose around them and Mavrone crumpled the paper and dropped it in the fire. The bottle was handed to him and he tipped it to his mouth, draining it to the last drop before he sent it crashing against the rocks. The violence of his action brought silence and he walked over to Carina. For the first time, he spoke to her.

'So, will your lover pay good money for your return?'

'I was with my aunt. We were on a pilgrimage—'

'I don't care what you were doing. I want to know how much you're worth to Prince Scalia.'

A small animal ran across the earth, scurrying between them. There was a squeal as a boot struck it aside. The sound skimmed the surface of Carina's mind as Mavrone took hold of the front of her dress. He drew her towards him until she was pressed against the length of his body. His hand went to her neck and he felt the rapid beat of the pulse beneath his fingers.

'Are you frightened, Miss Temple? Do you think you'll get your just desserts?'

Mavrone hoped to make her beg for mercy, but she would rather die than give him satisfaction. Carina raised her head, her voice cold and clear.

'I despise you, Captain Mavrone. But I wasn't the one responsible for your punishment. It was the guards I condemned to Scalia. If you were punished, then you brought it on yourselves by your actions.'

Mavrone towered over her and Carina raised her eyes to his shadowed face. When he spoke, his command was so quiet she barely heard it.

'Hold her still, will you?'

Ruffo held her by the arms and Mavrone moved behind her. The ropes binding her wrists became tight and Carina stifled a cry before she realised he was cutting her loose. Someone threw wood on the fire so the flames were high and Ruffo held her so she couldn't move. Mavrone lifted his knife to the side of her face. As the blade touched her cheek, her eyes glazed. She felt it trace a path down her neck to her throat. Then the knife was withdrawn and she heard his voice.

'The hostage is an Englishwoman, comrades. If we want the support of her country we must be circumspect.'

'I told Ruffo it was unlucky to bring her with us,' Paco's whiny voice joined in. 'What shall we do with her? She's seen too much.'

'If we don't return her, we'll get no help from England. If we free her, she'll go to Scalia and endanger all we've worked for.'

'So what do you propose? Make her disappear into thin air?' Ruffo was belligerent.

'I'll have to try and get her to Monteleone.' Mavrone's tone brooked no opposition. 'Scalia's men don't dare travel beyond Castelvano. It won't be easy but there's no other way.'

As the discussion moved from one to the other, Carina thought she discerned grudging acceptance. Where did he say he was taking her? Supposing, she thought wildly, he meant to deceive the bandits and set her free?

'I won't help you again, Ruffo. Next time you get up to your old tricks, leave the damned women behind.'

'May we enjoy her for tonight?' Paco asked.

'Let the capitano have her,' Ruffo answered gruffly. 'There's plenty of women for us in Marsala. If we made a mistake with this one, we made plenty of money too – and I'll drink to that.'

The men began to move away to sit by the fire and Carina's façade of courage splintered. Her legs gave way and, as she sank to the ground, Mavrone scooped her up in his arms. He carried her with his arm under her knees and her cheek pressed against the rough leather of his jerkin. Coming to the first hut, he bent his head under the lintel and kicked the door shut behind him before he put her down.

It was pitch black inside and reeked of sheep. Carina heard the bolt being drawn and Mavrone moving around. He struck a match and a small flame flickered into life. As he placed the candle on a table, she edged into the corner, backing away until her spine was pressed against the damp wall. Her hands were slippery with sweat and her voice hoarse.

'Tell me how much you want. I'll get it for you.'

'I don't want your money.'

Mavrone took paper and tobacco, rolling them together. He bent his dark head above the candle and she noticed he had shaved off his beard. It helped to stay sane by concentrating on small details and she must keep him talking.

'Are you going to set me free?'

'Not at this precise moment.'

'Then when?'

'When the time's right. You're lucky those scoundrels handed you over.'

'Are you saying you didn't plan this? It wasn't your idea?'

'I knew nothing about it.'

'But they're your men. I heard you give them orders.'

'They're outlaws, Miss Temple. I have no authority over them.'

'So why was he, you know … the man with you the day—'

'It so happened that Ruffo and I were detained at the same time. If I'd known what he planned today, I'd have stopped him and saved myself a lot of trouble.'

'You could have left well alone.'

'Don't play the innocent, Miss Temple. You know the men would rape you. The *banditti* are rather less fastidious than myself.'

Of all the abuse she had received, this last was the worst. How could he say that word in front of her? No gentleman spoke of such things. But Mavrone wasn't a gentleman! He was as cruel and coarse as the others. The insult was more than Carina could bear, unhinging the last part of her mind under control.

'You're not fastidious, Captain Mavrone. You're afraid you'll compare poorly with Riccardo Scalia!'

Mavrone dropped his unfinished cigarette and crushed the stub under his boot. When he reached Carina, he pushed her so hard against the wall she was lifted off her feet. One elbow rested above her head, his mouth above her lips and his breath rasping down her throat. The blazing light in his eyes terrified her. With an agonised cry, Carina twisted her head away and he let go of her so suddenly she almost fell.

'By God, ma'am, you deserve a bringing down.'

His voice cracked across the room and someone shouted from outside.

'Hey, Capitano! Hurry up! We're waiting for you!'

'*Pazienza!* I'm coming.'

The door slammed shut and Carina slid slowly to the floor. What had she done? Dear God, who would help her now? The candle spluttered and went out but the cold kept her alert. She heard the scraping of footsteps outside and was on her feet before Mavrone came back through the door. He relit the candle, its glow spreading to his face as he turned towards her.

'Don't look so frightened. I'm not going to hurt you.'

Carina did not hear his words. There was a rushing sound in her ears and the space between them lost focus. Her arms went out, flaying empty air, and Mavrone caught her as she fell. He laid her down on a pile of sheepskins and she felt his hand at the back of her head.

'Drink this …'

A flagon was pushed against her lips and into her mouth. Raw spirit scorched her throat and Carina gagged. She tried to spit it out but he held the bottle in her mouth until she swallowed. As her head fell back, liquid trickled from the side of her mouth and she thought she would be sick.

The brandy seeped into her bloodstream, dulling her senses. Her limbs felt too heavy to move, her mind too tired to think. She was dimly aware of Mavrone locking the bolt and snuffing out the candle before he lay down beside her. His arm dropped on her stomach and Carina rolled over on her side. She stared sightlessly into the dark but Mavrone did not stir. His breathing became light and, finally defeated by trauma and exhaustion, she fell asleep with his arm a dead weight across her waist.

Carina heard the creak of a door and could not think where she was. Her brain was befuddled by a sense of foreboding. She was lying on hard ground and every muscle in her body ached. Then she remembered the events of the day before. She prayed she was dreaming, but she was awake and the horror was real.

What devil made her taunt Mavrone with Scalia's name? She had alienated the one person who might have helped her. The ordeal must have shattered her wits, Carina thought with rising panic. There was no one she could turn to now. Her only hope was to escape. But how? She recalled the bushes near the entrance and the place where they had left the horses. Now that she was rested, she could run faster. If she could get to the horses, she might have a chance.

Carina opened her eyes. The only window was a small opening in the wall where stones had been removed and she saw Mavrone standing by the door. He had his back to her and his hunting knife lay on the table. He thought she was asleep and had left it unguarded. *Now*, she thought. *Now!* In one movement Carina came to her feet and grabbed the knife off the table, brandishing it in the air as Mavrone wheeled round.

'Unlock the door!' She ordered in a hoarse voice.

'I'm surprised you're so keen to join Ruffo and his friends.'

'Unlock the door. Then get out of my way.'

Carina jabbed the blade at Mavrone and he stood aside, but without slipping the bolt. He hoped to unnerve her, but she was the one with the weapon! She waved it at him again and he moved further away. Carina stepped cautiously towards the door. The iron bolt was stiff so she had to lift one hand off the hilt to open it. Glancing over her shoulder, she saw Mavrone watching her with an expression of absorbed interest. He thought she wouldn't make it but she was too desperate to contemplate failure. She opened the door a crack and looked out.

A couple of bandits were sitting around the fire while others were still asleep and she estimated the distance she had to run. If she kept behind the buildings she could get more than half-way before she had to break cover. Barefoot she wouldn't make a sound and Carina shoved the door wide open. Ruffo was kneeling by the fire poking it with a stick and she took a deep breath.

'*Figlio de puttante*, bring some coffee over here!'

Carina heard Mavrone's shout and spun about. He moved like lightning across the room and she went for him with the knife. The blade slashed through his shirt. Holding the hilt with both hands, she lunged at him again. Mavrone took a step sideways and his fist slammed down hard, knocking the knife out of her hands. It fell to the floor, sliding under the table beyond her reach. In a frenzy of rage, Carina threw herself at him, punching his chest until he hooked a foot behind her knees and kicked her legs from under her.

'Am I interrupting anything?' Ruffo walked through the door. Together they bound Carina and pushed her up against the wall.

'So she cut you, my friend.' He pointed to the thin red line of blood on Mavrone's shirt. His lips drew back in a smile that showed his yellow teeth. 'The knife – now that was careless.'

He had brought coffee and bread, which he placed on the table and Mavrone dipped a cloth in water.

'I've always been susceptible to feminine charms and this one's no exception,' he remarked as he cleaned his wound. 'It's only a scratch but she'd kill us all if she could.'

Carina sobbed in desperation and fury. If only she *had* killed him! Mavrone was treating her like an animal and she wanted him dead. For pity's sake, what was happening to her? Why hadn't she tried to negotiate with him? There was a chance she could have persuaded him to let her go. In less than twenty-four hours she had become as barbaric as her tormentors. Pain spliced her neck from the temple and she wondered if the blow to her head had affected her brain.

The smell of coffee made her stomach cramp with hunger. How long was it since she had last eaten? Not since yesterday morning but when Ruffo waved a mug at her, Carina shook her head. Mavrone dipped a hunk of bread in his coffee and brought it over and she clamped her mouth shut.

'You will eat, even if I have to force food down you. Don't fight me, Miss Temple. It won't do you any good.'

There was a hard look in his eyes as he pushed the crust into her mouth and Carina dared not spit it out. The bread had been softened by coffee and she swallowed it whole. Mavrone filled a mug with water and held it to her lips and she took a small amount.

'Make sure Prince Scalia pays a good price for her.' Ruffo leant down beside Carina, breathing sour liquor into her face. 'Behave yourself if you want to stay alive.'

'She'll soon learn. Now help make sure she doesn't escape.'

Everything Mavrone had said last night was a lie! Ruffo and the other bandits were under Mavrone's command. Why bother to deny it? As they dragged her over and looped a rope around her and the table leg, Carina shouted at them, heedless of the emotion in her voice.

'You won't get away with this! Never! Not even when you're dead and damned in Hell!'

'Maybe so.' Mavrone hunkered down and tied her ankles together. 'But until then it would be easier on us both if you were more amenable. Are you going to be quiet?'

Carina wanted to spit in his face but she saw the dirty cloth in Ruffo's hand. The idea of the filthy rag in her mouth made tears sting her eyes and she looked away so that Mavrone wouldn't see. There was no need for a gag. She could shout and scream all she liked, but no one would hear and he seemed to understand.

'Leave her be; only wolves pass this way.'

Mavrone retrieved his knife from under the table and wiped it clean before he tucked it into his belt. Ruffo was already outside, calling to his companions to hurry up, as Mavrone slung a knapsack over his shoulder and walked to the door. He stopped to look back and Carina dropped her head.

'I'll be away for a few hours and will return this evening. Be kind enough to wait for me until then.'

CHAPTER FOURTEEN

A fly settled on her nose and Carina tossed her head to get rid of it. Despair smashed into her like a battering ram. Where had Mavrone gone? How long before he would return? What if he never came back? To keep terror at bay, she concentrated on her discomfort; the cramp in her legs and the rope chafing her wrists. As the hours passed she recited lines from Byron and focussed her mind on thoughts of rescue.

Anna Maria must have been found and word sent to Palermo. The Scalia household would be alerted. No matter that she disliked him, the prince would do everything in his power to find her. He had troops at his disposal. His men would be searching the region of Santa Fiore by now. They could have picked up her trail already. It might take time, but they would come.

How could anyone find her in this godforsaken place? Reality forced its way in and tears filled Carina's eyes. They streamed down her cheeks and she wept until her heart was empty. Afterwards, she must have slept for when she awoke the light had dimmed. There was a snap of twigs underfoot and the door opened, letting a welcome draught into the stuffy atmosphere.

From her position on the floor, Mavrone looked taller and more imposing than ever. Walking over to the table he lifted the flap of the knapsack and took out her boots.

'I imagine these are yours?'

Mavrone tossed them onto the floor and went on unpacking. A bottle of wine with bread and strong-smelling cheese was laid out above her head. He took the pitcher outside and fetched fresh water. Then, without a word of explanation, he bent down and cut her loose. Not knowing what else to do, Carina stayed where she was, rubbing her chafed wrists.

'I don't need my boots. I'm not going anywhere.'

'Don't pin your hopes on Prince Scalia, Miss Temple. Ruffo backtracked to lay the search party off the scent. They won't find you here. No one will.'

'So what are you going to do with me?'

Mavrone took the bottle of wine and dug out the cork with the point of his knife before he cut a slice of bread.

'I'm not abandoning you, nor am I letting you go. Are you hungry?'

A hunk of bread was held in front of her. Carina turned away and he ate it himself. He did not offer her wine, but filled a mug with water and gave it to her.

'You should eat. We've a long journey ahead of us.'

When she shook her head, he replaced the cork in the bottle and returned the remainder of the food to the knapsack. Then he walked over to the sheepskins and lay down with his arms folded behind his head.

'I'm going to have a rest. Go outside and get some air.'

'Is it a habit of yours to abduct innocent women, Captain Mavrone?' Carina snapped at him. 'Do you do it for pleasure or for money?'

'On this occasion, neither. Now, if you don't mind, I'd like some peace and quiet.'

Carina walked out of the door and made her way to the fire. She looked up at the sky, scattered with white stars, and it seemed unbelievable that, only two nights before, she had stood on her balcony and gazed at the same sky. Her entire world had been swept away and everything familiar taken from her. There was no use trying to escape now. It was dark and she didn't even know if they had a horse between them. Hunger pains gnawed at her stomach and she should have eaten. The rational part of her brain told her it was stupid to refuse but resistance to Mavrone was the only way to hold on to her identity. If she gave in to him she was lost.

Carina knelt down by the fire, blowing the hot embers into life and thought of her grandmother. Poor Nonna would be distraught. She dare not think about her. What did Mavrone really want? Why was he being more lenient? Was he going to help her after all? She couldn't read his mind any more than she could anticipate his next move and her brain was tired from trying. When he emerged from the hut it was almost a relief.

Mavrone had her boots in his hand and he dropped them on the ground beside her before he went to the other side of the fire.

'There are a few things I want to set straight.' He spoke slowly as if she were hard of hearing. 'Firstly, we are both in a situation neither of us anticipated—'

'That's not true.'

'Secondly, I am in your debt.'

Carina's head came up, her eyes wide and uncertain. The glow of flames cast light on Mavrone's face and his expression was serious.

'After you alerted Enrico Fola of my capture, Baron Riso sent his men to free me. I'm sure it wasn't your intention to facilitate my release, but that's the fact of it.'

So Enrico had gone to the baron when he left her and Baron Riso had saved Mavrone. They were all in this together. The patriots shared the same ideals but Enrico would never associate with criminals like Ruffo. He would be horrified if he knew what had happened to her. Carina tucked her feet under her skirt and did not answer.

'In Sicily, every debt must be repaid in kind,' Mavrone went on. 'I owe you my life, or at least my present good health. I will negotiate your return to Palermo once we reach my home, Monteleone.'

'And where's that, may I ask?'

'On the west coast, not far from Marsala.'

'Why not nearer to here? Baron Riso can make arrangements for my return.'

'Sicilians are suspicious of strangers. There's not a village this side of Palermo that would offer you safe refuge. Now, will you put on your boots?'

He expected her to obey and Carina kicked the boots aside. It was a futile gesture, but she wasn't satisfied with his explanation. Why did he have to take her to his home? He could escort her back to the sanctuary of Santa Fiore, for heaven's sake! There was something Mavrone wasn't telling her.

He put her boots in the knapsack and stamped out the fire, then took hold of her hands, running his thumbs over raw patches of skin.

'I'd rather not tie you up again. Are you going to walk?'

'What happened to the horses?'

'I gave them to Ruffo in exchange for you. Not a good bargain on my part.'

She could take it or leave it, Carina thought. There was no way she could survive up here and Mavrone gave her no choice. She tracked his footsteps and they left the camp in silence. Passing through the thorn bushes, branches sprang back, scratching her arms and Mavrone was waiting on the other side. He set off at a brisk pace, his tall figure silhouetted against the skyline as they climbed and Carina struggled to keep up. She was weak from lack of food and perspiration poured off her neck, running down her arms and back. Then, as they neared the summit, she turned her ankle and fell, tumbling backward until she crashed against a rock.

'Breathe slowly. Slowly—'

Darkness hovered and Carina was aware of Mavrone lifting her up. He wiped the dirt off her face and brushed her hair out of her eyes. When the faintness passed, he probed the ligaments of her shoulders. Then he took hold of her knee and manoeuvred it upwards.

'Try to move your feet and wriggle your toes. If there's a fracture I'll have to splint your leg.'

Putting her weight on her hands, Carina straightened her legs and moved her toes.

'That's better. You've only sprained your ankle. A few hours' rest and you'll be fine.'

Mavrone wouldn't care if she broke every bone in her body! He was without pity and Carina turned on him like an angry cat.

'Why don't you just kill me while you're about it?'

'I don't want you dead. There's shelter in the trees up ahead. Come on, I'll help you.'

He bent down, reaching for her hand, and Carina gritted her teeth. She hung onto his arm, hopping on one foot until they reached a copse of trees bent sideways by the wind. There,

Mavrone let her rest but it seemed she had only just fallen asleep when his hand nudged her shoulder. A lark was singing and a thin coil of smoke drifted up through the trees. Carina stood up and an arrow of pain shot up her calf. Mavrone was busy with the fire so she crawled over to him on her hands and knees.

He poured black coffee into a mug and passed her bread with a chunk of salted meat. Carina took the food without a word. The meat made her jaws ache but the hot, sweet coffee revived her. She noticed his shirt was spread out on the grass; Mavrone had been swimming. His hair was wet and his hands cold as he examined her swollen ankle. She tried not to look at his bare chest but the pressure of his fingers made her groan.

'I can't walk! You'll have to find alternative transport.'

Mavrone reclined back on his elbows and his air of wellbeing infuriated her. 'So what will you do, Captain Mavrone? Are you going to carry me all the way to the west coast?'

'Once I've bandaged the ankle, your boots will give you enough support. There's a stream over there if you want to wash.'

Kindness had no truck here and Carina hobbled painfully to the stream. She longed to be home and a lump rose in her throat. I mustn't give up, she thought desperately. I must keep fighting. 'Pain your weapon and courage your strength.' It seemed a lifetime ago she had said those words to Enrico.

'Pain my weapon and courage my strength,' she murmured as she dipped her head and arms in the water, scrubbing off dirt that caked her skin and hair. She used her skirt to dry off and when she finished, Mavrone was packing up. He emptied the billycan on to the fire and folded the blanket, everything he did executed in the same methodical way. By the time she limped back, all traces of the camp had gone. Mavrone told her to sit down and Carina braced herself as he knelt in front of her.

As he bandaged her ankle, she found herself looking over his shoulder and saw a pattern of weals across his back. They were deep cuts and some not yet healed. The sight of them sickened her. The brutality of Scalia's punishment was not her fault, she told herself, but still she felt guilty.

'Not a bad effort on the part of Colonel Falcone,' Mavrone remarked as he laced her into her boots. Then he stood up and put on his shirt. 'I'm surprised you didn't stay to watch.'

'Abduction is a capital crime, Captain Mavrone.' Carina's eyes slanted up at him. 'It's not a whipping I'll come to next time – but a public execution.'

'Would it make you happy to see me shot?'

A smile lifted the corners of his mouth and Carina remembered the first time she had seen him. How bold and handsome she thought he was at Baron Riso's reception. She'd imagined he was some kind of hero and how wrong she had been.

'You were a good deal more friendly when first we met. It's a shame our amicable relationship was so short-lived.'

The sudden flash of attraction between them brought Carina to her feet. The magnetism that drew her to Mavrone upset and confused her. Never again, she had sworn. Never. Not ever again. The alert look in his eyes made her nervous and she knotted her fingers as he dropped on his haunches.

'I'm going to shorten your dress so you'll not trip again. Hold still, will you?'

Mavrone cut a wide strip off the bottom her skirt. His hand brushed her legs and when Carina flinched, he laughed softly.

'There's no cause for embarrassment, Miss Temple. The shorter length is perfectly acceptable under the circumstances.'

Before she could think of a stinging retort, there was a rustling sound and a large hare hopped into the clearing. It froze, long ears switching forward, then turned and disappeared into the undergrowth. To her surprise, Carina saw Mavrone had drawn a gun and watched as he unloaded it, dropping the bullets into his pocket and then put it in the knapsack. Her father had taught her to use just such a pistol and she was a good shot. If only she could get hold of the gun. The bullets would be more difficult to retrieve, but there was bound to be extra ammunition in the knapsack. Somehow, she would steal the pistol! Mavrone wouldn't laugh at her then, she thought, but he was already walking away.

The trek was long and hard across a barren, windswept landscape and followed no trail that Carina could discern. When they made camp at nightfall Mavrone did not light a fire. He threw the blanket on the ground and lay down. Exhausted, and with no other option, she lay next to him with her back turned. She shivered with cold so he drew her into his arms and she lay rigid until he was asleep.

The next morning they rose at dawn and walked until the sun was high. When they were thirsty they drank from streams that tasted of snow and all her energy was spent in keeping up. Her only thoughts were not to fall behind, the ache in her ankle and blisters on her feet. Hunger and fatigue alternated with the heat of day and cold of night and Carina could not get to the gun. Mavrone kept the knapsack strapped to his back as he walked and beneath his head at night and gradually the idea of trying to escape retreated to the back of her mind.

Weariness curbed her spirit and Mavrone became less abrasive. He allowed her to rest when she was tired and gave her more than her fair share of the food. Days and nights passed without sense of time but there was never a moment Carina was not aware of him, her eyes on his back as he strode ahead and his arms around her at night. He stayed close to her and when one morning she awoke to find herself alone the thought he had abandoned her filled her with panic.

They had spent the night in the hollowed-out trunk of a vast tree and she stumbled into the sunlight and saw him coming up the hill with a basket on his arm.

'I went to find us some breakfast. There's a farmhouse below and the owner gave me food. Let's have ourselves a feast.'

Mavrone tipped the food onto the grass and the smell of fresh bread and cheese made her mouth water. Sitting cross-legged on the ground, Carina ate until her stomach was full. She finished with an orange, sucking the juice from inside.

'You can see Castelvano from here.'

Almond trees blossomed in puffs of white smoke across the valley and he pointed to a walled town on top of a hill. A road snaked up the mountainside and Carina made out figures setting off for the fields. It was the first sign of human habitation she had seen since leaving Palermo and her gaze sharpened as a cavalcade of horsemen came into sight.

'*Perfidio!*' Mavrone swore under his breath. 'The Compagni d'Armi are garrisoned in town. Don't raise your hopes, sweetheart. They're not here for you.'

Had he seen the flare of excitement in her eyes? At once, Carina's exhaustion left her. Whatever Mavrone said, the cavalcade was a patrol searching for her, she was sure. Drawing a breath she remarked in a breezy tone of voice.

'You may leave me in the custody of the Compagni in Castelvano. My family will arrange an escort to take me back to Palermo.'

'How do I know you won't betray me?'

'I'll give you my word of honour.'

'Honour? There's no such thing in Sicily these days.'

His tone made her smart, but the stakes were high. Carina held her temper and tried to sound persuasive.

'You'll be rewarded generously for my safe deliverance. I have friends who will see to it.'

'Such as?'

Mavrone's expression was inscrutable. She couldn't tell if he was considering the proposal or had already cast it aside. Carina searched for an answer. When it came to her, she didn't know how she hadn't thought of it before.

'Enrico Fola will act for us. We both know we can trust him.'

She spoke with just the right amount of insouciance and Mavrone studied her in silence. Why was he looking at her with that gleam in his eyes? It was a perfectly reasonable proposition. Carina tried to assume an attitude of indifference, but she couldn't keep it up and her fingers plucked nervously at her skirt.

'As I told you before, I don't want your money.'

Damn him! Damn him to hell and back! He had led her on for the pleasure of setting her down and her eyes were bright with anger. His next words inflamed her further.

'You're very desirable when you're in a temper. I'm sorry to disappoint you, but your proposal is absurd.'

'So you won't consider it?'

'I'm afraid not. I enjoy your company too much. No amount of gold would compensate for being deprived of it.'

His gaze sought her lips and Carina made up her mind. If one tactic failed then she would try another. Scalia's men were garrisoned in town and would return this evening. If she could delay near the road, they would rescue her. Mavrone said there was no such thing as honour and she could be as dishonest and devious as he was. Sensing his desire, her mouth curved provocatively. 'I'm flattered by the compliment. I thought you would be glad to be rid of me.'

Carina held his gaze and Mavrone moved to lie on the grass beside her. Now what was she supposed to do? He was waiting for her to make the first move and she was at a loss. He was older and more experienced. Would he be able to tell she was a novice? She hesitated before putting her hand on his arm and he took her by the shoulders, turning her to face him.

Looking into his blue eyes, Carina saw none of the coldness she was used to. His regard was appreciative and warm. Worn and dirty as she was, Mavrone wanted to kiss her and she wouldn't stop him. It was the only way to get him to lower his guard and, before his steady gaze, her eyes fell.

He leant over and took her in his arms, one hand resting casually on her bodice. He cupped her chin with the other and kissed her slowly with warm, dry lips. She felt heat pulse in her veins as a surge of longing swept through her. All thought of subterfuge vanished. It no longer mattered who he was or what he had done. Carina's arms went round his neck and she began kissing him back, her tongue darting inside his mouth, until he rolled her over to lie on top of him. Mavrone's hand pressed her down and she felt the hard muscles of his thighs beneath her. Her arms were flung on either side of his head and her whole body trembling.

Then the cool breeze touched her face and sanity returned.

'Not like this, please. I want to be clean.' Her voice sounded small and unnatural. 'Can we wait until we reach Castelvano? How long will it take us?'

'A couple of hours at the most. We'll walk up this evening. I agree, you could do with a good wash.'

'Speak for yourself! You smell as bad as me!'

'No doubt much worse.' He grinned and his hands slid up her arms. 'What will my friends in Castelvano make of you, Carina? They're not used to finding a beautiful woman as my accomplice.'

It was the first time he had called her by her given name and Carina shifted her body to lie close to him. She raised herself up on her elbows and studied his face. There was mischief in his eyes and it gave her a glimpse of the boy he had once been. Remorse stirred her conscience. She had deliberately led him on and her surrender meant more to him than she realised. Everything was mixed up in her head. Mavrone spoke of her as his accomplice and suddenly she wished she were. If only it was always like this! The absurd idea of telling him her plan popped into her head. Instead, she heard herself say,

'Promise never to speak of this to anyone? My family could not bear the dishonour.'

'I promise to return you to Palermo with your reputation intact. When we get to Monteleone I'll send word to your family that you're safe. It may take some time. Are you happy to stay with me until then?'

Carina nodded and it meant nothing she deceived him, she told herself in the hours that followed. Mavrone slept and she positioned herself against the tree with his head on her lap. What was wrong with her? She had nearly gone too far and pulled back just in the nick of time. It was unnatural for a woman to experience such feelings. Carina had read about courtesans in books. Their motive was money while her reaction had been spontaneous, driven by a madness that she didn't understand.

Looking down at Mavrone her troubled gaze took in his tousled dark hair and long lashes. She wanted to remember him like this. He would never force himself on her. The danger came from within and her body's treacherous response went against all she had been brought up to believe was right. Love outside marriage was a sin and if she gave herself to him she would be ruined.

'The Compagni will not travel beyond Castelvano.' Carina remembered his words on the night of her abduction. She had been granted a God-given opportunity. Her ankle had recovered and when the patrol came by she would make a run for it. How did she know Mavrone would ever set her free? She must get away before it was too late.

CHAPTER FIFTEEN

She must have dozed, for Carina opened her eyes to find Mavrone ready to go. He had packed up and now helped her to her feet.

'We'll stay in Castelvano long enough to give you a chance to rest. It's time I took better care of you.'

He looked into her tense face and Carina felt her cheeks redden. He doesn't mean it, she told herself. He's only being nice because I let him kiss me.

'I won't thank you for being so hard on me before,' she said, trying to sound indignant.

'So you're never going to forgive me?'

'It depends on your future behaviour. How far is Castelvano to your home?'

'Four days' walk to Monteleone.'

'Monteleone ...' Carina repeated the name, rolling the vowels on her tongue.

'I've a hunch you'll be happy there – so much so, you may never want to leave.'

Why did she have to notice then how the grooves on either side of his mouth deepened as he smiled? For a brief moment

Carina longed for him to take her in his arms and kiss her again. Am I mad? she thought feverishly. I cannot change my mind. I know what will happen.

He was teasing her but Carina was so tense, she felt her nails cutting into the skin of her clenched hands and Mavrone bent down to pick up the knapsack.

'Don't worry, sweetheart. However much I may want to, I'm not going to kidnap you.'

Clouds gathered over the mountain peaks as they made their way down the hill and, afraid they were too early for the patrol, Carina affected a limp. Mavrone slowed his pace but did not stop until they were down in the valley. Donkey carts and mule wagons were making their way home and a girl in a red shawl, who was singing, sat perched on the one at the rear. Carina's nervous gaze searched down the hill. There was no sight of the Compagni. Why were they so late? In half an hour it would be nightfall.

Mavrone took her hand and spoke quietly. 'We'll keep off the road but cannot delay. If we enter after curfew we'll be taken in for questioning.'

'I must rest a while, please. My ankle's so painful.'

'Then wait for me here. I'll try to find a wagon.'

Had he put his hand to her neck, he would have felt the fast beating of her pulse, but Mavrone did not touch her and Carina watched as he moved stealthily from tree to tree. It was dusk already. The Compagni must come soon! She sat down, twisting her hair with her fingers until at last she heard the sound she was waiting for. The distant rhythm of hoof beats was faint at first, growing louder as they approached, and the cavalcade was travelling at speed.

Carina leapt up, ducking under low branches as she ran through the olive grove. She was clear of the trees and on open ground when a blur of horsemen came around the corner with their cloaks flying out behind them. A cloud of dust rose from under the horses' hooves and she shouted and waved her arms. The officer at the front lifted his arm to bring the troop to a halt. Carina was close enough to see his face before a shadow hurtled from behind and tackled her to the ground.

Mavrone fell with his full weight on top of her and his hand over her mouth. Her ear pressed to the ground and she heard muffled orders and bridles jingling as horses were reined in. A grassy bank rose above their heads and she began to struggle. She hunched her back, beating her feet on the ground and he threw his leg across her thighs. He was squeezing her jaw and she sank her teeth into the palm of his hand, hanging on as fiercely as a terrier at the neck of a rat. Her cries were muffled and she bent and twisted beneath him until she thought her heart would burst. Then she heard the command: '*Avanti!*'

In her mind's eye, Carina saw the officer wave his troop forward. They were so close. One of the men must look over the bank and see them! Then someone shouted to leave the lovers undisturbed and the drumming of hooves faded into the distance. Mavrone took his hand from her mouth and rolled off her. His fingers dug into her shoulders, he pulled her up and guided her back to where he had left her before. He thrust her down on her knees and she felt the bite of rope as he tied her hands. Then he put his hand under her chin and forced her head up. His face was black with fury and Carina thought he might break her neck.

'You didn't believe me! You knew all the time!' she cried out. 'You left me alone as a test!'

'The most dangerous part of our journey is ahead. I needed to be sure of you. My friends are bringing a cart. I trust your ankle's better?'

How could she have thought she had deceived him? The rope chafed her wrists, but Carina was too miserable to feel pain. She had taken a gamble and lost. Her mind was empty of anything except bitter disappointment. A shrinking feeling inside numbed her as she knelt on the ground until Mavrone was alerted by a birdlike call. He left her and when he came back two strangers were with him. Speaking to them in dialect, he threw a cloak around her shoulders and the small group made their way to the road.

A donkey cart was waiting and Mavrone pushed her up the bank and dumped her in the back like a piece of baggage. Carina lay with the side of her face on rough wooden boards as he climbed in beside her. Sacking was thrown over them and his breath touched her neck.

'If you make a sound I'll kill you. After your little performance, it would give me no pain to cut your throat.'

Bags of grain were added and the smell of corn filled her nostrils as the cart moved forward. They jolted and bumped along and when they halted they were at the gates. Voices rang with authority as they snapped questions to the driver and heavy footsteps marched to the back of the cart. A hard object prodded her side but Carina did not make a sound and the order to pass was given. When they stopped again, they were inside the town. The heavy bags were taken off and Mavrone lifted her out and stood her on her feet. There was a rumble of thunder and slow rain began to fall as the cart was led away.

With one arm beneath her ribs and the knife at her neck, Mavrone marched her through a maze of alleys and up a steep flight of stone steps. Reaching the top, he pulled her into the shadowed entrance of a church. Opposite was a bar with tallow burning in the windows. The door opened and a soldier in uniform of the Compagni stepped out into the rain. He stood with his legs apart, hand resting on the hilt of his sword. He seemed to be looking straight at them and Mavrone's blade touched her throat. Then the soldier belched and set off unsteadily down the street.

Mavrone let out a low whistle. 'You attract the Compagni like a bitch on heat! Let's move before other dogs catch your scent.'

They skirted the piazza and he lengthened his stride so Carina was forced into a run. Dogs were howling and she glimpsed a man with a snuff-coloured nose huddled against a wall but Mavrone ignored the beggars and strays of Castelvano. He made her go on until they came to a stairway leading off the street. An invisible hand opened the door and a boy's pale face emerged from the shadows.

Once inside, Mavrone took a candle bracket from the wall and gave it to the boy whose dark eyes gazed at Carina. He cut the rope loose and his hand closed around her arm in a grip hard as iron. The boy led the way along a subterranean passage with wet patches on the walls and places where the ceiling was so low that they had to bend double. And then, quite suddenly, they came out into a room filled with people.

Carina blinked in the bright light as an old woman came forward. She reached up to touch Mavrone on the forehead and a little girl tugged at his arm. Everyone was staring at her and she dropped her head so her hair fell over face. Mavrone leant down to speak to the child and then a man with an oil lamp ushered them down another passage to a stone cellar. He walked in and placed the light on the table. Carina saw an iron bed with a mattress and bed clothing rolled in a bundle and stood frozen in the doorway until Mavrone pushed her inside.

'These will be your lodgings. I've ordered you a bath.'

Two young men appeared with a wooden hip tub, which they dragged across the floor to the centre of the room. They returned with buckets of water, accompanied by a blue-eyed girl carrying a towel and clothes, which she put on the bed. The girl looked dubiously at Mavrone. He did not respond and she tossed her head so her black hair bounced on her shoulders and followed the boys out.

'Take off your clothes.'

As the door closed, the tension of the last few hours hit Carina all at once. Terror travelled down her veins so fast she thought she might faint. Her hands were shaking so she had to break the thread to get the buttons undone. She bent down to remove her boots and, wearing only her camisole and pantalets, walked towards the tub.

'I'm sure this isn't the first time you've undressed for a man. Take everything off.'

Carina tried to protest but her voice failed. If she disobeyed him, Mavrone would likely strip her naked himself. She turned her back, removing her underclothes and climbed into the bath, banging her hip on the side in her haste. He threw her a cake of black soap and she lathered herself all over, rubbing her legs and arms until the water was grey.

'That's enough. I want you clean – not scrubbed raw.'

Mavrone came to stand by the tub. His gaze raked over her and shame scorched her cheeks, spreading down her neck to her chest. He hauled her out and sat on the bed, pinioning her between his knees. Looping the towel behind her, he dried her before dropping it on the floor.

'You've only yourself to blame if I take up your invitation of this morning.'

'I wanted to get home.' Carina bit her lip to hold back tears. 'I wasn't going to betray you.'

'Well you made a damned good show if that's the case. It so happens I don't want you tonight. When I do, I take it you're willing to render me the service you offer your other lovers. Do you understand?'

Carina fixed her gaze on a spider crawling up the wall. There was a lump, like a small stone, stuck in her gullet and she did not answer.

'Do you understand?' he repeated.

Carina refused to submit, but a tiny sob escaped her lips. Her cheeks were wet and she buried her face in her hands as Mavrone collected up his belongings,

'Cover yourself before the lads come back,' he said tersely. 'They're honest fellows. I don't want them corrupted by your easy charms.'

They departed from Castelvano three days later and in that time Carina did not see Mavrone again. The black-haired girl brought her food, but she ate little. She was given clean clothes, a pair of loose trousers and a linen shirt, and allowed to rest undisturbed. When she was not asleep she listened to the rain pouring down outside. There were times she wanted to bang her head on the wall and bite her knuckles until they were raw. Mavrone punished me because I tried to trick him but I will never let him break me, she swore. I'll fight him to the end. One day I'll repay him for his treatment of me.

Late one evening two men came to the cellar. They had a quiet, professional manner and, with one on either side, Carina was taken from the cellar to the high-vaulted room she remembered from the night they arrived. An old man was smoking a clay pipe near the stove while children lay asleep on blankets on the floor. The women stood back and the girl with blue eyes stared her as she was led through their midst to the underground tunnel.

Mavrone was standing at the end and the light extinguished before they went out. When they reached the street, he walked so close behind her that his legs knocked into the back of her knees. With his hand on her shoulder, they made their way in silence to the guardhouse at the town gates. Beacons burnt inside and Carina saw soldiers sitting at a table with cocked hats tilted back on their heads.

'The duty officer will open the gate for us. When I tell you to walk, do just that.' Mavrone turned to the others. 'Stay back and cover us.'

The pale moonlight was as spectral as the fear that gripped Carina as the door of the guardhouse opened. One of the soldiers came out. He glanced furtively in their direction. Then he walked to the gate and unlocked a small door. Propelled by Mavrone, she stepped through and heard the bolt being drawn behind them. They were out of Castelvano, heading downhill, and she noticed that instead of the pistol he carried a rifle. When they halted, he lifted the muzzle to her cheek.

'I've better range with this and the aim is more accurate. Don't try to run away …'

I will shoot you if you do … The last sentence was unspoken, but Mavrone made her walk so hard and fast that night if an entire army had passed them by, Carina wouldn't have had the strength to run or the voice to call out. The pace he kept up was relentless. When they stopped she slept where she had fallen. The temperature dropped and it was bitterly cold but Mavrone no longer lay beside her. As she lay shivering on the ground, she knew he was not asleep and was watching her.

Making their way westward through forests freshened by spring rain, Mavrone avoided even the smallest hamlets. He rarely spoke and Carina kept her mind on the immediate future. When would she be able to rest? How long before the next bite of food or drink of water? They fed on stale bread and berries gathered from the bushes. One evening he shot a rabbit and roasted it on a wooden spit – she devoured the meat, tearing the flesh off with her teeth, and picking the bones clean. That night, for the first time since leaving Castelvano, she slept without the pain of hunger in her stomach.

They set off early next morning and now the streams they splashed across turned into fast-flowing rivers. Swollen by melted snow, they were increasingly perilous to cross. Carina came up behind Mavrone as he stood looking into a deep ravine where a waterfall crashed down with such force spray was thrown up into their faces. He deliberated for a moment before he unfastened his cartridge belt and laid the rifle on the grass.

'Give me your boots and I'll take them across.'

Carina sat down and took off her boots. She gave them to him and watched as he waded into the river. The water came up to his waist and he lifted the gun and rucksack above his head. A curtain of spray hid him and she craned forward until he emerged on the other side. He deposited his burden and then started back for her.

Too worn down to think of escape, she slithered down the bank and stepped into the river. Mavrone had his arm round her waist as they went forward together. Freezing water broke over their heads and the current whipped her heels. Carina lost her footing and clutched Mavrone's arm so that he staggered. Then her feet touched solid ground and he pulled her up the bank on the other side.

'Strip off and we'll dry out in the sun.'

They were in a glade of dappled sunlight and Carina was aware her wet clothes clung to her body. She took off her shirt and Mavrone waited until she removed her trousers. He went over to a tree stump and spread them out to dry in the sun. She kept on her vest and drawers while he undressed to his breeches, wringing the water from his shirt, before he stretched out beside her.

A bird was chirping, its range of notes bright and tuneful, and Carina sat with her knees hugged to her chest. Twisting her neck to ease the ligaments, she glanced at Mavrone. His eyes were closed and she studied him with vague curiosity, noting the firm muscles of his stomach and his long legs. It was strange that the sight of his body didn't shock her. All vestiges of civilised behaviour had been stripped away, she thought, and they were little better than savages.

There was a buzzing in her ears like the hum of a mosquito and a dull ache in her temples. Carina longed to sleep – but she could not rest with Mavrone half-naked beside her. To stay awake she picked up a pebble and sent it spinning into the water below.

'What makes you so restless? Do you want to make love?'

Carina took a shuddering breath. This was the moment she dreaded. I won't let him touch me, she thought. If he lays a hand on me, I'll throw myself in the river. She stood up and looked down at him, her face hard and taut.

'I despise you – or have you forgotten?'

'Sure you do – but it doesn't mean you don't want me.' The expression in his eyes belied the easy tone. 'Do you despise Prince Scalia as well?'

Mavrone had made her cry in Castelvano – but he would never find her so susceptible again. She knew how to hurt him and her voice filled with venom.

'Prince Scalia is a gentleman. No doubt that's why Bianca chose him for a husband and not—'

Mavrone was on his feet before she could finish with his fist raised above his head. Carina braced herself for the blow, but his arm stopped in mid-air.

'You'll keep Bianca Scalia's name out of your conversation or else—'

'Or else what? Will you beat me?' Her blood was up and Carina threw back her head. 'I dare say you enjoy assaulting defenceless women.'

Mavrone strode over to the tree stump and put on his shirt and boots. He turned around, letting his hand drop on her shirt and Carina experienced a rush of intoxicating energy. He was baiting her like a hunter with a trap and she began to walk towards him, her eyes on her shirt and the hand toying with the buttons. She was almost within reach when his voice checked her.

'So tell me about Prince Scalia. Does he make love to you like a gentleman?'

'He doesn't—'

Her answer ended in a rasping cough. A searing pain tore through her chest and Carina felt the strength drain out of her as fast as it had come. Her shoulders sagged and her arms were so heavy they felt glued to her sides. Thoughts formed and then broke off, drifting away. She tried to remember what she meant to say but the only thing lodged fast in her mind was the look on Mavrone's face when she spoke of Bianca Scalia.

With a bad-tempered gesture he threw the shirt at her feet and tossed her trousers over afterwards. He reached for his rifle, ready to go. Her clothes felt damp as Carina put her shirt over her head and pulled on her trousers. She followed at a distance and by the time they reached the coastal plain, Mavrone was well ahead. No longer wary of strangers, he greeted fellow travellers as they went by in their brightly coloured wagons. Children shouted as they hung out the back. When the same carts drove past her, Carina kept her head down.

Dirt was thrown up from under their wheels and she tasted grit in her mouth. The glare of light hurt her eyes and she stopped to wipe a hand across her face. In the far distance, she saw a ribbon of blue. It was the sea – they had reached the west coast but she was too sick to make anything of it.

She took a few steps and then halted again. Mavrone's figure was a shimmering mirage and Carina tried to call to him. Her voice came out as a wheezy rattle. She was shivering with cold and burning with fever at the same time. Every breath was agony, lacerating her lungs. Her vision was hazy as though someone had put a veil over her eyes and she imagined the sun spiralling through the sky towards her. The next moment she was incinerated in its heat and she pitched forward, falling headlong onto the dusty road.

CHAPTER SIXTEEN

'Signorina, you must wake up.'

The words were accompanied by a nudge and Carina felt herself being drawn out of deep slumber. She was lying on a feather mattress with her face pressed against sweet-smelling linen. The hand touched her again and she opened her eyes to see a woman with white hair looking down at her.

'Who are you?'

'I'm Selida. I've been nursing you. You have slept for two days.'

Selida brought over a tray and sat down by the side of the bed. She helped Carina to sit up and wrapped a napkin round her neck.

'The fever has broken, but you're still weak. Let me help you.'

Selida ladled a spoonful of broth into her mouth and a frown creased Carina's brow.

'I don't understand. Where am I?'

'You're at Monteleone,' Selida explained gently. 'Your carriage broke down. You were obliged to travel the last few miles on horseback. Benito is concerned for your welfare and asked me to take care of you. You must rest now and I will return later.'

When she left the room, Carina lay back on the pillows. Her carriage? Benito? Did she mean Mavrone? She had thought Selida was a housekeeper, but her quiet dignity suggested a more elevated position. Carina tried to recollect what happened after she collapsed. She had a dim memory of faces peering down at her and Mavrone lifting her onto a horse. After that nothing, until he carried her into this room – she recognised it now – and laid her down on the bed. Monteleone was Ben Mavrone's home and he had dragged her halfway across Sicily to bring her here.

Carina closed her eyes and slept until Selida returned. She followed her into a small room with a basin and a bathtub filled with water. Declining her offer of assistance, Carina poured water from the jug into the bowl and washed her face. Looking into the glass, there was no beauty in her hollow cheeks and her face was as pinched as a street urchin. She climbed into the bath and lay in the comfort of the warm water before washing her hair. When she returned to the bedroom, a young girl was with Selida.

'May I present Bella Campi? She's your maid. I will come to see you every day.'

Bella gave her an impudent look as she bobbed a curtsy. They left and Carina was relieved to be alone. The windows were open and she heard the sound of waves and a rake scraping on gravel. There were voices beneath her window and, looking down, she saw a courtyard smothered in blue wisteria. Mavrone was speaking to a small, well-dressed woman whose face was hidden by the wide brim of her hat.

Too tired to wonder who she might be, Carina spent the rest of the day in bed. She ate supper by the fire, wearing the wrapper given to her by Selida. Bella attended to her and Carina let her go as soon as she was finished. As the door shut, a draught made the candles flicker and she went over to close the window. Black night shut her in. Monteleone was a prison, she thought, as dark and forbidding as its owner. Her illness had left her weak and she hoped Mavrone would keep away as he had at Castelvano. She needed time to bolster her defences. And then, as if she had summoned him up, his voice came from behind her.

'I'm glad you're recovering. Take care not to catch another chill.'

Mavrone was standing by the door with a decanter of wine and two glasses in his hand. She walked slowly back and sat down, pressing her knuckles until the joints cracked. It will be different here, she told herself. There are people like Selida at Monteleone. Mavrone will have to behave himself.

He took the chair next to her – close enough for Carina to see nicks in his skin, where he had cut himself shaving, and smell his cologne. He poured wine into the goblets and gave one to her. The wine warmed her and she waited for him to go on.

'Are you feeling better?'

'Who was the woman with you outside today?'

'Greta Mazzini. She's an old friend and cousin to Italy's greatest political philosopher, Giuseppe Mazzini.'

Mazzini was an exile in London, Carina remembered, a radical intellectual whom Jane Parsons admired. Had Mavrone told Signora Mazzini she was here, she wondered? What reason might he have given for her presence?

'Greta has kindly agreed to write to your family – to inform them you're safe and no ransom is demanded. You will be returned to Palermo as soon as possible.'

'And when might that be?'

'When I can make the appropriate arrangements. Your disappearance caused quite a stir and Scalia's agents are still scouring the island. You've caused my fellow patriots a good deal of trouble.'

'That's hardly my fault!'

'And I wasn't the one responsible for your abduction.' Mavrone's glance swept her face. 'You're free to go as you please in the house and garden but no one leaves Monteleone without my consent. I advise a little patience. You never know, you may come to enjoy it here in time.'

His hand dropped over hers, stilling the restless movement of her fingers, and Carina snatched it free coming to her feet so fast she knocked over her glass.

'I've been with you long enough to be sure I will not!'

Mavrone picked up the goblet and used his handkerchief to mop up the spilled wine. Then he leant back in his chair and looked up at her.

'I've only one question for you. We were betrayed soon after the evening at the Palazzo Riso. Did you pass on any information you overheard to Prince Scalia?'

'I didn't betray Baron Riso.'

Carina shook her head. Mavrone must know she hadn't betrayed them. Why else would she have warned Enrico? She had used Scalia as a weapon against him – and what good had it done her? She was too sick at heart for another battle, too tired to go on fighting. The only thing she wanted was for him to go away.

'I'm not Prince Scalia's accomplice – nor am I his mistress. I loathe the man.'

'Do you really expect me to believe that?'

'I don't expect anything.'

'Are you saying your relationship with him was innocent? Riccardo Scalia doesn't know the meaning of the word.'

Carina fixed her gaze on the intricate carving of the mantel-piece. A nerve beneath her eye began to jump and she put a hand up to stop it. There was a bitter taste, like lemon pith, in her mouth and she swallowed.

'I've told you the truth.'

'And the scandal in London, do you deny that as well?'

'Is it beyond you to imagine I might have retained my virtue?'

Mavrone was on his feet and, meeting his incredulous gaze, Carina reached for the arm of her chair and sank down. There was no way of knowing what he made of her admission for he had turned his back on her. Reaching for the poker, he stirred the logs in the grate and stood for a long time looking into the fire.

Carina listened to the hiss of flames until he moved away from the hearth. Her eyes followed him as he took off his jacket and hung it over the back the chair. He went round the room extinguishing candles and then sat down to tug off his boots. The first one came off and dropped onto the floor.

'What are you doing?'

The question was superfluous, for it was quite obvious he was undressing. Mavrone, occupied with the other boot, looked up, for a moment uncomprehending. Then he pulled it off and stood up.

'It's late and I'm preparing to retire for the night.'

'You're not going to sleep here. This is my room.'

She broke off as Mavrone divested himself of his shirt. Firelight cast shadows on his chest and her heart began to race. She pressed her hands together, clenching and unclenching her fingers. Surely, tonight he could mean her no harm? A shiver ran down her spine as he moved his chair opposite her. He sat down and leant forward with his elbows on his knees.

'If what you say about you and Scalia is true, why didn't you tell me before?'

Carina kept her head low, taking care not to meet his eyes.

'I wanted to annoy you – and make sure you kept your distance.'

'And well I might have, had you not encouraged me otherwise.'

'So why didn't you let me escape?'

'Because if you betrayed us, the Compagni would have arrested every man of fighting age in Castelvano. We're preparing for war and cannot lose a single patriot. Nevertheless, I apologise for my behaviour and retract what I said about your virtue. You're under no obligation to me.'

So that was his answer. It was nothing personal. No matter he had hurt and degraded her. Words cost him nothing and Carina was silent.

'I treated you badly and I'm very sorry,' Ben added slowly, after a pause. 'I hate to be deceived and lost any sense of decency. Please look at me, Carina.'

He unpeeled her fists from the arms of the chair and took her hands in his own. Carina tried to pull back, but he held her fast. Unwillingly, she raised her gaze to his face. There was regret in his eyes and something else she had seen before. Ben said he was sorry, but that wouldn't stop him trying to seduce her. I swore never to let him come near me, she reminded herself. Let that be his punishment.

'If you want me to leave, I'll go immediately. The choice is yours.'

'Have you no principles, Captain Mavrone, no morality at all?'

'None whatsoever. I wanted you from the first moment I set eyes on you. I haven't forgotten our meeting in the Palazzo Riso.'

Ben lived outside the laws of society as he lived outside those of the state. With his good looks and silver tongue he expected her to yield, Carina thought. Beyond here lay the scorched wasteland of the fallen woman, ostracised by society and a disgrace to her family – but what did he care? Ben took any opportunity that came his way. It was the same as ever; his determination against hers, mind against body. Why did he have to torment her?

'Do you honestly think I'll let you ruin me?'

'If I ask you to marry me, would it make a difference?'

What was he talking about? He had no intention of marrying her! Carina would never know why she didn't challenge him then. She felt possessed by a devil, lurking in the shadows, waiting until this moment to claim her. Suddenly she was overcome by a sense of inevitability. Hadn't she known from the beginning her fate was bound up with his? Ben Mavrone had infiltrated her soul and she had neither the will nor strength to send him away.

Let it be … Let it be … Her head fell back and Ben knelt on the ground in front of her. He drew his finger from her chin down to the collar of her wrapper and planted a kiss at the base of her neck. Then he took the garment by the sleeves and pulled it down to reveal her bare shoulders. His hand made its way up her arm, returning to her elbow, brushing upwards again and across her collarbone to close over her heart.

'So what's it to be, sweetheart? Shall I go or stay?'

Tell him to leave now. Don't let him do this … The instructions hammered in her head but Carina ignored them. She longed for the comfort of his arms and warmth of his body. Fear and shame died away and Ben undid the sash of her gown and laid his head on her breast. She looked down at his hair, so dark against the whiteness of her skin, and pressed her lips to the top of his head.

'Stay.'

The conflict was over and Ben stood up and swung her into his arms. He carried her to the bed and lay down beside her. Moonlight fell across them and he ran his hand the length of her body. A rip of longing tore through Carina as Ben kissed the lobes of her ears before his lips came down on her mouth. She was on the brink of something from which there could be no return and did nothing to stop him until he nudged her legs apart. She stiffened and Ben lay still, gently stroking her hair and the side of her face.

'There's nothing to be afraid of, *carina*, my love.' He spoke her name as an endearment. 'It's time you learned the pleasure you've been missing.'

Carina remembered one brief moment of desperation that made her catch hold of his shoulders before her arms went round him. Her head was pressed down into the pillow and she smelled his clean, masculine scent. He was telling her he loved her, telling her she was beautiful. This was what she wanted; the feel of his body and his hands beneath her hips as they dissolved into one another, Ben taking her with him into the night, rising and falling in waves of sensation. She was aware of the pulse in her wrist and the surging of her heart. Sparks of electricity fired in her blood – there was no sense of time or space – only Ben in the warm, crushing darkness, the fusion between them and a wild, unknown thrill of surrender. Her last conscious thought was that she was disembodied and weightless, floating through water with her arms locked around his neck.

A long time afterwards her surroundings became solid and she lay with her cheek on Ben's chest. She listened to the quiet rhythm of his breathing and was unprepared for the tears that filled her eyes. They slipped from beneath her lashes and Ben's arms tightened about her. He held her to him and Carina cried until there were no tears left and she didn't know if they were for what she had lost or gained.

CHAPTER SEVENTEEN

When she woke up the next morning, Ben had gone. The memory of their passion was as sweet as the scent of jasmine wafting in through the window. For the first time, she had learned what it was to be loved. How strange that someone as aloof as Ben had revealed this to her! How surprising he had been so infinitely tender. Until last night, she hadn't known what it meant to be truly alive. Recalling her abandonment in his arms, Carina experienced a thrill of pleasure. Others might be outraged, but how could she be, when he had made her happy?

There was a knock at the door and Bella came in. She opened the shutters and, stifling a yawn, Carina watched as she laid fresh logs in the grate. Her wrapper lay discarded on the floor and Bella picked it up with a disapproving look. She went out, then returned with a breakfast tray, and a skirt of worsted material with a cotton blouse.

'Thank you, Bella,' Carina murmured as she sat up.

'Nothing to do with me, ma'am. The captain asked me to provide you with clothes.'

She buttered a roll and drank her coffee while Bella remained at the foot of the bed. She seemed unwilling to be dismissed and Carina wished Ben had come instead. She thought of his words in the night and wondered what it would be like when they met again. The thought made her pulse quicken.

When she had washed and dressed, Carina sat at the dressing table. The mirror showed her cheeks were pink and a new brightness in her eyes. She looked better already, she thought. Bella picked up a box of pins and Carina told her she preferred to leave it down. The next moment the box dropped onto the table and the girl marched to the door. She stood there with her hands on her hips and her head lowered.

'Suit yourself, ma'am. Quality don't come to Monteleone any more – only women of a different kind!'

Bella flounced out of the room, leaving the door open. As her footsteps rattled down the passage, Carina's grip tightened round the hairbrush she had unconsciously snatched up. She was shocked by her rudeness – but Bella had seen the crumpled bedclothes and much else besides. She would relay every detail to the other servants and she must find Ben and make sure he stopped her.

Carina hurried downstairs to a hall that was cluttered with walking canes and coats. The front door was open and she took a moment to study the house that was Ben's home. Monteleone was a white two-storey building around a central courtyard and its air of normality heartened her. She couldn't see Ben outside, and, trying the first door she came to, entered an oval room with French windows.

Miniatures and bronzes crowded the tables beneath old mirrors and the portrait over the fireplace arrested her gaze. At first she thought it was of Bianca Scalia. The likeness was such that they might have come face to face, only the young woman was dressed in the fashion of a generation before. It must be her mother, Isabella del Angelo.

The resemblance was so striking, Carina felt goose pimples on her arms. She thought of Paulo's story and Bianca Scalia's connection with Monteleone. Bianca had spent her holidays here. It was at Monteleone that she and Ben had fallen in love all those years ago – and here they had said their final farewells.

The room felt oppressive and, loosening the collar of her shirt, Carina stepped out on to the terrace. She walked to the end and went down a flight of steps to a garden aflame with red hibiscus. The sky was dazzling blue, the moss soft and springy beneath her feet and she followed a path to where a wooden bench was placed against the wall.

Sitting down, she tried sort out the chaos of her emotions. What happened last night was momentous. Nothing would ever be the same again. She would never be the same. For the first time she could remember, she had woken this morning feeling at peace. There had been lightness in her heart until the altercation with Bella dispelled her euphoria. Who were these other women who came to Monteleone, she wondered? Was it possible that Bianca Scalia was still in Ben's life? She must go and find him. When she saw him again, she would be reassured.

Carina walked back to the house, not looking at the portrait of Donna Isabella as she passed through the oval room. She searched the ground floor, but there was no sign of Ben. She would talk to him later, she decided and returned to her bedroom. She lay flat on the bed and was half-asleep when she heard Ben's voice in the passage. There was no time to put on her shoes or straighten her skirt, but she was out of bed in her stockinged feet when he walked in.

Ben was wearing riding clothes and his face was streaked

with dust. He was so handsome, Carina felt a clutch at her heart as he walked over and kissed her on the forehead.

'I'm away for a couple of hours and return to find the household in an uproar. Bella Campi's handed in her notice. Apparently, she finds herself unsuited to the position of lady's maid.'

'Really? Then it saves you the trouble of dismissing her.'

'What happened? Why did she upset you?'

'She was unpleasant and insolent.'

'There's only one person at Monteleone whose opinion is of any account and that is Selida.' Ben took hold of her hand and played with her fingers. 'I'm glad to say she's offered to look after you herself. What did Bella say that so offended you?'

'She said you don't entertain society at Monteleone – only women of a different sort.' Carina ignored the flicker of amusement in Ben's eyes. 'You presume I accept things as they are—'

'I presume nothing. You shouldn't care what Bella thinks.'

'But I do care!'

'Then you're not the woman I thought you were.'

All her life she had known who she was and where she belonged. Carina had been secure in that knowledge – and the ground had shifted beneath her feet. Who was she now and where did she belong? She searched Ben's face for an answer and found a look akin to pity for a child who fails to understand the adult world. Then he smiled, dropped her hand and headed towards the door.

'Don't let it upset you, sweetheart. Your status as my guest is of no significance to anyone but ourselves. Dinner is served at seven o'clock and I'll meet you downstairs.'

CHAPTER EIGHTEEN

Ben left the room and Carina heard him speak to someone outside before Selida came in. She smiled encouragingly and beckoned her towards the wardrobe.

'I've found you some lovely dresses. We brought them here this morning when you were in the garden.'

Carina was astonished by the number of outfits crammed into the small space. There were summer dresses and skirts, capes and riding habits along with boots and a selection of bonnets. An entire wardrobe was laid open before her and Selida held up a dress of sprig muslin with the high waistline in the empire style.

'Look, isn't this delightful? I am sure it will fit you.'

The dresses were old fashioned, not one had a wide skirt or crinoline, but they were pretty and a welcome distraction. Carina allowed Selida to choose and when it was settled she would wear the sprig muslin, she tidied her hair and set off downstairs. Her newfound elegance gave her confidence and she hoped Ben would be impressed. As she walked into the salon, he looked at her appreciatively.

'That dress must be thirty years old, but it suits you well enough. You look lovely.'

An elderly man in a white jacket shuffled in to announce dinner was served and Ben offered his arm and led her to the dining room. The table was large enough for twelve, with two places set at one end, and Ben seemed content to eat in silence. Looking at him now in his fine clothes, no one would imagine him as a convict in chains, Carina thought. Ben behaved as if the other side of his life did not exist. What had kept him all day so that he hadn't visited her until late?

When at last they were alone, she finished her wine and asked. 'Tell me about Donna Isabella del Angelo. Was this her home?'

'In a manner of speaking. It was the family's summer residence.'

'Is it true she was your benefactress?'

'I'm sure there's nothing about me that you don't know already. Why don't you give me your account of my past? It's bound to be more entertaining than anything I can tell you.'

His tone was relaxed and Carina gathered her thoughts before she began.

'I know you were involved in the '48 revolution. When it failed you were driven into exile. Where did you go?'

'I lived in Dublin for a time.'

Ben's eyelashes dropped and she went on more cautiously. 'Were you brought up at Monteleone?'

'My brother and I spent part of our childhood here. We inherited the estate when Donna Isabella died.'

'Why did she leave it to you and not her daughter?'

The question popped out without thinking and Carina put her hands under the table and pinched the napkin on her lap. On the day she collapsed on the road, Ben warned her never to speak of

Bianca – but she couldn't help being curious. Donna Isabella would never have bequeathed the property to Ben and his brother when she had an heir of her own. If Monteleone belonged to Ben, then it was Bianca Scalia who had given it to him.

'Donna Isabella's life was in Palermo.' Ben said with some reserve. 'I expect she trusted us to look after the place.'

'So you returned to Sicily with a price on your head to take care of Monteleone?'

'I came back because I'm committed to the cause of Sicily's freedom. And this time we will be successful.'

He pushed his chair back, bringing the conversation to an end, and stood aside to let her pass through the door ahead of him. Carina went to stand by the fire and felt his breath on her shoulder.

'You're shivering. Shall I fetch you a stole?'

'I'm not cold, thank you.'

'Greta Mazzini is coming to call on us in the morning. I'm sure you'll get on famously. Now, stay by here and keep warm until I come back.'

'Where are you going?'

'I'll be home by midnight, I promise.'

'What business can you have at this time of night?'

Carina heard vexation in her voice. She had waited for Ben all day and he was going out again. She was his lover now, not his captive. It shouldn't be like this! Her lips trembled and she clenched her jaw as she walked out of the room without waiting for his answer. Reaching the hall, she lifted the front of her skirt and swept up the staircase. She hoped to hear Ben's tread on the steps and feel his hand on her shoulder, but when she looked down he was going out of the front door.

How could he be so indifferent with the memory of their recent intimacy? Carina thought of his hands on her body and the rapture she had experienced in his arms. This morning she had been happy. She had broken society's greatest taboo believing that Ben would stand by her. Did such matters mean nothing to him? An awful suspicion came into her mind. Last night she had convinced herself Ben loved her – but perhaps she was the same as any other woman he had taken to his bed – and no doubt convinced them that he was sincere too!

Disappointment dropped in her stomach as she closed the bedroom door and leant against it. She had let Ben seduce her because she was worn down by deprivation and dependency. How could she have been so easily persuaded? If he cared for her, he would have come to her this morning and not left her alone like this! She would lock him out, Carina decided, but the key was nowhere to be found. She searched the room, on every ledge and in every drawer, then finally dragged one of the heavy armchairs and jammed it under the door handle. It might not keep Ben out, but he couldn't fail to get the message.

Worries darted through her head as she put on her nightgown and climbed into bed. Had she made a terrible mistake? What if she fell pregnant? Dear God, what then? The idea was so terrifying Carina scrambled out of bed. She found a flint and relit the candle. On the desk were writing materials and she gathered them up before going to sit by the fire. Chewing the end of the pencil, she imagined herself in the garden and began to write.

Shine on, calm crescent moon,
Shine on, beyond our sight,
Dispel dark and dusky gloom,
Absolve with limpid light.

Look down, star mantled sky,
Look up, soft singing sea.
Firmament of mother earth
Forbid all melancholy.

Breathe deep, sweet jasmine'd air,
Arabian flowers' delight.
Children of southern moon
Console my heart tonight.

Carina stopped and started, changing words and crossing out lines. The poem helped to control her panic and she made a final alteration, then left the paper on the desk. She went back to bed and snuffed out the candle. As the clock struck twelve, she heard the front door shut. A few moments later there were footsteps in the passage and the door handle rattled, followed by the sound of splintering wood as the chair crashed on its side.

Carina was so tense she could hardly breathe. She lay as close to the edge of the bed as she could. She felt Ben's knees touch the back of her legs and his hands on her shoulders. He began to massage her muscles and she kept her eyes shut, trying to keep still, but when he reached for the fastening of her gown, she clutched hold of it and he moved away.

The candle flickered into light and Ben turned her over on to her back. Placing his elbows on the pillow, he looked down into her face.

'What's wrong?'

'I won't let you do this!' Carina began. 'I'm not like your other women—'

'I agree – you're far more desirable and a good deal more difficult.'

'I'm at no man's command—'

'As I've found out …' Ben murmured and bent his neck to kiss her. Carina shut her mouth and he continued unperturbed. 'You remind me of a mountain cat my brother brought home. Alex was so sure he could tame that damn animal until it turned on him and mauled him half to death.'

It was the first time Ben had spoken of his twin and Carina looked him. She saw a shadow pass across his face and then he smiled.

'You're as wild as that cat and twice as dangerous.'

'Did he let the poor creature go?'

'I seem to recall he let it loose. It was shot dead the next week.'

'Well, at least he set it free.'

'But I'm not my brother, my love. I don't have his patience and nor do I have any inclination to tame you.'

'Ben, please! You know what we did was wrong—'

'There's no use shutting the stable door after the horse has bolted.'

He was mocking her and Carina twisted her head on the pillow, refusing to look at him.

'Listen to me, sweetheart.' Ben ran a finger down the inside of her arm.' I would love to spend every hour of the day with you, but I have other responsibilities. It doesn't mean I'm not serious in this matter.'

'But think what might happen if … if …'

'If you find yourself with child? Then I'll persuade you to marry me. I vowed long ago no offspring of mine would be born illegitimate.'

'Do you mean we'd live together as man and wife?'

'Not necessarily; I'm sure we can reach an accommodation that's acceptable to us both. You're a beautiful woman. It would be an honour to be your husband, even in name only. Besides, an annulment is easily obtained.'

Ben regarded marriage as a contract to be dissolved without a qualm of conscience – but she loved as fiercely as she hated. She would rather bear a child out of wedlock than submit to such an arrangement and her face tightened with determination.

'It would be a travesty of all that's right and decent.'

'Not if you prove you were forced into the marriage or your mind was unbalanced at the time.'

'By all that's sacred, I couldn't—'

'Hush now …'

Ben took her hand and guided it to his mouth, kissing the tips of her fingers. He hadn't listened to a word she said, Carina thought. She might have persisted, but he muffled her protests with his lips. She was aware of him removing her nightgown, leaning over and pressing kisses to her neck. Ben aroused feelings she had never known before. And now, for mercy's sake, what was he doing? The exploration of his fingers was insistent and Carina grabbed a handful of his hair and forced his head up.

'There's nothing to be ashamed of, sweetheart. It would be a sin against nature to waste that sweet ardour of yours.'

Ben looked down at her and the warmth in his eyes pierced Carina to the core. How could she resist when she had no desire to stop him? In his arms, fear and uncertainty slipped away. She would not think about tomorrow. Ben was no longer a stranger. She could close her eyes and see his face in the darkness. The passion between them was a raging fire, consuming her in its flames – and if this wasn't love, what else could it be?

CHAPTER NINETEEN

Darling Nonna,

I am glad to tell you I'm safe and well. You must have been so
worried, but my guardian angel protected me. I was rescued a week
ago and am now in the care of good people. When I return to
Palermo, you will see with your own eyes that I have come to no
harm ...

Carina chewed the inside of her mouth writing the last sentence.
She wanted to reassure her grandmother, but dare not say too
much. With the letter in her hand, she went downstairs to the
oval room where Greta Mazzini was waiting with Ben. Greta
wore a dark blue riding habit with a plumed hat perched on her
raven hair. She had a lively expression and an aura of vitality
that more than made up for her lack of stature.

'Greta is married to Stefan Bosco of Calatafimi,' Ben said as he
introduced her. 'But she's too proud of her connection to the
most dangerous radical in Europe to relinquish her maiden name.'

'Come now, Ben, only with my closest friends. To everyone
else I am Signora Bosco.' Greta spoke with a soft musical lilt

and smiled at Carina. 'Ben has told me of your predicament. I do hope I may be of assistance.'

There was generosity in her black eyes and Carina warmed to her. Greta was bright and friendly and she wondered how much Ben had told her. They were both waiting for her response, Ben with an amused, ironic look on his face, and she kept her tone light.

'I've been well taken care of since my arrival at Monteleone, thank you. Captain Mavrone has been very … attentive.'

'Well, it was the very least he could do! Your intervention saved his life – and, along with it, any prospect of our success.'

'I'm indebted to Miss Temple in every way.' The insinuation was clear as Ben came to his feet. 'Now I'm afraid I must leave you, ladies. I've business to attend to and you have a great deal to discuss. Good day to you, Greta. I will see you later, Carina.'

He lifted Greta's hand to his lips and his fingers brushed Carina's shoulder as he passed her by. Her eyes followed him and when the door closed Greta moved her chair closer.

'Ben's a remarkable man but he can also be impossible. Has he explained anything to you – or is that why I'm here?'

'He told me you have offered to write to my grandmother and I'm very grateful. Would you be so kind as to enclose this letter from me? I want to reassure her that I'm safe.'

'Of course – I shall write to Contessa Denuzio later today.' Greta took Carina's letter and placed it in her pocket. 'The story is you were abandoned close to our estate in Calatafimi. We've given you refuge and you'll stay with us until you are strong enough to travel. Our home is far enough from Monteleone to avoid any suspicion you might be in danger.'

Their eyes met and there was wry humour in Greta's expression. Carina coloured slightly and asked.

'Is there news of the uprising in Palermo?'

'Only that it's been postponed. Maniscalco's purge played havoc with our plans. There's only one man who can deliver us – and that's Giuseppe Garibaldi.' Greta eyes lost their focus and her voice became wistful. 'You can't imagine a man such as he! He's a new Messiah who will change the course of history.'

Carina was struck by the way she enunciated his name and the faraway look on her face surprised Carina. What was it about Garibaldi that induced such reverence? She recalled Enrico speaking of him in the same tone – as if there were almost something mystical about the man. She fiddled with the tassels of her shawl and it was moment before she spoke.

'Are you certain Garibaldi will come?'

'He'll come in the name of Italian unity. And now Ben's returned, we must prepare for action. For all his greatness, Garibaldi cannot achieve victory without the Sicilian patriots – and we can't be free without Garibaldi.'

With the briskness of a woman with purpose, Greta stood up, put on her gloves and straightened her hat. Her eyebrows drew together in two black crescents as she peered into Carina's face.

'Ben's confident you will never betray us. He's less certain of your political views.'

Surely Ben knew which side she was on! Her uncle and aunt might support the Bourbons, while Paulo was ambivalent, but she and Gabriella were patriots. It upset her that Ben questioned her loyalty and resentment glimmered in Carina's eyes.

'You may assure Captain Mavrone my sympathies are with the patriots.'

'Don't be angry.' Greta touched her hand briefly. 'Ben is vigilant to an extreme. He's been betrayed too many times to trust anyone.'

Greta knew Ben better than she did and Carina forgot her momentary annoyance. There was so much she wanted to understand – so much Greta could tell her about Ben. If only they had more time. But Greta was already taking her leave.

'I thank Heaven you've joined us, Miss Temple. Ben tells me you have the courage and fortitude of a lion. I believe in Providence and fate has brought you to us for good reason.'

CHAPTER TWENTY

Ben stayed with Carina all that night and every other night in the weeks that followed. Sometimes they dined together and when he was delayed she ate alone and he joined her later, coming to her room in the quiet of the night. She no longer resented his absences. They served to prolong the anticipation of his return and Carina did not question why she was at Monteleone. Her family knew she was safe and Ben was the centre of her world. There was no thought of going home, no thought of anything except Ben and the forthcoming revolution.

Greta sent a note asking permission to take her riding and Ben lent her his horse. They cantered through fields of green wheat and, when they came to the beach of Capo de Vito, galloped by the edge of the sea. Greta was an accomplished horsewoman and Carina was flattered when she complimented her on her ability.

'There's nothing I love more than being in the saddle! I've always understood horses better than humans.'

'Which is why you ride superbly. Garibaldi could do with equestrians of your skill. Will you enlist when the time comes?'

'Does Garibaldi allow *women* in his army?'

'He's never discriminated and his late wife was always by his side. Despite my husband's reservations, I'm determined to volunteer.'

Carina could shoot and ride as well as any man and she could barely contain herself.

'Then I'll volunteer with you! In what capacity may we serve?'

'As couriers and such like. I don't care so long as we can take part!'

She flashed a smile and Carina laughed out loud. Greta was unlike any other woman she had met. Her company was exhilarating and she was dying to ask her about Ben. She picked her moment as they were heading up the hill towards Monteleone.

'Have you known Ben all your life?'

'For as long as I can remember. The boys were five years older and I thought of them as my brothers.'

'Were the twins very alike?'

'They were identical in looks – and north and south in character. Ben was a rebel while Alexander never spoke of revolution. There was no justice in his death.'

Greta rubbed her riding crop against her cheek and Carina felt her distress. It must have been heart-breaking for all of them, she thought, and devastating for Ben. She couldn't imagine losing a brother or sister, let alone a twin. In the early days she had the impression of Ben as a man disinherited and alone. If what Paulo said was true, then his political activities had led to Alexander's death. Scalia was to blame, but Ben carried the burden of guilt and her heart went out to him.

'Why didn't Princess Scalia try to save Alexander?'

'Once she married Prince Scalia, Bianca del Angelo cut all ties with Monteleone.'

'I heard she was very close to Ben—'

'Bianca was close to *both* brothers,' Greta stated emphatically. 'I've no time for malicious gossip – and nor, do I imagine, do you!'

Carina blushed and Greta's tone softened. 'Ben's a good man. I can't bear to have him maligned. He needs a woman with spirit like you. But be sure to stand up for yourself – and don't let him go breaking your heart.'

Greta went from dark to light so fast that it was hard to keep up. She had stood up for herself all her life, Carina thought – only her relationship with Ben was different to anything she had experienced before. She needed Greta's guidance and would never mention Bianca Scalia's name again.

'Come on, I'll race you to the top.' Greta touched her spurs to her horse's flanks and called to her, 'Let the best man between us be the winner!'

Later that evening Ben came upstairs and put his arm around her.

'Greta tells me you ride like an officer of the Light Brigade. Where did you acquire such an excellent training?'

'I was an only child and spent most of my time in the stables. Horses were my best friends.'

'Do you miss your home?'

Her childhood and England felt as far away as the moon, her memories of Melton faded as old daguerreotypes. Not wanting to encroach on their present happiness, she had refrained from talking about the past, but they knew each other better now.

'I grew up in Yorkshire until I was fourteen and then moved to London.'

'Tell me about your parents.'

'My mother died when I was born. She never had the chance to bring me to Sicily.'

'And your father?'

She hadn't spoken about her father since his death, not even to Alice. The way Ben looked at her, so still and quiet, made Carina feel she could tell him anything.

'My father was killed out hunting.' The memory had been suppressed so long that her words came out in a rush. 'He jumped a stone wall without knowing there was a dyke on the far side. His horse fell and Papa broke his neck. He died instantly.'

It came back to her as if it had been yesterday. Carina saw her father's broken body being carried into the house. She remembered her stunned bewilderment in the beginning and the onslaught of grief that followed. There was a pencil lying on the table and she picked it up, squeezing it between her fingers.

'On the morning of his funeral, I took my horse over the wall where he was killed. It's what my father would have wanted. My courage was all I had to prove myself to him.'

The snap of the pencil made her look down. There were marks where the lead dug into the palm. Ben took the pieces from her and threw them onto the fire.

'Courage is a great quality.'

'Then I was fortunate for I was born with more than my fair share.'

'No one's born with courage, my love. Some people are born without fear, but that's different. Courage is acquired by degrees, layer upon layer. Brave men and women aren't those who don't know fear, but those who overcome and are strengthened by it.'

There was a serrated edge to his voice. Ben was going to tell her about Alexander at last, Carina thought. She waited and it saddened her when he was silent – but another matter pressed more urgently on her mind.

'Greta Mazzini and I intend to ride for Garibaldi when the time comes.'

'A battleground is no place for a woman. Would your father have let you take such a risk?'

Probably not, Carina thought, only she had come a long way since then. If Greta could volunteer, then so could she! Whatever Ben said, she would have her way. Her cheeks dimpled prettily and she changed direction.

'Greta speaks of Garibaldi as the new Messiah. Have you met him?'

'I fought beside him last year with the *Cacciatore dei Alpi*. He's a brilliant military commander. I admire him most for his integrity and humility.'

Ben walked over to the desk. He picked up her poem and brought it back with him. 'I read this earlier. Did you write it?'

She nodded, aware of the keen look in his eyes.

'I didn't know you were a poet. Are you still so melancholy?'

'Only when you treat me like a child—'

Ben laughed softly and Carina turned her face up to him. He kissed her with one hand pressed hard against the muslin that covered her breast and guided her towards the bed.

'You're made for love, not for war, sweetheart. It's a damned sight more satisfactory than any battlefield.'

Carina felt mildly irritated. Ben might not approve now – but she would wear him down until he agreed. She was going to ride with Garibaldi and no one could stop her! Seeing her expression, his eyebrows lifted in mock horror.

'My darling, don't look so fierce! You might frighten me away.'

Ben's tone was light-hearted, but his lips spoke a different language. Carina let him undress her and he tossed her clothes to the ground, kissing her all the time until she was breathless. When he knelt between her knees she had a dizzying glimpse of the brilliance in his eyes. There was no tenderness tonight. His hand twisted in her hair as he pushed her up against the headboard and Carina raked her nails across his back. His unashamed hands ranged over her body, as if he wanted to possess every part of her not yet made his own and Carina responded with desire as fierce as his own. Their passion for each other was insatiable, on and on through the darkness and danger of the night, until they fell back exhausted.

Later, Carina lay beside him with her hand playing across his chest. Ben was awake and she wondered what he was thinking.

'I've told you about myself, yet know so little about you. Are there secrets in your past?'

'None that would interest you, my love. There's no mystery about me – no riddles to solve.'

As he spoke, Ben reached for her. He drew her head into the hollow of his shoulder and she could imagine the look on his face. She had seen that blank expression before, warning her away whenever she came too close. Ben had encouraged her to talk about her parents and confessed nothing of himself. What was it that he would not admit even as he lay in her arms? How much longer must she wait?

I'll wait forever, Carina thought. Against hope, against reason, against peace, I love this man. I will defeat him as he has defeated me. I love Ben and will never give in until I capture his elusive soul.

CHAPTER TWENTY-ONE

March brought sun and showers and Carina sensed events were on the move. Strange men who came to the house were taken to buildings beyond the stable yard and covered wagons lumbered up the road almost every day. Ben was away so much and she was lonely without him.

Carina went for walks and picked the tiny red flowers of St Joseph for Selida. From her, she learnt the twins came from a village in the mountains. Selida had been employed by Donna Isabella as their nurse and stayed on at Monteleone ever since. She told her the boys had been educated at home, before they were sent to Ireland where Ben trained as a soldier and Alexander studied at university.

When he was at home, Carina sometimes caught Ben watching her with a speculative look in his eyes. What was he was thinking, she wondered? Surely, by now he knew he could trust her? She wanted to ask him when the revolution would begin but Ben put a finger across her lips. He made love to her, but didn't tell her where he had been or what he had been doing.

One night he was later than usual and Carina could not sleep. She tossed and turned in bed and then made up her mind. If Ben refused to involve her, she must find out what was happening for herself. Once, when she wandered too far from the house towards the stables, a groom had stopped her and told her it was out of bounds. Carina had let it pass at the time, putting it down to the obsessive secrecy of Monteleone, but it was there her investigation would begin.

The next morning she told Selida she was going for a walk and descended the back stairs, making a detour past the kitchen. The cook was rolling pasta and the smell of tomatoes and garlic on the stove followed her down the passage. Looking out from the back door, she saw two stable lads grooming a horse in the yard. One was holding the stallion's head while the other oiled its hooves. She waited until they finished, then slipped behind the loose box, walking swiftly until she came to a courtyard with high walls.

In front of her were storerooms with wooden doors and steps leading down to some kind of a cellar. Carina listened to make sure no one followed and then tiptoed forward. The door was open so she went down until her head was beneath ground level. As she pushed the door inward, cobwebs swept her face and she put down her parasol to brush them away. She could see stacked shelves reaching up to the curve of the ceiling. Why, it was only an old wine cellar! Carina smiled at her own foolishness. There was hardly space to move, let alone hold a secret meeting.

A shaft of sunlight came through the door as she turned back and the breath went out of her lungs in a gasp. Instead of wine barrels, she was staring at weapons. There were muzzle-loaders and bayonets stacked in rows, along with pistols and muskets. Wooden crates marked with skull and crossbones stood unopened on the floor. Here, Ben had assembled the military equipment for the revolution! Monteleone was to be the head-quarters and she would be at the heart of it!

The next moment Ben's voice exploded in her ear. 'What the hell do you think you're doing?'

There was a dangerous look on his face as he pushed her back into the dark interior. When he reached for the door, Carina thought he meant to shut her in but he left it open a crack, allowing a small amount of light into the cellar.

'Two of my men were watching you. They saw you come here and sent for me.'

'But the door was wide open.'

'The guards set you a trap. They don't trust you. In fact, they believe you're a spy.'

'Then tell them the truth—'

Carina broke off as Ben dropped into a crouch. He took hold of the front of her skirt and pulled it up above her knees. His hand slid from her ankle to her calf, running over her silk stock-ings to the top of her legs. She tried to keep her knees together but he forced them apart to search the inside of her thighs. When he straightened up, he unbuttoned her dress and felt roughly inside the bodice.

'Have you finished or shall I strip naked for you?' Carina cheeks flamed with mortification. Her hands were clumsy as she fastened the buttons and brushing her aside, Ben finished the job himself. Then he stood back, studying her face with the same scrutiny he had bestowed on the rest of her.

'I know how much you wanted my pistol and old habits die hard. If not a gun, what were you looking for?'

'I want to know where you spend all day and half the night.'

'You could have asked.'

'You wouldn't have told me! You never tell me anything!'

'I haven't told you because the more you know, the more dangerous it is for you. When you return to Palermo you will be interrogated – and possibly by Prince Scalia himself. The revolution is upon us, Carina. Indeed, I'm obliged to bring forward the date of your departure.'

Carina looked at Ben in disbelief. What was he talking about? She wasn't going back to Palermo. She was staying here with him. She heard his words but could not take them in.

'Baron Riso's staying here tomorrow night and will escort you back to Palermo. He's arranged for the British Consul to take you to your family. Between them, they'll conceal all traces of where you've been.'

Thoughts crowded her brain, one following so fast upon another that Carina felt stunned. How could Ben endure the idea of her being interrogated by Scalia? An overheard phrase drummed in her head. 'He's a man with a precise method of sucking the juice from the grape and then discarding the skin.' She couldn't remember where she had heard the remark, but it wasn't true of Ben. She refused to believe it.

'I've invited Greta and Stefan for the evening,' Ben continued with military efficiency. 'Francesco Riso believes you've been with them all the time. I've kept my promise, sweetheart. You will return home with your reputation unblemished.'

To hell with his promises! The day after tomorrow she would be gone from Monteleone. They might never see each other again. What about us, her mind screamed? Ben had asked her to marry him, for pity's sake! Furious, words sprang to her lips and Carina forced them down. Losing her temper would only make it worse. She lifted her chin and managed to ask quietly, 'When did you decide all this?'

'We received notice last week that Rosalino Pilo, one of

Garibaldi's best commanders, is on his way. Once Garibaldi hears the uprising is successful he will sail for Sicily.'

Compared to the great cause of Italy, their relationship was incidental and so, it seemed, was she. But Ben couldn't make her return to Palermo. She would write to Nonna and tell her she was delayed. Baron Riso could take her letter for Mr Goodwin to pass on. If Ben insisted she left Monteleone, she would stay with Greta Mazzini.

'I must get you back before your family take to their heels,' Ben's voice was kinder. 'Most of the nobility have abandoned Palermo for Naples already.'

Her eyes burned with obstinacy and Ben avoided her gaze as he led her up the steps. He escorted her across the yard and Carina walked on to the house alone. There's been a misunderstanding, she thought desperately. I must be cool-headed. Ben doesn't realise I'm committed to the revolution. It's the reason he won't tell me anything. I must talk to him and make him understand.

The rest of the day dragged by, and Carina took supper in her room. She hoped Ben would be early, but it was after midnight when he came to bed. His eyes closed straightaway, but she knew he wasn't asleep. She waited and then put her hand on his chest. Her fingers ran over his skin, skimming the flat surface of his stomach. Carina was astonished at her boldness. She wondered how much further she would go. Then his body tensed and Ben caught her by the wrist and pulled her hand away.

They lay face to face and Ben lifted her leg over his waist. Carina saw in his eyes the same hard elation she felt in herself. She moved astride him and tossed her hair back off her face. A smile played around her mouth and Ben swore softly. His resistance crumbled and he reached for her shoulders and pulled her down. He made love to her as if he wanted to impress himself upon her forever and her heart welled up with happiness. Ben couldn't love her like this and then send her away. Tomorrow, when she asked him, he would let her stay.

CHAPTER TWENTY-TWO

The twittering of small birds woke Carina soon after dawn. She had fallen asleep confident and woken up cold with apprehension. Supposing Ben denied her request? Would Greta be willing to have her to stay? If Greta wouldn't help her, then who could she turn to?

Ben had left early and, trapped in a state of nervous tension, the day seemed to last forever. It was past five when Carina heard Ben come in. She peered down from the landing to make sure no one was around before she crept downstairs to the library. She listened and then opened the door quietly. She needed to talk to Ben undisturbed and would wait for him here. He was bound to come soon.

Leaving the door ajar, Carina tried to rehearse her arguments, but could hardly think for the butterflies in her stomach. She ran her eye along the titles of the books. Dictionaries and periodicals were on the lower shelves with novels and poetry higher up. To distract herself, she climbed the library steps and took out the first volume that her hand touched.

It was an anthology of English verse and the flyleaf was inscribed with the name Alexander Mavrone. The binding had been stretched and she let the book fall open at will. The pages parted where a piece of folded paper acted as a bookmark and the lines of a poem by Byron were underlined in pencil.

> *When we two parted*
> *In silence and tears*
> *Half broken-hearted*
> *To sever for years …*
>
> *They knew not I knew thee*
> *Who knew thee too well,*
> *Long, long shall I rue thee,*
> *Too deeply to tell.*
>
> *If I should meet thee*
> *After long years*
> *How should I greet thee?*
> *With silence and tears.*

Beneath the quiet rhythm and simple words was a depth of feeling that haunted Carina. The folded bookmark caught her attention and she blew away a fine layer of dust, and spread the paper open. A curl of flaxen hair lay in the crease. She touched it lightly and then snatched her hand away. The image of Bianca Scalia's face swam into her mind and she shut the book with a snap.

'Did you find what you're looking for?' Ben's voice came from the doorway.

How long had he been watching her, Carina wondered? She put the book back and came slowly down the steps.

'Your library is a revelation.'

'My brother's library,' Ben corrected her as he strolled forward, his gaze scanning the surface of his desk. 'Perhaps my correspondence is of more interest?'

'I'm not in the habit of prying.'

'Of course you're not.' He was mildly sarcastic. 'Now you're here, why don't you sit down?'

Ben pulled up a chair and Carina sat down. The piercing blue of his eyes made her heart pound, but it was now or never and she held her nerve.

'I've decided not to return to Palermo. I'm going to volunteer my services to Garibaldi.'

'You know that's out of the question.'

'Please hear me out.' Carina lifted a hand, her voice gathering strength. 'I shall write to my grandmother and tell her it's unsafe for me to travel. I'm better staying where I am for now.'

'Which isn't true. In a few weeks Monteleone will be the most dangerous place in Sicily.'

'Then I'll stay with Greta Mazzini and her husband.'

'That's nothing to the purpose. You'll only be safe if you travel with your family to Naples.'

'I've no wish to go to Naples. I want to take part in the revolution. Sicily is in my blood. I have the right to be a part of our nation's future.'

'Please be reasonable, Carina. I'm not sending you away for my own convenience.'

'Then why are you?'

'I've no choice. I brought you here to save you.'

'Not from yourself!' Carina saw a muscle in Ben's jaw twitch and went on quickly. 'I'm sure Greta will agree. I'll discuss it with her later.'

'Greta and Stefan can't look after you. They know that it's madness for you to stay.'

'Then I shall find somewhere else—'

'For God's sake, Carina! It's time you went home.'

He sounded exasperated. And with the collapse of her hopes, despair and anger took over. Carina struck out with her hands, pointing first to herself and then to him.

'I thought my home was with you! You said you were serious and I trusted you! Were you afraid I wouldn't succumb unless I was convinced of your integrity?'

'Oh no, I knew you'd succumb from the first moment we met. Integrity didn't come into it.'

His words fell on Carina with crushing brutality. Did Ben know the hurt he caused? Was he being deliberately cruel in order to distance himself from her?

'Don't you understand what I've become? How can I go back to my family *now*?'

It was the last argument she had left to use and Carina looked into Ben's face. She saw the shadow in his eyes and tension in the hard line of his jaw. She waited, but he was silent. His mind was made up and no appeal of emotion nor reason would alter his decision.

Carina came to her feet and fled the library. She ran upstairs, taking the steps two at a time. When she reached her bedroom she slammed the door shut and fell on the bed. Pressure had been building up all day and she burst into a storm of weeping. She cried until her eyes were sore and her head throbbed. How arrogant to think last night changed anything! She had thought Ben cared for her – but he cared only for himself. He had lied to her and she had fallen for the oldest deception of all.

Some time later, Selida came in and sat down on the bed. She put a hand on her shoulder and Carina muffled her sobs in the pillow.

'Benito doesn't mean to hurt you. He's suffered more than you will ever know. You're on his conscience. He only wants what is best for you.'

After she had gone, Carina went through to the washroom and splashed cold water onto her face. I've done everything in my power to reach you, she thought. I have given you all of myself. I touch you, but leave no imprint. I am as wind blowing over rocks.

Never in her life had Carina accepted defeat, not in the sense she faced it now. She had lost her way before and recovered. It was not in her nature to yield and, standing by the basin with water dripping off her chin, she spoke out loud, 'I won't let you break my heart, Ben. I am as strong as you are …'

She would return to her family, but go no further than Palermo. When they left for Naples, she would find a way to stay in Sicily. With single-minded determination, Carina cast everything else aside. Selida had hung out a black evening gown, but it wouldn't do for her last evening at Monteleone. She searched the wardrobe until she found a dress the colour of poppies. Red for passion and red for Garibaldi.

The dress was of a later style and required stays, so she waited until Selida came back. Holding on to the bedpost, Carina made her lace her in until her waist was tiny. She soothed her eyes with pads soaked in cold water and buffed her cheeks to give them colour. Selida helped pin her hair into a chignon and, at her suggestion, she put a touch of cream to her lips. Then Carina thanked her and made her way downstairs.

Ben was walking across the hall as she came down and stopped to wait for her.

'You look beautiful this evening.'

She inclined her head as he ushered her into the salon where the others were gathered. Greta introduced Carina to her husband, Stefan Bosco, a tall man with a high forehead and gentle smile. Soon afterwards, Baron Riso arrived. He looked tired, Carina thought, as he bowed over her hand. Ben brought her a glass of wine and she settled herself on the sofa with Greta while the men talked together by the fire.

'I'm sorry you must leave us.' Greta's eyes were filled with concern. 'I worry for you alone in Palermo.'

'I've friends to support me and I won't be entirely alone. But what will happen when the authorities learn that I've been staying with you? They're bound to make enquiries.'

'We've had plenty of practice and know how to handle them.' Greta smiled mischievously.

'You must tell me all about your home. I need to be acquainted with every detail.'

'We're half an hour's ride south of Calatafimi. We have a smallholding with a few hectares of olive groves and ...'

Greta went on and Carina did her best to pay attention as her gaze strayed to the far end of the room. Ben had discarded his jacket and looked relaxed, but she knew how swiftly his pose could transform into action. He was the true soldier among the men, she thought. Baron Riso's courtesy made it hard to imagine him in hand-to-hand combat and Stefan seemed more a professor than an infantryman. The only other warrior in the room was Greta. Carina could imagine her on horseback, wielding a sword amidst the fray. Would she be kept from the battlefield, too, because she was a woman? Had their hope of riding with the Garibaldi been no more than a dream?

Dinner was announced and Carina was placed next to the baron, at the opposite end of the table from Ben. During the main part of the meal, conversation was general, but once the servants withdrew, talk shifted to the current situation.

'When does Garibaldi plan to set sail for Sicily?' The question came from Stefan.

'He will leave Genoa when he learns of our success.' Baron Riso's voice was compelling. 'I thank God the voice of freedom will soon be heard! We have bombs and firearms stored in the Gancia Convent and the day is appointed. I trust the *squadri* will support us, Captain Mavrone.'

'As soon as we receive your signal, we'll come down from the mountains and fight beside you in the streets of Palermo,' Ben answered.

'I would like to offer my assistance. I'll be in Palermo and the family home is at your disposal.'

Carina's announcement was met by stunned silence. She looked down the table and saw Ben frown. She expected him to protest, but it was Baron Riso who replied,

'We don't wish you to put yourself in danger, Miss Temple.'

'And yet you jeopardise the security of your wife and children? I'll not be excluded from the dangers that others face!'

'Brava!' Greta's eyes were bright as she clapped her hands. 'We womenfolk are ready—'

'You've a long journey ahead of you, Carina,' Ben cut her off and stood up. 'I'm sure you wish to retire. Let me escort you to the stairs. Will you excuse us, please?'

He came round the table and offered Carina his arm. She wanted to say a proper goodbye to Greta, but he barely gave her the time. They walked through the salon to the hall where the sconces had been extinguished and, leaving her at the foot of the stairs, Ben went to fetch a light. He returned with a candle and, as Carina reached for it, lifted it away and placed it on the base of the bannisters.

'Are you determined to frustrate me?'

'I told you before, I want to be part of the liberation of my country.'

'What am I to do with you, Carina Temple? You're utterly impossible but I'll miss you, my beautiful woman.'

Ben's fingers traced the contours of her face and Carina did not move. Cool and calm, she waited with her mouth slightly open until his arm went round her waist. Ben kissed her slowly and gently, his mouth pressing open her lips with a warmth that caressed her whole body. Remember this, she thought. He will come back to you …

There was no warning of the sound that broke in on them. One moment Ben was kissing her and the next, released her so abruptly that Carina lost her balance. She flung out her hand and sent the candle crashing to the ground.

'Please forgive me,' Baron Riso's voice came from somewhere near the door.

'Not at all.' Ben bent down and retrieved the broken candle. 'Carina was about to go up.'

'I'll get another light.' Stefan spoke next and returned with a candelabra from the dining table. With her hand on the rail, Carina climbed the stairs. An oil lamp was burning on the landing and she stopped to look down. Stefan held the candelabra aloft and Baron Riso coughed, putting his hand over his mouth – only Ben appeared unaffected by the moment. There was humour and admiration in his eyes as he smiled up at her. Then he put a hand on Baron Riso's shoulder and the small group headed towards the library, taking the light with them.

* * *

Carina departed from Monteleone early the next morning. She had said goodbye to Selida, whose niece accompanied her. The young woman sat on the seat opposite and she wondered whose idea it had been to provide a chaperone.

She could see Monteleone standing on its hill and the plain below, distinguished only by complexion from the sea beyond. How she wished this part of the journey over! Her papers would be checked along the way and she must practice her lines. She had to be word perfect to be convincing, but she was leaving Ben and sorrow strangled her heart.

He was to accompany them as far as the border of the estate and, as the carriage came to a halt, Carina leant out, craning her neck in search of him. Ahead on the road, a group of armed men gathered round the cavalcade. One of them began a chant and was joined by the others.

> *Come join them! Come follow, o youth of our land!*
> *Come fling out our banner, and marshal our band!*
> *Come with cold steel, come with hot fire,*
> *Come all with the flame of Italia's desire.*
> *Begone from Italia, begone from us now!*
> *Stranger begone, for this is our hour!*

Carina could see Ben now, standing in his stirrups as he motioned the men to silence. Baron Riso spoke a few words and then Ben sat back in the saddle and aimed his rifle in the air. A single shot rang out and the patriots waved their black hats and began cheering. Ben signalled to the coachmen to drive on. He was on her side of the carriage and her gloved hand gripped the rim of the window. As they drew level, he leant down from the saddle and said something but his words were lost in the din. The whip cracked, and, as the horses broke into a canter,

Carina put her head right out of the window to look back. Dust flew up, stinging her eyes, and she had a last glimpse of Ben on his black horse before they swept around the corner and he was gone.

CHAPTER TWENTY-THREE

PALERMO, APRIL 1860

Carina opened her eyes and looked up at the ceiling of her bedroom in Palermo. Her heart was heavy and she longed for Ben. She missed his warmth and dark head on the pillow. It was the same every morning. Depression faded with the activity of the day, but Ben was never far from her thoughts. Be patient, she told herself. You only left Monteleone ten days ago. It's not yet time.

Dawn sneaked in through the shutters and she cast her mind back to her arrival home. Despite endless roadblocks and checking of papers, the journey had passed without incident. At the city gates soldiers with foreign accents challenged them and Baron Riso took her on to the consulate alone. Jane and Mr Goodwin were waiting and she was whisked off to the Palazzo Denuzio, where she found her grandmother with Paulo and Gabriella.

'It was terrible not knowing what had happened to you.' Nonna held her hand tight. 'We were frantic with worry until your letter arrived. Thank God our prayers have brought you safely home.'

And it must have seemed like an answer to prayer when she walked in that night, Carina thought. Her grandmother's eyes never left her face and she had to answer a hundred questions before she was allowed to bed. She learnt that Anna Maria was rescued by a fellow pilgrim and Prince Scalia had taken personal charge of the search. Troops were deployed deep into the Interior, hundreds of suspects arrested and interrogated but to no avail. It was as if she had vanished into thin air – and only when they heard from Greta Mazzini, did they know she was safe.

Carina met with Carlo and Anna Maria the following morning. Her aunt wept and declared it a miracle she was alive, while Carlo was permitted to ask only the mildest questions. Carina would submit a written statement to the head of police, Nonna insisted, but nothing more.

'Use your influence, for once, Carlo! The child has suffered enough without having to face the trials of the Inquisition. I demand this matter goes no further.'

Her uncle reluctantly complied, and a report was duly submitted. Paulo seemed the only one unconvinced by her story. He did not contradict her, but there was a mocking look in his eyes and Carina wondered if he believed a word she said.

Palermo was an occupied city and every day more troops arrived. Foreign mercenaries were brought in to reinforce the Bourbon army and the sound of marching went on day and night. 'Disordered times, dangerous times ...' Those were the words on everyone's lips. The city was rife with rumours and Carina watched and listened, her hopes rising and falling with every piece of news. Carlo Denuzio decided to send his wife and mother on ahead to Naples. Nonna refused outright at first and only finally agreed on condition that Carlo kept his word and Carina would not interrogated.

Church bells calling people to Matins began to peal out across the city and Carina dangled her legs over the side of the bed. Would she receive a reply from Jane today? The situation of foreign nationals in the city was becoming precarious and she must know it was urgent.

My uncle and cousins leave for Naples at the end of next week. She had written to her three days before. *He has booked Rose a passage to return to England and I cannot remain in Palermo alone. Do you think Mr and Mrs Goodwin might be kind enough to allow me stay at the consulate? I would be forever grateful if you could act as my chaperone. Alice and my grandmother will be content if they know that I am with you, and under the consul's protection. I beg you to help me, dear Jane! I cannot leave Sicily in her hour of need …*

Carina could hear windows opening and footsteps on the stairs. The household was stirring and soon Rose would bring her breakfast. Matins must be over and she wondered why the bells were still ringing. Getting out of bed, she pinned her wrapper close about her and walked out on to the balcony. The streets around the house were deserted. There were no early morning hawkers selling bread and salami, no clattering of wagon wheels or the tramp of soldiers' boots. Apart from a group of nuns crossing the piazza, she could not see a single person.

The ringing of bells went on and her gaze scanned the churches and convents below with their campaniles rising above them. The pealing was coming from the old quarter of the city and now seemed to take on a different rhythm, ringing loudly and discordantly. Carina's heart stopped, then began to race. Could this be the signal for the insurgence? She was excited and terrified at the same time. And then, from nowhere, a flame of fire arched through the sky. There was a deafening explosion and she heard running feet behind her.

Gabriella appeared on the balcony in her nightgown, rosary beads in her hand. 'Lord save us, what's happening?'

'I don't know … What's the name of that church down there?'

'The convent of Santa Maria Gancia—'

The cannon boomed again and a shell detonated with a force that rattled the glass panes in the window. Carina grabbed Gabriella by the arm and pulled her back inside.

'Holy Mary, protect them! Mother of mercy, save our loved ones …'

Gabriella was on her knees and Carina didn't know whether to join her or tell her to get up. There were more loud bangs until, all at once, the bells fell silent. The quiet that followed was as chilling as the grave. Holding on to each other, the cousins stepped cautiously outside. A cloud of black smoke hung over the Gancia convent and Carina clasped a hand over her mouth. What had happened? Had the revolution been crushed as soon as it had begun?

'We must get dressed and find your father.' Carina tried to be strong but her voice shook. 'I'll meet you downstairs.'

Gabriella nodded, and, as she left the bedroom, Rose passed her in the doorway.

'Do you know what's going on?' Carina asked her.

'Gino says there's trouble in the east of the city. Seems it's all over now.'

Carina dressed quickly, not bothering with her hair. It might be nothing to do with the uprising, she thought as she ran down the stairs. Her uncle would know, but when she arrived in the gallery, both Carlo and Paulo had left the house. They had rushed off without saying where they were going or when they might be back.

Never had a day passed so slowly. The servants spoke in hushed tones and an eerie stillness hung over house. Carina and Gabriella could not eat and took turns walking up and down the gallery or slumped in chairs. Every moment they expected to hear carriage wheels on the cobbles but not until late afternoon were they alerted by noise in the courtyard. Both of them rushed to the top of the steps. Jane Parsons alighted from a *caleffini* and Carina ran down to meet her.

Jane instructed the driver to wait and put a finger to her lips, saying nothing until they were inside the house.

'I had to come and tell you myself.' She exhaled slowly as she sat down. 'The patriots were betrayed! Maniscalco's troops were waiting and drove them back into the convent. They rang the bells to call the people out – but there was no time! The doors were blown open by cannon. Three were killed and many more injured.'

She went on to tell them Baron Riso had been arrested and forced to march in chains all the way from the Piazza Bologna to the fortress of Castellamare. It was light and warm in the room but a chill wrapped itself around Carina.

'Those who lost their lives are true martyrs!' Gabriella spoke bravely but the blood had leached from her cheeks.

'Do you have news of Enrico Fola?' Carina asked, taking Gabriella's hand.

'I'm afraid not – I only know about Baron Riso because his wife sent a message to Mr Goodwin. I'm on my way to see her.' Jane plunged her hand into her reticule and retrieved a handkerchief. She held it to her nose a moment, then put it away and braced her shoulders. 'It's up to the *squadri* in the mountains now! They must keep the revolution alive in Sicily. For every man who died today, a hundred more will take his place.'

Jane's face was taut with strain as they went down to the

courtyard. Pietro stepped forward and Carina waved him away, handing her into the cab herself.

'Thank you for coming to tell us, dear Jane. Did you receive my letter?'

'We must no longer communicate by post,' Jane whispered as she settled herself inside. 'Of course you may stay at the consulate but travel only by *caleffini*. All the main streets are blocked and these drivers know every back alley and shortcut in the city. However, I expect your uncle will be delayed in Palermo rather longer than he anticipated.'

Carina watched as the two-wheeled gig trotted out through the gates. Purple bougainvillea cascaded over the walls and its garish display clashed with her dark mood. Ben had promised to fight alongside Baron Riso in the city and she imagined him waiting for the signal that never came. Renewed fear swept her. Now that the outcome of the revolution depended on the *squadri*; he would be in greater danger. And what of Enrico?

They were at the dinner table when Paulo came home. He threw his jacket onto a chair and loosened his necktie as he sat down.

'Papa sent me home to keep you calm,' he said and helped himself to a glass of wine, which he drank in one.

A plate was placed in front of him and Pietro served macaroni from a silver tureen. While they had no appetite, he wolfed down his meal. Paulo wouldn't eat like that if anything terrible had happened to Enrico, Carina thought. They remained silent until Pietro went out and Gabriella spoke first.

'Miss Parsons came by this afternoon. She told us the uprising has been crushed. Is Enrico safe? Please tell me!'

'Well, at least he's alive. He was arrested outside the convent.' Paulo cast Gabriella a pitying look as she crossed herself. 'They've taken him to the Vicaria prison.'

Gabriella lips moved but no sound came from her mouth and Carina answered for her. 'Enrico is a courageous man! Miss Parsons said that Baron Riso was also arrested.'

'Maniscalco believes your friend is the ringleader,' Paulo replied in a sanguine tone. 'Riso's in solitary confinement in the Castellamare – but there's no need to concern yourself unduly. Due to his rank he'll be granted a fair trial.'

Gabriella announced she would retire and Paulo went with her to the door.

'Try not to worry, Ella. Papa's promised to speak to the king on Enrico's behalf. He'll be home before we know it.'

Carina watched him hug his sister, his arm around her slight shoulders as he kissed the top of her head. She felt the warmth between them and Gabriella blew her a kiss before she went out.

Paulo closed the door and turned back into the room, scowling. 'How could Enrico be such a fool?'

'He acted according to his principles. He believes in a united Italy.'

'What are you talking about?' Paulo was derisive. 'There's no such nation.'

'I mean the new Italy that belongs to Italians – not to the Spanish or Austrians. The patriots sacrificed themselves for justice and freedom!'

'So you have been *mazzinified*! I hoped you had more sense than to be swayed by propaganda.'

Carina ignored the taunt and waited until Paulo sat down. 'What will happen to Enrico?'

'We must pray for clemency from the king. Scalia and Maniscalco's retribution is terrible to behold.' Paulo glanced at the tall case clock in the corner. 'Thirteen of the conspirators are condemned by court martial and will be executed at midnight. Can you imagine? The youngest is only fifteen years old.'

As the full impact of Paulo's words hit her, Carina's heart began to beat with hard, uneven jerks. She thought of the last time she had seen Enrico and the look on his face when he spoke of sacrifice. The memory was vivid and with it came to her a terrifying premonition. Enrico was alive, even if he was in prison, Carina told herself. He wasn't in danger and the events of the day were making her imagination run wild. She shook her head to get rid of unwanted thoughts, but the feeling of dread persisted and she could not shut it out.

Glancing across at Paulo, Carina saw his expression was bleak. An empty wine glass dangled from his hand. He must have witnessed terrible atrocities today and she admired him for keeping them from his sister. Gabriella was too young to withstand such horrors.

'We should visit Enrico, don't you think?'

'No one's allowed to see him, not even his family.'

'There would be no harm in trying.'

'I said no one.'

'Please can we—' Paulo stood up so abruptly the words died on Carina's lips as he came to stand over her.

'Don't even think about it! Your association with the rebels can only make Enrico's situation worse. Keep well out of this, I tell you!'

He had never spoken to her like that before and Carina stared at him. Did Paulo know she had been at Monteleone with Ben? No, it wasn't possible. There was no way he could have found out! She lowered her gaze and made an effort to sound contrite.

'I'm sorry. I didn't mean to interfere. Enrico's your friend and I know your family will help him. Let's pray the king is merciful. Now, if you don't mind, I'll follow Gabriella's example and retire.'

CHAPTER TWENTY-FOUR

It was barely light when Carina and Gabriella set out from the Palazzo Denuzio a week later. The landau was closed and heavy veils covered their faces as they handed their papers through the window for inspection. They could be turned back at any time and Carina was on edge every time they were stopped.

The visit had been hard enough to arrange and she couldn't have managed without Gabriella. It was her idea to involve Rose and Gino. They were sworn to secrecy and Gino instructed to make enquiries at the Vicaria on behalf of a young lady who wished to visit her brother. The prison guards said this 'sister' was by no means the first. They were inundated by such requests and prepared to oblige only if it was made worth their while. Between them, Carina and Gabriella had gathered a hundred scudi and divided the money into purses for Gino to distribute. Rose's task was to help them leave the house and make sure no one discovered they were gone. She would lock their bedrooms and wait for their return.

It was a day of showers and sudden gusts and they hung onto their bonnets as they hurried across the piazza. Gino was waiting with the landau in a side street and Rose had provided a basket of food. The journey passed in silence. Gabriella kept her eyes closed while Carina was too nervous to talk. She had never been inside a prison before. Paulo said 'gentlemen' were treated better than others, but the Vacaria had a gruesome reputation. They must be nearly there, she thought and lifted the corner of her veil to peer through the rain-spattered window.

Beneath stormy clouds, Mount Pellegrino hunched like a great beast over the fortress of Castellamare. It was a forbidding place and Carina shuddered as they went past. Somewhere inside there, Baron Riso was incarcerated. She hated to think of him in solitary confinement but now she could see the Vacaria. The prison's outer walls had small barred windows and a spiked rail running along the top. She nudged Gabriella, adjusting her veil as the carriage came to a halt. Gino opened the door and helped them out.

A rough-looking prison guard approached and said with a Calabrian accent, 'No more than ten minutes. That's what we agreed. So let's see what you've got in your basket.'

The basket was returned to the landau and its contents spilled on the floor and examined. When he finished, Gino handed him a purse and he gave a harsh laugh.

'Lover boy's a lucky fellow.'

Hardly, Carina thought grimly as they followed him to the entrance. Two guards joined them carrying truncheons and they passed through an arched vault and went down a steep slope. Most of the prison was underground, fortified by massive black stones with water running down the sides. Gate after gate was unchained, opened and locked behind them. There was no fresh air and the stench of human filth made Carina want to retch. She pinched the bridge of her nose and breathed through her mouth. It was worse than she could have imagined and when Gabriella stopped and bent over, she caught her by the shoulders as she was sick on the ground.

All around them the sound of groaning rose and fell. Lanterns in wall brackets gave out little light and the further in they went, the darker it became. The place was so cold they shivered despite their thick cloaks. The jailor stopped in front of a cave carved out of the rock. The cell was no larger than the inside of a carriage and the ceiling too low for a man to stand upright. At first Carina saw only one prisoner. Then two shadowy figures on the ground struggled to their knees and she realised they were manacled together.

Both men were dressed as common felons in devil's dust cloth. Heavy chains bound their ankles and wrists and their faces were black with grime. Gabriella shrank back as Enrico was wracked by a coughing fit. When he was able to raise his head, his eyes shone too brightly and Carina knew he was ill.

'We've brought you food,' she whispered. 'Don't speak. Save your strength.'

'Papa's petitioned the king. This is for both of you.' Gabriella pressed her face to the bars and pushed through a loaf of bread.

'I don't want the king's mercy. It's enough you've both come,' Enrico spoke with difficulty. 'You're my guardian angels.'

Carina took a step to one side to allow Gabriella to talk to him while she passed cheese and fruit to the other prisoner. She had the impression he was taller and older than Enrico. 'What's your name?' she asked.

'Max Corso. Have you news of Francesco Riso?'

'He's in the Castellamare. We're told his rank means he will be given a fair trial.'

'That would require an act of God.' Max Corso's light-blue eyes fixed on her face. 'Your friend is extremely ill. You must secure his release. He hasn't the strength to survive in here.'

Dear Lord, her premonition hadn't been so wrong! Carina felt a slither of ice slip down her throat. Enrico will not die, she swore silently. I won't let it happen. We must find a way to save him. The basket was empty and her gloved fingers brushed Max Corso's hand.

'I promise to do all I can. Trust me—'

'Basta! Enough!' The guttural voice of the guard was close by her ear. 'Hurry up now!'

It seemed they had only been there a few minutes when it was already time to leave. Carina went quickly to Enrico.

'God bless and take care of you. Stay strong, dear friend.'

'We'll meet again when the revolution is accomplished,' Enrico whispered and then they were being led away and heading back towards the outside world. Gabriella stumbled and taking her arm Carina saw her lips move in silent prayer. If only she were blessed with her cousin's faith and Enrico's hope! Orderlies passed them with foul-smelling soup and a fuse of rage ignited inside her. When a rat ran across her shoes, Carina scarcely noticed. This was Satan's kingdom on earth and the Bourbon regime was rotten to the core. Those who perpetuated such inhumanity must be destroyed! The revolution was far more than a political struggle. It was a war against evil and she had joined the crusade.

She was tempted to instruct Gino to withhold the payments; but the guards would only take it out on the prisoners and she watched in silent fury as the money was distributed.

Gabriella slept for most of the way back, leaving her to deal with travel permits. Carina was too agitated to care how many times they were stopped. Enrico's situation was grave and they needed to act fast. A petition to the king would take too long.

Who else had the authority to order his release? The answer that came turned her stomach. The thought of petitioning Prince Scalia made her feel physically sick. No, she couldn't do it! Gabriella must entreat her father to speak to the governor. Carlo Denuzio had the ear of the king. He could say that Enrico had been wrongfully imprisoned and demand his immediate release.

They were nearly home and alighted the carriage at the far side of the piazza. Skirting the church as the bell in the campanile chimed eight, they came to the door where Rose was waiting. She escorted them discreetly past the kitchens and the servants' quarters, up the back stairs where a housemaid was scrubbing the stone. Gabriella had rehearsed the story that they had been to early Mass and Carina went with her to her bedroom. When she came to her own, she removed her bonnet and kicked off her filthy shoes. Then she stripped off her gloves, washing her hands and face before she lay down on the bed.

Paulo had warned her not to interfere, she thought. She was a wiser woman now than the girl who left London a few months before. Enrico wasn't her responsibility. The sensible course of action was for her uncle to plead Enrico's case, only she had no faith in him. Carlo Denuzio was too weak.

Carina slipped out of bed and began to pace the floor in her bare feet. She loved Ben and must protect him. One false move and she might endanger the patriot cause. There were a hundred reasons to not get involved, but if she did nothing Enrico would die. Carina recalled Scalia's interest at the Villa Pallestro. He would not ignore a supplication from her. It was a loathsome prospect, but there was no other way and she went over to the desk.

For a long time she stared at a blank piece of writing paper. Then she took up the quill and dipped it in ink.

Your Excellency,

There is a matter of great urgency I need to discuss with you and pray you will receive me at your earliest convenience. I beg you request permission from my uncle to attend upon your Excellency at the Palazzo Reale. The matter to which I refer is of a delicate nature and I would be grateful if the application came at your bequest rather than my own.

I trust upon your kindness and remain, sir, your most obedient servant …

Carina signed her name at the bottom and addressed it to the prince under the direction of the Palazzo Reale. She sealed the envelope, inscribing her initials above the wax. Then she walked over to the bell pull. She would instruct Gino to deliver the letter this afternoon before she could change her mind. Prince Scalia was not a man to be easily deceived. If he responded to her request, the interview would be a trial by fire. She must be clever, duplicitous and use every weapon in her armoury.

CHAPTER TWENTY-FIVE

'Garibaldi is an unprincipled opportunist.' Carlo Denuzio was standing with his back to the window and in full flow. 'Piedmont will never join forces with him against our beloved king.'

They were in the salon, waiting for Paulo to return for dinner, and Carina was sitting beside Gabriella. Her cousin was concentrating on her crochet and did not answer.

The door opened and a footman entered, bearing a silver salver with a letter, which he carried over to her uncle. Carina watched as her uncle took a paper knife and sliced open the envelope. He took out a piece of thick writing paper and was unfolding it when Paulo walked in.

'I'm sorry to be late—'

Carina hushed him and indicated towards her uncle. Carlo read the letter, frowning, and then returned it to its envelope.

'I have received a summons from His Excellency, Prince Scalia. He requests an interview with you in the morning, Carina. I'm to escort you to the Palazzo Reale at nine o'clock.'

Carina let out a long breath. So, the prince hadn't forgotten, and had responded sooner than she expected! There was no way out now and she lowered her head.

'But, Papa, you promised Nonna! You can't break your word!' Gabriella's cheeks flamed as she stood up and faced her father.

'I agree. Our grandmother will have you flayed alive,' Paulo commented drily. 'Unless, that is, you intend to keep her in the dark?'

Carlo Denuzio took off his spectacles and held them to the light. He inspected them minutely and replaced them on his nose, shifting his weight from one foot to another.

'If you accompany me, Uncle Carlo, then I've no objection to an audience with Prince Scalia,' Carina said and looked up. 'It may provide an opportunity to plead Enrico Fola's case. There's no need to inform Nonna, it will only upset her.'

They were all staring at her, Gabriella with her mouth open, Paulo curious, while Carlo beamed with relief.

'Thank you, my dear. We must all do our duty in these difficult times. However, I advise you not to speak on Enrico's behalf. Evidence has come to light that he is not as innocent as we believed.'

The words hung in the air and Carina's gaze went to Paulo. He spread his hands in a gesture of hopelessness and she turned a sharp eye on her uncle.

'If I may not speak openly with Prince Scalia, then there's no purpose to the interview. You may tell His Excellency that is my answer.'

Carlo Denuzio didn't appreciate his authority being challenged and Carina wondered if he would give way. A glance at Gabriella and she saw her cousin had turned pale. A slight breeze came in through the window, stirring the warm air and Carina sat motionless until her uncle answered.

'You may speak to Prince Scalia as you wish. But I shall be with you throughout the interview, Carina. I've given you my advice and expect you to take heed of it.'

Carina remembered his words as the carriage drew up at the front steps of the Palazzo Reale. She had hardly slept, but was alert as a sprung cat and she had considered every contingency. If necessary, she would agree to Scalia's demands but with no intention of honouring her word. The prospect ahead was daunting, and she must be on her guard from beginning to end.

She chose a suitably modest dress with a high collar and a bonnet trimmed with blue feathers. On her way downstairs, Carina caught a glimpse of herself in an old mirror and stopped to tilt the hat at a more rakish angle. There wasn't a hint of softness in the face that gazed back at her. Her eyes were hard and her mouth set in a determined line. It wasn't the face to beguile a man. She should appear more appealing and vulnerable. Turning her head, Carina fluttered her eyelashes and practised a pretty smile. She made her lower lip tremble as if she was about to burst into tears. That was better! She hadn't forgotten her old tricks and was on her mettle, ready for the battle ahead.

They were met by a court official who escorted them up the stairs to the palace. He held his mace of office high as they passed through the crowded hall and people fell back to make way. Carina's gaze passed over the petitioners. She could see fear and desperation on their faces and the furtive eyes of police spies as they mingled among them. No one was safe, she thought. How could her uncle align himself with a government that depended on torture and denunciation?

They climbed a second staircase, crossed an inner courtyard and came at last to the throne room. At the far end, dwarfed by the scale of the architecture, stood the throne raised on a dais and next to it the desk reserved for the governor of Sicily. Prince Scalia sat behind the mahogany escritoire and rose to his feet as they were ushered forward. According to the dignity of his station, he did not bow but proffered a hand first to her and then to Carlo. Flunkeys pulled up two chairs and Carina studied him from beneath her eyelashes.

His small stature gave a false impression. Prince Scalia was the most powerful man in all of Sicily, she thought and was conscious of his hooded eyes on her as she arranged her skirts.

'We've been most concerned for your welfare, Miss Temple.' Scalia spoke first.' I'm glad to see you look better.'

'I thank you, sir. I am almost myself again.'

'Do I have your permission to ask Miss Temple a few questions, Carlo?'

'My niece submitted a written statement for Count Maniscalco.'

'I've read it and certain parts require greater clarification.' Prince Scalia's tone was impatient. 'Tell me, Miss Temple, do you have reason to suspect there was a political motive behind the crime?'

'I don't believe so. The men were common criminals.'

'Countess Denuzio told us one of them recognised you. Isn't that so, Carlo?'

'It was my wife's impression at the time.'

'A most unfortunate coincidence.' Carina's eyes met Scalia's dark stare. 'Their leader was an escaped convict who had seen us riding near the Villa Pallestro. No doubt he expected Your Excellency to arrange a ransom for my safe recovery.'

'Is that so?' The prince seemed genuinely surprised. 'Would you be so kind as to tell me what happened after you were kidnapped?'

In a toneless voice, Carina repeated the account she had given so many times before. She described the ambush and her subsequent abduction. Again, she stressed that she had been unconscious and didn't know how far they rode that day. When the ransom was not forthcoming, she was finally abandoned near to Calatafimi.

'I was cared for by the family of Stefan Bosco. They insisted I stay with them until I was well enough to travel home.'

Prince Scalia rested his chin on his fingertips, his unblinking eyes missing nothing. One false note, careless word or breath of anxiety, would betray her, but Carina did not falter. When she finished, he sat back in his chair and looked her in the face. 'Apart from general mistreatment, were you molested in any other manner?'

It was obvious what he meant and Carina shook her head silently.

'Why do you think they detained you so long?'

'I presume they kept me hostage against further reprisals by yourself.'

Carina answered too fast and Scalia was quick to catch her. 'So there was a political motive?'

'They were without decency or respect. It's painful to recall ...'

'Forgive me, my dear. I didn't mean to upset you.'

Carina took out her handkerchief to wipe her eyes and Scalia stood up. Carlo followed suit and the prince motioned to her to stay where she was.

'I would appreciate a moment in private with Miss Temple. It's difficult to speak of before an audience. Would you be so kind as to wait in the antechamber?'

Before Carlo could object, Scalia rang the bell on the desk. A side door opened and a stern-looking official marched forwards.

Her uncle was escorted out of the room and the prince came round the desk and took his chair.

'And what is this delicate matter you wish to discuss with me?'

'I'm most grateful to Your Excellency for granting me an audience. Enrico Fola has been wrongfully arrested. He is innocent of any crime. I'm here to plead for clemency on his behalf.'

'So you hope to save your liberal friends. Do you petition for the traitor Riso, too?'

'I've no interest in Baron Riso,' Carina lied smoothly. 'Enrico Fola is a friend of our family. I plead only for him.'

'You may rest assured, Enrico Fola's unlikely to face execution.'

'But he's extremely ill … If he stays in prison, he will die as surely as if you shot him by firing squad. There must be somewhere else he can be detained?'

'Is young Fola your lover?' Scalia's hand dropped over hers, his grip hard and painful.

'Enrico is sweetheart to my cousin, Gabriella.'

'In that case, we may reach an accommodation.'

Scalia let her go and stood up. He moved to sit at the far side of the desk and rested his hands on the arms of the chair. 'You're aware that mercy comes at a price?'

'I'm sure his family will pay any amount necessary.'

'My dear, don't let's dissemble further. In return for Fola's release, I expect you to render me a service.'

She had prepared herself for this. If Scalia demanded an assignation, she would consent and then make herself scarce. It was risky, but the prince wouldn't dare snatch her from under her uncle's roof. If it came to the worst, then she could always seek sanctuary in the consulate. She could promise him anything and still slip through his fingers.

Carina opened her fan and moved it slowly in front of her face. 'Pray, tell me what kind of service you require.'

'I want you to gather intelligence from the English community. We've reason to believe the British Consul is aware of Garibaldi's plans. You are well placed to find out what they are.'

The prince lifted his hand and took up a pen. He wrote a single line on a piece of paper and placed it on the blotter. Carina watched as he folded the parchment in two. He handed it to her and she placed it in her reticule.

'I'll send my carriage for you in ten days' time. The princess is in Naples so we may meet in private at the Palazzo Scalia. As for your young friend, when you provide us with information, he'll be sent home under house arrest. Are we agreed?'

'I will only agree on the day Enrico Fola's released from the Vacaria.'

'And why should I trust you?'

The emphasis was placed on the last two words and the look in his eyes implied: You think you can deceive me, but you're mistaken. I will get from you what I want … Carina despised Scalia's machinations as much as the man himself, and her temper flared.

'I will give you my word. If that's not good enough for you, then I withdraw my petition.'

Carina met the prince's gaze defiantly until he picked up the bell. Moments later Carlo stalked in, his face puckered with frustration.

'Thank you for your patience, my friend.'

'Indeed … Indeed. Now, how may I be of assistance?'

'A matter of importance has come up, a mission that entails your leaving for Naples at your earliest convenience. I'll come to it presently, but first I crave a further indulgence. Count Maniscalco requests your niece remain in Palermo a few days longer. They've arrested a suspect in Marsala. If Miss Temple can identify him, then judicial proceedings may begin.'

Scalia had come up with this in the last few minutes, Carina thought. His cunning took her breath away. She looked at her uncle and saw he was sweating. Carlo gave a small cough to clear his throat before he answered.

'I can't leave Carina without protection. It would be most improper—'

'I wouldn't ask such a favour, but His Majesty is in need of your counsel. By all means take Gabriella with you. Paulo may remain in Palermo as her guardian. I will personally guarantee their security in your absence.'

Lord, he was devious! The prince had made Carlo envoy to the king to get him out of the way. The suggestion of Paulo as her guardian was as calculated as it was absurd. The prince didn't trust her cousin and wanted to keep him under his eye. At a stroke, he had engineered an arrangement so that neither of them could escape.

Scalia held out a hand to signify the audience was over. They returned downstairs and she wasn't certain, exactly, what had been agreed – but a pact had been made. Passing the line of supplicants who waited in a disorderly queue on the stairs, Carina felt their despair. There was no mercy or justice in this place. The petitioners were downcast, as if they knew already their pleas would go unheard. Would she succeed where so many had failed? The interview had taken all her skill, but Prince Scalia held all the cards. It was up to him to make the first move. There was nothing more she could do now but wait and hope.

* * *

She could see but she couldn't open her eyes and Ben was walking away. Carina tried to call out but her tongue was frozen to the roof of her mouth. She was paralysed, suffocating in the darkness. If she didn't open her eyes she would die …

She woke up in fright, tucking her knees up under the coverlet as she stared into the black night. The nightmare was fading but a miasma of fear clung to her. Where was Ben? With Baron Riso in prison, she couldn't get a message to him. Scalia remained in Palermo and yet there came no word of Enrico's release. Maniscalco's agents had arrested a suspect in Marsala. If it was Ruffo or one of the others, they would betray her!

Stop this! Carina ordered herself. You're the one who requested the audience with Prince Scalia. You're not a coward and nor are you alone. Gabriella and Carlo left yesterday and Rose the day before, but Paulo is with you – and Mr Goodwin and Jane are still in Palermo.

The consul would be up to date with the latest intelligence and might have news of Ben. Scalia had given her a permit to travel freely in the city and would expect her to call at the consulate. That's what she would do, Carina decided. She would make arrangements in the morning. It had only been a dream – a dream and not a premonition. Tomorrow she would visit Jane and her courage would return.

CHAPTER TWENTY-SIX

I hope you are well, dearest, ran Alice's letter to Carina, who was reading it outside. *As I haven't heard from you these last weeks, I feel certain you are in better heart. We are now residing in Northumberland, which is greatly to my liking. Salford Manor is a comfortable house, situated south of Berwick and only two miles from the sea. When the weather is clement Anthony and I drive along the coast. As soon as you return to England, you must come to visit us …*

It was a warm evening and Carina returned the letter to its envelope as she waited for Paulo. The air was fragrant with orange blossom and she watched as bats swooped down in jagged flight. She was glad Alice was happy and Jane's news had made her spirits soar. General Garibaldi had set sail for Sicily and was expected to land within a fortnight!

Telegraph messages crackled to and fro between Palermo and Naples. Prince Scalia must be aware of Garibaldi's plans. Would he keep his side of the bargain now, Carina wondered? The ten days since their meeting were almost up and she would learn his intentions soon enough.

Jane had also told her the revolution was gaining momentum in the Interior. A squadron under Captain Mavrone had attacked and crippled a mobile column of the Neapolitan army just days before.

'Captain Mavrone? Are you sure?'

Carina's intervention was so sharp that Jane stared at her. 'I was with Baroness Riso yesterday. Her husband may be in prison, but she knows everything that's happening.'

'So this is where you're hiding.' Paulo's voice startled Carina as he sauntered through the door. 'I have good tidings! Pietro's bringing a bottle of wine to celebrate.'

'Has Garibaldi landed?'

'Enrico is home and under house arrest.'

'That's wonderful news! When was he released?'

'Yesterday, I'm told. I've sent a letter to Ella by the night packet. I don't suppose your audience with Scalia had anything to do it?'

'How is he? Have you seen him?' Carina felt a burden lifted off her.

'The house is under heavy guard and no one allowed near. On the square, Carina – what did you promise the old goat in order to persuade him?'

Pietro brought a lantern and tray, which he set on the table. He poured out two glasses of chilled wine and Carina took a sip before she answered.

'I told him Enrico was innocent. Prince Scalia may be more benevolent than we supposed.'

'Nonsense!' Paulo turned down the corners of his mouth. 'Scalia has no dealings with clemency – but I'm glad to say we're rid of him for a few days. The king's finally lost patience. Sicily's to have a new governor and Scalia is summoned to court. He departs for Naples tomorrow.'

It was almost too good to be true, Carina thought, Enrico was out of prison and Scalia about to leave for Naples. It had turned out better than she dared hope.

'How long will he be away?'

'Long enough for us to make our escape. We'll cross over to Naples as soon we hear he's on his way back. Our ships will pass in the night …'

'I'm not leaving Palermo.'

'What are you talking about?'

'I want to stay and take part in the revolution.'

'Don't devil me, Carina! You're no more of a revolutionary than I am. If you want to stay, it's for another reason entirely.'

'What are you saying?'

'You're in love with Captain Mavrone.'

Carina had taken a gulp of wine and choked as she swallowed. Spluttering and gasping for breath, she grabbed a napkin, holding it over her mouth as Paulo went on.

'When I heard of your abduction I wrote to Enrico. He replied that you were safe and there was no need for concern. I thought it strange at the time. It was only when I returned to Palermo and learned you saved Mavrone's life that I rumbled you.'

Carina was too confounded to answer. She gazed at Paulo and he lowered his head so their eyes were on the same level.

'It's true, isn't it? Mavrone kidnapped you and you fell in love with him. That's why you want to stay in Sicily.'

'You're not as brilliant as you think you are.' Carina found her voice at last. 'Captain Mavrone did not abduct me. He rescued me from the brigands—'

'And left you in the care of Stefan and Greta Bosco for over a month.'

'Precisely; until I was strong enough to return home.'

'Balderdash! I haven't forgotten Baron Riso's reception—'

'Desist this minute, Paulo! I entreat you!'

'Then tell me the truth.'

Darkness had fallen and shafts of light beamed down from upstairs windows. The cicadas began their nocturnal chatter and soon they must go in for dinner. This was a conversation they would never have again. Paulo had known all along, Carina thought. There was no point lying to him now.

'If I trust you with my heart, you must promise not to betray me?'

Her cousin nodded and leant forward, his intent gaze on her face.

'I was happy with Ben, happier than I have ever been in my life.'

'I knew it!' Paulo punched an arm in the air. 'The first time I saw you, I said to myself: there's a girl after an adventure. You've exceeded all my expectations.' He paused, a frown furrowing his brow. 'Even so, you can't remain in Palermo alone. It's far too dangerous.'

'I've been offered refuge in the consulate. Jane Parsons will act as my chaperone.'

'And what happens if Garibaldi's defeated?'

'His army won't be defeated—'

'Garibaldi doesn't have an *army!*' Paulo expostulated. 'The Thousand, in their red shirts, are doctors, lawyers and heaven knows what else – but they're not trained soldiers—'

'The Sicilian patriots are well equipped and will fight alongside them.'

'And how many are they? Three, maybe four hundred, at the most? They don't stand a chance against a Bourbon army of twenty-five thousand. Mavrone might be killed. Have you thought of that?'

Of course she had. How could she know if Ben would come through alive? The only thing she knew for certain was that she must stay in Sicily. Carina had never told anyone of her premonitions. She was glad to have helped save Enrico, but if she tried to explain to Paulo, he would think she was out of her mind.

'I'm not staying only because of Ben Mavrone,' she answered after a moment. 'I truly believe in the cause. The Bourbon regime is evil. How can you remain immune to their cruelty and tyranny?'

'Because, despite the government's failings, I'm a realist. If your revolution is successful, which is unlikely, what do you hope to achieve?'

'The liberation of Sicily from bondage and oppression! You can't remain neutral, Paulo. Not now, when it's all about to begin!'

'There'll be bloodshed and countless lives lost – and, when it's all over, we Sicilians will carry on as we did before. We have a long history of invasion and learnt to live with occupation. You should have followed my example and kept out of it.'

Passive fatalism lay at the heart of Paulo's nature, Carina thought. She couldn't change him any more than he could pretend to be someone he wasn't and she waited for him to go on.

'What about Prince Scalia? How do you intend to deal with him?'

'I'm not in danger, if that's what you mean.'

'Not at present, but Scalia plays a long game. He never forgives those who outflank him.'

It was a timely reminder and Carina remembered then what she should have before. Prince Scalia had made his move and would expect her to respond. She couldn't afford to be complacent.

'We must convince the authorities I've left Palermo with you.' She rubbed her forehead hard, speaking her thoughts aloud. 'You'll book two berths on the ferry and register one in my name. After you've gone, I'll go to the consulate and disappear from sight. Scalia will believe I'm in Naples and no one will suspect that I'm here. Please, Paulo! I can't give over on this.'

A gong rang from upstairs and Paulo came to his feet. 'You realise Nonna will murder me?'

Paulo was waiting by the door and Carina hurried over and laid a feverish hand on his arm. 'It's up to you to reassure her! Say that, as a British citizen, the consul advises me to place myself under the protection of Her Majesty's government. He'll be responsible for my safety and she's not to worry.'

'And how do you propose we prevent Papa informing Scalia of your whereabouts?'

'You must blackmail him! If he breathes a word to Scalia, Gabriella will tell Nonna he broke his promise to her. He forced me to meet with Scalia, who interrogated me most cruelly.'

'Hang it all, Carina! I never knew you were so ruthless. No wonder you always get your way.'

'Not always—'

Carina broke off, unaware Paulo was watching her and that her expression changed, bringing sadness and uncertainty to her eyes. There was a time she believed that she could achieve anything she wanted. No longer. Ben was her nemesis and a ragged pain tore at her heart.

'Tell Nonna from me that if she's not back in Palermo by the summer, I'll come to see her in Naples.'

'With Ben Mavrone in tow, no doubt.' Paulo grinned and covered her hand with his own, pressing it against his arm as they went inside. 'The rascal will give you a run for your money – but if he's in your sights he doesn't stand a chance. Do you know, I feel sorry for the poor chap already?'

CHAPTER TWENTY-SEVEN

Carina did not move into the consulate and, after Paulo's departure, the household was reduced to a minimum. She installed herself in a bedroom next to the contessa's sitting room with its own door on to the veranda. The rest of the house was closed off, blinds drawn and the furniture covered in dust sheets; only Gino, with Pietro and his wife, remained on duty.

Prince Scalia had returned to Palermo and Carina dared not go out – but it was her decision to stay and she kept herself occupied. There were books to read and letters to answer. Many were from Harry Carstairs, who was upset he hadn't heard from her. He made no mention of a romantic interest for himself, but his correspondence was full of other gossip.

The London season is about to begin – and without the presence of Lord Danby! The scoundrel has finally had his comeuppance and been charged for unpaid gambling debts. There's even talk of him being asked to resign from the club. Can you imagine such a thing?

There was another letter too, from Alice.

*Please write soon, dearest. And reassure me you're in no danger.
The British newspapers are on fire with speculation about General
Garibaldi. Is it true he is on his way to Sicily? Will he really invade
the island?*

Carina's answer was deliberately ambiguous:

*I am sorry to have been so late in replying to your last letter. Great
events are taking place and everyone in a state of wonderment as
to how the present crisis will be resolved. We pray for news of
Garibaldi's arrival every day. My family and Jane Parsons are well
and send you their warmest regards.*

She was equally misleading to her grandmother:

*Mr Goodwin has taken me under his wing and Jane Parsons is a
delightful companion. I miss you all but I am in good spirits.*

Deception was paramount and she was becoming skilful at
artifice. Nonna and Alice would be appalled, Carina thought,
but it was crucial her family believed she was in the consulate
– and Prince Scalia that she was in Naples. How else could she
stay on in Sicily?

The army patrolled the streets day and night and Gino was
her only source of information. He told her of posters put up
by the secret committee, announcing 'Garibaldi is coming!'
They were torn down by the police only to reappear the next
day and the mood in Palermo was febrile. The government
ordered a demonstration of loyalty to the king and Gino
described what happened. Twice, Maniscalco shouted: 'Long
live the King of Naples!' to be greeted by silence from the huge
crowd. Then a single voice shouted 'Long live Italy.' The people

began to cheer and stamp their feet and the Royal Guard opened fire on them. More than a hundred people, including women and children, were wounded and twenty shot dead.

In the days that followed, Carina was stalked by doubt. Threatened with such brutal retaliation, the citizens of Palermo were frightened. She was frightened. Would the Sicilians find the courage to rise up for Garibaldi? Would they? Everything depended on the answer to that question.

Later the same week, Gino came running up the steps with a newspaper. Catching sight of the headline, Carina threw her hands in the air.

On 11th May, an act of flagrant piracy culminated in the landing
of armed men at Marsala. It is estimated they number at least
eight hundred and are commanded by Garibaldi.

The article was dated 17th May and was already out of date. What had happened since? She had to know and must send a message to Jane at once. The curfew forbade carriages, so Gino would have to go on foot wearing her uncle's badge and livery. The Denuzio name still counted in a city governed by the Bourbons and he was unlikely to be challenged.

'What news?' she wrote, then folded the paper and gave it to Gino.

Carina was on tenterhooks as she waited for his return. She stood on the veranda and looked up to mountains of the Conca d' Oro where a hundred bonfires glimmered in the darkness. They were lit by rebel groups as a threat to the government and symbol of hope to the people below. Was Ben with them, she wondered? She would like to think he was, but knew he was likely on more deadly business; harrying enemy battalions that ventured into the Interior.

By the time Gino returned, it was midnight and Carina had bitten her nails to the quick. Yes, he had given her letter to the doorman at the consulate. No, he didn't know if Mr Goodwin or Miss Parsons were at home because he hadn't enquired. Gino's expression suggested he had gone beyond the call of duty and Carina bit back her frustration and thanked him.

She was late up the next morning and walked into the sitting room to find Pietro standing by the door. He held a silver salver on which was placed a small white envelope. His expression was so serious, Carina felt the blood drain from her face. Could Maniscalco's agents be at the door? Gino might have been followed last night and they had come to investigate who was home. God forbid, it might be Prince Scalia himself! There was no one who could save her from him!

Carina plucked the envelope from the tray, took out the card and let out a small cry. 'Please show the consul in immediately!'

Pietro went to fetch him and Carina tried to compose herself. Relief followed so fast upon panic her cheeks were pink and she dabbed her face with a handkerchief, stuffing it up her sleeve as Mr Goodwin was shown in. He was wearing his official uniform with sash and badge, and looked uncomfortably hot.

'How good of you to call.' Carina proffered her hand and then walked out onto the veranda. 'Pietro, please bring some lemonade for His Excellency.'

Mr Goodwin came forward, taking off his gloves as he sat down. Pietro filled their glasses and then withdrew.

'Until last night, we had no idea that you were in Palermo. I have orders from London to evacuate all British citizens immediately—'

'So Garibaldi is marching on the city!' Carina broke in. 'Has there been a confrontation?'

'Indeed there has. Despite reports to the contrary, General Garibaldi won a decisive victory at Caletafimi.'

Good news at last! Carina was so excited she wanted to jump up and shout 'hurrah'. She restrained herself watching a small lizard run across the terrace, disappearing down the steps as Mr Goodwin continued.

'Sir Rodney Mundy and I called on Count Maniscalco to enquire as to measures being adopted for the security of British personnel and property in the city. It was made clear to us if the patriots incite the people to rebellion, the city will be shelled by artillery fire. Hence my visit.'

'How close are the Redshirts? Do you know?'

'No one knows. Every scrap of information is contradicted by the next, which is exactly how Garibaldi wants it. The element of surprise is crucial to his advance.'

'And the *squadri* in the mountains? Do you have news of their campaign?'

'Skirmishes continue with casualties on both sides. Garibaldi lost one of his best men recently.'

Carina gripped the sides of the cane chair and asked in a whisper. 'Do you have his name?'

'Rosolino Pilo was killed two days ago. Acting on false intelligence, Garibaldi ordered him to occupy the high ground above Monreale. Four columns of Bourbon infantry were in the town. He died with a pen in his hand, trying to summon reinforcements.' Mr Goodwin stopped, alerted by the look in Carina's eyes. 'My dear, I hope he wasn't a personal friend?'

'Rosolino Pilo was an outstanding soldier. It's a terrible blow indeed.'

'I've secured you a berth on Admiral Mundy's flagship anchored in the harbour.' The consul nodded, rearranging his face into a formal expression. 'The port is packed with refugees and my wife and Miss Parsons are expecting you to join them. You will be taken on board first thing tomorrow.'

She had sought his protection and Carina was embarrassed. It felt shabby to turn down the offer, but when the Redshirts entered Palermo it was here that Ben would come to find her. She could not leave now!

'I'm very grateful, sir, but I prefer to remain at home. We're out of range of Bourbon cannon and stocked with provisions. The house will be kept securely locked until hostilities are over.'

'If Garibaldi tries to take Palermo, the Bourbon government will destroy the city. Houses belonging to the liberal nobility have already been ransacked—'

'But my uncle's not of the liberal persuasion, sir. No Bourbon troops will be sent to his home.'

'Please consider my proposal and send a message to the consulate by this evening.' Mr Goodwin finished his lemonade and stood up. 'It is my duty to ensure your safety. However, if you're determined to place yourself in danger, there's nothing I can do prevent you.'

The consul made a stiff bow before Pietro escorted him out. I've made him angry, Carina thought, but Jane will understand. A poem was streaming through her head and she must set it down. She hurried to the bureau and collected a sheaf of paper. Carrying the inkwell outside, she put them on the table and started to write.

> *A thousand men, no more, no more,*
> *A thousand men, no more,*
> *For Italy and Freedom*
> *Sailed to Sicilia's shore.*
> *For Unity, Italia's name,*
> *A thousand went to war*

O sons of brave Italia
Praise be forever more!

Twenty thousand five and more,
Twenty thousand five.
Enemy with cannon fire
Redshirts to survive.
'Italy or death' they swore!
Gallantly they charged,
Garibaldi to the fore,
God above their guard!

A thousand men, no more, no more,
A thousand men, no more,
For Unity, Italia's name,
Cast strangers from our shore.
For Sicily and Freedom
Raise high the tricolour!
O sons of brave Italia,
Praise be forever more!

The poem came so fast that she scribbled the words, smudging the paper and staining the blotter. When she had it right she would translate it into Italian. It was her tribute to Garibaldi and, given a chance, she would present it to him. A gust of wind blew the papers off the table and Carina went down on her hands and knees, scrabbling on the ground to retrieve them. She stood up and saw black clouds over the mountains. The Sicilians were deeply superstitious, but the oncoming storm was not a bad omen. Garibaldi and the Redshirts would be victorious!

CHAPTER TWENTY-EIGHT

Early on the 27th of May, when the first shell was launched on Palermo, Carina was asleep. The cannon boomed again and she put a pillow over her head to block out the noise. A shell screamed over the house, its vibration knocking the clock on the mantelpiece to the floor and she leapt out of bed and ran outside. Her grandmother's apartments were too low to see the city, but she could hear church bells pealing. They had been silent so long, Carina was terrified they might stop but they were ringing from every quarter of the city. The people had risen in support of the revolution – or else Garibaldi had already captured Palermo!

She was going too fast. If the government had surrendered, the bombing would be over, but the whine of shells started again. The sound of them was ear-splitting as they ripped off roofs and tore masonry apart and one landed so close the house was shaken to its foundations. At any moment the wooden veranda might collapse. How could this be happening? A barrage from the harbour couldn't reach this far and Carina shook her head in disbelief as she hurried inside.

She had told Pietro and Nella not to come in, but Gino was here. Throwing open the wardrobe doors, she took out the first outfit her hand touched. Without a crinoline, the skirt was too long so she caught up folds of material and tied them in a knot above her knees. Then she found a pair of low-heeled boots and sat down to lace them up before setting off down the dark passage.

Instead of fresh coffee, her nostrils caught the whiff of sulphur as she unbolted the front door. Above the din, Carina heard the whinnying of frightened horses. Gino would be with them in the stables and she called to him. The boom of cannon drowned out her voice so she waited for a lull and then shouted again. There was too much noise and she would have to go and find him. Carina was halfway across the courtyard when a shell exploded outside the walls. Its detonation was so powerful the top of the gate was ripped off and she was thrown backwards. Sitting on the ground, she tasted mortar, thick as chalk in her mouth, and rubbed her sleeve across her face as Gino came running towards her.

'You must take cover, signorina. In the cellars or the garden?'

Gino helped her to her feet and Carina tried to think. If they received a direct strike, the house would collapse with the cellars buried beneath it. The garden would be safer – but first, she must find out how long the bombardment was likely to last. As she ran up the stairs with Gino beside her, she recalled the day Paulo had shown her his father's sabre, demonstrating it so carelessly he had cut his hand.

'Get the count's hunting guns. Make sure they are loaded! And bring me his sword! The one hanging on the wall.'

It was dark in her old bedroom and Carina stopped to catch her breath. Then she heaved open the shutters. The bells were still ringing and the sound gave her courage as she stepped out onto the balcony. The sky was the colour of blood and the barrage coming from a squadron of Neapolitan battleships outside the harbour. Shells were being launched, not only from the sea but also from higher ground. Everywhere she looked, there was devastation. A gaping hole was gouged out of the church roof and she saw lifeless bodies strewn over the terraces below. Huge tongues of flame leapt in the air, showering cascades of sparks down and setting houses on fire. One shell followed another in quick succession and there would be no end to it until Palermo was flattened!

A sob thickened her throat as Carina went back into the bedroom. God help them all! The Bourbons would rather murder Sicilians than surrender. Should they open the gates and offer refuge to those fleeing from the destruction? The house would be swamped and more killed if they received a direct strike – better they escaped the inferno of the city into the countryside.

She bolted the shutters and headed back, meeting Gino halfway down to the courtyard. He had the sword, but no guns. Her uncle had locked them away or taken them to Naples and the sabre was so heavy she had to use both hands to grasp it by the hilt.

'Get an axe from the woodshed! They're killing our people!'

Gino ran down ahead and, as she came to the bottom of the steps, Carina stopped and stared at the gate. There were loud voices outside and a hard object was being rammed into the wood. She stood, petrified, as the hammering went on until the gate caved in and Bavarese mercenaries poured into the courtyard. Their faces were blackened by smoke and their uniforms covered with blood. Drunk on violence and liquor, they were shouting and raising their fists in the air. Then they caught sight of her and fell silent. One of them swaggered forward and spat on the ground at her feet.

Carina looked at his filthy beard and greedy expression and such anger filled her that terror fell away. She lifted the sabre so the blade was pointing at his heart, her eyes like fire in her white face. As the mercenary made a lunge, a volley of shots rang out and the man's face snatched sideways. He leapt in the air and then fell at her feet with half his head blown off.

The sabre dropped from her hands as more shots were fired. All around her was a kaleidoscope of movement and noise. Chunks of masonry came crashing down and a hand caught her by the arm and pulled her out of the way. Carina glimpsed a hunter's black hat and the red tunic of the Garibaldini. She squeezed her eyes shut and opened them again. The courtyard was crowded with Redshirts and the Bavarese were being rounded up. She stared at them stupidly before turning to the slender figure beside her.

'By the devil!' Enrico Fola's expression was thunderstruck. 'What on earth are you doing here?'

Enrico and his troops gathered around her and the dead soldier was dragged away. His body left a trail of blood on the ground and Carina thought she might be sick. Gino appeared with the axe, jaw dropping as he took in the scene.

'Why aren't you with the British contingent?' Enrico asked curtly.

'I was offered a berth on Admiral Mundy's flagship ...'

'Then why the hell didn't you take it?'

His harshness so unnerved her, Carina nearly burst into tears. 'I thought ... the bombardment couldn't reach us ...'

Enrico appeared to be in charge and yet uncertain what to do. Carina stood twisting her hands until one of the soldiers shouted the grounds were clear and he made up his mind.

'You'll have to come with us. Leave your man here to guard the house. We'll give him guns and ammunition. Get your stuff – but only as much as you can carry in one hand – and hurry!'

Enrico was pale but his voice rang with authority and Carina dashed down the passage to her bedroom. She collected a few belongings, stuffing them into a bag, and hurried back. A make-shift attempt had been made to repair the gate and Gino was armed with Bavarese guns. Carina spoke briefly to him and then followed Enrico outside.

He broke into a run and they headed downhill, avoiding the streets crowded with people fleeing the bombardment. Adrenaline gave strength to her legs so Carina managed to keep up until they reached the ancient quarter where Enrico slowed to a walk. The thunder of cannon seemed further away in this no-man's-land. Faces peered out from behind half-closed shut-ters before they moved quickly out of sight. Then, without warning, Enrico halted. Carina looked over his shoulder and saw they had come to a wide street.

Stretched across the road and less than thirty paces away, an overturned cart formed the basis of a barricade. An assortment of planks and barrels were piled on top and it was manned by Redshirts. There seemed to be a hiatus in the fighting until shell rocketed out of the sky and exploded in front of them. Cobbles were torn up and shrapnel rained down, but no one moved until Enrico gave the command.

'*Avanti*! To the barricade!'

One moment they were squashed together in a doorway and the next bolting down the street with Carina dashing after them. As she reached the barricade, a sharp pain tore into her upper arm. Enrico threw her to the ground, protecting her with his body. There was blood seeping through her dress and he cut the sleeve from cuff to shoulder.

'Let's hope it's only a flesh wound. I'll bandage it, as best as I can.'

He worked fast, wrapping a tourniquet tight around her arm before he climbed up to join the others. The Redshirts were returning fire, standing up and ducking down, while she crouched beneath the ramshackle structure. Bullets ricocheted around her and fusillade seemed to go on forever until the gunfire ceased. Carina heard cheering and lifted her head. Enrico came down and helped her to her feet and her eyes went from his face to the men on the barricade. They were waving their muskets and clapping each other on the back. Enrico was laughing and then she was laughing too, the pain in her arm forgotten as she threw her arms about his neck.

'We must hurry to the Piazza Pretoria,' Enrico said, disengaging himself. 'Before the day's out we shall raise the tricolour in Palermo!'

Carina's heart was on fire as she fell into step with the men. Enrico could have led her through the gates of Hell and she would have followed him. For the rest of her life she would remember this day, she thought, marching through the streets of Palermo with the applause of a free people ringing in her ears. Women and children stood on the balconies, shouting greetings while boys in rags ran on ahead, turning somersaults as if leading a military band in a carnival. When a shell landed not far in front, a young boy sprinted forwards and threw himself onto the smoking missile. He extracted the fuse and then leapt high in the air, holding the piece in his hand – to be rewarded by clapping and cheering for his daring performance.

Arriving in the Piazza Pretoria, the atmosphere was markedly different. The square was crammed and the hot sun beat down on an army of wounded and exhausted men. Injured soldiers sat with their weapons at their feet, passing water skins from one to another as donkey carts arrived with more casualties. Redshirts on stretchers were passed over the heads of the crowd and Carina saw a soldier, with skin hanging off his face and blood pouring down his neck. He seemed to be staring at her before his knees buckled and he went down in the dust. Suddenly she began to shake uncontrollably. Afraid she might collapse, she undid the knot in her skirt, letting it fall to the ground.

'Where are the casualties being taken? I'd like to help …'

'That won't be necessary, ma'am,' the officer with Enrico answered. 'Garibaldi has set up a hospital in the Royal Palace. We have more nursing volunteers than we need.'

'You're in need of medical attention yourself, Carina. I've friends to take care for you.' Enrico took her bag and turned to the officer. 'May I leave my platoon under your command? I must see to my companion.'

She was relieved, dammit! She was worn to the bone and her arm throbbing. Carina longed to breathe fresh air and escape the misery surrounding her. She was so weak that Enrico put his arm round her waist, supporting her as they picked their way between rows of casualties.

'I'm taking you to my old tutor and his wife. You'll stay with them until the bombardment is over.'

Carina was too dazed to answer. They came to a side street where it was cooler and stopped in front of a house at the far end. Enrico used the stock of his musket to bang on the door. The shutters were closed and he hammered again, shouting to those inside.

'Enrico Fola wishes to speak to Monsieur Carot. Please open the door!'

There were voices inside speaking in French; a man's raised in argument and the quieter tones of a woman. A few moments later Carina heard the creak of bolts being drawn. The door opened a hand's width and an elderly gentleman peered through the gap. He might have shut the door in their faces if Enrico hadn't placed his foot across the threshold.

'It's me, *maitre*! Enrico Fola at your service. Please don't be alarmed. I beg your assistance. This young woman is injured.'

Monsieur Carot's spectacles slid from his nose to hang from a chain around his neck as he stared at Enrico. 'I cannot believe it! Does your father know about this?'

'My father's in Naples. I'm in charge for the present.'

'But you're ... you're ...'

'I am myself, dear friend. May I present Miss Temple – the granddaughter of Contessa Denuzio.'

It was absurd to be making formal introductions at such a time, Carina thought, as Enrico's hand pressed into the small of her back. He pushed her forwards and Monsieur Carot stepped out into the street, looking one way and then the other.

'First the bombardment – and now the red devils camped next door! I never thought I'd live to see this day. *You*, Monsieur Enrico! *You* in Garibaldi's uniform!'

He bent to draw the locks but Enrico put a hand on his shoulder. 'I can't stay, but I'd be grateful if you could provide for my friend. She needs medical attention—'

'*La pauvre petite!*' Madame Carot came bustling through, taking in the situation at a glance. 'Don't you fret, Henri. I'll take care of her, Monsieur Enrico – be off with you now and don't bring any of your new friends back with you. Where are you hurt, young lady?'

She spoke to all three of them in the same breath, her eyes on Carina as she led her to a chair. 'You're very pale, my dear. You should sit down.'

Madame produced a phial from her pocket, which she uncorked and waved under Carina's nose. The smelling salts cleared her head and Carina caught Enrico's quick smile before he lowered his head and stepped into the street. She wanted to tell him to be careful, but the door slammed shut and Monsieur Carot slid the bolts before she could get the words out of her mouth.

CHAPTER TWENTY-NINE

'But, monsieur, the bombardment is over! Surely you'll permit me the benefit of fresh air?'

They were sitting at the kitchen table and for the last few mornings the conversation had been the same. Every time she begged to go out, Monsieur Carot refused point blank. Her wound had festered and, as Madame Carot applied hot bran poultices to draw out the poison, she told her of the desolation the Redshirts had inflicted on Palermo. Carina did not believe her. Now her injury had healed, she was desperate to get away.

In that instant there was a loud rap at the door. Before anyone could stop her, Carina ran to open it. Enrico was standing on the doorstep wearing freshly laundered uniform, and she took him through to the kitchen where he spread his arms in apology.

'Forgive me for not coming before now.'

'Have they gone?' Monsieur Carot asked.

'The last ship, taking Bourbon troops to the mainland from Palermo, sailed last night.'

'*Sacre Coeur!*' Madame Carot pressed her hand to her mouth

while her husband's gaze rested nervously on Enrico as he continued.

'General Garibaldi secured an armistice and there's has been a ceasefire for four days. Surely you're aware of that?'

'We've had no news. We were waiting for you.' Carina was impatient. 'Please tell us everything.'

They sat round the table and listened as Enrico described how the battle lasted three days and nights with victory balanced precariously between the two sides until the Bourbons were confined to an area surrounding the Royal Palace. Cut off from supplies and reinforcements, they called a truce and proposed a conference on board Admiral Mundy's ship. At this point Carina made a small sound, then nodded vigorously, urging Enrico to go on.

'Miss Parsons sent you many messages, Carina. I'll come to that later. A cease-fire was agreed and Garibaldi appealed to the citizens of Palermo for help. Men, women and children worked all night, building barricades and repairing weapons. General Lanza was so confounded by their support for Garibaldi, he telegraphed the king and received the order to evacuate by return.'

'So Garibaldi's in charge of Palermo?' Monsieur Carot enquired fretfully.

'*La municipalite c'est moi.* That's what he said, only in Italian.'

Madame Carot's cup rattled in its saucer and Carina shot Enrico a cautionary glance, which he ignored.

'The general's taken up quarters in the Royal Palace. You're invited to a reception there tonight, Carina. Miss Parsons told Garibaldi how you refused to take refuge aboard ship and stayed to help the Redshirts. You are quite a heroine!'

'But that's nonsense! I don't believe Jane said any such thing!'

'Why else does he want to meet you? I'm here to take you home so you can make yourself ready for this evening.'

Enrico did his best to reassure Monsieur and Madame Carot while Carina fetched her belongings. She thanked them for their kindness and, once in the carriage, her eyes began to sparkle.

'I couldn't believe it when I saw you at the palazzo. How did you escape from house arrest?'

'I was rescued by agents of the Secret Committee. They bribed the guards and took me to the *squadri* in the mountains. Fortunately, I had time to recover before Garibaldi attacked Palermo.'

So it was Enrico, and not Ben, stoking the fires and watching over Palermo, Carina thought as they jolted along. Flagstones had been ripped up to make barricades and the roads were precarious, with potholes and mounds of rubble to negotiate. Some of the finest buildings in the city had been destroyed, but from the burnt-out ruins came the sound of laughter and singing. Tricolour flags were draped from shattered windows and Enrico assured her the palazzo was in good order. He had called by yesterday and the servants were preparing for her return.

'What's the purpose of this evening?' Carina enquired.

'To celebrate our victory and rally the support of the municipality. One and all are fascinated by Garibaldi – whether they attend is a different matter.'

'Have you news of Captain Mavrone?' Finally, she asked the question foremost in her mind.

'Mavrone's well and promoted to colonel. I am sure he'll be there tonight.'

His tone gave nothing away, but disquiet stirred in Carina and Enrico turned towards her.

'Nothing stays the same in times of war. We must prepare ourselves for change. I only wish Gabriella was here to share in our victory.'

'Have you heard from her?'

'I've written, but my letters are returned unopened.'

Carlo meant to punish Enrico for his politics, Carina thought, and she wasn't having any of it.

'Then we must arrange this among ourselves. Nonna loves Gabriella. Between us, we'll find a way to circumvent my uncle.'

They drove into the courtyard and she outlined a plan as it came into her head. She would write to her grandmother and enclose a letter from Enrico to Gabriella. He must bring one for her tomorrow. If the contessa agreed to act as go-between, they could correspond under her seal. There was no time to say more for they had arrived and Pietro was letting down the steps.

Enrico led her to the door and Carina waited until the gig drove out through the gates. She went inside and walked to the sitting room, barely aware of Pietro as he took her bag to the bedroom. Tonight she would be reunited with Ben! Every day for the last two months had been destined to lead to this evening. Suddenly, she was apprehensive. Would Ben be pleased to see her? 'Nothing stays the same …' Enrico's words came into her mind. Was he trying to warn her? Pietro said there had been no visitors. Ben was in Palermo, but he had not come to find her. How would it be when they met each other again?

CHAPTER THIRTY

Carina was among the last guests to arrive at the Royal Palace. She had been busy all day and visited every room in the house. The main gate was repaired and Carlo's sabre polished and hung back in his study. It was there Pietro found her to inform her the carriage would be at the front door within the hour.

She took time to have a bath and wash her hair. By all accounts General Garibaldi was a man of simple tastes, so she chose a plain silk dress with a scalloped neckline, and left her hair loose. Only at the last minute did she remember her poem and ran back to collect a copy from her bureau. It was written out on a single piece of vellum and she folded it in her reticule.

As she climbed the steps of the palace, Carina thought of her last visit. Where were Scalia's police spies now, she wondered? The palace was transformed, the marble-columned hall festooned with red, white and green banners as ordinary citizens of Palermo mingled with the Revolutionary Guard. There were smiling faces everywhere she looked. Men and women in national dress conversed with gentlemen in tailed coats and ladies in crinolined skirts and she joined a line at the bottom of the stairs.

'Miss Temple! We've been waiting for you. Come on up!'

Jane made herself heard above the hubbub and Carina looked up and saw her friend with Mr Goodwin. They were at the head of the queue, beckoning to her, and she made her way up, muttering apologies to the ladies and gentlemen who stood aside. When she reached the top, Jane kissed her and the consul shook her hand.

'We're so proud of you!' Jane's face radiated happiness. 'Mr Goodwin was in high dudgeon when you refused Admiral Mundy's offer. I told him you always acted upon your principles.'

Jane's opinion might be different if she knew the half of it, Carina thought. Then the municipal brass band struck up, playing loudly and rendering further conversation impossible. Passing through the upper hall, she looked around for Ben. There were Redshirts gathered by the open windows, along with fellows in check jackets with notebooks who looked like newspaper correspondents. Drawing near the terrace, Carina craned her neck, hoping to catch a glimpse of him outside.

'We must wait our turn, my dear,' Jane spoke in her ear. 'General Garibaldi has promised us a private audience.'

Ahead of them, officers were selecting a small number from the line and taking them out to the terrace. Carina saw Baron Riso leaning on a stick and Admiral Mundy in full naval uniform. She thought she glimpsed Greta Mazzini's dark head, but there was no sign of Ben. She was flushed with nerves and she fanned herself until a soldier came to fetch them. He led the way, whisking them past others, and brought them up behind Admiral Mundy. As the admiral stepped aside, Carina found herself face to face with Garibaldi.

The general held out his hand and Carina had the absurd idea she should curtsy. Her first impression was of his eyes, brown or very dark blue, deeply set with well-defined eyebrows. It was an open, pleasant face and his gaze was mesmeric. She understood immediately the effect he had on those who met him and couldn't have looked away, even had she wanted.

'Miss Parsons told me of your bravery, Miss Temple,' Garibaldi's voice was deep and melodic. 'We owe a great debt to people like yourself.'

'I'm sure Miss Parsons greatly exaggerated.'

'I hope you'll stay for dinner after the reception.' Garibaldi smiled, his clear gaze on her face. 'I've a great many people to greet, but afterwards we'll celebrate in true Sicilian style. Please honour me with your presence at my table.'

'We shall be delighted. The honour is entirely ours,' Jane answered.

Carina had not uttered more than one sentence in the whole exchange. Yet, in her simple dress with her hair about her shoulders, she had secured a place at Garibaldi's table. Tonight she would be the envy of every female heart in Palermo! It was silly to be gratified, but she had been hidden away so long a delicious kind of warmth enveloped her. Baron Riso limped over to talk to them. He made little of his ordeal but his shoulders were stooped and his hair had turned white.

A sudden quiet fell upon the company and Carina looked to the doorway as a tall, statuesque beauty stepped out onto the terrace. She had long blond hair and wore breeches and a military jacket. Ignoring those waiting in line, she walked straight up to Garibaldi and kissed him on the cheek.

'Who is she?' Carina whispered to Jane.

'Her name is Anne Lamartine. She sailed with the Thousand ...'

Everyone was looking at the tall beauty, but Carina had seen the man who followed. Ben was tanned and clean-shaven, his hair falling across his forehead as he loped down the steps. For a moment she thought he might not see her and walk straight past. Then, as if caught by the strong pull of her gaze, he stopped and swung round. His glance swept from her pink cheeks to the low neckline of her dress and came back to her face.

Before they could say a word, Baron Riso stepped between them. He greeted Ben, kissing him twice in the Sicilian fashion, and then presented him to Jane and Mr and Mrs Goodwin. Carina had pictured this moment so often in her mind but never like this! A noise like the roar of the sea filled her head until Anne Lamartine's voice shafted through her senses.

'Do hurry up, Benito! The general wants to know what you've been doing these last few days.'

The Frenchwoman was standing beside Garibaldi with her thumbs tucked into her belt. She spoke Italian with a heavy accent and Carina saw Ben frown. She thought he meant to ignore her, but Jane was smiling and urging him on. He waited a moment and then, with a brief apology, walked over to the general.

Ben couldn't be with that woman! It was pure coincidence they had arrived together, Carina thought. First impressions were often wrong. She only had to get through dinner and they would meet up afterwards. Then a hand touched her shoulder and she turned to find Greta Mazzini beside her.

'I'm so happy to see you. I knew you would stay in Palermo. I told everyone you wouldn't desert us!'

The genuine pleasure of seeing Greta helped Carina endure the next hour and later, when she looked towards Garibaldi's entourage, Ben had gone. Anne Lamartine was holding court, her gestures as affected as her manner of dress. Jealousy was not an emotion Carina recognized in herself, but Lamartine was a show-off and the type of female she instinctively distrusted.

The crowd began to disperse and, from the corner of her eye, Carina saw Ben standing at the top of the steps. Guests drifted off and now only Redshirts and the British contingent remained. Dinner was announced and she noticed how Garibaldi brushed the interruption aside. This was her opportunity and she touched Jane's shoulder.

'Please excuse me …'

Carina did not miss Jane's shrewd look as she left her and walked over to Garibaldi. There was a soft glow in her eyes as she took the poem from her reticule and handed it to him.

'These are a few poor verses I wrote after the battle of Calatafimi. Please accept them with my deepest admiration.'

Garibaldi glanced down at the lined paper, reading it over before he put it in his pocket. He offered Carina his arm and spoke to Anne Lamartine.

'Please join us at our table, madame. And bring Greta Mazzini and Colonel Mavrone with you.'

Carina gave the Frenchwoman a cursory glance, noting how Lamartine pursed her lips as she tucked her hand into the crook of Garibaldi's arm. He led her across the terrace and as they passed by Jane, she made a signal indicating she had been waylaid. The general stopped to talk to Ben and she pretended to admire the view as they discussed arrangements for the next day.

Carina was aware of Ben standing to attention and, as they were about to move on, Garibaldi said, 'May I present Colonel Mavrone?'

'We've met before.' Ben answered in a level voice. 'A pleasure, as always, ma'am.'

'Along with our dear friend, Rosalino Pilo, Colonel Mavrone kept the fire of revolution alight. We couldn't have defeated General Lanza without the noble *squadri*.'

'And without Garibaldi, Sicily would not have won her freedom.' Carina smiled.

'I expect not.' The general had an easy way of casting flattery aside. 'Now, I've kept everyone from their dinner long enough. We must eat our macaroni pie before it gets cold.'

Ben stood back and Carina saw a flicker in his blue eyes. He didn't care for her audacity but she would rather annoy him than be ignored and she lifted her head and walked on. In the great hall trestle tables were set out, laden with food and flagons of wine, and Redshirts stood around talking. Catching sight of Enrico, she waved to him. He lifted his arm, then, seeing who escorted her, dropped it to his side. Guests were left to find their own places and, as soon as Garibaldi sat down, everyone followed in a disorderly scramble.

Benches scraped the marble floor and Anne Lamartine forced her way to the front. Carina was on Garibaldi's right. She hoped Ben might be next to her, but Stefan Bosco was on her other side. The general had invited Jane, too, and she looked around until she spotted her seated at a table some distance away.

There was no formality between Garibaldi and his officers as they talked together, and, when supper was over, Carina glanced down the table to where Lamartine sat opposite Ben. She watched her put a cheroot between her lips, inhaling before she handed it to him and said something that made him laugh. Pain slashed at Carina's heart. Never before had she felt inferior to another woman and she could not bear Ben's indifference.

He was behaving as if there had never been anything between them and Carina leant closer to Garibaldi so that her bare arm brushed his sleeve. Her eyes were luminous beneath their thick lashes and she gave him her rapt attention until he swung his leg over the bench and turned his back on the others. How long had she been in Sicily, he asked? What had brought her to the cause? Garibaldi spoke to her as if she was the only person in the room. No one could tell, from her bright eyes and brittle smile, the chaos raging inside. It was well known that Garibaldi liked to retire early and Carina hoped Ben noticed it was past eleven before the general stood up.

'Friends and comrades, you have given all of yourselves for your country. Seek only the glory of Italy – for the destiny of our nation is that of all the world. May we thank God for the strength to drive out the vermin who have devoured all that is rightfully ours.'

He spoke slowly, articulating each word, and Carina's eyes sought out Ben. He was leaning forward, listening attentively, and she willed him to look at her. He only had to turn his head a fraction to catch her eye, but he seemed oblivious to her presence. Heartbreak swept her and hot tears pricked her eyes. She was afraid she might give herself away before Garibaldi's next words banished everything else from her mind.

'I've been presented this evening with a poem by Miss Carina Temple. Her verses say more eloquently than I can, the emotions that are in my heart tonight. Hear them and be proud!'

Garibaldi began reading her poem and Carina forced herself to sit still. Her verses weren't meant for this! They were a personal tribute, not a public oration. For mercy's sake, the lines didn't even scan in Italian! She felt hot colour rise in her cheeks as he came to the end.

> For Unity and Freedom
> Raise high the tricolour!
> O sons of brave Italia,
> Praise be forever more!

When Garibaldi finished, there was a moment of silence. Then someone shouted 'Bravo!' and there was a loud rumbling of applause. People were clapping and stamping their feet and Garibaldi held up his hand for silence.

'I thank you, Miss Temple. You risked your life to stay in Palermo during the bombardment. We're blessed by your courage and the beauty of your verse.'

Carina didn't know where to look. Garibaldi expected her to answer. The whole room was waiting and there was a stranglehold in her throat. Not knowing what she was going to say, she made as if to stand up when a male voice pre-empted her.

'Generale, you must come at once! There's an urgent message from Messina.'

Carina thanked God for the staff officer's intervention. Without another word, the general left the table and strode towards his private apartments. He walked with his head held forward, his legs carrying his sturdy body with a swagger and she was aware of a different man, determined and ruthless, with no time for prevarication. Before he went through the door, Carina knew he had dismissed her from his mind.

Following Garibaldi's departure, guests pressed in on every side. Stefan clapped her on the back and Greta hugged her. She saw Jane trying to get through and being blocked by others. A man with a ginger moustache, who said he was from *The Times* of London, asked for a copy of the poem. Carina declined, but it was half an hour later before she could get away and by then the room was almost empty.

Tobacco smoke clung to the air and she looked for Jane and Enrico. She was desperate to go home, but she couldn't leave without saying goodnight to her friends. They were probably outside on the terrace, she thought. It was dark and cool as she stood on the steps. Carina breathed in the sweet night air, listening for Jane's voice among the masculine tones of her companions. She was about to go to her when Ben spoke at her elbow.

'A pretty poem. Well done.'

She turned to face him. There was not enough light to see his face clearly and she answered coolly, 'I'm glad you think so. I'm on my way to say goodnight to my friends. So, if you'll forgive me—'

'Forgive you for what – for flirting outrageously with Garibaldi? You certainly made an impression.'

'Really? And why do you say that?'

'Because the general is receptive as any man to feminine wiles. You can behave as you wish, but he has a reputation to maintain.'

Ben was goading her, but she refused to rise. Carina stayed silent and his hand touched her arm.

'I must talk to you alone. It's impossible here. May I call on you tomorrow?'

For the first time in the evening, relief stole over Carina. Ben was annoyed with her for flirting with Garibaldi and nothing more! She was acutely conscious of his hand on her arm, the physical connection between them so powerful his lightest touch made her tremble. If only she could take him home with her now! Once they were alone there would be no need for explanations.

'There you are, Benito!' Anne Lamartine's voice cut between them. 'I've been looking for you everywhere! I hope I'm not disturbing a secret tryst?'

Her gaze switched accusingly from Carina to Ben as she came down the steps. For all her masculine dress, Lamartine exuded sensuality and Carina wished her at the other end of the earth.

'Why don't you introduce us, darling?' Lamartine's hand dropped possessively on Ben's shoulder. 'You know any friend of Garibaldi is a friend of mine.'

'Miss Temple, may I present Madame—'

'I'm afraid I can't delay,' Carina interrupted rudely. 'Good night to you, Colonel Mavrone.'

With a withering glance at Ben she pushed past him, forcing Lamartine to step out of her way and heard her raise her voice.

'What an ill-mannered creature! And as for that poem, did you ever hear anything so sycophantic?'

Nothing would induce her to stay a moment longer. She would send her apologies to Jane and Enrico in the morning and she hastened through the hall. The tables and benches were stacked on top of each other, wax from the dying candles dripping on the floor and sticking to the soles of her satin slippers. When she came to the staircase, she ran down. As she reached the hall, Ben called down from above.

'Carina, wait!'

Carina hesitated. Why hadn't he sent Lamartine packing? The strain of the evening had left her exhausted and disappointment clouded reason. Women swarmed round Ben like flies. Why should she wait when he had Lamartine, and plenty others, to entertain him?

She could see the landau on the forecourt with Gino asleep, his head bent sideways, and hurried across the gravel. She would drive home herself, Carina decided. She hitched up her petticoats to climb onto the driving board and, with a crack of the whip over their heads, set the horses off at a canter.

Gino woke up and grabbed the headboard as the carriage skidded round a corner, narrowly missing a wall. He shouted at her that she was risking the horses' legs taking them at such a pace, but Carina did not slow down until they began to climb. By the time they crossed the piazza and trotted by the damaged church, she was calmer. Had she been unfair to Ben? She didn't think so – and one thing was for certain: he would not be permitted to call until he rid himself of that woman. They weren't at Monteleone now. If he wanted to see her then he must show her more respect.

CHAPTER THIRTY-ONE

'Signorina, there's a gentleman to see you.'

It seemed she had only just gone to sleep when Nella opened the shutters.

Carina rubbed her eyes. 'What time is it?'

'Seven o'clock, ma'am. A gentleman called earlier, but I sent him away.'

'Did he leave his name?'

'No, ma'am, not even a card.'

'Please inform him that I don't receive visitors before ten o'clock.'

'But he left his horse with Gino—'

'Then kindly ask Gino to stable his horse and instruct the gentleman to return later.'

Nella's expression implied she would rather resign than do any such thing and Carina reluctantly sat up.

'All right, then ask your husband to tell him. Where's Pietro anyway?'

'He's in the courtyard talking to the gentleman.'

'Please pass on my instructions. And I'll have my coffee while you're about it, thank you.' Carina watched as Nella scuttled out of the bedroom. What did Ben think he was doing, disturbing the household at crack of dawn? Not only was Gino obliged to provide for his horse, he was passing the time of day with Pietro! Whatever next? She wouldn't be surprised if he ordered breakfast while he was about it.

Carina had gone to bed upset and woken up fractious. She was in no mood to be hurried and it was past ten o'clock when she walked into the sitting room. Ben was sitting in an armchair, reading an old newssheet and came to his feet as she entered. He returned the newspaper to the rack and Carina noted he wore the same red shirt and breeches as the night before. She hoped he was sorry, but there was an air of confidence about him and in the way he spoke.

'The newspapers fail to give Garibaldi the credit he deserves. We were on the brink of disaster at Calatafimi – and he alone saved us from defeat. The general was accidentally hit by a rock and shouted the enemy was throwing stones because they'd run out of ammunition. It wasn't true, but he gave us the courage to make a final assault.'

Carina made no comment and walked past him out onto the veranda. Opening her parasol, she descended the steps and heard Ben's boots crunch on the gravel behind her. She walked on to where a statue of Venus presided over a stone bench scattered with cushions and sat down.

'How very enticing.' Ben glanced up at the naked goddess as he joined her. 'Do you receive all your visitors in such charming company?'

'Only those I wish to talk to in private. What brought you here at such an unearthly hour?'

'I was afraid you might not receive me after madam's performance last night.'

'You're right. Is she your lover?'

'How could you possibly think such a thing?' Ben's eyes creased at the corners as he smiled. 'A woman addicted to glory and gunpowder is hardly my type.'

She had forgotten how handsome he was with laughter in his eyes. Ben's smile melted her heart. Carina desperately wanted to believe him, but she was guarded.

'Why didn't you come to find me before now?'

'Our intelligence indicated you had gone to Naples with your family. Besides, I had a few other things on my mind. Cannon fire and nights without sleep can make a man forgetful. What other excuses can I think of?'

'That you no longer care for me?' The cloying scent of carnations filled the air and a bee buzzed close by her head. Carina waved it away. Ben thought for a moment before he answered.

'I've missed you, sweetheart. Life's been very dull without you.'

'Even in the midst of revolution?'

'Even then. I heard you were wounded in action?'

'A bullet grazed my arm. It was nothing.'

'May I see?' Carina undid the buttons of her cuff and pulled her sleeve up above the elbow. The wound had left a small scar and Ben's finger passed gently over the bruise. Then he took her hand, turned it over and pressed his mouth to her palm.

'You're an exceptional woman, Miss Temple. Has anyone ever told you so?'

Ben was about to make a declaration! For one mad, fleeting instant Carina was convinced of it. She saw the flame in his eyes and held her breath before he caught her in an embrace that sent the parasol spinning to the ground. Bending her back over his arm, he kissed her like a man starved. With her head on his lap, he slid one hand across her collarbone and his fingers dipped inside her bodice. Warm, swimming giddiness enveloped her, and Ben kissed her until the sky was no longer blue but a million different colours. When he raised his head, the light was so bright she put a hand over her eyes to shield them. Ben helped her into a sitting position and picked up her open parasol, shaking off the dust before he gave it to her.

'Shall we go inside?' His voice was hoarse and a ribbon of sweat slid down Carina's spine. There must be somewhere they could go! There were too many people downstairs and rest of the house was shut up. Ben would have to come back later when Pietro and Nella had gone home. Carina straightened the neckline of her dress. When she answered, her voice was as strained as his. 'You said you wanted to speak to me.'

'I hoped we might converse somewhere more comfortable.' Ben opened her hand, circling her palm with his fingers. 'I want to talk about the next few months. Garibaldi intends to invade the mainland while the momentum is with him.'

Carina wondered what he was leading up to. She wasn't interested in Garibaldi's plans for the future. Her only concern was for them.

'I would like to take care of you, Carina. When the army moves on, I want you to stay in Palermo.'

Carina rested the handle of her parasol on her shoulder to shade her face from the sun. From the recesses of her mind came the memory of Ben making her leave Monteleone. She had begged him to let her stay and he had been implacable. It was different now. She was an independent woman and could do as she wished.

'I'm going to ride for Garibaldi with Greta Mazzini. I'm as good a horsewoman as she is.'

'I know you are, but Greta has a husband to look out for her. Stefan's in the rear guard while my duty is to lead every charge beside Garibaldi. I can't be responsible for you.'

'I'm not asking you to be responsible. I can look out for myself.'

'The campaign ahead is far more dangerous than anything we've encountered so far. We might be defeated and driven back. You must stay in Palermo so you're safe.'

He made it sound as if it was for her sake, and happiness drained out of Carina. Moments before, she had been confident. She had even imagined Ben was going to propose. He had raised her hopes only to dash them. Enrico was wrong, she thought. Ben was the same as ever and nothing had changed. 'On what terms do you propose I stay?' She asked, breaking the silence at last.

'I hoped we might continue as at Monteleone. I'll return to Palermo as often as I can.'

'Are you asking me to be … your … your mistress?' It was a difficult word to get out. Ben wanted her, but not enough to take her with him. He needed her, but not enough to make a lasting commitment. Even if he loved her, it wasn't enough to give up his precious freedom. And if he didn't love her, what kind of woman did he think she was? Her heart told her any kind of arrangement was better than none. She must stay close to Ben. To lose him again would be unbearable, but her brain reminded her of the past. He'll make love to me and then leave, she thought. I can't let him do this to me. Where's your pride, Carina Temple?

She fought a hard, swift battle with herself and stood up.

'I'll not be your mistress, Ben. I had no choice at Monteleone. Now that I'm a free woman, I respect the code of morality that society demands.'

'You've always broken the rules and been proud of it! What's happened that you no longer have the guts to follow your instincts? "I had no choice …"' Ben's voice seared with scorn as he mimicked her words. 'You wanted me as much as I wanted you – and you still do. Damn your code of morality! Where was it when you were in my bed?'

He was so angry that Carina thought Ben might pick her up and shake her. Hot words rushed up and she flung them at him, not caring that they hurt. 'You're the one who's a coward! You don't dare to love and that's the truth! You haven't the guts to risk your wounded heart.'

They were standing so close Carina saw Ben flinch as if she had struck him. There was a flash of pain in his eyes before his lashes dropped and she turned on her heel and started back towards the house. Halfway there, she broke into a run. As she came to the steps, Ben caught up and grabbed her by the arm.

'I pledged to marry you if you were carrying my child. It doesn't appear to be the case, but I've been faithful all the same. What a bloody waste of time!'

Neither of them had noticed the two figures on the veranda. Ben released her and as Carina looked over his shoulder she saw Enrico with another man, standing under the awning in the shade. They must have heard every word and she blushed to the roots of her hair. She had forgotten Enrico was to call today and wondered vaguely who was with him. Looking back at Ben, the anger of moments before had vanished from his face. He was amused by her embarrassment and she glared at him. Then, mustering as much dignity as she could, she lifted the front of her skirt and went up the steps.

'Good morning. I'm sorry to have kept you waiting.' She sounded breathless as she held out her hand to Enrico.

Enrico saluted as Ben appeared and he touched the back of his hand to his forehead.

'I'm glad to catch up with you, Captain Fola. The general has a staff meeting at three o'clock and requests your attendance.'

Ben walked over to Carina and bowed. 'Thank you for the tour of the house and garden, Miss Temple. I shall report to General Garibaldi on the state of your property. I'll see myself out.'

With that he was gone and Carina was left speechless, staring after him. She tried to collect herself as Enrico presented his companion and then sank deep into a chair. She had no interest in the Englishman and did not trust herself to speak. Staring into the middle distance, she let the two men make conversation.

'You may recall we met at the reception last evening, Miss Temple.' Mr Barrow's voice distracted her. 'You were kind enough to say I might have a transcript of your poem.'

She remembered him now. He was the correspondent from *The Times*. She was sure she never said any such thing, but Carina was in no frame of mind to argue. She rose and went over to the bureau. Searching among her papers she found an early draft, which she gave him. It no longer mattered what became of her poem. Mr Barrow could claim he wrote it himself for all she cared! The only thing she desired was to be left alone. Pleading a headache, she took the letter for Gabriella from Enrico and then rang the bell for Petro to show them out.

CHAPTER THIRTY-TWO

She had hoped for too much, Carina thought. Ben had offered his protection and pride made her refuse. She wasn't sorry for what she had said – but she had been so sure they would be together. What was her future without him? If she refused to accept his proposition, how could they ever set things right between them?

Her mind went round and round searching for answers. If only they could talk, but Ben made no attempt to see her again. I can't stop loving him because we had an argument, she thought. War has its own rules. Who knows what might happen? Ben could be wounded or killed. I must find a way to be close to him. I've the skill and courage to ride with the Redshirts – but how is this to be arranged?

Temperatures soared during the day but when the scorching sun set behind Mount Pellegrino, sea breezes refreshed the city and life returned to normal. A steady flow of correspondence arrived from her grandmother, each letter containing one for Enrico from Gabriella.

Dearest Carina, Nonna wrote. *We were concerned when we learnt of the bombardment and glad to know you were safe on Admiral Mundy's flagship. I am most grateful to Mr Goodwin and Miss Parsons for taking care of you. As you can imagine, there is great consternation at court. The king and queen remain in Naples for now. How long they will stay, depends on Garibaldi's intentions …*

Enrico came regularly and Carina longed to ask for news of Ben, but every time she thought of him she struggled to hold back tears. I can't go on like this, she thought in despair. I have to find out if Greta Mazzini is still in Palermo. She's the only person who can help me.

The next time Enrico brought a letter for Gabriella, she rustled up her courage and asked him.

'I believe she's staying at a pensione in the centre of town.' Enrico gave her a straight look. 'Stefan's gone home to look after the farm at Calatafimi. They have an unconventional marriage, as you probably know.'

She didn't know, but Carina nodded. 'They were very kind to me. I would like to call on her. Do you have an address?'

Enrico scribbled the directions on a piece of paper and, when he left, Carina called Pietro and requested the landau be made ready.

'But it's impossible, signorina! Tomorrow is *Festinu*. The procession of Santa Rosalia is tonight! No carriages are allowed in the city.'

How could she have forgotten? The feast day of Palermo's patron saint was the most important celebration of the year. Carina asked Pietro to order a *caleffini*. She remembered Jane telling her the drivers knew every route in the city and one of them would get her to the centre.

Less than an hour later, she was in a gig and on her way. The driver told her the pensione was close to the Piazza Garibaldi and dropped her off as near as he could. From there, she would have to go on foot. There were hundreds of people milling around and a murmur of excitement ran through the crowd as the procession of St Rosalia approached.

The statue of the saint was dressed in white, placed high on a boat-shaped chariot and illuminated by a forest of candles. As she came nearer, children dashed in front of the horses to throw blossom in her path. A young woman fell to her knees in the middle of the road, bringing the procession to a halt and those next to Carina genuflected. She bowed her head and when the statue moved on everyone began to sing.

> *Notti e ghiornu farìa sta via!*
> *Viva Santa Rosalia!*
> *Ogni passu e ogni via!*
> *Viva Santa Rosalia!*

Santa Rosalia was a real person to them, Carina thought as she joined a stream of people heading towards a piazza where a band was playing. Wall brackets lit the dark alleys and she checked each door until she came to the pensione. The upper windows were open and music and laughter drifted out into the night. She lifted the heavy knocker and a housemaid opened the door and showed her upstairs. Someone was singing a Venetian barcarole and as Carina hesitated by the entrance, Greta glanced round.

'At last! I've been waiting for you every evening. Where've you been all this time?'

Greta was wearing national dress; a black jacket and red skirt adorned with flowers. Her hair was tied up in a scarf and her black eyes shining as she presented Carina to the company.

'I'm sure you all remember our distinguished poet, Carina Temple?'

There was a round of applause and Carina was introduced to the pianist, whose name she didn't catch, and a French woman called Angela Pourri. A group of Redshirts came forward and one seemed vaguely familiar.

'Our guardian angel, if I remember correctly? Max Corso at your service, ma'am,' the soldier said. 'It was a mercy you secured Enrico Fola's release.'

Carina looked at the young man with blonde hair and blue eyes. At first she couldn't think who he was. Then it came to her. He was the prisoner who had been with Enrico in the Vicaria! Max Corso was younger than she had thought, no more than twenty-five, and good-looking with regular features.

'I'm sure it had very little to do with me. When were you set free?'

'On the day Garibaldi entered Palermo. The citizens blew open the gates and stormed the prison. They attacked the guards and carried us out as heroes.'

'It was a wretched, evil place. I thank God you survived.'

'I'm fortunate to be blessed with the constitution of an ox. We heard Fola's sentence was commuted by order of Prince Scalia himself. You must have gone to extraordinary lengths.'

Carina smiled and moved on. Prince Scalia had taken to his heels with the rest of them. He could do her no harm, but the memory of that time made her shudder. She wondered how Max Corso had found out. If he or anyone else asked her, she would deny her involvement outright. Everyone in the world had a secret and this one was hers. It was the only truly worth-while thing she had done in her life and she would take it with her to the grave.

'Come on! It's time for a tarantella!' Greta exclaimed as the pianist struck up a lively tune. She had never danced a Sicilian folk dance before, but Carina found herself on the floor between Greta and Angela with a tambourine in her hand. The men danced in a circle around them, clapping in time to the music. Then it was the women's turn and she was on her feet, picking up the rhythm and clapping the tambourine on her hip and in the air as they snaked through the men. They danced in circles and spun round in pairs, the tempo becoming faster and wilder until the dance ended with a loud cheer.

They were all hot and breathless and Greta declared they must go to the piazza for an ice cream.

'This is the one night of the year that we're safe. There are no pickpockets when *Santuzza* is in town. They wouldn't dare!'

The party began heading for the door and Greta was halfway down the stairs when Carina called to her. 'Please, Greta, can you wait for a moment? I must speak to you before I leave.'

'You can't possibly go home tonight!' Greta looked up briefly. 'You can sleep my bed and we'll talk tomorrow. Now come along or we'll miss all the fun!'

When Carina opened her eyes, Greta's head lay on the pillow beside her; she was asleep. They had strolled back from the piazza in the early hours and Carina had slept in her petticoats. Her dress hung haphazardly from a hook in the wall and the smell of coffee wafted up from downstairs. A church bell was tolling and she counted to seven. She didn't want to disturb her friend, so she quietly washed and dressed, waiting until Greta stretched her arms and yawned.

Coffee was sent up and she perched on the end of the bed with a cup in her hand while Greta propped herself upon pillows.

'So, we must talk about Ben?'

'No, not at all.' Carina was taken by surprise. 'I came to ask you about riding with the Redshirts. I need to know who to speak to.'

'You should ask Ben. He has the authority.'

'He won't let me volunteer. He insists I stay in Palermo.'

'The reason Ben doesn't want you near the battlefield is because he cannot be distracted in any way.'

'So no one is distracted by Anne Lamartine?' Carina protested.

'Precisely; you are different.'

'But you don't understand! We had an argument. I refused to—'

'You refused to be left behind?' Greta drew up her knees and rested her chin on her hands. Her eyes were kind and her voice firm. 'The next confrontation is likely to be the bloodiest of the campaign. Ben wants you to stay in Palermo so you're safe.'

'And if Garibaldi is victorious, may we volunteer then?'

'I sincerely hope so. In the meantime, I must return to Stefan in Calatafimi. I've an appointment with the general this afternoon and will request he sends for us both when the time's right.' Greta curled a lock of hair round her finger and tucked it behind her ear. 'There's something I must ask you, Carina. Max Corso told me you appealed personally to Prince Scalia for Enrico Fola's release. Do you know about the vendetta between Ben and Prince Scalia?'

Carina nodded silently and felt her face stiffen as Greta went on.

'The whole world can change, but devils remain constant. A vendetta lasts until death, no matter the circumstances. You must be careful – especially if you and Ben have feelings for one another.'

She had brought the conversation back to Ben and Carina finished her coffee and put down her cup.

'I don't know if Ben has feelings for me – or for anyone else.' She answered in a low voice. 'Have you met Madame Lamartine?'

'Anne Lamartine is a vain, ambitious woman. Her quarry is Garibaldi and she'll use any means she can to stay close to him. She may try with Ben, but she won't get far.'

How can you be sure? Carina wanted to ask. She was desperate for reassurance, but in the depths of Greta's eyes she saw compassion and stayed silent.

'When Ben returned from his years of exile, he was a changed man,' Greta spoke with care. 'He had no love or trust to offer any woman. At least, I believed that was so, until I saw him with you. I was struck by your effect on him from the first day I met you at Monteleone.'

So much had changed since then, Carina thought. The young woman, brimming with the golden confidence of youth, had gone forever. Her presence at Monteleone had had no lasting effect on Ben. She had learnt that men only cared for women if it is on their terms. She had refused Ben his, and there was an ache in her heart as she looked at Greta.

'I cannot stay in Palermo when the army leave. I won't be able to endure it.'

'Then we must both be patient.' Greta slipped out of the bed and went over to the wardrobe. She searched among the clothes until she found a clean shirt. 'I take it you can ride astride?'

'I rode astride when I was young and can borrow my cousin's breeches and boots. What happens if Garibaldi's defeated?'

'He will return to Palermo and consolidate his power in Sicily. He won't be defeated in the long run.'

Ben had tried to explain all this to her, Carina thought, and she hadn't given him the chance. But Greta was to meet with Garibaldi today. She would put her name forward and it was enough to give her hope.

'Thank you with all my heart.' Carina embraced Greta as she said goodbye. 'You have no idea how much this means to me.'

'I have every idea.' A smile touched Greta's mouth. 'There may be a rift between you now – but don't give up on Ben. He needs you.'

If only that were true, Carina thought as she walked back to the piazza – and it was Ben who had given up on her, rather than the other way around. Passing through the crowd, she was cheered by the festive atmosphere and excited voices of children. Men and women were dressed in their best clothes and only black-frocked priests, fearful of Garibaldi's anti-clericalism, walked by with their heads down. At the far corner stood a line of *caleffini* and she was about to cross over when a clatter of hooves made her look round.

Two riders were coming down the street and, with a lurch in her heart, Carina saw Ben in the lead with Lamartine close behind. She pushed back into a shadowed corner as they went past and stopped by the fountain. Lamartine swept off her sombrero, laughing as she shook out her hair. Then Ben tossed a coin to a boy to hold their horses and they strolled towards a trattoria.

Carina waited until they were inside before she skirted round the other side of the piazza. Hidden behind a cab, she watched as they joined Max Corso and Angela Pourri. Max pulled up extra chairs at their table and Lamartine sat close to Ben. She took off her gloves and placed her hand on his arm.

Carina wanted to cry. Until now, she had believed that somehow she and Ben would be reconciled. Oh God, how could one ever know anything? Seeing Ben with Lamartine drove everything Greta had said from her mind. Ben had discarded her as carelessly as a piece of old rag. He could have any woman he wanted. So why choose Anne Lamartine? Had he lied about her, too, on the morning after Garibaldi's reception?

Carina scrambled into a cab and gave directions to the driver. As they set off, she leant back to keep out of sight and dug her nails into the leather upholstery. I hate him, she thought with hot violence. I hate Ben for making me feel worthless and ashamed. I wish he had never come into my life.

CHAPTER THIRTY-THREE

It was past nine o'clock and Carina's hair was wet from the bath when she went out onto the veranda. She had arrived home at midday and survived the afternoon without breaking down. Now, everyone had gone and she was alone. There was an ocean of tears inside her, but if she started to cry she might never stop. I won't let Ben destroy me, she thought. I must find the courage to live my life without him.

With all the will of her strong character, Carina told herself it was over between her and Ben and reached for the carafe. She poured a generous quantity of wine into her glass and gulped it down. Pietro had left an oil lamp on the table and she placed it on the floor to prevent it attracting mosquitoes. There was a rumbling of thunder in the distance and an electric storm was on its way. Soon it would burst over the city and cool the sweltering streets. How she longed for rain to wash away her misery!

She had not eaten all day and Carina picked at the food Nella had left before she pushed the plate aside and helped herself to more wine. Behind her, the house lay dark and still. It was stiflingly hot and she must open the door to her bedroom to let in some air. She felt giddy as she stood up and walked unsteadily along the veranda. She wasn't drunk – just a little off balance – but she forgot the lamp was on the floor and stumbled over it on the way back. Crouching down, she set it on the table and fumbled around until she found the tinderbox. She dropped the first match, but her second attempt was more successful – the flame caught light.

Carina picked up the decanter and was surprised to find it almost empty. The wine eased the pain in her heart and she needed a little more to help her sleep. Just one more glass would be enough. Leaning back in the chair, she hitched her nightgown up to her knees and stretched out her legs. There was a bird caught in the creeper on the balustrade and she could hear it rustling the leaves. She should get a stick and set it free – but there were flashes of lightening over the sea and the storm almost here. First she must clear away her supper.

The tray was so heavy Carina had to brace her arms to lift it and she would have to come back for the lamp. She was about to go in when she heard the crack of a branch near the steps, followed by the sound of breaking glass as the decanter tipped off the tray onto the ground.

Pietro had locked the gates hours ago and no one could be in the garden! One of Gino's dogs must have escaped the kennels and was prowling around looking for scraps. Still holding the tray, Carina stood barefoot amidst the shattered glass, her eyes fixed on the darkness at the top of the steps. There was a shadowy movement and then the head and shoulders of a man emerged.

'You!' Carina stared at Ben before the fright he had given her detonated a reaction. 'What the devil do you think you're doing?'

'The front door was bolted and no one answered the bell. I was obliged to scale the wall.'

Ben walked over to her and took the tray from her. Placing it on the table, he hunkered down and picked up the shards of glass, depositing them in a pile on the tray. He rubbed his hands to shake off the dust and Carina wondered why he took the trouble.

'I didn't mean to frighten you. I apologise—'

'If you had any manners, you'd have gone away. As it is, you're not welcome.'

'Calm yourself, Carina.'

There was a note of command in his voice, but Carina had seen a fruit knife on the tray. She grasped hold of it, waving it in front of his face.

'You're trespassing on private property. I don't want you here. Go away!'

'If you send me away, you'll miss what I have to say. I've an important message from General Garibaldi.'

'That's not true. You're lying—'

'Have I ever lied to you?'

Of course he had, so many times she had lost count. Her brain wasn't functioning properly and she wished she had drunk less wine. It crossed her mind that Ben might have intercepted Greta at headquarters and prevented her speaking to Garibaldi. What if he had? She would speak to the general herself and Ben couldn't stop her! There was something that was different about his appearance. For a moment Carina couldn't place what it was – and then saw he was wearing the jacket of a cavalry officer.

'Did you steal yourself a new uniform? I can't say I like it.'

'I've been given command of a cavalry regiment.'

'Why? For courting favour with Garibaldi's concubine?'

'I didn't come here to trade insults. Do you want the general's message or not?'

Carina put one hand on the back of a chair to steady herself. There was a jug of water on the table and she put down the knife, concentrating hard as she filled a glass. She drank to the last drop and hiccupped.

'Well,' she said, finally, 'what is it?'

'Garibaldi is leaving Palermo later tonight. He instructs me to inform you that he returns on Sunday and requests an audience at eleven o'clock. He has business to discuss with you.'

'What kind of business?'

'How do I know? If he wasn't so occupied with preparations for the campaign, I'm sure he'd have come himself—'

'But he sent you, didn't he? Why you and not a friend of mine like Enrico Fola?'

'I volunteered because I am leaving in the morning. I came to say goodbye, Carina.'

Ben had not come to undo Greta's work. He had come to say goodbye, no more and no less. 'Let thy servant depart in peace …' Words from her father's funeral; nonsense jangling in her head. Ben was holding out his hand and Carina stretched her arm, stiff and straight, across the table. He lifted it and brushed her fingers lightly with his lips.

'Your departure is very sudden …' It was a ridiculous thing to say, but the whole situation was ridiculous, with her in her nightgown and Ben so formal in his uniform. Carina wanted to laugh or make a joke to ease the tension, but she couldn't laugh in case she began to cry and she had to keep talking.

'Who else is coming with you?'

'I ride out in the morning with Enrico Fola and the *Cacciatori d'Etna*. All soldiers who are fit enough to fight will follow within a week.'

'I see …' But she did not see because tears filled her eyes. Ben was leaving her and they might never meet again. She had convinced herself she hated him, but now she couldn't bear to let him go. As Carina searched for words of farewell, the cicadas ceased their chatter and in that long moment, in the long, hot night, the absence of their company was deafening. Ben glanced upward and a flash of lightning turned the veranda dazzling white. There was a crash and heavy rain slammed down on her head. Ben moved so fast she couldn't think of what he was doing. He grabbed her hand, dragging her with him towards her bedroom.

Another flash ripped across the sky as Ben came in and shut the door behind him. Water dripped from his hair onto his face and he gazed about the room, his expression changing to one of surprise. Then he ran a hand through his wet hair and laughed.

'I didn't intend to confine you to your bedroom. I thought we were taking refuge in the salon.'

Carina watched as Ben shook himself, scattering drops of water onto the polished floor. He walked across the room, unfastening his jacket and slinging it over the chair. The way he moved reminded her of when they had been on the run. It was as if the storm exhilarated him, stripping away his veneer of sophistication and she eyed him suspiciously.

'I hesitate to offer advice, but you should get out of your wet clothes.'

There was devilment in his blue eyes and Carina knew her shift was soaked through and transparent. The next crack of thunder shook the glass panes in the window, but she did not move.

'Don't be alarmed, sweetheart. I'm aware you're a paragon of virtue and will leave as soon as the storm is over. There's nothing to fear.'

How casually he said the words! There was nothing to fear because Ben had another woman to warm his bed and would return to her tonight. That thought was the last thing Carina remembered clearly of what followed. His mocking tone set loose madness in her brain and she looked around wildly for an object to hurl at him. As she made a grab for a bronze statuette, Ben crossed the room and caught her in his arms.

'Get out of my life!' She beat her hands on his chest and screamed at him. 'I don't want to see you again! Never again! Never! Leave me alone—'

Carina sobbed as she gave way to days and nights of strain and Ben crushed her against him.

'Hush, Carina, that's enough.' Her wet cheek was pressed against his shirt, his fingers stroking her hair and his voice gentle. 'It's all right – be quiet now. Please don't cry, my love.'

He put his hand under her chin and tipped her head back so Carina was forced to look at him. She couldn't hide what was in her heart and the terror of losing him was plain in her eyes. Ben lifted her up and carried her over to the bed.

'Try to rest. You're exhausted. You need to sleep.'

He laid her down with her head on the pillow. As he straightened up, Carina thought he meant to leave and caught hold of the front of his shirt. Kneeling up on the bed, her arms reached up and hooked around his neck. There was no shame or pride left. She clung to him as if her life depended on it and when he tried to free himself, cried out.

'Please don't go! Not yet—'

'I don't want to take advantage of you – not in the state you're in.'

'Stay with me, please. Stay just a little while!'

'Then give me a chance to get undressed.'

Ben sat on the edge of the bed and Carina watched through half closed eyes as he stripped off his shirt. He bent down to take off his boots and when he came to her, took her shift by the hem and pulled it over her head. Streaks of lightning illuminated the room through the slatted shutters and he studied her as if he had never seen her naked before. His hands moved over her body and he kissed the corner of her mouth, his lips lingering and caressing her neck.

Tonight when he tried to leave, she had begged him to stay. Ben was a sickness in her soul and Carina longed to be soothed by the comfort of his arms. Then she thought of Anne Lamartine. Did Ben make love to her with the same tenderness? How many women were there for him? In the name of mercy, how many more beside herself?

Carina sat up. Ben had hurt her and the urge to smash the pain inside was the same impulse that made her turn on him. He reached for her shoulder and she struck out and caught him across the cheek with the back of her hand. She would have hit him again, but he pulled her down on the bed beneath him. She was saying she hated him, saying she loved him until his lips covered her mouth and the retaliation of his body obliterated all else.

Ben possessed her completely and carelessly, their union as primitive as the violence that preceded it. Never before had Carina called out her love and need for him as she did now. Their passion for each other was undiminished, stronger than ever, carrying them to fulfillment black as night and bright as the blinding light of day – a beginning and an end, like death itself.

Ben lay with his head on her shoulder, her lips touching his forehead long after the storm had passed. Carina was only dimly aware of him getting up. He must have opened the shutters for the draught, the scent of wet leaves coming into the room. He pulled the sheet up to cover her and she felt his weight compress the mattress. His hand brushed her face, wiping the damp hair off her forehead and he kissed the side of her cheek.

'Take care of yourself, my beautiful woman.'

Carina was too drowsy to speak or open her eyes and did not hear him leave. His footsteps were silent as he picked up his boots to put them on outside. Before he had gone from the room, she was asleep.

CHAPTER THIRTY-FOUR

The sun shone in a clear blue sky as the paddle steamer headed for the open sea. Hanging over the ship's rail, Carina caught sight of the schooner belonging to the famous author Alexander Dumas. The scene was so colourful it was hard to believe they were on an expedition to war. Boats in the harbour were decked with flags and crews of frigates at anchor shouted jubilantly as the old paddle sounded its horn. Garibaldi had left Palermo, taking his army overland two weeks before, and the campaign that would carry the revolution to Italy was about to begin!

Last night Carina had written to Alice, in haste:

Please forgive a brief letter. You will have heard of Garibaldi's success in Palermo. Now he plans to cross to the Straits of Messina and lead the Redshirts onto the mainland! He has recruited Jane Parsons and myself as auxiliary nurses and we leave for Messina tomorrow. We are not allowed near the field of battle and in no danger. In case I cannot write again, I will do so as soon we reach Naples …

Passing the headland of the bay, the steamer picked up speed and Carina thought of Ben. On the night of the storm she had been overwhelmed by her love for him. She didn't care if the servants talked or what they thought. Garibaldi and the revolution had changed everything. The old order had been swept away and this was a new world where everyone was free. Alice and Nonna might not agree, but one day they would understand. She couldn't worry about them now, not when they were on their way to the front.

Arriving at Garibaldi's headquarters, Carina had found Jane and another woman with him. The general was eating an orange and wiped his hands on his handkerchief before he introduced her to Jessie Mario, the wife of one of his staff officers.

'Jessie's the most important woman in my campaign. She's a political writer as well a doctor,' Garibaldi said admiringly, of the broad-shouldered Englishwoman. 'I've asked you here this morning, ladies, to request your assistance. I'm concerned that our ambulance arrangements are inadequate for a sustained military campaign. We have doctors among the Thousand but no nurses.'

'There are plenty of nurses in Palermo,' Jessie responded robustly.

'I'm not talking about Palermo, Jessie. We need medical facilities for the field,' Garibaldi answered. 'I came to fight the cause of all Italy and not of Sicily alone. The time has come for us to cross to the mainland.'

They all knew that in going ahead without explicit support from Piedmont, Garibaldi was taking a great risk. The Bourbon army was ready to defend Messina to the last man. Yet hearing him speak and meeting his calm gaze, how could they refuse? As the meeting drew to a close, the general thanked them in turn. They were almost out of the door before he called Carina back.

'Greta Mazzini tells me you're a skilled horsewoman and wish to volunteer. If Jessie can spare you, I give you my word you'll ride with the Redshirts. It will be arranged once we gain the mainland.'

She had been right to put her faith in Greta, Carina thought as they left the palace. Jane, normally so calm, was pink in the face and pressed her hands to her cheeks.

'To think we will be part of the great campaign!'

'And you'll be a second Florence Nightingale, I suppose,' Carina teased her.

'Don't be frivolous. You may prefer gallivanting about on a horse, but I'm happy to follow the example of that eminent lady.'

Since then, life had been such a bustle there hadn't been time to think or a minute to spare. Under the supervision of Jessie Mario, she and Jane collected medical supplies, rolled bandages and filled bed ticks until everything was ready to be shipped. They visited the hospital to learn first aid and Carina went to bed each night exhausted.

A confrontation between the two armies was expected any time and soon their training and preparation would be put to the test. She had written to Greta, arranging to meet her in Messina, but beneath the brave exterior lay tension and fear. No one knew what the next few days would bring and Carina was as nervous as everyone else. Pray God Garibaldi would defeat the Bourbons and Ben would be unharmed!

It was dusk when the steamer dropped anchor in a bay west of the town of Milazzo and Jane and Carina were taken by mule cart to their lodgings. They drove past fields bordered by plated cactus and as they bumped along the darkening road, Carina plied the driver with questions. He replied with grunts and she persisted until he answered, 'I don't know who's winning and I don't care.'

The man spat a piece of chewed tobacco on the floor and she could get no more out of him. They had to wait until they reached the village where Jessie Mario was waiting. The wagon drew up at an old farmhouse where she stood in the doorway, holding a lamp as they alighted.

Jessie paid their driver and led them inside. There was soup on the table and she sat down with them.

'Action commenced at first light. It's been a bloody battle. Over eight hundred of our men were killed or wounded.'

'Dear Lord, why so many?' Carina asked.

'The Bourbon army is well disciplined and performed with credit. They suffered half as many casualties as we did.'

'Then there must be a great deal for us to do!' Jane said briskly. 'Shall we start tonight or in the morning?'

'In the morning. We've set up a hospital in the Capuchin convent. The wounded will be brought in during the night.'

Jessie showed them to their quarters at the back of the house. The room was spartan, furnished with a couple of chairs and a table on which stood a basin and a pitcher of water. There was a large bed for the two of them and Carina kicked off her shoes. Without a thought for modesty, she stripped off her dress and folded it on a chair, only taking the time to wash her arms and face before she lay down.

When she awoke, Jane was already up and Carina dressed quickly. She could hear cannon fire not far away as she pinned her hair under a starched cap and then went through to the kitchen. After breakfast, Jessie outlined their duties for the day. They were to nurse the most severely wounded and assist the doctors in whatever way needed. She handed them two large white aprons with ties at the neck and waist.

'Remember all that you've learnt. You may be shocked by what you see today and must have stout hearts.'

They made their way to the square and passed by a squadron of Redshirts preparing themselves for combat. Their equipment was battered and there wasn't an officer among them, but the soldiers waved and one blew Carina a kiss before he gathered up his musket and marched away. The sight of his jaunty swagger made her proud. Jessie needn't fear they would be faint-hearted, she thought, but when they reached the Capuchin convent, her confidence left her.

Passing through shady cloisters, they came to a refectory where wounded men lay shoulder to shoulder on straw pallets. Two doctors were performing surgery on the ground and the floor was running with blood. The place was filthy and Carina ran back to fetch a mop and bucket. Some of the injured were unconscious while others groaned, clutching wounds where dried blood stuck to their torn uniforms. The dirt and stench of unwashed bodies in the blistering heat, the staring eyes and swollen tongues of the dead made Carina want to vomit. Then a hand touched her apron and she looked down to see a young soldier with blood frothing on his lips. He was mouthing soundlessly and she dropped to her knees.

'Drink please …'

'Yes. I will bring you water.'

She was already on her feet when Jessie stopped her, telling her she must go and help the doctor in her place.

'But this man is dying!'

'Then we will need his place for others. You will work with Dr Bernadotti.'

Carina was thankful that Jessie gave her no choice. How else could she have endured the horror of that day? Swarms of flies crawled over open wounds and the smell of gangrene nauseated her. No amount of training could have prepared her for the shattered bodies and faces burnt black by gunpowder. If only she could block her ears to the screams and shut her eyes as the scalpel cut into putrid flesh.

The only way to carry on was to concentrate on the task in hand. Carina cut thread, forcing it through the needle eye, and tore strips of cloth for tourniquets. With a basin of water, she took the doctor's instruments, wiped them and handed them back. As soon as one patient was attended to, surgery was performed on the next. There was no quinine and only a limited amount of iodine. Chloroform was kept for the worst cases and cheap brandy the main antidote for pain. She poured it down the throats of young men who gagged and choked. Carina held them still, trying not to look, until the doctor finished stitching up and moved on. They must have performed more than twenty operations before Dr Bernadotti took his bag of instruments from her.

'I visit the field this afternoon and will need you again this evening. Take some time in the fresh air. You must keep up your strength.'

The doctor shuffled off with the gait of an old man. Carina was exhausted but she could see Jessie cradling the head of a solider in her lap as she removed shrapnel from his neck. She could not rest while Jessie and Jane worked on. When Jane came to find her, the three women went outside. Too tired to speak, they sat sipping tea and nibbling sweet cakes brought by the monks. Dr Bernadotti returned and stirred plenty of sugar into his coffee before he drank it and put the tin cup on the ground.

'They're bringing in more casualties this evening. We don't have enough doctors to perform surgery. You're a trained doctor, Mrs Mario. You will deal with the gunshot wounds.

Miss Parsons will help you and Miss Temple will continue as my assistant.'

So the endless process of cutting and patching up began again and all the time more casualties were coming in. For those they saved, twice as many died. Orderlies with grim faces wrapped still-warm corpses in sackcloth and carried them away. There was no time to change mattresses or to provide clean straw, no time for kindness or consolation. The living, dying and dead followed each other in a morbid procession until, close upon midnight, Dr Bernadotti declared they must stop until morning.

Carina walked home with Jessie and Jane and they ate in silence. Warmed by soup and bread, they took turns to wash before they fell into bed. Carina awoke early and, afraid she might lose her nerve, set off ahead of the others. She arrived at the convent to find Dr Bernadotti already at work. He told her to clean his surgical instruments, so she sat on a stool with a bucket of water, scraping off particles of skin and clotted blood. When would this nightmare end? What good was the agony of surgery when bodies were carried off with such depressing frequency? There were only ten nurses among a hundred patients and, despite endlessly scrubbing floors and boiling bandages, death became commonplace.

Conscious only of the misery around her, Carina hadn't noticed it was getting dark when Jane came running to find her.

'Dottore, I must speak to Carina. Can you spare her, please?'

Carina was fixing a tourniquet and Dr Bernadotti did not answer. Hearing the urgency in Jane's voice, she stood up and wiped her hands on her apron. Jane's face was ashen and deadly fear went through her heart.

'What is it, Jane? What's happened?'

'Come outside with me.' Jane took hold of her hand. 'You must be brave, dear. We've just learned Enrico Fola was killed in yesterday's action.'

Carina stared dumbly at Jane. Enrico had been killed! No, it couldn't be true! Not Enrico. Oh God, poor Gabriella! She wanted to howl like an animal but Jane's grasp tightened, forcing her to listen.

'Jessie has sent for you. She needs you immediately.'

'Tell Jessie I'll come later!' Carina's self-control snapped. 'You're the one meant to be helping her, aren't you?'

Her eyes were half-blinded with tears, but she saw the distinctive jerk of Jane's chin.

'Colonel Mavrone has been brought in. He's critically wounded. Jessie wants you to attend him.'

Carina was too shocked to understand and Jane went on rapidly. 'He's in a coma. I told Jessie you're his friend. They hope Colonel Mavrone might respond to a familiar voice. She wants you to talk to him.'

Her brain swirled with panic. Enrico was dead and Ben was critically injured. He was here in the hospital! Her knees were shaking and Jane held her arm as she led her towards the cloisters. The monks had evacuated their cells to provide more space and Jessie was talking to a young doctor at the far end. They looked so serious Carina stopped, heedless of Jane tugging at her sleeve, until Jessie walked back and dismissed her with a nod of her head.

'Colonel Mavrone has been unconscious since this morning. We hope it's bruising and not bleeding in the brain. Talk to him and try to make him respond. Stay with him until I come back.'

Jessie took her to the cell where half a dozen men lay next to one another on the floor. Carina was aware of the doctor's hand on her shoulder and he indicated a figure nearest the wall.

Lifting her skirt, she climbed over the bodies crammed into the small space, and knelt down beside Ben. He lay on his back, with his jacket rolled up under his head, and blood seeped from a bandage below his hairline. His eyes were shut and his breathing so light she put her ear to his mouth. When she spoke his name, there was no reaction. Searching in her pocket for a clean handkerchief, Carina found water and squeezed it into his mouth. The liquid trickled down the side of his jaw and she put her finger between his lips. They were cold and she held his wrist and took his pulse. The rhythm was faint, but she could feel it. Ben was alive.

'It's me, Carina,' she whispered. 'I'm here to take care of you.'

A soldier lying close by called for his mother but Carina was powerless to help him. All her attention was on Ben. She kissed his forehead and tasted blood on her lips.

'Wake up, my darling. I'm with you now. Please open your eyes.'

Not a muscle in Ben's face moved as she crouched beside him and Carina lost track of time. It could have been minutes or hours later when she heard footsteps stop outside the cell. Turning her head, she saw two orderlies standing in the doorway holding a sackcloth shroud.

'There's no one for you in here,' she hissed at them.

'But we were told—'

They came forward and bent over the man lying next to Ben. To her mortal shame, Carina realised they had come for the young soldier who had called for his mother. She had shown him no kindness and there was none for him now. With rough efficiency, the men pulled off his boots and dumped him in the sacking. Then they slung his weight between them and carried him out.

'I won't let them take you, Ben. I swear they won't have you. Please, darling. You must wake up!'

Still there was no response and Doctor Calvi came into the cell with two stretcher-bearers. There was scarcely room to move, but they laid another wounded soldier down on the straw pallet. He, too, was the son, brother or husband of someone who loved him. He too would die alone with no one to comfort him or say a prayer – but not Ben! She would stay with him until he opened his eyes and his heartbeat was steady.

Carina watched anxiously as the doctor lifted Ben's wrist and placed a hand over his mouth.

'Did he respond in any way?'

'Yes. I'm sure he did.'

'Dr Bernadotti asked me to find you.'

'I can't leave. Colonel Mavrone recognised me ...'

Her voice trailed off as the doctor took her arm and helped her to her feet.

'You can come back later. Nothing will change in the next hour.'

Doctor Calvi tried to reassure her, but he was taking her away from Ben. Looking back from the door, Carina saw his eyes were still closed and when they came to the cloisters, Jessie told her to sit down. Too worn out to protest, she sat on the ground and Jessie went to fetch her coffee, returning with a Garibaldini officer.

'The women are exhausted, dottore. Is there no one else?'

'We'll stay for one more hour,' Jessie answered. 'Then we'll go home.'

'If my wife's mind is made up, I'll not sway her,' Alberto Mario conceded. 'How is Colonel Mavrone? The general sent me to find out.'

'It depends on what happens in the night. He will either regain consciousness or his brain will cease to function.'

'He knew me!' Carina lied and came so swiftly to her feet the little group stared at her. 'I must go back to him at once.'

'Dr Bernadotti needs you.'

'Someone else can assist the doctor! I'm the only one who can help Colonel Mavrone.'

'His survival depends on the will of God.' Jessie's retort was like a glancing blow. 'Please report to Dr Bernadotti immediately and take him some coffee.'

She didn't believe in the will of God! How could a merciful God permit the obscenity of this place? Blasphemous words sprang to her lips and Carina bit them back, her eyes angry and defiant.

'You can stay with Colonel Mavrone all night, if you wish.' Jessie's tone softened. 'I'm only asking for an hour of your time.'

A mug of coffee was thrust into her hand and Carina made her way to the refectory and put the coffee down beside Dr Bernadotti. She was clumsy and dropped an ice bladder pressed to an amputated arm to freeze the severed nerves.

'*Merda*, woman!' The doctor swore under his breath. 'Are you too weak to do the job properly?'

'I'm sorry ...' From then on, Carina's hands were steady. She fetched fresh swabs as Dr Bernadotti stitched the wound of a boy no more than twelve years old. He clung to Carina, crying in her arms until he fell asleep and she held his head on her lap.

'Let no one say Sicilians lack courage.' The doctor leant over her shoulder. 'I've seen greater bravery here today than on any battlefield.'

'Let no one say Sicilians lack courage.' Carina repeated his words as she walked back to the cell where Ben was waiting.

She wasn't sure she believed in God, but she prayed all the same. 'Don't let him die. Please, God, let Ben live. Please save his life,' she whispered as she peered into each cell, her footsteps resounding on the stone floor until she came across a young nurse.

'Have you seen Doctor Calvi?'

'He was here not long ago.'

'The officer in the end room? What news of him?'

'The orderlies collected a body not long ago.'

The girl had made a mistake! How could she know which cell the orderlies had visited? If someone had been taken away, it wasn't Ben. I'll see him when I look in. He will be there … Carina ran down the corridor and stopped at the last cell, her fingers clutching the rough wood of the doorframe. She waited until her eyes became accustomed to the dim light and then looked inside.

Every part of the floor was occupied and she let out a breath of relief. Unhooking the lamp, she climbed over the bodies and fixed it on a nail in the wall above where Ben lay. Nothing appeared to have changed, but something was wrong. Carina sensed it at once and instinct, stronger than fear, impelled her to look down. Where Ben had lain, a soldier with a shattered arm was stretched out with a knapsack under his head. She heard a cough behind her and cast a terrified glance towards the passage. Dr Calvi stood in the doorway and his expression told her what she already knew. In her absence, Ben had been taken from her and this man, one of the last casualties of the battle of Milazzo, had been given his place.

CHAPTER THIRTY-FIVE

Jane's face came slowly into focus. I must have fainted in the hospital, Carina thought listlessly. Then memory came back and her voice came out in a rasp.

'Is he dead?

'Try not to think of Enrico Fola.'

'Is he dead? Tell me!'

'I told you yesterday.' Jane looked puzzled and then her expression cleared. 'You mean Colonel Mavrone? No, he's not dead. He walked out of the hospital on his own two feet.'

Carina blinked, trying to take in her words. 'I thought they'd taken him away …'

'He regained consciousness and discharged himself. Dr Calvi came to tell you but you collapsed.'

The sun came through the window and relief was choked by pain. Ben had survived, but Enrico was dead. Dear, honourable Enrico. Why him of all men? Carina thought of his beautiful hands and eyes like pools of deep water. Poor darling, little Gabriella. She had known with such terrible certainty and prayed that she was wrong. Premonition was not a gift. It was an affliction and in the old days she would have been burned as a witch.

She was aware of Jane sitting with her back to the window, her needle moving in and out of the material as she repaired an apron. For a long time, neither of them spoke. Then Jane folded her mending and looked across the room.

'You're not allowed in the hospital today. I'm staying here until lunchtime. You must keep quiet this afternoon.'

After Jane had gone, Carina slept again and later felt strong enough to get up. She washed and went through to the kitchen where she found Jessie. She had come to collect oranges for the hospital and Carina helped her gather them from the larder.

Jessie pinched the oranges with her fingers, picking out the ripest. 'Head injuries are always unpredictable. Colonel Mavrone should have stayed where he was. Alberto says he's gone off to lick his wounds in private.'

Jessie's apron was full and she looked Carina in the face. 'You were right. He did recognise you. He asked Dr Calvi what you were doing in the hospital.'

Ben had frightened her out of her mind, but he was alive and Enrico was dead. Carina wanted to cry but her eyes had burned dry, her grief too deep for tears. There was so much to do in the hospital and she returned to work the next day. Every time she nursed a dying soldier, she imagined it was Enrico and her distress was fuelled by silent anger. She believed in the revolution – but too many men had died. What cause on God's earth could be worth such terrible suffering? Those who fell on the battlefield were fortunate compared to the wretches who lingered here. For that small mercy granted Enrico, Carina was grateful, but for the rest she felt only sorrow.

A week later Dr Bernadotti arrived at the hospital and made an announcement.

'General Garibaldi has negotiated the evacuation of enemy forces from Messina! All of Sicily is liberated at last! The sacrifice of our gallant soldiers has not been in vain!'

Everyone cheered the doctor in the dark refectory that afternoon. Soldiers with amputated arms and legs shouted 'Bravo!' from their straw pallets and even the weakest whispered a faint hurrah. Faces emaciated by pain brightened and men on crutches waved one feebly in the air. Garibaldi's victory lifted spirits as no amount of nursing could and, for the first time, Jessie and Carina left the hospital early.

The village was deserted and they strolled home, swinging their nursing hats by the ribbons.

'You and Jane have proved excellent nurses. I'm proud of you both.'

'Wait for us, ladies!' Alberto Mario shouted from behind them. He caught up and there at his side was Ben, with a clean bandage over his wound and a bruise like an ink stain spread across his forehead.

'We missed you at the hospital. I wanted to thank you.' Ben's gaze went from Carina to Jessie and Alberto. 'May I speak with Carina in private?'

The village square had a stone ledge along one side and Ben led her over to sit under an oriental plane with thick leaves that blocked out the sun.

'I'm very sorry to hear about Enrico.' He put his arm round her shoulders. 'He was a fine man and a brave soldier.'

Unshed tears choked her and Carina was beyond utterance. Tremors started to move up through her abdomen and down her arms. Her breath came in short, ragged gasps and Ben held her to him until the paroxysms ceased.

She sat up and smoothed back her hair, patting it flat against her head.

'Enrico was in love with my cousin,' she said, wiping a hand across her face. 'Gabriella is in Naples. Will they publish lists of casualties over there?'

'To the last name, and invent many more besides. Sadly, your cousin will find out soon enough.'

'How did Enrico die?'

'He fell in the first cavalry charge. He is buried with our other brave men who died in the battle.'

From somewhere in the distance, Carina heard the bray of a donkey and cartwheels on cobbles. It was unbearable to think of Enrico buried in a mass grave. She half expected him to walk round the corner and greet her with his quick smile. Turning her head, she noticed Ben was pale beneath his tan and touched his cheek.

'I was afraid I might lose you as well.'

'It will take more than a knock on the head to finish me off.' Ben took her hand, his fingers moving from her wrist to her elbow in long low sweeps. 'I came to know Enrico well this last month. He said you were responsible for his release from prison. He implied you even went so far as to appeal to Prince Scalia.'

Max Corso must have told Enrico, Carina thought. The risk she had taken had been for nothing and Ben must believe her because if he didn't, she would get up and leave.

'Enrico would have died if he'd stayed in the Vacaria. Prince Scalia was the only person who could save him. I know he's your enemy, but I had no choice.'

'And what did Scalia demand in return?'

'He asked me to find out Garibaldi's plans from the British Consul. As it turned out, events moved so fast he found out without my help.'

'It was a noble and brave act, Carina. There's nothing more terrible than to rot to death in prison. Enrico died with honour. I hope that may be some small consolation for your cousin.'

Ben's brooding gaze went through and beyond her. His hand stilled and Carina knew he was thinking of Alexander. They were identical twins. Alex would have been the same height as Ben with dark hair and blue eyes. Did he talk in the same way and move with the same grace? Would she have been able to tell them apart? Alexander. Monteleone. Bianca … She had suppressed her suspicions for so long, why did she have to think of Bianca Scalia now? I must ask Ben, Carina decided. We love each other and I trust him to tell me the truth. It was a delicate question and she decided to begin with Alex.

'Please tell me about your brother.'

'Alex was the steady, sensible one.' Ben's gaze came back to her. 'He was a scholar and hoped to become a teacher. He was more of a gentleman than myself. You'd have liked him.'

'Would he have approved of me?'

'I dare say he would. He had an eye for a beautiful woman – that was one weakness we shared.'

Ben let go of her hand and cupped his palm around the nape of her neck. He kissed her gently and, when he drew back, there was a glow like a small flame in the depths of his eyes.

'I couldn't believe it was you in the hospital. I dreamt you were an angel sent from heaven to collect me.'

'Garibaldi asked me to assist the medical corps.'

'Well, I'm glad he persuaded you to forget your other idea. We lost three of our best couriers in the battle.'

If she told him of Garibaldi's promise, they would have a quarrel. Ben was recovering from a serious injury and she must not upset him. How could she explain she had no vocation for nursing – that the only thing she wanted was to be with him? Bianca Scalia was put aside and she swung to a different tack.

'Stars above, Ben! How could you disappear from the hospital like that? You were at death's door.'

'Do you think I'd have survived long in there?'

Soon Ben would re-join his regiment, Carina thought. He could be taken as swiftly and cruelly as Enrico. She would rather die than be without him and this might be her only chance. She must ask him now.

'Please will you take me with you when leave?'

His eyebrows went up and Carina's resolve wavered. Ben was studying her face in that disconcerting way of his, his gaze penetrating and guarded. What else could she say? She had seen the desperate faces of women searching for names of loved ones on casualty lists and would not be one of them.

'I want to be close to those I love, not laying out their corpses.'

Ben looked down at his scuffed boots and spoke without looking up. 'I'm to lead an advance party across the Straits. Garibaldi is determined never to suffer such heavy losses again. The main army will only follow once we've secured a position on the mainland. You know I cannot take you with me.'

'Then I'll cross over with General Garibaldi.'

'You will travel with Jessie Mario and the ambulances.'

'Relief nurses arrive from Palermo tomorrow and I'm released from my duties.'

'Please, my darling, we can't go through this again.' Ben raised his head and looked at her through tired eyes. 'Believe me, there's nothing to be gained by competing with Lamartine for Garibaldi's favours.'

It was an unnecessary jibe and Carina stood up. Ben came to his feet and put his hands on her shoulders.

'War's no time to make commitments, my love.' There was both frustration and tenderness in his voice.' God willing, the

Pioneers will gain the headland successfully. I promise we will be together in Italy. Is that good enough for you?'

Everything she had fought for so long was in the balance but they must not have an argument. If Ben couldn't take her, then she had to manage this by herself. Somehow, she must find a way to follow him and soon Greta would be here to help her.

A group of people strolled into the square and caught Carina's attention because of their smart clothes. They looked like foreign tourists. One of them seemed to be pointing towards her. Then a young man detached himself from the group and began to walk across the square. He was dressed in the finest broadcloth jacket and peg top trousers Carina had seen since leaving London. As he broke into a run, her heart stopped. She forgot Ben was standing beside her and waiting for her answer. Her mind went blank as Harry Carstairs swept her up in his arms and spun her round.

'Your poem was in *The Times*! You're famous, Carrie! You've been away long enough and are free to come home!'

CHAPTER THIRTY-SIX

'You must give us your news first. We've heard nothing from England in weeks.'

Jane was insistent as they sat together on the small patio behind the house. Carina had brought Harry home and he was smoking a pipe.

'You can't imagine the brouhaha when Carina's poem was in *The Times*! Every newspaper in England covered the sailing of the Thousand. The country is infected with Garibaldi fever. He's regarded as the hero of our age! Anyone who knows him is exalted.'

How fickle people were, Carina thought. She was glad her poem had been published and more so that Jane was keeping Harry occupied. She needed time to collect herself. Harry had given her a shock and by the time she had recovered and looked for Ben, he had gone. She watched as Harry unrolled his tobacco pouch and took out a small amount, compressing it with great attention. He hadn't changed, she thought. With the addition of a top hat and cane, he might have been about to take a stroll down the Mall.

'How did you learn we were here?' Jane was inquisitive as Harry lit a match and drew on his pipe.

'Sir Oliver Temple gave me permission to enquire at the Foreign Office. Mr Goodwin advised them of your whereabouts and they passed the information on to me. I travelled with correspondents from a dozen newspapers.'

'How long do you intend to remain here?' Carina asked pointedly.

'I'll stay until you're ready to come home to England.'

Harry spoke of England as home but it was no longer her home. And why had he thought it necessary to ask for Oliver's permission? He knew she despised her uncle. Carina's foot began to tap a rhythm on the ground and Harry hurried on.

'Faith, I don't mean right away! Another sea voyage would be the death of me!'

Jessie appeared at the door to call them in for supper. She had invited Harry, along with her husband Alberto, who was waiting in the kitchen.

'One more Britisher!' Alberto declared as Harry was introduced. 'We have more foreigners than Italians fighting for our nation's freedom.'

'Now don't you start getting at Mr Carstairs!' Jessie said as they sat down at the table. 'He's a gentleman and not used to your soldierly talk.'

'Well, thank heavens he's not another journalist. I've had enough of those vultures feeding on our pickings.'

'The pen's as sharp a weapon as the sword,' Jane retorted firmly. 'The British newspapers have changed the world's view of Italy. We should be grateful to them.'

'And since when have newspaper editors won Garibaldi's wars for him?'

'Come now, Alberto, stay quiet and eat your supper,' Jessie scolded mildly as she ladled out soup. 'A full stomach will put you in better humour.'

They ate in silence for a time. Alberto polished off his plate with a crust of bread and then turned to Carina.

'I'm glad we found you this afternoon. Colonel Mavrone was most anxious to speak to you.'

'I can't think why … He seemed to have recovered well.' Carina stumbled over her words and blushed, annoyed with herself. 'Do you know when Garibaldi plans to cross the Straits?'

'The British are with him all the way!' Harry interjected. 'The Prime Minister and many others have contributed to his funds.'

'A thousand Redshirts wrapped in English banknotes!' Alberto smiled at Harry.' Garibaldi will take his decision in the next few days. Now, where's that spaghetti you promised me, Jessie?'

When supper was over, Jessie and Jane insisted Carina leave the clearing up to them and sent her outside with Harry. They drank coffee and, as Harry talked, she tried not to think of Ben.

'I'm glad you've come round to Miss Parsons. I wrote to your aunt and dare say she's relieved that you're together.'

'And why did you do that?'

'I thought it polite to tell Lady Farne I was setting out to find you.'

'Did you also inform your father? I take it he gave you his blessing?'

'Better to keep the old man in the dark. He dislikes foreigners and abhors revolution.'

His response nettled Carina. Her own father had served in the navy and met her mother when he was stationed in Sicily.

As far as she knew, Harry had never left England before and displayed an irritating superiority that was common to his kind.

'Garibaldi's campaign has nothing to do with you, Harry. You should have stayed away.'

There was a full moon and Carina saw happiness wiped from Harry's face. She didn't mean to be cruel, but his arrival was a complication she could do without. Her life with Ben was about to begin and she must explain this to Harry. It was his first night and she would talk to him tomorrow, Carina decided as she walked with him to the gate and gave him the lantern.

'I hope you've found decent lodgings. The accommodation in Milazzo may not be up to the standard you're accustomed to.'

'I've booked a pensione beneath the castle and am assured the beds are clean. Will I find you here in the morning?'

'Yes, if you're up early enough. We're handing over to the medical team from Palermo tomorrow.'

Harry held the lamp up so that its light shone down on her face. 'To be honest, Carrie, I didn't come to join the revolution. You know why I'm here—'

'Be off with you now! It's time we were all in bed.' Carina cut across him not wanting to hear his next words, her gaze following the bobbing light of the lantern until it disappeared. Harry had written to Oliver and Alice. Why hadn't he forewarned her? Was he afraid she might have stopped him? They were friends, not sweethearts! She had learnt to bat away uncomfortable thoughts, but Harry was as dogged as she was – and the sooner she told him about Ben, the better.

Disquiet scratched her as she thought of Ben. He wasn't yet fully recovered and could have a relapse. The Neapolitan navy might sink his boat. Anything might happen to him and they hadn't even said goodbye. Ben had more lives than a cat, she told herself. There was no use worrying about him, but she wished with all her heart Harry had not come. She was bound to make him unhappy. If only she could pack him off home on the next boat for England.

CHAPTER THIRTY-SEVEN

Two days later, with Carina free of nursing duties, Harry hired a pony and trap. They drove to visit Garibaldi's army, bivouacked on the beaches where the Redshirts were preparing for the invasion of the mainland. The men's faces had the same determined look Carina had seen in Palermo. They were scorched in the sun by day and chilled by sea mists at night but morale was high for the Pioneers had successfully crossed the Straits. Ben was safe and Carina longed to be with him.

'A penny for your thoughts.'

Ben was so strongly in her mind, Carina did not hear Harry.

'I said, a penny for your thoughts.'

She was wearing a wide straw bonnet and Carina fiddled with the bow as she turned her head. 'I must talk to you, Harry. Please stop the trap so we can speak?'

'I told you already; I don't want to know about the last six months. You've done your penance and now it's over.' Harry flicked the reins on the pony's back so she broke into a trot. 'I hope Garibaldi is in no hurry for I've no stomach for bloodshed.'

'Then why don't you go home? You can tell your friends in White's how you served in Garibaldi's campaign without ruining your best coat!'

Harry's mouth twitched and his cheeks went red. She should be ashamed of herself, Carina thought – but if only he would listen to her! She had tried to tell him about Ben so many times. Harry regarded her sojourn in Sicily as a punishment – when it had been the best time of her life. His refusal to let her speak maddened her. When he dropped her off in the village without giving her another opportunity, she made up her mind. Harry was afraid of what she had to say but it could be put off no longer. This evening, without fail, she would tell him she was in love with Ben. She would sit him down before supper and make him hear her out.

'There you are, my friend!'

Carina heard a familiar voice and saw Greta Mazzini running down the road. She wore a red tunic that reached below her knees and was out of breath as she wrapped her arms round her.

'I've been looking all over for you. I couldn't believe it when I received your letter. Just imagine, Carina Temple as a nurse!'

'I wasn't as bad as all that – but not so good either!' Carina laughed. 'I'm so glad you're here. Is Stefan with you?'

'Yes.'

'Come back to the house and I'll tell you everything.'

It made her happy to be with Greta and, as they walked the short distance, Carina told her about the meeting with Garibaldi and the horrific casualties after the battle of Milazzo. Greta had heard about Enrico and held her hand as they spoke of him. There was a horse tethered outside the farmhouse and they went inside to find Alberto Mario standing by the sink, pouring water from a pitcher.

'I've just ridden from Messina and am dying of thirst.' Alberto gulped down the water and refilled his glass. 'I hoped to catch Jessie on my way to meet Colonel Bavari at the barracks.'

'Then I'll make some coffee.'

'No, thank you – I'm already late. Garibaldi leaves tonight and I'm sailing with him. Please will you tell my dear wife?'

'And when do we follow?' Carina grasped Alberto's arm. 'The general promised us we could ride as couriers. We're waiting for his summons.'

'What are you talking about?' Alberto's gaze went to Greta. 'Miss Temple is a nurse—'

'Garibaldi gave me his word,' Greta replied with a winning smile. 'He won't be surprised, but he may need reminding.'

'I'll come with you now unless you speak for us!'

'Then it appears I have little choice,' Alberto Mario said, removing Carina's hand from his sleeve. 'Does Jessie know about this?'

'No, but I'll tell her as soon she gets back.'

'I'll pass on your message.' Alberto strode towards the door. 'When you arrive in Reggio, report to staff headquarters.'

'So we'll ride with the Redshirts, after all!' Greta grinned as he went out. 'It's lucky Alberto Mario's used to strong-minded women! And now I must go and find Stefan. Shall we meet on the ferry tomorrow?'

Greta took care not to mention Ben, Carina noticed as she waved her off. When Jessie and Jane came home, she told them Alberto's news and her own plans. Jane raised her eyes to Heaven and Jessie said she was sorry to lose her, but they didn't try to change her mind. Too animated to go to bed, the women talked late into the night until, one by one, they fell asleep around the kitchen table.

They were woken at dawn by a loud banging on the door.

Rubbing the sleep out of her eyes, Carina went to open it and found Harry on the doorstep, dressed in plaid trousers and green frock coat.

'Garibaldi's landed in Italy! Four thousand Redshirts sailed overnight and are camped near Reggio. I'm travelling with the newspaper reporters. I hope victory will be secured by the time I get there!'

There was no time to delay. Jane was to accompany the ambulances the next day, while Jessie and Carina were in the advance party. They spent the morning loading bandages, medicines and surgical equipment on to a mule cart and, with her bag containing Paulo's breeches and boots, Carina sat between Jessie and the driver as they lumbered down the dusty road to the beach.

The trawler requisitioned as a ferry was packed to the gunwales and Greta had saved a place for them in the stern. Once their precious cargo was stowed, Carina sank down on a pile of sacking with her grip bag under her knees. They had been on the go since dawn, but she was too excited to be tired. Greta had brought a basket of food. She handed out cheese and bread with slices of watermelon and Carina's gaze travelled over the crowded deck. Anne Lamartine was standing in the bow, accompanied by an officer of the *Cacciatore d'Etna*. As the boat moved away from the beach, she took off her hat, waving it above her head and shouting, 'Viva Garibaldi! Viva Italia!'

The Frenchwoman's long hair flew out behind her like a banner and everyone on board took up the chant, apart from Carina. Gradually the singing died away and the passengers became quiet, all eyes fixed on the opposite shore. Carina made out a long, sandy beach. A flotilla of fishing boats rowed out to greet them and, within an hour, the passengers were disembarked and the trawler set off to collect its next load.

Greta left them to meet up with Stefan and, as their supplies were being loaded onto a wagon, news came through that Garibaldi had taken Reggio. The Redshirts had entered the town by night and, after an hour of ferocious hand-to-hand combat, the enemy had surrendered. The bells were ringing when they arrived and an ecstatic crowd was out on the streets. As Carina alighted, two boys caught hold of her hands and dragged her into a dance. She lost her bonnet and would have been swept away, if Harry hadn't appeared and pulled her free. He retrieved her hat and Carina tucked it under her arm.

'Isn't it wonderful? This is what it was like after the liberation of Palermo.'

'I have to say the Latin temperament is too ebullient for my taste.'

'Oh, Harry, don't be such a dry stick. Don't you want to join in?'

'I'd prefer supper and a good night's rest.'

For all his assumed diffidence, Harry's eyes were bright and when they gained the corner of the square, he clapped Alberto Mario on the back.

'Well done, sir! A tremendous victory!'

'Indeed it was.' Alberto managed a weak smile. 'Now, Miss Temple, you're to come with me. Garibaldi is expecting you.'

'You're not serious! You can't let Carina consider such rashness.'

Not Harry too, Carina thought with a ripple of annoyance. Taking no notice of him, she turned to Jessie. 'May I borrow your husband for ten minutes?'

Jessie offered to keep her bonnet and Carina followed Alberto down the main street to where Garibaldi had taken lodgings at the edge of town. Two soldiers guarded the entrance and stood to attention as they saluted Alberto.

'From now on you're on your own. Good luck.' Alberto cast a glance over his shoulder as he headed back. 'What's Jessie supposed to do with Mr Carstairs in your absence?'

'Tell her not to worry about him. Harry can look after himself.'

The guards moved aside and Carina did not hear Alberto's reply. The door swung open and she stepped into a smoky kitchen with a low ceiling. Ben standing by a window and Garibaldi sitting at the table with Lamartine leaning over his shoulder. A newspaper was spread open and he was reading aloud. When he caught sight of her, he stopped and stood up.

'I'm glad to see you, Miss Temple. You are most welcome. Come in, come in.'

The general introduced her to his senior members of staff and Carina recognised the names of the gallant men who had fought at Calatafimi and Palermo, the heroes of Milazzo and Reggio. It was beyond her wildest dreams to be among them but when they came to Ben, he bowed and turned abruptly away. *I should have told him in Messina*, Carina thought with sudden misgiving. *He's angry because this isn't what he planned. I should have been patient and waited.*

Garibaldi indicated the chair next to his own and as she sat down, Carina met Lamartine's hostile stare.

'Well, what a surprise.' The Frenchwoman said, throwing back her hair, 'When did you arrive, Miss Temple?'

'I travelled from Messina on the same boat as you, along with Jessie Mario who's in charge of the ambulances.'

'We've no need of your rags and plaster now! Isn't that so, Generale? From now on our progress will meet with no resistance.'

Garibaldi leant forward, absorbing himself in the broadsheet, and Lamartine pitched her voice higher. 'How will you occupy yourself? Are we to be favoured with more of your charming poetry?'

'I'm here to ride with General Garibaldi and the Redshirts to Naples.'

Garibaldi put down the paper and everyone stopped talking. Carina was conscious of Ben watching her from where he stood by the window. There was a moment of suspense before the general answered. 'I gave you my word in Palermo and I intend to honour it, Miss Temple. You will ride in the company of my personal bodyguard.'

'But she has no experience—' Lamartine exclaimed.

'Great courage is required for nursing our wounded soldiers.' Garibaldi interrupted her mid-sentence. 'Miss Temple is an excellent horsewoman. I pray no more blood will be shed between fellow Italians, but her training can only be a benefit. We leave at three and I suggest we now retire.'

Garibaldi rose, the two women flanking him on either side, and spoke to Carina first. 'I propose Miss Temple stay here as my guest tonight. I'm sure Colonel Mavrone will make the necessary arrangements for you, *chere madame*.'

He made the announcement as if she had already given her assent and Carina felt colour rush into her cheeks. Ben can't leave me here, she thought wildly. He knows I want to be with him not the General. Why doesn't he say something? Her eyes searched his face, but Ben ignored her appeal. There was a hard line to his mouth and he looked her over briefly before turning to Lamartine. 'Shall we go?'

Garibaldi had foisted Ben with Lamartine while she had no choice but to stay here! The implications of spending the night with Garibaldi became clear and Carina's gaze bored into Ben's back as he went out of the door. Too late, she understood why he warned her not to compete with Lamartine. Garibaldi was a man who took whatever was on offer and that was how her eagerness had been perceived. She had disappointed him once, at the reception in Palermo, and he would be incensed when she did so again. But that was nothing compared to what Ben must be thinking at this moment!

Had she learnt nothing in all this time? It wasn't her fault. Ben should have insisted she went with him! Instead, he had abandoned her and now matters were beyond her control. The kitchen emptied, and when everyone had gone, Garibaldi led her up a narrow staircase. Carina was in such a panic she stumbled and he gave her his hand. They reached the top and a figure in a nightcap shuffled onto the landing.

'This is my manservant, Basso. He'll give up his bed for you tonight. He is used to sleeping on my floor.'

Carina was too distraught to feel any kind of relief. Ben would think she had deliberately set out to secure the general's attention when it was the last thing on her mind. He would be furious. There was a suffocating feeling in her throat and she did not answer.

'Try to get a good night's sleep.' Garibaldi stroked one side of his moustache as he looked at her. 'Thank you for saving me from Madame Lamartine this evening. Don't worry, my dear. Colonel Mavrone will come to his senses by the morning.'

As he lifted her hand to his lips, Carina supposed Greta must have said something to him. If he knew about her relationship with Ben, then he should have sought his permission beforehand! Garibaldi was inspirational, charming and utterly ruthless. He had manipulated them all to his advantage – but he didn't know what Ben was like and anxiety left her speechless.

'Basso will provide you with the uniform of my bodyguard in the morning.' Garibaldi's gaze was calm and unrepentant.

'Don't be concerned, Miss Temple. No one will question your honour when you ride at my side into San Giovanni tomorrow.'

Carina stayed awake so long worrying, she had only just fallen asleep when Basso woke her. Stiff from lying on the narrow pallet, she stretched her arms to ease her cramped muscles. Basso brought her warm water, clothes and a comb. She put on Paulo's boots and breeches and a red shirt with a belt and holster. Then she tugged the comb through the hair and tucked it under the distinctive cap of Garibaldi's bodyguard. She packed her clothes and gave her bag to Basso before going downstairs to join Garibaldi and his officers.

Sitting round the kitchen table drinking strong coffee, she listened as they planned their strategy for the day. Ben was not present and Lamartine only made an appearance as they walked down the street to mount up in the square. Carina was allocated a sturdy cob and was adjusting the length of her stirrup leathers when the Frenchwoman rode up beside her.

'A word of advice, if I may?' Carina made no reply and Lamartine nudged her horse closer. 'All men are bastards. Don't ever expect them to be faithful. They're all selfish bastards – to the very last one of them.'

With that, she touched her spurs to the horse's flanks and rode off. She should know, Carina thought – but to whom was she referring? Had she been with Ben last night? The thought made her feel sick. Garibaldi said Ben would come to senses by this morning, so where was he? Catching sight of Greta, she rode over to her.

'I hoped to find you with Garibaldi yesterday evening.'

'Stefan preferred to keep away. We stayed in town and dined with your friends.'

There was no time to find out more for they were off. With Garibaldi at their head, the cavalcade left Reggio while its citizens slept. Once the town was behind them, they headed inland, riding in single file through terrain bleached bare by heat and lack of rain. The sun came up, turning the landscape blazing white and they had been in the saddle for over three hours before Garibaldi reined in.

The general stood in his stirrups and put his spyglass to his eye to survey the layout of the land. Carina saw a fortified town by the sea with encampments along the beach. Columns of their own infantry, who must have marched during the night, were strung out in battle formation and as close to the enemy as they could get. No one spoke until a plume of dust rose from the road. The main body of cavalry was approaching and when Garibaldi gave the signal, they began their descent, slowly at first and then at a canter as the general galloped ahead.

Garibaldi's grey horse and red poncho made him stand out and Carina watched nervously as a volley of shots from the battlements of San Giovanni exploded around him. Seemingly indifferent to danger, he dismounted and climbed onto a rock, shouting to his men not to return fire. The general stood there alone, a dramatic and formidable figure, showing himself to five thousand Redshirts as they swept up the coast.

In their black hats with bayonets and daggers in their belts, they looked like an army of bandits, Carina thought as she followed the others to take shelter behind rocks. Bullets whistled overhead and black canister shot rained down so she pulled her neck scarf over her nose and mouth. Her instructions were clear; she must stay close to Garibaldi at all times. She was ready to mount up when, in front of her, she saw an infantryman lying wounded and unconscious on open ground.

Tossing the reins of her horse to an officer nearby, Carina grabbed a medical bag and ran forwards. A shell exploded, covering her with earth and grass as she ducked and knelt beside the injured man. She wound a tourniquet round his thigh, using her teeth to secure the knot, then beckoned to the men behind her. As the soldier was dragged to safety, she dashed back to the rocks. Enemy fire began to slacken and Carina counted time between the volleys until they stopped altogether. She stood up and spoke to the captain who held her horse.

'What's happening?'

'Garibaldi's negotiating a surrender. You're meant to be with him, aren't you? You'd better hurry up!'

Looking around, Carina saw the other members of the bodyguard had gone. The field was aflame with Redshirts and Garibaldi could be anywhere among them! She had forgotten her first duty and as they cantered down the hill, the captain shouted to her. 'Better stick closer to the chief from now on!'

They had reached Garibaldi's entourage and Carina saw him sitting cross-legged on the ground, smoking a cigar, as relaxed as if he were on a country picnic. He gestured to her to join them and one of the men handed her a water skin, which she tipped into her mouth. Succulent peaches and slices of black bread were passed round and they watched as the gates of the town opened. A small detachment of Bourbon officers marched up the hill towards them. They looked uncomfortable, sitting on the ground in their gold-braided uniforms, and one of them made a long speech.

Garibaldi sat in silence, puffing on his cigar until the senior officer demanded the Redshirts withdraw.

'I can make you prisoners or push you into the sea!' the general's voice rang out. 'You may return home in defeat or retain your rank and serve under my flag. The choice is yours, but I'll not hold back all day.'

The enemy could not hope for a conditional surrender, but went on blustering until Garibaldi pulled his hat down and gave an ultimatum.

'I never make bargains and I refuse your offers on any terms. You have twenty minutes before I attack.'

He took out his watch and the Bourbon officers scrambled to their feet. They hurried back towards the town and Garibaldi shouted for his mount. His mood changed in a lightning stroke and Carina ran to her horse and vaulted onto its back. With his bodyguard behind him, he galloped down the hill, cavalry and infantry closing in on all sides and brought them to a halt close to the gates.

The horses snorted and stamped and Carina's heart beat faster than the seconds ticking away. Her gaze scanned the high castle walls and she saw a white flag hoisted on the battlements. A loud cheer came from the ranks of the Redshirts and was echoed from inside the walls. Precisely twenty minutes after he had given his ultimatum, the garrison of San Giovanni surrendered and Garibaldi took the town without firing a shot.

CHAPTER THIRTY-EIGHT

She had been born for this moment, Carina thought as she rode into San Giovanni. Her heart overflowed with pride for the men who had given their lives so that Italy might be free. The sacrifice made by Enrico and many others had achieved far more than unity. It had broken the bonds of slavery forever.

All the same, she was alert as she rode close behind the general. The Bourbon soldiers looked wretched, smoking cheap cigars and spitting into the gutters, but they were still armed. Carina's hand rested on the stock of her revolver and the bodyguard hemmed him in until they reached the centre of the town, where Garibaldi rode forward and spoke from the saddle.

'Soldiers, you too are the sons of Italy and are at liberty! Anyone who wishes to join my army may apply to General Cosenz. Those of you who want to go home may do so.'

This unhoped-for clemency was too much for the defeated men of King Francis. Their reaction was spontaneous. As they threw down their rifles and rushed towards the general, Carina thought they meant to pull him from his horse. She drew her gun to fire over their heads and then saw they were kneeling and trying to kiss his boots. Doors and windows were thrown open and people poured into the streets, cheering and shouting as they crowded around him.

Mothers held up their children to be blessed and an old woman dressed in black limped past with tears pouring down her cheeks. '*Il nostro gesu Christo!*'

'Not quite … but it makes a change,' a Genoese officer who rode beside Carina remarked drily. 'Last week they called him the Devil Incarnate. Garibaldi won't want his sanctity impaired by such earthly beings as a bodyguard, so we'd better make ourselves scarce. If we don't find stabling in the next hour there'll be none to be had.'

He was right, Carina thought as they rode up the narrow streets, making their way against a flowing tide of people. This was Garibaldi's victory and his moment of triumph. There would be time later to offer him her congratulations. She twisted her neck, looking for Ben. She hadn't seen or heard of him all day. The Redshirts had suffered minor casualties, but she would have heard if he was injured. There was no sign of Greta or Stefan either and she hoped he was with them.

The captain negotiated a price for livery and invited Carina to join him for supper in the square where the patron gave them a front table. His wife took her inside to wash and she wiped her face and scrubbed her hands, rolling up her sleeves to scrape off dirt and pieces of shot from her arms. It was stiflingly hot and she shook out her hair and tucked her cap into her belt. Then she went back to the table where two more members of the bodyguard had joined the party.

Spicy pasta was washed down with red wine. The food and company eased her fatigue, but Carina was restless. More than once she turned in her chair to search for Ben. The square was heaving with people, but he was tall enough to stand out and she couldn't see him anywhere. Instead, her gaze alighted on Harry. He cut an eccentric figure in his green frock coat among the ragged uniforms of the Redshirts and Carina stood up and waved.

Harry saw her and came straight over. His face was flushed and his voice too loud. 'Where were you last night? I thought I'd never see you again.'

'There was no need to worry.'

'We expected you to come back. I waited up until daybreak.'

'I stayed the night at Garibaldi's headquarters.'

'Is it a habit of the general's to offer hospitality to single ladies?'

'Please keep your voice down!' Aware of her companions, Carina tried to calm him. 'I'm a member of the general´s body-guard. There are other women besides myself.'

'But not many who share his lodgings overnight!' Harry made no attempt to lower his voice.

'Well, now you've found me, why don't you join us?'

'I need to talk to you urgently. You must come with me this minute!'

Harry was insistent and Carina apologised to her comrades, trying to gather her strength as she left the table. Harry took her by the hand pulling her along. The brightly lit square was left behind and they walked through dark, narrow streets until they came to the town gates. There was no one about and through the archway Carina saw the coastline of Sicily with the setting sun tipped on the horizon. On any other occasion the view would have been spectacular, but she was alarmed by the wild look in Harry's eyes.

'This may be the last chance we have to talk – that's if you carry on as you are—'

'I thought you were coming to Naples!'

'There's something I must say to you, Carrie. I should have told you long ago.'

Carina's eyes went sharply to Harry's face. She knew what was coming and threw up her hands in an attempt to stop him.

'I'm in love with you! Always have been but never had the courage to tell you until now.'

'Don't! You don't know what you're saying!'

'You could love me – I know you could, if only you'd give me a chance.'

'But I do love you, Harry. You're my oldest friend.'

'I don't want your friendship. I want you to be my wife!'

Harry took her hands in his and bowed his head. His grip was so strong Carina thought he might break her fingers.

'You're hurting me!' Her voice lifted in desperation. 'I've tried to explain so many times! I love someone else—'

'I don't care what you've done.' Harry's arms went round her. 'You've had your fill of adventuring, darling. Come home and marry me before I lose you to General Garibaldi or anybody else—'

'I'm afraid that's out of the question, Mr Carstairs.'

The sound of Ben's voice gave Carina such a fright that she let out a cry. She wrenched herself from Harry's embrace as Ben emerged from the shadows. He walked towards them and did not favour her with a glance.

'You see, Miss Temple is already betrothed – to me.'

How she collected her wits Carina didn't know. Harry was staring at her, his eyes glazed with shock and Ben's tone was demonic.

'You may deny our betrothal, Carina. But I hope you have the honesty to admit to Mr Carstairs you're my mistress.'

Harry had gone white, his mouth tight beneath his moustache and his expression was so stricken, Carina thought he was going to faint. She reached for his hand and he flung her aside with such force she fell on her knees. With his arms by his sides, his hands balled into fists as he looked down at her.

'Is this true? Are you this man's mistress?' he demanded in a cracked voice.

The lines on Harry's forehead and around his mouth narrowed as he battled to keep control. Yes, she would tell him Ben was her lover! She was desperate for Harry to know – but not with Ben standing over her, forcing her to confess. The words stuck in her throat and Harry's eyes slid away. He turned on his heel and stumbled towards the shelter of the streets. When he reached them, he clutched at the walls like a blind man. As he disappeared from sight, Carina leapt to her feet and turned on Ben in fury.

'How could you be so cruel? Who do you want to hurt, Harry or me? Which of us do you hate the most?'

'Mr Carstairs has a right to know the truth.'

'I was going to tell him—'

'I'm not surprised he's so upset.' Ben stemmed her words. 'I couldn't credit the way you pursued Garibaldi yesterday. Oh, the sweet poison of a woman's charms ...'

'I didn't know he would ask me to stay. I came to find you!'

'It was perfectly obvious what you were after.'

'Garibaldi behaved impeccably—'

'Did he now? How very disappointing for you.'

Carina could feel the barely controlled violence in Ben. The steely glint in his eyes indicated how far he might go, but never in her life had she lacked courage. Not once, in all the time she had known him, had Ben admitted he was wrong. He hadn't declared openly he loved her as Harry had done! Who did he think he was to defame her? She wanted to hurt him as much as he had hurt Harry and her voice filled with venom.

'You said no commitments! Well, you needn't have bothered! I never belonged to you and never will. It was lust – not love – that drew us together!'

Ben sucked in his breath and the side of his lip curled down in disgust. Carina saw in his eyes the same contempt she had witnessed before. In that instant she hated him. She hated him with a rage that made her want to smash his face with her fists. As she struck out, he caught her by the wrists and twisted her about. Carina kicked at his shins with her boots, shouting and swearing, as he pushed her ahead of him. When she dug her heels into the cobbles and threw her weight back, he jerked her arm painfully, not caring if he hurt her. This wasn't the man she loved! She was at the mercy of a rough and cruel stranger. What did Ben mean to do? Where was he taking her?

'I've arranged accommodation for us outside of town,' he answered as if she had spoken aloud.

With only the moonlight to guide them, Ben made her walk in front until they came to a house lit by red lanterns. The windowpanes were stained scarlet and above the door was a sign: *Senora Vacavi's Establishment*. There was a piano thumping inside and, through the thin net curtains, Carina glimpsed soldiers with scantily dressed girls. Ben had brought her to a brothel and her voice broke with rage.

'How dare you bring me here?'

'If you're too tired to walk, I'll carry you inside.'

'I'm not going into that place!'

'Tonight, for once, you'll do as you're told.'

'I won't go in, do you hear?' Carina shouted. 'If you try to force me, I'll scream the place down! I hate you ... you bastard!'

'And a bastard's what you deserve, Carina – not a great man like Garibaldi, nor even a pretty gentleman like Mr Carstairs.'

'Damn you, Ben Mavrone! You're a famous liar!'

'Leave it now, both of you, please!'

Greta Mazzini's voice came out of the night and Carina flinched in surprise. Ben released her and Greta stepped from darkness into the garish light. Carina saw a revolver holstered at her side and stared at her in bewilderment. How could Greta be here?

'Stefan's found lodgings. You're staying with us tonight. He's waiting with a wagon just over there.' Greta faced Ben, her hand resting on the stock of her gun. 'Shall we go? It's been a long day.'

'I'm sure Carina's grateful for your hospitality, but I must decline.'

'I'm sorry, Ben, but you're coming with us.'

Greta's tone was uncompromising. Carina glanced at Ben and saw the frightening glitter gone from his eyes. For a time the three of them stood in silence. Then he shrugged and set off in the direction indicated.

It was inconceivable Ben could be made to walk at gunpoint by his best friend, Carina thought as he led the way along a narrow path beneath the walls. Greta walked directly after him while she trailed last. When they came to the road, Stefan was waiting and squeezed her hand as he helped her into the back. Ben climbed up beside him and Greta on the driving board. They headed away from San Giovanni and down a bumpy track to a farm building, waiting outside while Stefan stabled the mule. As they went into kitchen, Greta unloaded her gun, dropping the bullets into her pocket.

'Carina will sleep in my bed tonight. You can share with Stefan or sleep here, Ben; whichever you prefer.'

The smell of cigar smoke drifted upward as Carina followed Greta up the stairs and closed the bedroom door. She undressed, leaving her clothes on the floor, and slipped into bed before Greta blew out the candle.

'How did you know?' she whispered in the darkness.

'Stefan was with Ben all evening. When Ben followed you and Mr Carstairs, Stefan came to find me. We were afraid this might happen.'

'What are you saying?' Carina was too dazed to comprehend her meaning.

'We couldn't let Ben do something stupid. We're too fond of you both.'

'Oh, Greta, Ben was brutal to Harry. And to me. I couldn't believe it of him.'

'Perhaps it was the only way for Mr Carstairs to accept the truth.'

'He frightened me. I thought Ben had gone mad.' Tears started in Carina's eyes and Greta's arms went round her.

'Sicilian men are driven mad by jealousy. Why else do we have so many crimes of passion in our country? No Sicilian will let another man near the woman he loves.'

'But I'm not his woman and he doesn't love me.'

'That's where you are wrong.'

Greta kissed her on the cheek and lay down. Carina was dropping with exhaustion, her heart numb with pain. Nothing made sense anymore. She must wait until morning and then ask Greta what to do. Greta understood Ben far better than she did. Thank God for her this evening. Thank God for Greta and her good friendship.

White clouds scudded across a blue sky and Carina could hear the tinkling of sheep bells in the distance. The house was quiet when she woke up, so she assumed the others must have left already. Near the basin she found a note from Greta saying there was coffee in the kitchen and they would return later.

Had Ben stayed here overnight, she wondered, or had he walked back to San Giovanni?

Carina tried to isolate in her mind the mistakes they had both made. She had failed to believe Ben when he gave her his promise. She was too impatient and Ben too quick to condemn her. She had underestimated Garibaldi and Ben had believed the worst of her. Hatred was the counter side of love, but it was Ben's capacity for cruelty that hurt the most. He had wanted to humiliate her and would have done so if Greta hadn't intervened. She still loved him, but the darkness in Ben was as impenetrable as the darkness of Sicily itself. How could they go on after last night?

First things first. She would have something to eat and then walk to town to collect her horse and find Greta and Stefan. She must report to Garibaldi's headquarters and was bound to run into Ben. She wouldn't have the courage to face him unless they were with her. Carina dressed and noticed that her holster was empty. She couldn't remember where she had left her gun, but it must be in the house somewhere. She picked up her boots and carried them down the narrow staircase.

'Good morning. Did you sleep well?'

Ben's voice startled her and Carina looked around the kitchen. He was alone and she sat down at the kitchen table without answering. As she put on her boots, Ben poured coffee into a mug and placed it in front of her, along with freshly baked bread he must have brought back with him. Through the open door Carina saw his horse unsaddled and tied to a rail in the shade. Ben had been waiting for her.

'Stefan and Greta dropped me in town early,' Ben said, tipping his chair back in the usual way. 'I called on Harry Carstairs and asked him to accept my sincere apologies. I said I was drunk and my allegations were totally unfounded.'

Carina took a sip of coffee. It was so bitter she almost spat it out. She could not rage at Ben now, but nor could she bring herself to meet his gaze.

'Did he believe you?'

'He said he hoped never to set eyes on me again. He asked me to leave before he had me thrown out. I don't blame him.'

'What do you want, Ben?'

'I want to say I'm sorry. My conduct last night was unforgivable. There was no excuse.'

Her revolver was lying on the table. Ben picked it up and Carina watched as he broke it open. 'So, she took your bullets too. Never let it be said Greta Mazzini is not thorough. You'll need to get more ammunition.'

He put down her gun and Carina lifted her head to look at him. Ben was unshaven and there were dark shadows under his eyes. He hadn't slept, she thought and waited for him to go on.

'If Harry Carstairs proposes again, you should accept his offer. I was mistaken in my opinion of him. He will make a good husband.'

'I hardly think you're qualified to offer advice.'

The ghost of a smile touched Ben's lips and then faded. Carina dipped the roll in her coffee and chewed it slowly. She was glad of the breeze coming through the window and took her time.

'What came over you, Ben?'

'I was jealous and lost control.' Ben ran a hand through his hair, pushing it off his forehead. 'I'm not a good man, Carina – not even a half decent one like your friend. I've hurt too many people.'

Carina studied the coarse grain in the wood of the table. It might help Ben to damn himself, but it wasn't enough for her to forgive him and soft anger stirred inside.

'How could you be so vile? What were you thinking?'

'I was thinking you were a beautiful flirt who'd stop at nothing to get what she wanted. Me, Garibaldi, riding with the Redshirts – that it was all a game to you before you returned to your safe life in England. The fact I was wrong makes no difference.'

The low note in his voice brought Carina's head up and Ben leant forward and put his elbows on the table.

'We cannot change the nature of our souls. Even you, with your dogged persistence, won't succeed in that endeavour. A better man than myself would have let you go long ago. Lord knows, I tried—'

'I've one question,' Carina interrupted. 'Why are you jealous of Harry?'

For a long moment, Ben said nothing. When he finally answered, Carina sensed the effort it cost him.

'Harry Carstairs can give you everything you deserve. He'll make you happy and I will not. The time has come for us go our separate ways.' Ben paused and drew a long breath. 'I hope one day you can find it in your heart to forgive me.'

The finality in his voice hit Carina like a blow to the stomach. How much easier to fight in hot blood than with cold logic! They had both asked themselves the same question and Ben reached his conclusion. He articulated what he believed to be right – but she had vowed never to give up. She had fought so long and so hard. They couldn't let it end like this! Ben could change. She could change. They could find a way back together.

Ben was watching her face and made an impatient gesture with his hand.

'For God's sake, Carina! You can't make everything right with your bloody-minded tenacity. I'm jinxed. I've destroyed anyone who has come close to me and I will destroy you. I don't mean to – but that's the way it is. We're going to put an end to this right now.'

'I love you—'

'I recall you saying much the same to Mr Carstairs.'

'You were unforgivably cruel to Harry—'

'And what about you?'

Carina did not reply. For as long as she could remember, Harry had been her steadfast friend. His only fault was in loving her too much. She wasn't the person he believed her to be – but she couldn't think about Harry now. Ben wasn't jinxed! It was just another excuse not to commit himself. She must have faith. How could she convince Ben there was still hope – that it wasn't too late for them?

Carina began to chew the nail of her thumb and Ben broke the silence first.

'Harry's devotion is such that he'll forgive you anything. Marry him, Carina. For the first time in your life do what is right for yourself.'

'And if I refuse?'

'Then we're both damned.'

Ben stood up and went to the window. He had his back to her and Carina looked down at her hands. With their calluses and torn nails, they reminded her of the lonely child and unhappy girl she had once been. She had exorcised her demons while Ben was still tormented by his. He wanted to save her from himself, but she would not help him.

Ben is the only man I will ever love, she thought. It doesn't matter that I don't always understand him. No human being truly understands another. I love him and can endure anything if he's with me. Without him I am lost.

Carina breathed in to fill her lungs. Then she rose from the chair and walked across the room. Standing behind Ben she leant her head between his shoulder blades. The side of her face pressed into his back and she felt the tautness in his muscles.

'It's not my nature to do what's right. You should know that by now.'

Ben turned slowly and looked down at her. 'Have you been listening to a word I said?'

'I'm prepared to take the risk.'

'Then you're out of your mind.'

'Maybe so …'

'I can't promise never to lose my temper again. What will you do then?'

'I will kill you.' Carina answered with quiet force. 'I don't want to marry anyone else. I want to be with you.'

'I've no desire to ruin your life, sweetheart.' Ben's gaze shifted over her shoulder. If she hadn't known better, Carina might have thought there was someone standing behind her. Then his eyes came back to her face. 'Above all, I want you to be happy.'

'I can only be happy with you. I love you, don't you understand?'

Ben looked at her so long and hard, the suspense was excruciating. How could she know what was going on in his head? Carina saw surprise and self-deprecation in his face; then something new to her, the look of a man resigned to his fate caught unawares by a last-minute reprieve. She was so tense she twisted a lock of her hair around her finger, tugging until it hurt.

Then, without warning, Ben went down on one knee. 'Will you marry me, Carina Temple?'

He held out his hand and Carina thought he was joking. Looking into his blue eyes, she saw that he was serious and her breath came fast.

'When?'

'Tonight. Tomorrow. As soon as I can get a licence.'

'By the devil, Ben Mavrone, you're a hard man to pin down!'

'Will you be my wife – for richer or poorer, for better, for worse and all that?'

'Why?'

'Why do you think? Because I'm in love with you, darling.' Ben took hold of her hand and pressed it to his lips. 'Are you going to keep me on my knees all day? For the last time, Carina Temple, will you marry me?'

'I will.'

Ben stood up and pulled her to him. He held her so tightly she thought he would crush the life out of her, kissing her with a passion that made her dizzy. One hand was at the collar of her shirt and she clung to him, overrun with happiness and relief. By a hair's breadth they had snatched victory from the jaws of defeat! Her love for Ben was invincible and Carina was ablaze with triumph. Whatever lay ahead, whether for better or for worse, they would be together. The man she loved was secure in her heart and she would never let him go.

CHAPTER THIRTY-NINE

Dearest Alice,
I am writing this in the town of San Giovanni and will explain
everything to you when we reach Naples. I have the most wonderful
news! Tomorrow I am to marry Colonel Ben Mavrone. I know this
will come as a shock, but please trust me. I met Ben this spring and
came to know him well after the Redshirts entered Palermo. He is
the best of men and I love him dearly. As soon as the campaign is
over, I will bring him to England to meet you. Then you will
understand my happiness ...

Carina was awake, but too tired to open her eyes. Her spine was
pressed against Ben's stomach and, for the first time in weeks,
they were alone, lying on the softest spring mattress in the
whole of Naples. How Ben had found the hotel, she had no
idea. It was late when they arrived and the double bed and snug
apartment seemed like paradise.

And what a day yesterday had been! They had travelled the
final lap of the journey with Garibaldi on a train that was
crammed to bursting. Enthusiastic demonstrations greeted

them at every station and when they reached Naples and Garibaldi descended onto the platform, a crowd of supporters surged towards him. Knocking down barriers, they swept past the guard of honour, drowning out the welcome speeches of the officials. Ben had shouldered a way through the melee and they had managed to get to the open carriages before the procession through the city began.

Once or twice Garibaldi took off his hat and inclined his head, but he neither waved nor smiled. Only when they passed the port, where the sailors hung like monkeys from the riggings and broke into a cheer, did he raise his arm in a salute. Arriving at the Royal Palace, vacated by the king only days before, he addressed the crowd from the balcony.

'This is the beginning of a new era for Italy! Today we pass from the yoke of servitude to become a free and great nation. I thank you for your welcome. I thank you for your courage in the name of all Italy.'

Something had surprised Carina then. She and Ben were standing beneath the balcony and her gaze strayed to the group of people behind Garibaldi. One man caught her attention because he was wearing court dress. She had imagined for a moment it was Prince Scalia, but she must have been mistaken. The king had fled north to Gaeta and taken his court and ministers with him. Snuggling closer to Ben, she dismissed the memory and let her mind drift back over the last weeks.

Ben had found a priest in San Giovanni and they were married quietly in a small chapel with Greta and Stefan as witnesses. There was no time to invite anyone else. Greta gave her a clean red shirt and helped tie her hair with a white ribbon. As she stepped forward to stand beside Ben, Greta pressed a small bouquet of white carnations into Carina's hand. They had taken their solemn vows and, hearing Ben's voice pledging his love and fidelity, Carina thought her heart would break with joy.

She had been with Ben and the Pioneers ever since and Carina had never ridden so hard or so fast in her life. This was the life he loved, she thought. She noted every detail about him, the way he took decisions, his easy manner with subordinates and the warmth in his eyes when they met hers across the campfire. When Ben slung their bedrolls down side by side on the ground, she had wished they were alone, and last night was her reward. Not waiting to have supper, Ben had dropped their bags on the floor and taken her straight to bed. Thinking of it, Carina stirred restlessly.

'Are you hungry, my love? Shall I order breakfast?'

'I'm starving. I said so last night, but you wouldn't listen.'

'I recall other appetites demanded satisfaction first.'

His hands were under her hair, lifting her head, and Carina's lips fluttered against his mouth. When he made love to her all other thought was scattered to oblivion. It was only later, as she looked up at cherubs and satyrs painted above the bed, Carina remembered. It *was* Scalia she had seen yesterday! How could he have been in the official ceremony for Garibaldi? Could Bianca also be in Naples? Had Ben seen him too, and drawn the same conclusion?

Carina slipped out of bed and wrapped a sheet round her as she went to the window. The street below was crowded with men and women waving banners and chanting Garibaldi's name. She leant forward to get a better view until a whistle from the opposite balcony made her step back.

'Your beauty isn't wasted on the menfolk of Naples, my love. A little more modesty, please, or we'll have the entire male population of the city barracking our hotel.'

Ben smiled and Carina gave a toss of her head as she went to the antechamber and immersed herself a tub of cool water. Ben came through and knelt down. He tried to duck her head under water so she threw the soap at him and when she scrambled out, he climbed into the tub himself.

'I've been looking forward to a bath for weeks!' Carina feigned indignation. 'You might have let me enjoy it.'

He made a lunge for her, but she escaped and put on her clothes before she tugged the bell pull to summon the porter. After some time the man appeared, yawning as he buttoned up his jacket.

'We would like coffee and as much bread as you can find.'

'But everyone's out in the streets, signora.'

'But you're here and I'm sure you'll be kind enough to fix something for us. My husband has an appointment with General Garibaldi. We mustn't keep him waiting.'

Garibaldi's name had a magical effect and within half an hour Carina was sitting by the window, dipping panini into milky coffee. When Ben emerged from the bathroom, he had shaved off his beard and her heart skipped a beat. Oh how she loved him! His good looks and engaging smile caused havoc in a woman's heart – and she must take care not to lose him in this riotous city.

Ben sat down and flicked a breadcrumb off the front of her shirt. His hand lingered a moment before he sighed and withdrew it to fill his cup with coffee. Carina wondered if she should tell him her suspicions about the prince. She didn't want to spoil the happiness of the morning but had vowed to keep nothing from him.

'I thought I saw Prince Scalia with Garibaldi yesterday. Could it be possible?'

'Scalia and Liborio are snakes in the grass. As soon as they deserted one master, they crawled straight to the next.'

'How can Scalia remain at liberty? I don't understand.'

'One of Garibaldi's strengths is pragmatism. The king is holed up in Gaeta, but he's determined to reclaim Naples. The general knows the populace is fickle. He's prepared to accommodate a few turncoats until Victor Emmanuel accepts the crown.'

'But Scalia's the most evil man in the two Sicilies—'

'And one of the most powerful in Naples. He has greater influence here than in Palermo.'

'Mercy! Will we never be rid of him?'

'Scalia will be punished in time. Garibaldi will deal with him when he's no longer of any use – but I agree. I find it reprehensible he does business with murderers.'

Ben stood up, and walked over to the cabinet where he had left his revolver. He checked the hammer before tucking the gun it into the holster. Carina was prepared for a shift in his mood but it passed swiftly.

'And now, and now, sweet wife, I must attend to your trousseau. I'm going shopping.'

'May I come with you?'

'Heavens, no! What would the couturiers of Naples say? Trust me, darling. I'm told I have an excellent eye for feminine fashion.'

He was bound to be away hours, so Carina set about fixing her coiffure. Her hair had grown long and she brushed it, combing out the knots, before she attempted a chignon. Standing in front of the glass with a mouthful of pins between her teeth, she tried to remember how Rose had put it up. It was far harder than she knew. No sooner was her hair rolled in one place than the pins fell tumbling to the floor. In the end she gave up and waited impatiently for Ben to return.

He walked in, his arms stacked with boxes, which he tossed on the bed. Packed within layers of tissue, were dresses and petticoats, underclothes and corsets, and Ben made her try everything on. He had rather too expert a hand, she thought, as he laced her into stays and fastened buttons until she stood before him in a dress of moiré silk. Carina was impressed by Ben's good taste, including a delightful bonnet with a wide brim and ribbon that matched the colour of her eyes.

'Thank you, my darling.' She stood on tiptoes to kiss him. 'They're lovely.'

'This is our honeymoon and you look beautiful. I shall be the envy of every husband in Naples.'

There was undisguised admiration in Ben's eyes and Carina took him by the hands and whirled him round the room. He laughed and told her she was behaving like a child, but she didn't care. Ben arranged for a lady's maid to come each morning to dress her hair, and she did not think about Prince Scalia or Bianca again. The weather was perfect and Naples a vibrant, bustling port surrounded by antiquity. They drove out to the slopes of Vesuvius and looked in wonder at the volcano. Another day, they visited a museum packed with treasures from Pompeii where the mosaics were fresh as yesterday and sculptures so lifelike they looked like flesh and bone.

Ben cut a dashing figure in the city and Carina was aware of the impression he made when entering a room. She noticed the eyes of other women following him and how they blushed as he bent over their hands. More confident than she was in conversation, Ben could be provocative or as tactful as a diplomat. She never knew what he might say next or which opinion he would favour. Carina listened to him talk of matters about which she knew nothing and regretted her lack of formal learning. She wanted to be Ben's equal in every way and was ashamed of her ignorance.

'But you have youth on your side!' His eyes danced when she told him. 'You've plenty of time to learn about the world. There's no need to rush.'

Nevertheless, Ben took the trouble to explain current issues to her and bought her newspapers to read. He asked her questions and listened to her answers, encouraging her to form her own views. He could be serious or funny, making her laugh until she cried. When he gave her a book of Keats's poetry, he said that he preferred her verse to all the Romantic poets put together. He was teasing, Carina was sure, but she was pleased with the compliment.

On the surface Ben was sophisticated and urbane, but he never lost the look of a man who has lived with danger too long to be careless. He was unstintingly generous and attentive, yet his core of isolation remained. Occasionally, Carina turned her head and caught a brooding look on his face. His mind was far away and his expression so serious she wondered what he could be thinking. The moment he felt her eyes on him, Ben would get up and kiss her or tell her a story to make her smile.

Then, for two consecutive days, he left her alone in the hotel. He gave no explanation of where he had been and Carina knew better than to interrogate him. Ben had always been secretive and she wouldn't look for shadows in the sunlight. She had known how it would be and there were no regrets. Ben was her beloved husband and, for the most part, seemed as delighted with married life as she was herself.

One evening they were invited to dine with Garibaldi at the Palazzo D'Angri, arriving late to find the antechamber crammed with journalists. Scores of hands darted in the air, beseeching them with questions until they reached the private apartments where Garibaldi embraced Carina. He congratulated Ben on his good fortune and she was overjoyed to find

Greta and Stefan among the guests, along with Jane and Jessie and Alberto Mario.

'We've only just heard of your marriage. Congratulations to you both!' Jessie wagged a finger at Ben. 'You've found yourself a remarkable woman, Colonel Mavrone. Make sure you take care of her – no more running off as you did after Milazzo!'

'I've been dying to talk to you. Do you mind if we sit down?' Greta took her hand, leading Carina to an open window.

She was pale and Carina looked at her with concern. 'What's wrong, Greta? Are you ill?'

'I'm told the sickness is normal and will pass in a month or so.'

'You don't mean? You're not—'

'In an interesting condition? Yes, I am! Can you believe it? Stefan and I've been married for five years. We'd almost given up hope.'

'Why, it's wonderful news! When did you find out?'

'I saw the doctor yesterday and the baby's due in April. Stefan's mortified that he let me ride as a courier. He insists we return to Sicily at the earliest opportunity. And you, dearest? Are you happy?'

'Oh, Greta … When I think how Ben and I almost lost each other. We owe all our happiness to you. How can I ever express my gratitude?'

'By coming home and following my example.' Greta opened her fan to cool herself. 'I shall spend my confinement with my mother and rely on you to visit every day. Now I've found a woman after my own heart, I intend to keep her my friend forever.'

The others joined them and Jessie cast a knowing glance over Greta. 'Well, Senora Bosco, it's fortunate your services are no longer required on the battlefield.'

'What news of the ambulances?' Ben asked.

'They arrived from Reggio yesterday. I'm glad to say we've been allocated the finest convent in Naples as our hospital. Never again will we be unprepared as we were at Milazzo.'

'Garibaldi hoped no more blood would be shed between fellow Italians,' Carina said quietly.

'No king gives up his throne without a fight and the Bourbons are the worst of the lot.' Alberto Mario answered. 'I'm afraid it's not over yet.'

The next night they went to the opera at the Theatre San Carlo for Verdi's *Nabucco*. Carina hoped to hear the famous chorus, but the audience was over-excited and the performance constantly interrupted. The opera stopped and started so many times, they left at the interval, walking along the marina before returning to the hotel. When she thought about Harry, Carina hoped he had returned to England, and tried not to feel guilty. She must write to him but nothing was so important that it couldn't wait. Happiness was not a dream. It was here and now and every moment too precious to waste.

They were sitting at a pavement table in the morning sun and waiters in long aprons hurried from table to table. Smartly dressed men did business over coffee and Ben was reading a newspaper. At the far end, a man sat with a book propped in front of him. Carina noticed him because, more than once, he lifted his head to stare in their direction. When she caught his eye, he looked quickly away and soon afterwards summoned the waiter for his bill. The next day she saw him again. She was with Ben, buying cigars, and he was standing outside the shop window.

Touching Ben's arm, she indicated with her head. 'Who is that man?'

'Which one?'

'That bald fellow over there. I am sure he's following us.'

'You're a beautiful woman, darling. Every man in Naples would follow you if they had time.'

He wasn't taking her seriously and when Carina looked again, the stranger had gone. Ben was right. Why shouldn't the man frequent the same restaurants and visit the same shops as they did? He was probably one of the many journalists who followed Garibaldi from Sicily and now had nothing to do. During the next few days there was no sign of him and Carina put him out of her mind.

She had discovered the Villa Denuzio was an hour's drive from Naples and sent a letter to her grandmother.

Darling Nonna,

I am sorry not to have written before but these last weeks have been a whirlwind. I pray you are well. Please, can I come and see you soon? I have some good news I wish to convey to you in person …

An answer, written in a spidery hand, was delivered to the hotel the same evening. Nonna wrote that Carlo and Anna Maria were in Gaeta on the command of the king, while she remained in the villa with Gabriella and Paulo. She looked forward to Carina's visit. When might they expect her?

Carina replied there was someone she wanted her to meet and she would bring him for lunch the day after tomorrow. She was confident Ben would win Nonna over but when she thought of Gabriella her mood darkened. She felt so desperately sad for her. What could she say that could possibly be of any consolation? They were driving home and, with these thoughts on her mind, Carina sighed as she rested her head on Ben's shoulder.

'You're tired, my love. I'll take you back and then I must return to headquarters.'

'But you were there only an hour ago.'

'Something's come up.'

When they arrived at the hotel, Ben walked her to the door and Carina entered the dark lobby alone. She was about to go upstairs when she heard her name and looked round as Harry rose from a high-backed chair. He walked over and then, as if it were the most natural thing in the world, invited her to join him in a glass of lemonade.

'I've been looking for you but only thought of enquiring at the Palazzo D'Angri this morning. They told me you were staying here.'

'I meant to write to you. Dear Harry, I'm so sorry.'

Harry poured her a glass of lemonade. He sat straight and stiff in his chair and took a sip of juice.

'When I heard you were married I couldn't believe it.'

'Can you forgive me?'

'Nothing to forgive, old girl. Had a feeling something was up and hoped I was wrong.' His sentences were patently rehearsed. 'I sail for England on Friday and couldn't leave without saying goodbye. We've been friends for too long.'

'Dear Harry, you're like a brother to me—'

'And too much of a fool to realise it!'

Carina dropped her gaze to her lap. It was awkward enough and she didn't want to make it any worse. There was a commotion in the street outside but no one came in and Harry put down his glass.

'I know it's not my business, but are you sure you made the right decision?'

'I promise you I am happy. I know Ben behaved badly in San Giovanni and I apologise. He was upset that night but he's a good man and I truly love him.'

'Will you stay in Italy?'

'Sicily will be our home but we'll visit England once the campaign is over. I want to see you and introduce Ben to Alice.'

'Does Lady Farne know of your marriage?'

'I've written to her and will tell my grandmother tomorrow.'

Harry began to fiddle with his watch chain. He was disinclined to continue the conversation and Carina studied him over the top of her glass. His hair was bleached the colour of pale straw and he looked older than his twenty years. How she wished she hadn't had to hurt him! There was a long silence, then he took a card from his wallet and, in a curiously formal gesture, placed it on the table in front of her.

'Please will you do me the honour of dining with me tomorrow evening? I would like to be on better terms with your husband before I leave. I'm staying at the Hotel Garibaldi. Shall we say seven o'clock?'

'Why, thank you! How very kind.'

Carina stood up to kiss him but Harry put on his gloves and shook her hand. After he had gone, she made her way up to the bedroom. Harry had left an English newspaper and she was lying on the bed reading it when Ben returned. She would have jumped up and run to him but the serious look on his face stopped her.

'I'm afraid there's trouble in Palermo. The Sicilians are claiming Garibaldi's deserted them. He's asked me to take charge of the situation.'

'Why you? Why not someone else? How long will you be away?'

The questions followed one upon the other and Ben sat down on the bed beside her.

'I'm the most senior Sicilian officer in Garibaldi's command.'

'When do you go?'

'At first light tomorrow.'

'But we're visiting my grandmother—'

'I know and I'm sorry. I will pay my respects as soon as I return.'

Carina swung her bare legs over the side of the bed. There were other officers who could do the job just as well! Why did Garibaldi have to choose Ben? He was a well-respected and high-ranking officer, she reminded herself. Ben was under the general's command and must obey orders. He had other responsibilities, apart from attending upon her.

'I've booked you on the same ferry as Greta and Stefan on Thursday. I'm not leaving you alone for long, my darling.'

Thursday? Why, today was Tuesday! It was the day after tomorrow and Ben was taking her with him to Palermo! How silly to think he would abandon her in Naples. Those days were behind them. She was his wife now and he would never leave her again.

Ben came to bed and pressed her hand against his heart so she felt its strong, steady beat. Carina sought his mouth impatiently. She held him close to her and when he tried to raise himself up, pulled him back down. She was intoxicated with this man who was her husband. She loved the taste of him, the feel of his hard body and his cool skin. Ben kissed her, gently at first, and then passionately. He turned her over, his lips brushing her shoulders as he lifted her onto her knees. Carina felt his body against hers, his finger tracing the deep groove of her spine and she abandoned herself to him entirely. He is mine, she thought …

Carina lay with her head on his lap, her hair spread across his stomach as Ben propped himself up on the pillows, not knowing if she stayed awake or dozed in the hours that followed. The clock struck three and she heard him moving around the room.

She kept her eyes shut until he came back and knelt by the bed, taking her in his arms.

'I've paid the bill and left you money with your travel papers in the desk. Stefan has your ticket for the ferry. Remember your pistol, sweetheart. Promise to have it on you always.' He took her face in his hands and kissed her forehead and then her lips. 'I'll see you in Sicily, my darling. Behave yourself while I'm away.'

Ben stood up, collected his knapsack, slinging it over his shoulder as he walked towards the door. He stood for a long moment with his hand on the knob looking back at her and then went out. As the door closed, Carina experienced a sense of loss so acute she bit down on her knuckle to stop herself crying. She didn't know why she was so upset. They would only be apart for two days. It was no time at all. Her love for Ben was making her soft, she thought as she walked over to the window.

Carina watched Ben cross the street below, his stride long and purposeful as he headed towards the port. When he was lost from sight, her gaze travelled over the tiled rooftops to the bay. The sea was smooth as polished gunmetal and he would have a good crossing. Tomorrow was a busy day. She must try to get some rest and she went back to bed, curling up in the place where the sheets were still warm.

CHAPTER FORTY

There was no warning of the sirocco that swept up the western seaboard late that afternoon. The morning had dawned bright and it was only as she left Naples in a hired diligence, Carina realised she had forgotten to tell Ben about meeting Harry. The dinner engagement would be more difficult without him, but she must go all the same. As they arrived at the Villa Denuzio, she looked out and saw a pretty pink stucco house surrounded by mimosa trees. Paulo came striding across the gravel to open the door. He gave her his hand and peered into the interior.

'Where've you hidden him? We expected your husband. Nonna will be disappointed.'

'Mercy, how do you know?'

'Papa was informed. He told Nonna you married one of Garibaldi's officers without asking her permission.'

'It was a private ceremony! How could he—'

'No doubt the priest told the bishop, who told the cardinal, who told the pope, who told my father. It doesn't matter. What have you done with him?'

'Ben had to go to Palermo this morning.'

'So the damned man's deserted you already?'

The teasing note was still there, but Paulo's face was drawn and Carina saw the dark look in his eyes as he led her up the steps.

'Oh, Paulo. I'm so sad about Enrico. You must be devastated.'

'Enrico was too fine a man to die. What a stupid, tragic waste!' Paulo answered roughly as they stood in the cool of the hall. 'What difference does it make if we're ruled by a dictator or a king? It's not a cause worth dying for!'

Carina wanted to tell him he was wrong, but Enrico had been Paulo's friend. Caution checked her and she asked, 'How is Gabriella?'

'My sister is stronger than I am. You will see.'

As they walked through the house, Carina had an impression of the same dilapidated grandeur as in Palermo, rooms full of old pictures with faded furniture and windows shuttered to keep out the light. Paulo took her out onto a terrace where Nonna was sitting in a wicker chair under a canopy of vines. She asked Paulo to leave them for a while and Carina took a seat beside her.

'I hoped to be the one to tell you, Nonna. I wanted you to meet Ben and for you to give us your blessing. Sadly, he received orders to return to Palermo this morning.'

'Then I look forward to making his acquaintance at another time,' Nonna answered brusquely. 'I gather I've been misled as to your activities over these last few months. I hope you will now do me the courtesy of telling the truth?'

Carina was determined to be honest, but it was harder than she anticipated and would have been impossible had Ben been there. How devious she sounded, admitting that she had lied on her return to Palermo! How sordid her confession that she had been with Ben and not Greta Mazzini all that time! She faltered more than once and Nonna listened in silence until she came to the wedding. 'We were married in the parish church of San Giovanni. I should have asked your permission. I'm sorry, but there was no time.'

'Carlo will be vexed your union had the benefit of clergy. He hoped it was a secular arrangement that might be annulled.'

'I'm sorry if I've disappointed the family.' Carina coloured slightly. 'I love Ben and would do the same again tomorrow.'

'A gentleman would have sought my permission. Did your husband fear it wouldn't be forthcoming?'

'You may not consider Ben a gentleman – but he's good enough for me.'

'Even so, I cannot condone your duplicity.'

They were stern words and the two women fell silent. Nonna looked small and old. The skin of her face was creased and her neck bent with the strain of holding up her head. Her grandmother was frailer than when they had last been together, Carina thought. And she had changed too, far more than she realised. How otherwise could she have lied so blatantly to Nonna and Alice? She had hoped Nonna would be pleased and smarted under the reprimand. Six months ago she would have defended herself, but Carina held her tongue. Nonna was an old woman. How could she understand the extent of her love for Ben?

Bees were humming in the lavender and Carina looked over the garden walls to the sunburnt fields beyond the gate. There were clouds massing on the horizon. She wondered if it would rain and whether she should leave before lunch – but she couldn't go without seeing Gabriella.

'I'm not made of stone, Carina,' her grandmother said at length. 'I understand that for you love is everything. It was the same with your mother.'

'Then why are you angry?'

'Because you should have told me the truth. Were you afraid I might be shocked? When I was young it was considered the greatest misfortune not to experience a grand passion. I know what it is to be ruled by one's heart.'

Nonna's mottled hands folded over the top of her cane and her gaze turned inward. Her grandmother had lived through the age of the Romantics, Carina thought. She had been alive at a time when Byron was in Italy. How presumptuous to assume she knew nothing of love! She dismissed her hurt, smiling at Nonna, who beckoned her closer.

Carina shifted her chair, lowering her head, and her grandmother traced a cross on her forehead.

'I give your marriage my blessing, dear child. Ben Mavrone has made you happy and that is all that is important. If your mother were alive she would bless you both. It's time we had some good news in this house.'

A breeze rustled the vine leaves as Paulo and Gabriella came through the door. Gabriella's face was white as a china doll with dark smudges beneath her eyes. She was so thin her shoulder blades stuck out through the thin muslin of her dress and Carina was shocked. During lunch, she took care not to speak of Sicily. Afraid of saying anything that might break Gabriella's brittle composure, she described San Giovanni and Garibaldi's progress to Naples. Paulo pretended not to listen, but she was aware of Gabriella's covert attention and, when they returned to the terrace, Nonna made an excuse to leave them alone.

Gabriella walked to the balustrade, resting her elbows on the top. Her back was turned and Carina spoke gently, 'I know how much you loved Enrico and he loved you, dearest. I'm so very sorry.'

Only the stiffening of muscles in her neck gave any indication that Gabriella had heard. She doesn't want my sympathy, Carina thought. If Ben died, I would be the same. Sympathy doesn't make you strong – it only makes you cry. She searched her mind for inspiration and noticed Gabriella wore a band of red, white and green ribbons around her wrist.

'I wish you could see the tricolour flags and banners on display in Naples. Every balcony of every house proclaims the New Italy! All that you and Enrico believed in and fought for has been realised.'

'Enrico was proud of you.' Gabriella gave a slight lift of her shoulders and turned to face her. 'He said you were valiant. That was the word he used.'

'Foolhardy, more like! Did he mention that he saved my life?'

'He told me everything. I'm so grateful you made it possible for us to write. His letters are a great comfort.' Gabriella paused and a tear slid down either side of her nose. She took out her handkerchief and wiped them away. Then, with a fortitude that defied her years, she went on.

'It's God's Will that Enrico was taken from us. I cannot count his loss against the greatness of what has been achieved.'

Faith glowed in her dark eyes and Carina felt a lump rise in her throat. Her cousin was awash with sorrow, but behind her suffering lay a hinterland of courage. Gabriella is the valiant one, she thought. She's the youngest and bravest of us all.

'The triumph of Liberty gives me strength to endure,' Gabriella went on after a long pause. 'If only Paulo could understand that Enrico didn't die in vain. Will you talk to him, Carina?'

She could try but it would do no good, Carina thought. Paulo did not share Gabriella's idealism. He might never accept Enrico's sacrifice but he was a survivor. With his charm and agile mind, he would carve out a career for himself, under whichever regime prevailed. Her cousins had steel in their bones, the same gritty resolve she felt herself, and she was proud of them.

'Will you promise to visit us in Naples when we return from Sicily?' Carina lifted her hand to her cousin's cold cheek. 'And bring Paulo with you! He's far too curious to resist.'

'Holy Mary! I forgot to congratulate you on your marriage! Do you know that Enrico and Colonel Mavrone became friends? He told me all about him in his letters.'

'What did he say?'

'Enrico considered Colonel Mavrone the finest leader of men in the Sicilian army. He was also of the opinion you were in love with each other – and both too proud to admit it!'

It wasn't often she was lost for words, but Carina was never to remember how she answered or whether she responded at all. Paulo joined them and they sat outside talking until the first drops of rain began to fall. She said goodbye to Nonna and Paulo held an umbrella over her head as he escorted her to the carriage. At the last minute Gabriella came running out of the house and thrust a cloak through the window.

'Take this or you'll be soaked before you reach Naples …'

'And next time don't forget to bring your husband!' Paulo shouted.

The force of the storm unleashed a downpour on their heads and they ran back to the shelter of the portico. As the diligence moved off, Carina leant out to wave. Her cousins were standing on the top step and an image of them burnt into her mind: Paulo, with his arm bent at the elbow like an artist's maquette and Gabriella, standing on tiptoes waving her white handkerchief, until they were hidden by a curtain of rain.

CHAPTER FORTY-ONE

By the time they reached Naples, the rain had stopped and a wind was getting up. She would call in at the hotel and change before dinner, Carina decided, and engaged the driver to wait and take her on. The lobby was empty and the porter absent from his desk so she fetched her key herself. Then, with a quick look around, she lifted her damp skirts and went up the stairs. No one had bothered to light the lamp on the landing and when she reached her bedroom door, she stopped outside and felt through her skirts for her gun.

The pistol was in place, strapped to her thigh, and Carina turned the key to let herself in. She hung Gabriella's cloak over a chair and took off her wet shoes. As she was tidying her hair, the window banged shut, making her jump. She was as nervous as a kitten – but was only because Ben wasn't here and she must hurry or be late for Harry.

Carina searched for a dry pair of shoes and was about to put them on when she heard the creak of floorboards behind her. As she swung about the blood froze in her veins. The door was wide open and a heavily built man stood on the threshold. She stared at him, her eyes wide with shock. Her first terrified impulse was to try and make a run for it. She might just bolt past him and get downstairs but he was blocking the doorway.

'I believe you have come to the wrong room, sir.' She tried to keep her voice steady. 'If you ask the concierge, I am sure he will redirect you.'

The stranger stood where he was, menacing and silent. Without taking her eyes off him, Carina slipped one hand into her pocket. She reached through the opening in her skirt and touched the stock of her pistol. Before she could remove it from the holster, the man stepped into the room. In two strides he was at her side and towering over her. Carina screamed before a blow sent her flying backwards. She fell against the table and tried to save herself, but a second blow sent her to the floor. Her body smashed onto the marble and she lay stunned.

She was dimly aware of the stranger beside her, lifting her into a sitting position. His hand was round her neck and a pad of material was clamped over her nose and mouth. Carina recognised the smell of chloroform and clawed frantically at his fingers. She tried not to breathe, but her lungs were bursting and she choked against the gag as she inhaled. With each breath her movements became weaker. Her vision blurred and she saw solid furniture melting in front of her eyes. She was falling, plummeting off a cliff into a swirling vortex, and seconds later collapsed on the floor unconscious.

Carina had the sensation of being cast adrift on a sea that was rolling and pitching beneath her. Her head ached and drowsiness pulled her under. Awareness slipped away until she was forced awake because she was going to be sick. Bending her head to one side, she retched. Then she dropped her chin on her chest until the nausea and giddiness passed.

Taking long, slow breaths, Carina opened her eyes. She was tied to a chair with her arms bound. Light from a flare flicked ghostly shadows over the walls and she was in a low, vaulted cellar with a portcullis gate. Over her own rasping breath, she heard the scratching of rats. Vermin infested this dark, dank place and she cast about desperately, trying to think what had happened. There had been a stranger in her room. He had drugged her and brought her here. She thought of the man who followed her and Ben, but there was no obvious connection. For the love of God, where was she?

There had been harrowing accounts in the newspapers of cells dug into the hills, where opponents of the old regime were condemned to a living death. They had been evacuated by the Redshirts but there might still be a guard. Carina called out. Her cries echoed around the chamber and came back to her and she let out a whimper of terror. No one would even know she was missing! Harry would wait in vain and assume she had forgotten or changed her mind. He wouldn't think to raise the alarm. But if she had been brought here to die, why was a torch still burning?

Whoever he might be, her abductor meant to return. Carina felt the weight of the holster strapped to her thigh. It was hidden beneath her skirts. Thank God he hadn't found the pistol! She began to rock backwards and forwards, trying to loosen the rope that bound her arms. She twisted her wrists, working at the knot. Then, from a long way off, she heard the sound of voices.

'Help me! I'm down here!'

There were hurried footsteps and a shadowy hulk stood outside the gate, stooping to turn the key. As the gate swung open, her kidnapper emerged from the darkness.

'Now you're awake there's someone who wants to talk to you.'

'My dear Carina, this is a long-awaited pleasure.'

The big man stood aside and Carina turned her face towards the voice. With an attention to detail that distanced shock, she noticed that Prince Scalia was dressed for dinner. He had removed his gloves and held one hand over the other, stroking the signet ring on his little finger.

'Fetch me a chair and leave us alone. Come back in half an hour. Make sure we're not disturbed in the meantime.'

The man found a stool and Scalia locked the gate behind him. He dropped the key into his pocket. His face was close to hers and Carina felt her skin crawl. She should have guessed Scalia was behind this – but what did he want? Enrico was dead and he had joined forces with Garibaldi. She was no longer his enemy. Fear and revulsion made her heart pound, but she kept them out of her voice.

'I've friends in Naples who will be looking for me.'

'No one would think of searching here. Did you really think I was taken in by your charade in Palermo, Carina? I knew by then you had fallen in with the rebels.'

'So why did you release Enrico Fola?'

'Fola was of no consequence to us. I hoped to entice to you into my bed – but I've no taste for second-hand goods, particularly cast-offs from Captain Mavrone.'

Scalia sat with his legs wide apart and his hands clasped. Ben should have killed him when he had the chance, Carina thought and lowered her gaze to hide what was in her eyes.

'You can't keep me a prisoner here.'

'I've no intention of keeping you a prisoner. Our business won't take long …'

Scalia paused and Carina was swept by disgust. She loathed this man, with his small white hands and cruel face. Raising her eyes to meet his gaze, her lip curved contemptuously.

'Do I revolt you, Carina? The scars you find so unattractive are your husband's doing.'

'To avenge the murder of his brother!'

'You don't believe in that old fiction, do you?' Scalia gave a hollow laugh. 'Mavrone never forgave me for stealing Bianca from him.'

'That's not true—'

Carina broke off as the prince stood up and kicked the stool aside. He reached into the pocket of his waistcoat and took out a small heart-shaped locket, which he dangled in front of her face.

'Bianca sailed for Sicily with Mavrone this morning. They've spent time together in Naples. I have a record of all their assignations. She left this behind so that I would know she was with him.'

Carina recognised the locket. She remembered Bianca fidgeting with it the first time they met, clasping it as a talisman in the Villa Pallestro. She was never without it. Scalia must have ripped it off her neck – but it wasn't evidence of Ben's infidelity. The prince was playing a grotesque game. Bianca hadn't gone to Sicily. Where was she, she wondered suddenly?

'Let me show you the portrait my wife wears so close to her heart.'

Scalia leant down and snapped open the clasp. Carina glanced at the tiny painting inside. The portrait looked like Ben, but it wasn't him.

'The portrait is of Alexander, the man you executed,' Carina spat the words at him.

'It's of Ben and not his brother. Come now, my dear. You know as well as I do that your husband's still in love with my wife.'

Unwanted memories swam to the surface: Ben's unexplained absences these last few weeks and the look on his face when she had first spoken of Bianca. But Ben had arranged for her to be with him in Sicily. He hadn't betrayed her and Scalia was lying. She watched, transfixed, as he threw the locket aside and took a small dagger from his belt. Its blade was no longer than that of a man's finger and Carina went cold with horror. Scalia wasn't going to kill or rape her. Cruelty was his life's blood and he had something else in mind, something that made the gorge rise in her throat.

'You're the weapon I shall use against Mavrone. He'll never look at you again without being reminded of me. This is the last act of the vendetta.'

Carina tried to tip the chair backwards, but Scalia put one foot on the seat to hold it upright. He bent over her, his smile extended by the scars. His eyes shone feverishly, saliva brimming at the corner of his mouth. Carina couldn't bear to look. She squeezed her eyes shut and felt the knife slice open the front of her dress, Scalia's fingers moving from her throat to the top of her basque. The cold edge of the blade touched her skin and her mind reeled in terror. God save me! Then agonising pain spiralled upwards and she fainted.

A hand was slapping her face, becoming harder until Carina was forced awake. She was lying on the floor with Scalia standing astride her. A burning sensation in her chest made her groan as she pushed back on her elbows.

'Goodbye, Signora Mavrone. I don't expect we'll meet again.'

Scalia put on his gloves as he walked towards the gate. Warm air bathed her skin and Carina felt blood trickling from her chest down to her stomach. Her fingers stretched out and as her hands touched damp straw, she stared at them. The rope had come undone! Scalia had untied her or else it had fallen off, and she could defend herself.

'I will kill you for this!'

The prince turned to face her, but Carina was no longer on the ground. She was kneeling up with the pistol in her hand. Somehow, she had removed it from the holster and the barrel was aimed at his heart. Scalia was telling her to give it to him. He was walking towards her and holding out his hand. Her finger crooked on the trigger, but the hammer caught the edge of her cuff. She tore at the material with her teeth to free the action and he halted, the pupils of his eyes dilating.

'Don't be a fool. Give me the gun and I'll let you go.'

Carina steadied her wrist and pulled the trigger three times in quick succession. A deafening explosion accompanied each shot. Through a cloud of burning gun-smoke, she saw Scalia stagger. He swayed on his feet but did not fall. She thought she had missed him and raised the gun to fire again. Now there were four scorched holes in his waistcoat turning from black to red, spreading into a pool of blood across his chest. Scalia fell on his knees. One hand clawed the air, and then he toppled forwards and lay still.

The prince lay on his stomach with his neck twisted towards her. His eyes were filmy and blood lathered his lips. A rigour made his body hunch up and a rattling sound came from his throat. Carina dropped the gun. She thought she would be sick or faint again, but did neither. Her mind seized on one thought – she must escape before the other man came back.

Scalia's dead eyes were staring at her and the key was in his pocket. It was safer to stay low and she crawled across the floor on hands and knees. Gritting her teeth, she groped in one pocket and then the other. The prince's arm moved in a final spasm and she cried out in fright – but she had the key and she staggered to the gate. The flare had burnt low and she had to feel for the keyhole with her fingers. The key was in, but wouldn't move. Wiping her hands on her skirt, Carina tried again. The lock gave way and she leant against the heavy gate and shoved it open.

A moment later, she was running down a tunnel in pitch darkness. She tripped over the hem of her dress and fell. Her face hit the ground and Carina tasted mud in her mouth. Lifting her head, she saw a slither of light in the distance and stumbled on. Scalia's accomplice must have heard the shots! He would be waiting to ambush her. She must be careful. With her back grazing the wall, she inched forward, listening for footsteps, but the only sound she heard was the howling wind outside.

When she came to the light, Carina crawled through a narrow opening, grimacing as she squeezed through the earthen tunnel. Fresh air touched her face – the fresh air of the living world not the fetid stench of the subterranean prison – and she was standing on a rocky escarpment. She wiped the back of her hand across her eyes and made out an outline of buildings not far below. Dark clouds buffeted across the moon and, between them, Carina caught a glimpse of the metallic sea. A surge of relief energised her and she began to run, not stopping until she came to a stone paved street where the wind was funneled into gusts.

It was the sirocco, the hot African wind detested by Sicilians. Its wailing lacerated her brain and she crouched down, her hands clasped over her ears. The wind sounded like Prince Scalia screaming. Carina imagined him hurtling towards her with blood pouring out of his stomach. Deranged by the vision, she stared wild-eyed up the street. A wine barrel had broken loose from its moorings and burst open, bumping down and spilling its contents as it gathered speed and went past her.

She began to walk, keeping her balance by running a hand running along the wall. Three men were coming up the hill towards her and stopped beneath a street lamp. Her mind was rank with death and Carina saw their shirts were red as the blood on Scalia's body. They were devils sent from hell in vengeance! With a muffled scream, she darted past them and careered blindly on, swerving round corners and down flights of steps until she came to the bottom of the hill. There she stopped and bent over to drag air into her lungs.

The wind was no longer warm and she shivered as it gathered up pieces of confetti, the remnants of a victory parade, and sent them swirling in a storm of snowflakes. Carina looked nervously over her shoulder. Why was she so afraid? Who was it that followed, keeping his distance hiding in the shadows? A man passed on the other side of the street, holding on to his hat as he bent into the wind. Robert Danby cast a furtive glance in her direction and hurried on. Snow would muffle the sound of carriage wheels and she must get home! How far away was she from Mount Street?

Wincing with pain, Carina forced herself on until she came to a cobbled square. On the far side was a hotel with lamps burning in the windows. She limped over to the entrance and read the sign above the door. The Grand Hotel Garibaldi. Of course! What in the world was she thinking? She was in Naples and not London – and this was where she was meant to be! How could she have forgotten Harry was expecting her for dinner? She hadn't had time to dress properly. Carina couldn't remember what had kept her, but Harry would understand.

She felt she had achieved a miraculous feat and stepped into the foyer with her head high. As she knew he would be, Harry was waiting. She saw him get up, his jaw dropping as he clutched the back of the chair. He was staring at her as if she were a madwoman. The wind slammed the door shut and a concierge came out from behind his desk, shouting at her and waving his arms about like a pantomime character. He looked so funny that she burst out laughing; a high-pitched, hysterical laugh that ended as Harry's arms went round her.

CHAPTER FORTY-TWO

OCTOBER 1860, NORTHUMBERLAND

She was asleep and dreaming she was at Melton. Paddy was in the loose box, grooming Papa's bay hunter. He looked up and smiled. Carina saw him clearly before he disappeared. Now she was in Palermo with Nonna – or was it her mother? They looked so alike. She tried to reach out to them but they vanished. Faces assembled in strange disguises, then fractured into tiny pieces. Nothing was real …

Voices at the edges of her memory; Harry asking questions, harsh and insistent. Carina wanted him to go away. He stopped her listening, listening for the only voice she wanted to hear.

She tried to turn her head and a woman said softly, 'Stay quiet, dearest. There's nothing to fear. I am with you.'

Carina opened her eyes. She was lying in bed and Alice was beside her. She was holding her hand, gently stroking her fingers. Alice wouldn't let her go.

'You had an accident in Naples. Harry Carstairs brought you home. You arrived yesterday.'

She wanted Ben. Where was he? Carina felt tears rolling down her cheeks.

'Please don't cry, darling.' Alice wiped her face with a hand-kerchief. 'You're safe now. Trust me … all will be well.'

'Camomile tea will calm her anxiety.' A man's voice with a northern brogue. 'She needs rest, peace and quiet. Our Northumbrian air will do her good …'

But she wasn't in Northumbria. She was in Italy. She wanted to tell them but she had forgotten how to speak. Darkness closed in again.

When she awoke, Carina was sitting in a chair wrapped in blankets. She didn't recognise this room with blue curtains. She was due to catch the ferry to Palermo. Where had she left her cloak? She tried to stand up.

'Not yet, dearest.' Alice touched her arm. 'You're not strong enough. Dr Crawley says you can come downstairs in a few days.'

Carina shook her head. Her lips struggled to form a question. It came out in a soundless whisper. 'Where am I?'

'Don't upset yourself, dear one. I'll explain everything once you are well.'

Carina closed her eyes. Pigeons cooing outside the window. The yapping of a small dog. Sounds drifting through her head in snatches. She wanted to sleep, but something was changing. She was losing control, her mind rushing upward towards an invisible surface. She had been safe deep down on the seabed but Alice was drawing her into the light. Suddenly she knew where she was. She was staying with Alice and Anthony in Northumberland. She was meant to be in Sicily with Ben. He was waiting for her. Her heart cried out for him. Why was she here?

★　★　★

'I must speak openly with you, Mr Carstairs.' Alice was sitting with her back to the window. 'I'm afraid Carina's return to England has done her more harm than good.'

'Are you suggesting I should have abandoned her in Naples?'

'You were placed in a difficult situation.'

'What else was I supposed to do?' Harry sounded peevish. 'I hate to think what might have befallen Carina if I hadn't been there.'

Alice held her sampler up to the light. A stitch seemed to be at fault and she took out her scissors to snip the thread. 'Carina wrote to me of her marriage. She sounded happy, therefore her present state of health has come as a great shock. Pray, tell me what you know of her husband.'

'I only met Colonel Mavrone once. Didn't take to the fellow. He's certainly not a gentleman – but I never thought he'd assault Carina.'

'Did she say he had done so?'

'When she arrived at the hotel, she was wild with terror and covered in blood. They must have had an argument. Ben Mavrone's a jealous man with a savage temper. It's obvious he was the culprit!'

'How much did she tell you?'

'Nothing beyond Mavrone's name, over and over again. Anyone would have understood she wanted me to know who had attacked her. When I suggested calling a doctor she went berserk. It took two glasses of brandy to calm her down.'

'And what happened on the voyage home?'

'At first, she seemed calm but distracted, suffering from the shock of the attack, I dare say. I tried to question her, but she became angry and increasingly withdrawn. Sometimes she would talk to herself in Italian, but I couldn't get a sensible word from her. I hoped she would be better once we arrived in England. It grieves me to see that so far it's made little difference.'

'And you consulted a doctor in London before coming north.' Alice spoke in the same quiet voice. 'What was his professional opinion?'

'That her wounds are superficial and will heal, ghastly though they are – but the mental shock will take much longer. He insisted that Carina must never set eyes on her assailant again if she's to have any chance of full recovery.'

'But we don't know what Carina wants, do we? It's possible there's more to this than she's able to tell us at present. Do you think she's in love with Ben Mavrone? Why else did she marry him?'

'Asked myself the same question a hundred times.' Harry stopped and blew his nose loudly. 'I believe Carina was obliged to marry Colonel Mavrone – for the sake of appearances, if you take my meaning?'

'And not because she's in love with him, is that your meaning, sir? You know very well my niece has never felt obliged to conduct herself in accordance with proprietary.'

'Maybe so, ma'am, but I'm sure that Carina was afraid of him.' The stamp of Harry's footsteps began on the hardwood floor. 'The morning after the assault, I went to their hotel. Mavrone had taken to his heels so I bribed the porter to let me into the bedroom. The place was a shambles. A stroke of luck that I found Carina's travel documents.'

'Were you able to confer with her grandmother before leaving Naples?'

'I didn't have time to find out where she lived and Carina was in no state to enlighten me. I left a letter for Colonel Mavrone. Told him I was bringing her here. The man knows where she is. If he's innocent and wants her back he'd have come by now, or sent a letter.'

'So you took it upon yourself to remove Carina from her husband, without her or anyone else's consent?'

'Someone had to save her from the blackguard!' Harry's voice rose, loud and agitated. 'The scoundrel assaulted and deserted Carina. The sooner she starts proceedings for a divorce, the better—'

'A divorce! Whatever are you talking about?'

'I'm prepared to stand up in court and bear evidence against Colonel Mavrone. Happy to do so, ma'am. The man deserves horse whipping!'

'My dear sir, it's not your place to pass judgement on Carina's husband.' Alice put her sewing on the table and stood up. 'I'm confident that we will hear from Colonel Mavrone soon. Are you certain you gave him our address?'

'Do you doubt my word, ma'am?'

'Indeed I do not. You have been a good friend to Carina and I'm grateful. However, we have encroached upon your time too long.' Alice's voice was unnervingly calm. 'Your parents must be anxious for your return. I will ask Anthony to make arrangements for your journey south as soon as is convenient.'

It was the note of anger in Alice's voice that made Carina stop as she went past the morning room door. She was on her way to the garden, and, hearing voices, paused, her bonnet under her arm as she listened. She could see Alice, but not Harry who was standing by the hearth. To begin with, she didn't understand what they were saying. When Ben's name cropped up she was confused by Harry's answers. Why did he say Ben had attacked her? Harry knew she loved Ben. She wasn't afraid of him! What was he talking about? Harry went on and on, taking no notice of Alice and when he spoke of divorce, Carina pressed her hand to her mouth. She heard his offer to testify against Ben, followed by her aunt's firm dismissal, and ran up upstairs to her room.

Carina locked the door and slung her cape and bonnet onto a chair. She perched on the edge of the four-poster bed with her arms around her body and her head bowed. She had suffered concussion as a child. From the moment of falling off her pony until she woke up, all memory was wiped from her mind. It was the same again now. She remembered meeting Harry in a hotel lobby but nothing immediately before or after that, until she had found herself in a ship's cabin. Bewildered and disoriented, she had looked out of the porthole and seen the rock of Gibraltar. A cannon boomed a salute from the castle and it was then she realised they were on their way to England. Harry hadn't saved her. He had stolen her from Ben!

Flashes of memory, fleeting and insubstantial, disturbed her recollection of the rest of the journey. When Ben came to her in dreams, it was like dreaming of the dead and she knew she was being punished. She had done something terrible. Her mind was unfreezing and it was all coming back. She had shot Prince Scalia! Why had she killed him? He had hurt her, she knew – the scars she bore told her that afresh every day. But there was something else, something her mind only let her remember now: Scalia had said Ben was in love with Bianca. She didn't believe him, but she had shot him all the same.

She had been too ill until now to understand. Scalia had unhinged her mind and she had murdered him. Dear God! Carina's jaw began to tremble so she had to clench her teeth to stop it. Don't think about it, said a voice in her head. This has to be gone through with, but not yet. Wait until you're stronger.

Alice is sending Harry away. You'll be better once he's gone. Alice will help you. Don't think about it now …

In the days after Harry's departure, Carina did her best to put herself back together. Slowly, carefully, she began to talk again. Rose came from London with a portmanteau of clothes and she let her fuss over her. When they spoke of Sicily, it was only of small things. Rose attended to her hair, but Carina insisted on dressing herself. She had become used to it, she said, and gradually her health improved.

Alice encouraged her to take the pony and trap for short excursions. Driving along the coast near Bamburgh helped clear the fog in her mind. What happened after she left Naples, she wondered? Greta and Stefan would have gone to the hotel and found her missing. Ben would have learnt of her disappearance when they arrived in Palermo. He must know that she hadn't left Italy of her own accord! Once he returned to Naples and read Harry's letter, he would set out to find her.

On waking each morning Carina forced hope into her heart. Today there would be a letter from Ben. Post was delivered regularly, but there came no news of his imminent arrival. There was good reason for the delay, she told herself. The weather had been atrocious and the postal system on the continent was famously unreliable. Alice had told her that a final battle between the two sides was expected any day. How could Ben leave Italy when the future of the revolution hung in the balance? She could not – would not – believe that Harry had spoken the truth.

How could I not love thee, my heart was aflame?
No one before thee, beloved thy name—

Carina began a poem, then tore the paper into tiny pieces and threw them on the fire. Why was there no word from Ben? If he could not travel then at least he could write. She tried to summon up her old resilience. She would go and find him, she decided, then changed her mind. The man who had abducted her knew that she had killed Scalia. When she landed in Italy, she would be arrested and charged for murder.

There was no going back and, try as she might, the suspicion implanted by Scalia could not be rooted out. Ben had spoken of annulment. Now Bianca was free, was it what he wanted? Did Harry have proof they were together? Was that the reason he was so willing to testify against Ben? 'All men are bastards. Don't expect them to be faithful.' Anne Lamartine's words circled her mind like vultures. She had only loved one man and trusted him completely. Now, the very action that prevented her returning to Italy had set Bianca free to fall into his arms ...

Upset by the smallest mishap, Carina often found herself on the verge of tears. She was nervous of strangers and shut herself away when visitors came to the house. Alice tried to comfort her, but the only person she could talk to was Ben and he wasn't here. Perhaps she should write to him. Where was he now, she wondered? What if he was with Bianca? She could not bear her suspicions to be confirmed in the cold formality of a letter. It would send her mad.

When Carina caught sight of herself in the mirror, she saw a white-faced stranger with sunken eyes. I look like a terrified child, she thought. I was always so strong, I believed myself indestructible. How could I fall so in love with Ben that all my happiness, even my sanity, depends upon him?

In the stony reality of his absence, Carina stopped asking herself what the next day might bring. She, who always fought her way out of trouble, was trapped in a situation from which there was no escape. She had never known this type of misery and helplessness. Cut off from those around her, she felt locked behind glass in a world where she no longer belonged. She went on living, getting through each day without feeling she was alive. Time passed her by and gradually hope ebbed away.

There was a night when Carina dreamt Ben was in bed beside her. She heard him breathing and slid her hand over the cold sheet. Her eyes flew open and she sat bolt upright, weeping until she was exhausted. I can't go on like this, she thought in anguish. If I can learn to live without hope, then I will live without despair. I must accept the truth. Ben doesn't love me. I must crush him out of my heart and lock down my pain. No one will ever hurt me like this again.

'This is splendid news!' Anthony Farne lowered the newspaper and looked across the morning room to Carina and Alice.

'It's reported Garibaldi fought one of the greatest battles of his career at Volturno. The Bourbons were routed and Victor Emmanuel is proclaimed King of Italy.'

'I'm delighted to hear it,' Alice exclaimed. 'What will the great man do now?'

'Garibaldi was offered an estate, a dukedom and enough money for a lifetime, but refused them all. He's retired to his home on Caprera, taking only two horses named Calatafimi and Milazzo. You were fortunate to have born company with such a man, Carina.'

Carina continued leafing through the sketchbook of Alice's Sicilian watercolours. The names touched a raw nerve. She didn't want to think about Garibaldi and looked out of the window to where leaves of beech and maple were dying in a burst of autumn colour.

'I wonder if I may take the trap to the picnic house by the beach this afternoon?'

It was a beautiful October day and the sun was warm as Carina drove through the park to the beach. When she came to the small stone bothy, she hitched the pony to the post and left her bonnet and cape in the trap. She unlocked the door of the hut and took out a chair, sitting in the sun for a while before she decided to walk down to the sea. The tide was out and her boots sank into wet sand as she stood at the water's edge. Seagulls swooped overhead and she watched as they dived low on the incoming tide.

A wave swept over her feet and Carina turned to make her way back. A flock of birds rose up and flew away all at once. She could see the pony standing on the dunes with its neck arched and its ears pricked forward. The pony whinnied and she looked over her shoulder. A horseman was riding by the sea and she recognised Anthony's big chestnut hunter. She had been away too long – Alice was worried and sent him to find her.

Carina held a hand over her eyes and stopped to wait for him. The rider seemed taller than Anthony as he approached. She admired the way he rode with long stirrups, giving the horse its head as they cantered across the sand. Dear God, was it a trick of light that made him seem suddenly familiar? For a moment her heart stood still. Surely, she was mistaken?

Curbing an irrational urge to run, Carina walked so fast by the time she reached the dunes, she was out of breath. She stopped at the top of the bank and put her hands to her sides. How ridiculous she must have looked scuttling across the beach like that. How stupid to lose her head! She only had to put the chair back and lock up before she drove home. Then, it seemed the next moment, she heard the clink of irons as the horse was pulled up, followed by a soft thud of boots on the sand.

She hadn't let herself believe it was Ben. Yet he was here and standing right behind her! She could feel him in her bones and a spasm of pain made her put her hand to her chest. She splayed out her fingers and pressed down until the ache subsided. Keeping her eyes on the chair in the porch, Carina waited until she was calm. She knew why Ben had come. He had travelled a great distance and she must hear what he had to say. Unclenching her fists, she dropped her arms to her sides and turned to face him.

CHAPTER FORTY-THREE

Ben was standing beside Anthony's horse with his arm resting on the animal's neck and his hand tangled in its mane. How long had it been, Carina wondered, one month or two? His hair was windswept and his face lined and weary. She looked at him and felt no leap of happiness. There was an iron chain around her heart and she passed her tongue over her lips.

'How did you know I was here?' she asked.

'Your aunt gave me directions and Sir Anthony lent me his horse.'

'I meant in Northumberland. Did you get Harry's letter?'

Ben led the horse up the bank and looped the reins next to those of the pony. He reached inside his jacket for a crumpled piece of paper and handed it to her.

'Read this, if you will.'

Carina spread the note open and scanned the brief contents.

*Miss Temple instructs me to inform you she has placed herself
under my protection. Should you attempt to write or to meet with
her, she will seek your indictment on the charge of grievous harm
against her person.*

    Harry Carstairs

Surely, it must be a forgery? Carina read it again. Harry's signature was unmistakable. She felt her palms prickling and her hands begin to shake. The letter fluttered to the ground and Ben stooped to pick it up.

'When Greta and Stefan arrived in Palermo without you, I caught the next ferry to Naples. Mr Carstairs's letter was waiting. Did you instruct him to write to me?'

So Ben had arrived in Naples the same day they sailed for England. They had missed each other by only a few hours. Harry had deliberately misled him – But why? Carina saw disillusionment in Ben's eyes and answered stiffly.

'I didn't know Harry had written until a few weeks ago. He told my aunt he had informed you that he was bringing me here. He assured us you were aware of my whereabouts.'

'Did he now? So, Harry Carstairs isn't quite as honourable he would have us believe? I suppose he's still in love with you and hoped to get me out of the way. But let's not pin all the blame on him. Did it not occur to you how I might feel when you disappeared without any kind of explanation?'

She hadn't let herself, Carina thought. In her madness and misery, she had been tormented by the thought of Ben and Bianca together. Why make it worse by speculating on how Ben felt when he found her gone? Relief, she imagined now. There was too much to disentangle and she did not answer.

'I searched all of Naples and then paid a call on your grandmother. She received me kindly and I was sorry to alarm her.

When Lady Farne's letter arrived, she sent your cousin to tell me. It was only then any of us knew you were alive. Honestly, Carina! How could you be so careless of those you left behind?'

'I wasn't myself. I cannot remember …'

'Will you try, please? I know you've been ill, your aunt has told me that much. So, unless you prefer to be outside, I suggest we avail ourselves of the hut.'

Ben guided her towards the door and picked up the chair as they went past. He placed it inside and motioned for her to sit down. Carina remained on her feet. Whatever he had to say, she preferred to hear it standing up. Her glance passed over him, taking in his travel-worn clothes. Ben felt like someone she had known long ago. How could it be like this?

'What happened to you after I left Naples? Please tell me, Carina.'

Ben held his hand out to her and Carina folded her arms across her chest. Before the coldness in her face, his expression hardened. He took a cheroot from his case and struck a match to light it, blowing a ring of smoke into the air.

'You're aware Riccardo Scalia is dead,' he said.

It was a statement, not a question and Carina was silent. She stood, looking out of the door and concentrated on tiny particles of dust dancing in the light.

'His body was discovered after you left Italy.' Ben continued. 'The authorities treated it as a political assassination. They were unable to identify the killer and Garibaldi has since declared the case closed.'

He was giving her the facts, but Ben couldn't feel the emptiness inside. Did he suspect that she was involved? It seemed like a lifetime ago. What did it matter now?

'I've had no news from Italy,' Carina chose her words carefully. 'I don't suppose anyone was very sorry.'

'I was questioned by the police on my return from Sicily. They showed me the gun used to kill Scalia. It was very similar to the one I gave you. Tell me, do you still have the Colt pistol?'

'Harry took charge of my affairs. He may have left it in Naples—'

'But you're not sure?'

'I suffered from memory loss.'

'Do you remember why you ran away? Was it to get away from me?'

'And if it was?'

'I'm sorry you didn't have the decency to tell me yourself. I am your husband – or did you forget that as well?'

Ben was twisting what she said, making it sound as if it was all her fault, and resentment fired Carina's spirit.

'I haven't forgotten. Surely that's why you're here? You've come to obtain an annulment of our marriage.'

'An annulment? On what grounds, may I ask?'

'Adultery with Bianca Scalia. I've been kept well informed.'

'Is that what you think – that Bianca and I left Naples together?'

Carina ignored the bitterness in his voice. They had come to the point sooner than expected. At last, the truth was out in the open. She must get this over before she lost her nerve.

'Why not? You've been in love with each other for years.'

'Or so Riccardo Scalia told you!'

'Yes, if you must know—'

'And you *believed* him?'

'He showed me Bianca's locket, the one she always wears. He said she left it to prove that she was with you. He said you were lovers ...'

The words died on her lips as Ben dropped his cigar butt on the floor and crushed it beneath the heel of his boot. He was looking at her as if she had said something so stupid it was beyond credibility. Ben was good at this kind of thing, Carina reminded herself. He would try to manipulate her and she must not let him.

'Do you think I'd have married you if I loved another woman?'

'I don't know what to think? How can I when you never confide in me? You warned me never to speak of Bianca. Why was that – unless you had a secret to hide?'

Carina wasn't aware she raised her voice and threw out her arms. Ben's hands came down on her shoulders and he leant his face so close to hers she felt his breath on her cheek.

'I'm not in love with Bianca and she did not travel to Sicily with me. Scalia had her committed to a hospital for the insane six months ago.'

There was a dark look in his eyes, not of anger but the pain of returning memory. Ben was as tense as a cat ready to pounce and Carina braced herself for whatever was coming next. When he spoke, his voice was so low she strained to hear his words.

'Riccardo Scalia lied to you. Bianca is not my lover. She is my sister.'

How she came to be standing outside, Carina did not remember. Ben must have moved the chair to let her pass for she was aware the tide had come in and water covered the beach. In her mind she was in the library at Monteleone, reading Lord Byron's poem: 'They knew not I knew thee who knew thee too well ...' It was rumoured Byron wrote the verse for his half-sister by whom he fathered a child. Nothing was impossible. Ben might have been in love with Bianca. He had gone to see her in Naples. There were meant to be no secrets between them – so why hadn't he told her?

Carina heard Ben speaking, his voice reaching her from a distance.

'My brother and I were the result of a liaison Donna Isabella had before she married Bianca's father. We were brought to Monteleone after her husband died and didn't discover the truth until years later. Before he proposed to Bianca, Scalia made extensive enquiries and discovered our true parentage. Donna Isabella was terrified the scandal would destroy her daughter's prospects. She told us everything on the day we were packed off to Ireland.'

'And your father?' Carina turned her head slightly.

'Patrick Mavrone was stationed in Sicily after the war. Quite a shock when his illegitimate sons turned up years later – but he did his duty by us. He paid for our education and gave me refuge when I was in exile.'

'I came across a bookmark in your brother's book, a lock of Bianca's hair.'

'I placed it there when Alex died.'

Everything fitted into place and Carina believed him. She should have felt sorry for Bianca, but Ben could have been talking about someone she had never met. Ben was the man she had loved more than life itself; yet she felt as far removed from him as when she first saw him riding on the beach. She had thought her love was invincible and she was wrong. Her heart had turned to stone.

Carina stood motionless, her attitude as unyielding as her state of mind and Ben's arm went round her shoulders.

'I've come to take you home, sweetheart.'

'Please will you leave now?' Throwing him off, Carina backed away. 'If you hurry, you can catch the last train. Take Anthony's horse! I'll arrange for its collection later.'

'What the devil—?'

'I'm not coming home with you!'

'Why not?'

'Because I prefer to stay here. I'm better off in England.'

'Not in your aunt's opinion. She's invited me to stay until you're well enough to make the journey.'

'Name of Mercy, do I have to spell it out? I don't want to return to Italy. I'm never coming back!'

'What are you afraid of, Carina? Did Scalia make a coward of you?'

'Yes, I'm a coward.'

'You've never been a coward in your life.' Ben spoke without raising his voice.' Do you know what I think? I think you're one of those women who love the thrill of the chase and lose interest once they've hunted their prey to ground. Did I fail to live up to your expectations, Carina? Were you bored by the constraints of married life? Give me an honest answer, but don't dare say you're afraid of loving me.'

Carina looked at the sandy turf and rushes growing at the edge of the dunes. Ben's taunts were deliberate, forcing her to where she didn't want to go. Her pulse was beating at such a rate, she felt dizzy. She tried to hold on, but her mind was moving too fast. Hellish memory crashed in, shattering the paralysis that guarded her spirit and she was back to the darkness and terror of that night. She saw Scalia's contorted face, saliva dribbling from his mouth. She smelt his blood and felt the sweat on his fingers as he touched her. Carina reached for the collar of her dress, her hands working frantically at the buttons until they were undone. Then she pulled the bodice open down to her corsage and stepped forward.

'Here's your answer, Ben! See what hatred and revenge have done to me!'

The wounds had healed, their scars vivid on her pale skin.

Two lines were scored diagonally one across the other, running from the tip of her collarbone to the rise of each breast, in the mark of vendetta. The same blasphemous cross was burnt into the trees of Calabria and carved into rocks on the hillsides of Sicily. Carina saw in Ben's eyes the awakening horror she experienced every day in her room. Her voice dropped to a whisper.

'Scalia said it was the last act of the vendetta. I killed him because of you. I damned my mortal soul on your account.'

Ben was the only person on earth who could share this with her. She did not expect an appeal for forgiveness. It was hardly Ben's style, but she longed for him to say something that might help through the years ahead. If he had put his arms around her, she would have accepted any strength he had to give but he was too shocked to speak. Ben turned away, his profile rigid as he stared out over the charcoal sea. Everything they had been through together was drawing to a close.

The trembling in her hands ceased and Carina refastened her bodice. 'Go home to Sicily and seek whatever comfort you can. Leave me to find my own peace.'

Ben turned his head and gave her a long look that went through her in the absent, brooding gaze she knew so well. She must get back and convince Alice there was no point in prolonging his visit. Carina began to walk to where the pony was hitched to the post. Ben would not call her back or try to stop her. If he had spoken it might have acted as a spur, but he was silent and the short distance to the trap felt like a progress to the gallows. Carina was exhausted but, tired as she was, her mind ran on. Nothing in life will be so hard again. Don't pity the man you are leaving behind. Ben will manage well enough without you. He always has …

Carina unhitched the driving reins and climbed up onto the driving board. Reaching down, she retrieved her cloak and wrapped it around her shoulders. The chestnut stamped restlessly as they moved off and she turned the pony's head away from the sea down the rutted track that led to the house.

It was past nine o'clock when Carina went to bed. Rose had brought her supper on a tray but she could not eat while Ben was in the house. She had begged Alice to find him lodgings in Salford village. Her aunt looked at her despairingly and said she would not dream of being so inhospitable. Colonel Mavrone must stay tonight and leave in the morning. It was the very least they could do for him. She had even gone so far as to put Ben in the room adjoining her own, and was now entertaining him downstairs.

It was a cold, still night and sounds carried. Carina heard dinner being cleared and the servants going to bed. When Alice tapped on her door she snuffed out the candle and pretended to be asleep. The door opened and then shut. Ben would be having a cigar with Anthony and come upstairs later. She had taken the precaution of locking the connecting door and would stay awake until the light beneath it went out.

She had been half-dead before but now every nerve in her body was on fire. Her heart would not be quiet. She hadn't intended to confront Ben this afternoon. She had put all the blame on him when it was not his fault. I've done exactly as Scalia intended, she thought. He marked me in order to hurt Ben and destroy our love. Harry deceived us both – but I was the one who lost faith – not Ben. He came to take me home and I sent him away. Tomorrow he will leave my life forever. What if I still love him? Don't be a fool, an inner voice answered. You told Ben all he needs to know. He will never look at you again without horror and disgust. How can you live together as man and wife?

There were footsteps in the passage and Carina sat up as she heard his bedroom door shut. Her curtains were open and there was enough light to see the key safely in the lock. Ben was undressing and she waited for him to try the door. The light from the oil lamp dimmed. Soon he would extinguish the candle and she lay back on the pillows. Noises that usually went unnoticed were loud, the murmur of wind in the leaves and the distant hoot of a barn owl. Ben must be asleep, so why was there still light beneath the door?

The clock on the landing chimed eleven and Carina got out of bed and tiptoed across the floor. She put her ear to the door. There was no sound from his side. With her heart in her throat, she turned the key. She glanced around the dressing room with its dark oak furniture and saw Ben's motionless form on the bed. Just as she had thought, he had fallen asleep and left the candle burning on the table beside him.

With her hand at the neck of her nightgown, Carina crossed the threshold and stopped. Alexander came so forcefully into her mind that she could not move. She imagined him standing by the bed. He was the same height as Ben, with the same profile and dark hair, only younger as he had been in the miniature. If she wasn't careful, her sixth sense would bring him to life and she would hear him speak. Alex was Ben's identical twin, she thought. They had been conceived as one. The empathy and understanding between them was unlike any other. When he died, Ben had lost a living part of himself. Every time he looked in the glass he saw, not his own reflection, but the image of his dead twin. How could he ever accept that Alex was dead and he was alone?

It struck Carina with sudden, blinding clarity. The part of Ben hidden from her belonged to his twin. It was Alexander and not Bianca he kept in his heart and no one could take his place.

Now, at last, she understood his distrust and fear of commitment, the pain and madness that drove him to revenge. Ben had suffered terrible and inescapable grief. Selida had tried to tell her, but she had not listened. She had wanted more from Ben than he was able to give.

The image of Alexander faded as she walked over to the bed and looked down. Ben was asleep with one arm bent under his head on the pillow. His handsome face was ravaged by exhaustion and her heart wrenched. She felt more sorry for him than she had felt for anyone before. The vendetta and all that had followed had led to this moment. If he stayed with her, Ben would be reminded of Alex's murder every day for the rest of his life. He deserved to be free of his past. And, if she loved him, she must let him go.

Self-sacrifice went against the very grain of her nature and Carina fought with her conscience. I can't do this! I'm not noble and unselfish like Gabriella. I love Ben with all my heart. How can I give up the one person who is more precious to me than anything in the world? God give me the strength to do what is right, not for myself, but for Ben.

A tear fell on her cheek and she wiped it away. Carina lifted her hair off her face and traced a cross on Ben's forehead. He did not move and she held her breath and bent down to kiss him lightly on the lips. A draught came through the window as she straightened up and snuffed out the candle. She could see the open door to her bedroom and was about to make her way back when Ben's fingers encircled her wrist. Carina let out a gasp as he shifted over and drew back the bedclothes. His face was in shadow and she stood trembling until he reached for her and pulled her next to him on the narrow bed.

Ben put his arms around her and she lay with her head in the crook of his arm. Her whole body was shaking until his warmth and stillness infiltrated her senses. Tension and sorrow left her and peace fell on her spirit. 'I love you. I love you,' she whispered in the darkness, hoping Ben might hear, but he was already asleep.

Carina woke up as Ben left the bed and went to shut the window. She heard him use the bellows to blow the embers alight, and, when he came back, turned on her side to face him. He put his hand on her cheek and drew his finger over her lips and down her chin. How she loved the feel of his hands, the comfort of him close to her. Looking into his eyes, Carina felt he could see into her soul.

'I'm not leaving without you, sweetheart.'

'But how can I return to Italy? I'll be charged with murder.'

'Enough evidence of Scalia's atrocities has come to light for Garibaldi to have him arrested and executed. You saved him the trouble of a public trial. No one apart from ourselves will ever know.'

'But Scalia wasn't going to kill me. I shot him in retaliation.'

'God will reward you for ridding the world of a monster.'

'How can you be so certain?'

'Scalia committed crimes for which he will be damned. His treatment of Bianca was beyond forgiveness.' Ben's voice was heavy with impotent anger. 'He locked her up in a lunatic asylum on grounds of mental instability. When I found her in Naples she was barely alive. Greta and Stefan helped me move her to the convent of Santa Lucia. Now she's in the good care of the nuns, I pray she will be at peace.'

So, Prince Scalia was aware Bianca was half-sister to the twins and yet he executed Alexander all the same. Did Greta and Stefan also know the truth?

'Selida is the only person alive who knows that Bianca is my sister.' Ben read her mind. 'When Alex died, I vowed never to let anyone close to me again. I was insane during the years of my exile and afraid to go back to that time. How could I expect you to understand?'

'You could have tried.'

'And you could have written to me. Why didn't you?'

They had both made the same mistake, Carina thought, both too proud to admit weakness and seek reassurance from the other. Only honesty could save them now.

'I was never certain that you loved me.'

'Why else would I marry you?'

'You're a possessive man. You didn't want anyone else to have me.'

'Oh, my darling. The moment I laid eyes on you I knew you were put on this earth to cause me trouble. I had never met a woman like you. I was captivated by your beauty and courage. When Ruffo dropped you into my lap I knew I had met my match. I should have been kinder but you fought so hard, you drove me beyond restraint. I wanted to protect you and sent you away from Monteleone so that you would be safe. I did everything in my power to forget you, but I could not. Then there you were in Palermo on Garibaldi's arm. Every time I tried to hold on to you, you flew away. Every time I tried to leave you, you caught up with me.'

Ben had cared for her for longer than she had known. How could she have ever doubted him? There was so much she had failed to understand. I should have believed in him, Carina thought. She was silent and Ben took her face in both his hands with his thumbs beneath her chin.

'Your stubborn, unconditional love saved me, my darling. When I failed to persuade you to marry Harry, I convinced myself Scalia was no longer a threat. I should have known better. Name of God, I never meant you to come to any harm.'

Carina had never before heard him speak with such emotion. She looked at Ben and, for the first time, saw him as he really was – a man who needed to love as much as to be loved. Their hearts and minds were at one but there was something she had to say, even now, at the risk of losing her last chance of happiness.

'I won't let you take me back out of duty, Ben. I'd rather die than endure your pity.'

'Pity's not an emotion you arouse in those who love you, Carina. Besides, how would I dare face Greta if I came home without you?'

Ben's fingers moved to the ribbon of her nightgown. He undid the bow so it fell open to the waist. Carina's hands went up to cover herself and he took hold of them and placed them by her side. She felt his lips touch her skin, his mouth moving along the lines left by Scalia's knife. He planted tiny kisses on the scars and her closed eyes were wet with tears. When he raised his head, she pressed his cheek to her own and he took her in his arms.

'Never take your love away from me. I love you and cannot live without you. I will love you until the end of time, my darling, brave, beautiful woman.'

ACKNOWLEDGEMENTS

I owe a debt of gratitude to three remarkable women:

Joanna Frank, editor of the first draft, for her advice and faith in the book.

Diana Beaumont, my literary agent, for her guidance and perseverance.

Genevieve Pegg, publishing director of HarperNorth, for her creative skill in preparing the book for publication.

Thank you to my family, above all, for your unfailing loyalty, support and encouragement. This book is for you, with my love.

AUTHOR'S NOTE

This is a work of fiction. The historical events are true but, apart from General Garibaldi, Francesco Riso, Jessie and Alberto Mario, the characters in the book are products of the author's imagination. Any resemblance to actual persons, living or dead, is purely coincidental.

Harper North

BOOK CREDITS

HarperNorth would like to thank the following staff and contributors for their involvement in making this book a reality:

Hannah Avery
Fionnuala Barrett
Claire Boal
Charlotte Brown
Sarah Burke
Alan Cracknell
Jonathan de Peyer
Anna Derkacz
Tom Dunstan
Kate Elton
Mick Fawcett
Simon Gerratt
Alice Gomer
Monica Green
Matthew Richardson

CJ Harter
Elisabeth Heissler
Graham Holmes
Nicky Lovick
Megan Jones
Jean-Marie Kelly
Alice Murphy-Pyle
Adam Murray
Genevieve Pegg
Rob Pinney
Agnes Rigou
Florence Shepherd
Emma Sullivan
Katrina Troy

For more unmissable reads,
sign up to the HarperNorth newsletter at
www.harpernorth.co.uk

or find us on Twitter at
@HarperNorthUK

Harper
North